For my amazing friends and family who have supported me through everything

1

Hope took a deep, shaky breath.

Her large eyes stole a glance at her cracked mirror. She bravely smiled, noticing the way her bright eyes seemed to pierce the almost shattered glass. Hope had tried to look her absolute best for today's test. She had brushed her golden hair through and through and put on the prettiest outfit she owned, in her opinion.

Today's the day, she thought nervously.

Only a matter of minutes until I find out my future.

However, this was not an ordinary test. There was no way to prepare for what obstacles she would have to face. Passing this test meant living a normal and happy life. Failing meant something worse than death.

Anyone who had failed had gone down in history. It was rare for someone to fall victim to defeat.

This unordinary test decided how dangerous a person was. Everyone took this test exactly one month after they turned 18 years old. Anybody who failed had to be an especially terrible person to be considered dangerous. Sometimes, seemingly harmless people would be declared a threat, and it was a large shock to everyone. It was impossible to know if your neighbor could secretly be planning murder.

I am not dangerous, Hope repeatedly told herself. *I would never hurt anyone.* Of course, she rationally knew she wasn't even close to being dangerous. But no matter what she told herself, her mind was never quiet with the buzzing of nerves. She would lie awake at night, overthinking all the possible outcomes of her fate.

You will be fine.

Hope leaned in carefully to apply mascara to her blonde lashes.

"Hope!"

The girl jumped, jabbing her mascara wand into her watering eye.

"What, mom?" she yelled back, gently dabbing her eyelid with a tissue. With a jittery sigh, she wiped up the line of mascara on her lid and began to start again.

"You're going to be late!"

"I'll be right down!" She applied the dark mascara to her other set of lashes quickly. Hope glanced at her reflection once more and dashed down the stairs, her arms keeping herself upright.

"Wait," a voice whispered. Her step-sister, Haylee, took a deep breath as she spoke. "What if you're dangerous?"

Hope chuckled uncomfortably, feeling her nerves soar.

"Don't you have faith in me?"

"Of course," Haylee muttered, nodding. "But what if you are?"

"I won't be, I promise," Hope reassured, giving her a soft, anxious look. "I'll be back in an hour."

"She's right," her mother added, walking through the room. "You have nothing to worry about, Haylee." Her gaze turned to Hope. "Ready?"

Hope gave a weak smile.

"Ready."

She hopped into her mom's blue faded car. When they had first bought the car, it had been a beautiful sky blue. The cracked paint filled her with nostalgia of when she was a little kid, not ever having to worry about being known as some dangerous freak. Hope looked up and saw Haylee waving out of their 6th story apartment building. Their home looked minute compared to the towering skyscrapers all around them. She waved back, putting her thumbs up.

The pair drove together in complete silence. The knot in her stomach kept her silent while she listened to all the noises her massive city had to offer. Her mom's worried eyes darted to the small mirror at the top of the vehicle. Her daughter's knee was bouncing up and down quickly, and Hope was beginning to feel the panic of anxiety that she knew so often. The blonde adult rolled down her window, wishing that the crisp, cool morning air would distract her from her own mind. Time seemed to stretch endlessly.

Finally, the car slowed. Her mom parked in front of a windowless white building. Hope felt her stomach leap.

"Good luck, honey," her mom said, trying to hide the worry from her large eyes.

"Don't worry Mom, I'm fine. I won't be dangerous," Hope reassured her. She got out of the car in a rush, grabbing onto the handle for balance.

"Hope, wait!" Hope's head spun around. "I remember when I took my test," her mom said quietly. "I know you'll do fine. Don't be nervous. Don't be nervous."

Hope chuckled uncomfortably.

"Are you saying that to me or yourself?" Her mom snickered.

"Both, I suppose."

"Mom, we've been over this," Hope reminded her. "I know I'll be fine, I just get nervous for everything, you know that." Hope turned away, taking a deep breath. "Love you!"

"I love you too," she replied quietly. Hope grinned weakly, locking her eyes with her mother. She took a long, deep breath. The sun shone down brightly, and a slight breeze filled the air. The thought that she might never breathe in this warm summer air again was terrifying.

You'll be fine, she chided herself. Hope began slowly walking to the place where her fate would be decided.

She hesitantly pushed open the steel doors of the building. The tiny knot of fear in her gut became more prominent as soon as she took her first steps in. Her footsteps echoed on the marble floor as she nervously walked down the long hallway. Hope turned to a doorway on the right.

"M'am," said a dull voice. Hope spun around, a small gasp escaping from her mouth. "The room is that way," a lady said, pointing mechanically to the left.

"Sorry," the young adult muttered. Embarrassed, she quickly turned and followed the woman's directions.

She pushed open a door, taking one last breath. She was greeted with numerous pairs of eyes as she stepped through. She looked away as she carefully sat down, hating the attention she was receiving. No one was talking, which wasn't a surprise. No words could form in such a place of fear.

Hope brought up her head and took a look at her surroundings. The entire room was the same dull gray color. The first word that came to mind was *prison*. A bright light flickered slightly on the ceiling, causing her to shield her eyes with her shaking palm.

You're fine.

A moment later, a woman came out of a sliding door in the wall. Her black hair was pulled back in a tight bun. It was styled so tightly that Hope noticed a deep blue vein in her forehead, which made her chuckle quietly to herself. The stranger cleared her throat and began to speak.

"Welcome, young adults," she said plainly.

"27 years ago, prisons became overcrowded and overused. The United States of America was given a bad reputation due to the amount of criminals and dangerous children. To solve this problem, the government decided to put the harmful onto an island in the sea. Our country was no longer infected with the criminally insane." The woman's voice had a mechanic touch to it; it was obvious that she had delivered this speech countless times before. "This is a test in which your mental health will be rated from one to ten on a scale."

Hope knew this information already. Everyone at her school had nicknamed the device 'The Psycho Scale'.

She sat up straighter, smoothing out her hair. Hope's heart was racing in anticipation to get to her part of the test. "Any number that is 4 or below is considered harmful. If you are concluded as so, you will be dropped off on an island in the middle of the sea.You shall remain with the other criminals on the island for the rest of your life."

Hope had known this since kindergarten. Schools across the country had made it a huge deal to tell young kids the horrific details. Hope could remember her young five-year-old self learning the gruesome tales of what was found there. She had even seen some of the bodies that were brought back, meant to show kids just how much they should want to behave. However, hearing this statement as she was about to take the test sent goosebumps all over her body.

I'm not dangerous, she told herself firmly and nervously. *I would never, ever hurt someone. I'm not dangerous.*

"This will depend entirely on your own decisions as a person. Make smart choices, young adults; you don't get a second chance," the lady continued. "When I call your name, come with me. First, Gabbie Aarons."

Hope rubbed her clammy hands against her loose, bright blue blouse. For the next few minutes, she watched all the faces of the testers as they walked in. A curvy brunette's face looked smirky and arrogant as she glided through the metal entrance. Clearly she didn't think anything about the island speech. A petite redhead was bouncing up and down, her hands sticking to her shirt in fear.

Wow, all these people have the same birthday as me. Hope gave a sarcastic grin. *Happy birthday.*

She drummed her fingers on her black leggings, ready to jump up when she heard her name. *Ok Hope,* she thought to herself. *When they call your name, you're going to get up, look mentally stable, and walk into the room like you're not about to have a heart attack.*

"Alyssa Sarry," said a different but still female voice. Hope chomped on her lip, wincing at the taste of metallic blood in her mouth. *Oh god, she's on 'S'.*

She watched as the young adult named Alyssa walked stiffly through a sliding door. Afterwards, three boys and one girl were called into the office. Each of them made it out with their results as harmless. *You got this, Hope. If they can do it, you can do it.*

"Hope Samuels," said a bland feminine voice.

Hope stood up. As soon as she did, her legs shook beneath her, and all of her mental preparation crumbled. A small girl sitting next to her kindly grabbed her arm and steadied her. Hope slapped herself, hard, as if that would get rid of all the fear inside her.

"Hope Samuels," the voice repeated, now with a tinge of impatience. Hope quickly cleared her mind and forced her legs to move. She slowly, rigidly walked into the private office. As she walked in, the metal door behind her slid shut. Hope was greeted by a gray-eyed woman who seemed as though she had lost the ability to smile. She gestured to a gray metal chair in the middle of the small room.

"Sit right there, Miss," the woman said in her robotic tone. Hope's hands shook slightly as she sat on the cold metal. The lady reached into a black leather and pulled out a syringe filled with a murky blue liquid. Hope felt a stab of fear as her eyes locked on the silver needle.

"There's a needle?" she squeaked. The stranger's eyes didn't even look up as she scribbled something on her clipboard. "Miss?"

"Yes, Miss Samuels?" Her voice came out as a snap. Hope flinched at her suddenly aggressive tone.

"Will it hurt?" she asked nervously. The woman shrugged her shoulders.

"Possibly," she responded. Hope's impossibly green eyes grew wide. Before she could say anything, the lady pressed the needle into her neck. She felt the sharp prick of the needle before she fell unconscious.

Hope opened her eyes, an entirely new location in front of her.

Panic was the first thing she felt. She had absolutely no clue to where she had gone, or how she'd even gotten there.

The girl took a deep breath, stopping the bubbling fear inside that threatened to overpower her. She was in a pure white room with no windows or doors.

"Help!" she screamed to no one. Hope opened her mouth again when she remembered that she was completely alone.

No, her mind told her. *Nobody can hear you. Stop. Don't be stupid.*

Hope stopped yelling as she took a deep breath.

Outside, she heard the unmistakable siren of a police car. She hesitantly walked out of a door that wasn't there moments earlier. *Thank god, the police are here.*

An officer stepped out of the blaring car. His eyes met hers, and she gasped. His iris was a deep, piercing black. Hope froze, ice flooding her veins. He waited a moment before he broke out into a sprint, rushing directly at her.

At that moment, a gun caught her eye on the sidewalk next to her. Hope quickly picked it up, and without thinking, her shaking hand pulled the trigger.

She watched as the bullet hit the man in the middle of his chest. She was bitterly thankful that it was already loaded.

Oh my god.

She wanted to get as far away as she could from the dead man's body. Before she could run, the scene in front of her dissolved into a dark alleyway. She stopped dead in her tracks, slapping her hand on a rough wall.

"What just happened!?" she shouted to nobody. Without warning, a sinking feeling of dread plummeted in her stomach. Hope turned slowly around.

A man was standing there, his hand snaking out toward her throat. Instinctively, she dove to the side. She looked back up, any rational thinking gone. The strange man's hand was slowly inching toward her, and somehow she knew that his intent was to kill.

"Stop it!" she yelled urgently. He paid no attention to the frightened girl's order as he came closer and closer. She backed up, terrified for her life.

"Come here," the man snarled. His voice sent chills down Hope's body. Realizing that she was weaker on the ground, she jumped up. The man was still walking menacingly toward her.

Suddenly, he lunged at her, making her shriek in surprise. His hands were to the side, leaving his face vulnerable. Without thinking, she clawed at his eyes, slightly aware of the screams escaping her mouth. She couldn't remember the moment when he transformed into an elderly man.

"Help," he croaked. As he reached for her, she jumped back even farther. She could sense that he was *off*, somehow.

This time, she was full of more frustration than fear. Without a second thought, she kicked him, not looking where she struck. She didn't look back as she sprinted away once more.

Again, her surroundings dissolved.

In front of her were two children, hitting what looked to be an animal.

"Stop!" she shouted to the kids. It made her sick to think that this helpless body was being assaulted by two young kids. They ignored her demand as they continued. Hope bit her lip angrily as she ran closer to them.

"I said quit it!" she yelled, more desperate. One of kids stood up and stopped the assault.

"Thank you," Hope said, heaving an audible sigh of relief.

The young boy walked over to her, an emotionless expression plastered on his face. Without warning, his hand reared back and smashed her face.

Dimly, Hope knew that the strength was impossible for a child his size. He started laughing loudly, grinning at the pain and anger in Hope's eyes. He skipped back to the other boy, still attacking the animal.

Anger and tears blurred her vision. Her eyes darted around, looking for anything that would stop the two kids. She noticed a piece of loose cement to her right. With red blocking her senses, she picked it up, walking stiffly over to the two boys.

"Stop right now," Hope commanded. The small kid put up his middle finger, making her jaw drop open. The boy stuck out his tongue and gave one hard punch to the now unconscious animal. Hope took a calming breath, but it had no effect. Some part of her mind knew that she shouldn't be this aggravated, but that part was small. In her blinding rage, the cement smashed on the head of the kid who had slapped her. He fell unconscious, his head loudly smacking against the ground. The other boy looked at her, pure terror in his wide eyes.

His fear, that was what brought her back to reality. She stared down below her at the boy, whose head had begun gushing blood. The second boy backed up, twitching.

"You're a monster," he whispered, running away.

Hope breathed in, then out, now understanding the true horror of what she had done.

You're a monster, Hope.

She felt a sharp sting on her arm, and her mind went black.

3

Hope opened her eyes.

The shrill sound of blaring sirens rang in her ears.

The woman who had given her the test was looking at her with fear in her eyes.

No, not fear.

Disbelief.

Hope looked back in surprise and terror.

"What's going on?" she practically yelled. The woman slowly shook her head, her mechanical touch gone.

"I don't understand…" her voice trailed off. The metal door slid open to reveal a line of people in black suits. None of their faces showed through the frightening dark masks they were wearing, but by their body shape, she guessed they were males. The menacing group marched toward her. Hope looked at them, her body giving a nervous jolt.

"Who are you?" Hope asked fearfully.

Powerful hands forcefully grabbed her out of the chair. She had a bad, bad feeling in her gut. *This is wrong*, she thought. *Why can't I just exit like everyone else?*

They dragged her to a door in the corner of the room. One of the men slid his badge in a slot, and she heard a loud beep. The door opened, and they roughly carried her to the back of the building. A gigantic black truck with tinted windows was parked on the side of the wall. *Wait a second,* she thought. *A truck?*

"What's going on?!" Hope yelled. Anxiety was seeping into every part of her body.

Am I dangerous?

Hope gulped.

"No, of course not," she reassured herself firmly, clenching her fists. "You are *not* dangerous. There's no way." Her quivering hands were forced together roughly with rusted handcuffs.

"What are you doing!?" Hope shouted hysterically. One of the men took off his mask and glared at her.

"We're sending you where the other dangerous and unpredictable people are. You'll be stuck on a deserted island with the murderers, thieves, and other hazardous kids who are just like you." Hope's eyes grew large in urgency.

"I'm not even close to dangerous!"

"In your test, you assaulted and killed more than three humans. Not to mention you punched a man who did no harm to you." Hope's eyes looked him up and down angrily, her stare lingering on his badge.

"He was trying to kill me, *Tom*!" she shouted, using the name on his uniform. "I'm not dangerous at all! *You have got to be kidding me!*" Tom's hand shot up, startling her into silence.

"You are considered unpredictable and therefore must go with them," he explained, tying her hands to a pole inside the truck. "So, girl, say goodbye to your home." Hope realized what kind of horrors were in store for her, causing her to feel fear for the umpteenth time again today.

"That's not fair! I only defended myself!" she cried out. The man shrugged.

"I'm sorry. You know how the test works."

"The results are wrong!" she said desperately. "I promise you, I would never kill anybody, even my worst enemy. I swear it."

The man looked at her roughly.

"Listen kid, clearly you must have some dangerous tendencies. Why else would you be here?"

"But I don't!" Hope yelled. "I'm not harmful!"

"Are you calling the government a liar?" Tom asked quietly. Hope hastily shook her head.

"No, but the system might be wrong. Please don't send me to an island, I swear I'm not a criminal. I can't be around criminals, they'll kill me!"

The man's hard eyes looked at her for a second. Hope thought she saw something in his eyes; regret, maybe? But it went away so fast that she didn't know if she imagined it or not.

"Sorry," he said blandly. "You're going to this island. The tests don't lie." Hope didn't even struggle against her bonds. There was no point. Tom lessened his force when he saw her resistance crumble.

"Are there any other 18 year olds there?" she asked. The man ignored her as he walked to the front, leaving Hope in the corner of the massive vehicle. The large truck was slammed shut, the only light coming from the front of the car. Tom then slid a clear wall between him and her.

Hope felt the vehicle start to move. She made herself as comfortable as possible and lied down. Before she could stop herself, she began to feel tears in her eyes.

"Mom," she whispered.

Then, she sobbed uncontrollably for what seemed like forever.

A few hours later, Hope sat up groggily. She brought her hands to rub her puffy and itchy eyes, but she remembered angrily that she was tied up.

"Get me out," she muttered through gritted teeth. She started pulling frantically on her rope, only burning her hands more.

She slowly stopped struggling as Hope realized something had changed; the truck had ceased moving.

A moment later, the large door was slowly lifted open. Sunlight blazed into Hope's watery eyes.

Tom was there, mumbling something into his walkie-talkie. He reached in with a knife and swiftly cut the thick rope off of her numb hands. He grabbed her roughly and pulled her out of the vehicle. Hope's feet landed unstably on the concrete below. She caught a glimpse of a large building close by.

"Where are we?" Hope asked. Her voice came out raspy, and she cleared her throat. The man looked hesitant to tell her anything. "Come on, I'm about to go die on an island. Just tell me where we are," she begged.

"Long Island," he finally said. Hope looked at him oddly.

"Why are we here?"

"Alright, we're boarding a plane now," Tom said, ignoring her question. "Don't try anything."

He shoved her none too gently into a small, cramped helicopter. The walls were a dull white-gray, which oddly described how Hope felt, in a way; boring, plain, and depressed.

"How long will I be here?"

"Shut up," he said, without any emotion. He pushed a button on some switch that was located on the outside corner of the helicopter.

"How long will the ride take?" Tom shot her a glare.

"Be quiet!" His tone rose to an angry yell. This time, he slid a steel wall between the front seats and the back. Hope raised her eyebrows but didn't say anything after that, afraid of the man's sudden outburst.

For the first hour, Hope had only one thing on her mind: her family. She would never see her little sister or her parents again. The thought was like a knife to her heart. Her loving, kind mom who did everything she possibly could to make her happy. Her step-sister, who was her best friend.

I promised her I'd see her again.

This depressing thought brought on a new wave of sadness. The second hour rolled around, and Hope did what she did best; overthink. She imagined at least 20 ways she could die on the island, ranging from dehydration to brutal murders. She thought of being there all alone, and this inspired a new fear. *Oh God, please let there be kids my age. Please, I'll do anything,* she thought silently.

The third hour came, and Hope began to feel some frustration replacing her sadness. *Why is this taking so long?* She thought about yelling the question to Tom, but his outburst popped back into her mind.

By the fourth hour, she stopped thinking about anything at all. She was struck with overwhelming numbness. All Hope did was stare at the Atlantic Ocean. It looked like a murky grey mess instead of the sparkling blue waters she had seen so many times.

A sudden noise snapped her out of her mind. It sounded almost like the air being let out of a balloon. She glanced around anxiously, looking for the source of the sound.

The noise stopped. Hope's eyes narrowed slightly, but she stared back out of the window. A minute later, she saw a little wisp of smoke puff out of the wall. Her eyes squinted in confusion. A second later, another wisp came. This time, it was double the size. Finally, another wisp came, the largest of them all. Right away, Hope thought the small plane was having difficulties.

It's ok, she reassured herself, only feeling a little panic. *This is a government plane. It won't crash.* A moment later, two puffs of white mist came out of the wall. Suddenly, numerous small bullets of smoke poured out of the walls. Hope's breath began increasing rapidly. *What if we crash?*

A few seconds later, much more of the strange gas kept puffing and puffing out of the walls.

"Help me!" Hope screamed, pounding on the metal wall. "What's going on?" More smoke came leaking from a million tiny pores. When it was obvious that the man wouldn't help her, she tried holding her breath. After 45 seconds, her lungs couldn't take it anymore. She gulped in a huge amount of air, almost tasting the smoke enter her system. Hope coughed and even tried to throw up. Her mind began to feel hazy as the whole area was engulfed in the mist. She didn't recall the exact moment her eyelids felt too heavy to stay open.

After what seemed like an eternity, she woke up. The plane was safely on the ground, wherever it was. Two men jumped out of the seats in front of her and grabbed her arms. Much too forcefully, they threw her down onto the outside ground. She stood up and aggressively brushed the dirt off from her now stained blouse.

"Was that really necessary?" she asked, locking eyes with the man she had first met. He shrugged halfheartedly.

"We're here."

Hope's green eyes looked up in wonder. She was astounded at how beautiful the place she was sentenced to looked. There were volcanoes in the distance and what looked like a jungle to the far right. There was a thick line of golden sand in front of the glistening blue sea. Hope made sure to take a mental snapshot of this perfect moment. Who knew if she would ever feel peaceful again?

Tom must have seen her radiant eyes widen, because he said, "Don't get your hopes up. Even though it looks like paradise, it's far from it. Believe me, we check up on this island once a year." Hope still thought this island didn't look nearly as bad as he described it to be.

"You should see all the dead bodies there are," he said in a warning tone. She felt her smile falter.

"Like, *murdered* dead or just, *dead* dead?" The man looked at her blankly.

"Lady, I have no clue what you are trying to say. Now I need you to take ten steps that way." He pointed ahead. Hope knitted her eyebrows together.

"Why?"

"So you can't somehow stab or maim us right now," the man answered simply. Hope threw her hands up in the air.

"But I'm not dangerous at all! Why would I ever stab you?" The man shrugged halfheartedly.

"I don't know, it wasn't my test, you tell me. Now take your steps." He held up a gun. "Or I will make you."

Hope put her hands out in front of her.

"Fine, I will. You don't have to threaten me." *Now who's violent?* she thought smugly to herself. Hope backed up, still keeping out her hands.

"Goodbye now," the man said, taking steps back to the helicopter. A different government official sarcastically waved to her from the tiny plane.

"Stay safe!" His tone was much too cheerful and bright for Hope's liking. Tom hopped in the pilot's seat and began to start up the vehicle. He shot one last look at Hope. His facial expression looked softer and more sympathetic than it previously had.

"I'm sorry, kid. Really. It's your brain, not you."

He suddenly put his hand over his mouth, but Hope had other worries on her mind. The plane finally took off, leaving her alone to fend for herself.

"Well, this will be fun," she muttered. The previous joy of seeing the beauty of the island was now rapidly fading away. All of her thoughts on the helicopter were now rushing back into her mind. Hope scanned the area, looking for any source of food, water, or shelter. She could barely comprehend that she would live here for the rest of her probably short life. Hope began to slowly walk to the thick jungle, carefully looking for any danger. She held out her arms weakly in defense.

Hope took a deep breath as she stood in front of the rich green trees. The girl took one last glance at the stunning ocean. As soon as she took a step into the jungle, all sunlight seemed to disappear.

"Hello?" she yelled. Almost immediately, she swore in surprise and anger, squeezing her fist. *What on earth are you thinking?* She had just openly invited any criminal her way.

Frozen, Hope held her breath in fear. She stayed poised like a statue until she was certain that, impossibly, no one had heard her yell.

As she was still, she bitterly realized that she couldn't be more unprepared. The only thing she had were the clothes on her back, and that was useless in helping her survive.

A weapon, she thought suddenly. *I need a weapon.* What else was there besides branches?

Don't panic, she ordered herself. *Think.* There was nothing surrounding her except trees.

Hopes eyes were filling with water when she noticed a dark but narrow line of smoke in the distance, over the countless trees. Hastily wiping away her tears, she squinted even more.

Yes, it was definitely smoke. The only question was, what was it from?

On this beautiful yet awful island, there seemed to be only two outcomes; good or bad. Grimly, she knew that the bad possibility was much more likely.

I'll soon die away, Hope thought with sudden sick amusement. *Maybe this will just make it faster.*

Slowly jogging, she took off in the direction of the unfamiliar smoke.

4

Hope's face had turned maroon by the time she finally reached the source of the smoke. Broken, vandalized buildings lined an old road in front of her. The town was much farther than it had seemed.

Found it, she thought happily. Then, she collapsed from exhaustion on the worn pavement.

There she stayed until she was ready to find a place to stay for the night. She grimaced as she slowly dug stray pebbles from her hand.

The booming footsteps were what made Hope's eyes look up in fear. The sight ahead of her was what finally made her realize what truly littered the island.

There were multiple men before her, all much older. The looks on their faces were enough to make Hope's hands quiver. They slowly continued their walk to her, Hope too paralyzed to move or run.

"Hello, girly," the largest man smirked. His lower lip was split, and his hair was growing back in small patches. His black shirt was practically shredded to pieces, barely hanging on to him. He brought up his hand to scratch his ear, and Hope noticed all of the pink scars lining his hand.

"Hello," she said, attempting to calm the shakiness in her tone. "What do you want?"

"It's not often we get new people on this island," the man chuckled. "Especially young girls that fall so willingly into our grasp." His eyes had a haunting touch to them that made Hope want to get up and run far away.

"No," she suddenly said. "Leave me alone."

"I don't think so," the awful man whispered. "I don't think I will, blondie."

Dread was the only thing that she felt now. She was in no position to fight one man, let alone five others. Hope's eyes looked toward the ground, goodbyes running through her mind.

The footsteps toward her grew louder and louder.

Make it quick, she begged to no one. *Please.* She knew, though, that whatever they had in store for her would not be quick at all. The man wouldn't be licking his lips and grinning if all he wanted to do was kill her.

The man's sick laughter turned into shouts of alarm. Screams pierced the air, but the yells were much higher than his. Hope snapped open her eyes, looking up in terror. She heard the man in front of her give a growl that sent chills up her arms.

Hope's heart leapt in her chest when she felt a pull on her arm. Her immediate reaction was to throw her fists in every direction.

"Stop, stop!" a voice called. Hope calmed herself enough to understand that a girl's voice was yelling to her in the chaos. She put her flailing arms down to her sides, making fearful eye contact with a brunette girl. "Follow me," the girl whispered urgently. "Don't think, just run."

Speechless, Hope followed her order. The stranger grabbed her wrist and roughly pulled her. Filled with terror and relief, Hope began to sprint with the girl despite her previous exhaustion. The stranger began to slow after three long minutes of nothing but running. Hope desperately wanted to stop, but getting far away from the horrible men was her main priority.

Seven minutes passed. Hope's lungs were on fire, and she didn't think she had any energy left whatsoever. Although they were only jogging, she would collapse at any moment.

"Where are we going?" Hope puffed out. The girl spun quickly around, a corner of her mouth perked up slightly.

"We're almost there." Although she was gasping as well, her voice sounded silvery and clear. She picked up speed again, and Hope barely missed sprawling across the ground. It took only two more minutes of jogging to reach the place where they were going. Hope knew she couldn't run anymore. She slipped her hand out of the girl's grasp and fell to her knees, gasping. She stayed like that for five minutes, her throat clawing for air. The sweltering heat didn't help at all as she panted for oxygen. The stranger was gasping as well, but not nearly as hard as Hope was. A minute passed, and she was able to stand and breathe steadily.

"That was horrible," Hope said, her hand over her racing heart. "How in the world are you not on the ground?" The girl shook her head, her breathing becoming slower as well.

"I've spent a lot of time running." Hope nodded through the pain of her dry throat.

The stranger looked over. She slowly walked over to Hope, who was now sitting on the hard ground again. "Here," she said, her voice ringing through the air. "Let me help." She reached into the pocket on her short khaki shorts. The girl grabbed a small canteen of water and threw it to Hope. Hope gave a small smile before she drank.

In front of Hope's eyes, there stood a building, only one story high. The windows were shattered, and Hope could see that they were boarded up tightly.

"What's with the windows?" she asked, not liking the spooky feel of it. The brunette girl snorted, but Hope didn't think she found anything funny.

"Oh, that? Well, the other people on this island aren't very cordial to us," she said, glancing at the windows as well. "We have food, others don't. You know how people get when they're desperate. The boards are for our safety."

"Yikes," Hope said. She couldn't imagine having some creep breaking in, using glass in hopes of hurting her. The girl shrugged.

"Oh well, as my mom used to say, 'Es lo sí que es.'" Hope looked at her blankly, making her chuckle. "It's spanish for 'it is what it is'." She smiled slightly.

"Let's go inside now. It's quite hot, if you didn't notice." Hope nodded, grateful for the girl's suggestion. The stranger got up, holding the door for her. Hope walked in, taking in only room the building had to offer. There were small, dirty mattresses set up, and there was some cans of food stored in the corner. Hope noticed all of the writing and pictures on the wall.

"Oh, excuse that," the stranger said, pointing to the pictures. "We like to draw when we get bored." Hope nodded, marveling at one picture in particular. It was a diamond shape, outlined by a beautiful combination of blues, purples, and pinks.

"Who's we?" Hope asked. "And what's your name?"

"My name's Cassidy," the girl responded, locking the door behind her. "And my friends played a large part in saving your life, too." She chuckled. "And your name is?"

"I'm Hope," she said with a smile. Cassidy glanced at the blonde girl, taking her appearance in.

"Hope... nice name."

"Thanks." Hope paused, the true fear of what just happened sinking into her system. "Um, Cassidy, how did you guys find me so quickly? Thank the lord you did, but how?"

"You know those guys you just saw?" she asked. "They've started to do this thing where they when they see a helicopter, they hide out and wait. This poor excuse of a town is really the only place to go if you actually want to stay alive. I saw what they did to the last person who arrived." Cassidy gave a small shudder. "I would tell you, but I don't want those words coming out of my mouth. Let's just say that I would rather lose my sanity that go through what that poor boy did." Hope bit her lip in anxiousness.

"We want to help as many people stay alive," she continued. "Once we see a helicopter now, we get ready to help, just in case. Luckily it was just you, and not someone who was actually crazy."

A loud bang sounded outside the door.

Hope jumped, staring at it wide-eyed. Cassidy looked at her, a glint in her eye.

"Who's that?" Hope whispered in a shaky voice. Cassidy unwillingly smiled.

"My friends." Hope covered her face in her hands, embarrassed, when she realized that they weren't in any danger.

"Sorry, I should have told them to be quiet," she apologized through laughter. She quickly hopped up and opened the door. Staring at Hope sympathetically, she walked back over. "I really am sorry. They probably shouldn't have done that." Hope's heartbeat was racing like crazy.

A loud bang sounded once more.

"Open the door!" a shrill voice screamed from outside. Cassidy rolled her eyes, an amused smile spread across her face.

"It's open!" she screamed back. A second later, the door was aggressively thrown open, making Hope jump once more. A boy dashed in with six people following him.

"They didn't stand a chance," the boy called to the group, laughing. He faltered when he noticed Hope staring at them, frightened. Cassidy saw her expression and said, "Don't worry, Hope, these are my friends. They helped save you." The boy, who couldn't have been more than 20, came up to her. She noticed a small amount of disbelief and fear in his light green eyes. The look vanished, and he shook Hope's hand enthusiastically.

"Hi there! I'm Ethan! I like to kill people and commit robberies!" Hope's eyes grew wide as she quickly slipped her hand from his grasp.

"He's just kidding," Cassidy said quickly, with a stern look at Ethan. He largely grinned, walking back to the door.

"Guys, this is Hope, one of the new ones," Cassidy explained.

"Really? Cass, I hadn't noticed," Ethan muttered. The girl glared at him once more.

"Hey, Hope," she began, "would you genuinely consider yourself dangerous?" Hope thought for a moment, nervous at what they would do if she said yes. *Why am I hesitating?* she thought. *I didn't do anything wrong!*

"No," she finally said. "All I did in the test was defend myself. Isn't that the normal thing to do?"

Suddenly, for some unfathomable reason, Hope felt the same anger she had experienced in her test. She wanted to *hurt* the people who dumped her here, the people who ripped her from her family.

"That's all I did! All I did was defend myself in their stupid test! What else was I supposed to do? And now I'm stuck here for the rest of my life! *I want to leave.*"

Ethan was looking at her, nodding his head slightly. She suddenly wanted to punch something, as if that would take care of all her worries. Hope desperately wanted to scream, but she knew that wouldn't be a good first impression for these new people. Cassidy nodded, her face in an expression of sympathy.

"I know, I know. But I think there's something you need to know." Hope mentally calmed herself and looked up at Cassidy.

"What's that?"

"I knew from when I saw you that you couldn't possibly be dangerous," the brunette girl started. "In fact, all of the people in this room aren't looking to harm anybody. Well maybe Maya, but we'll talk about her later," she said, gesturing to a snickering redhead. "There must be a reason we're all here."

"I know why we're here," Ethan piped up. Cassidy rolled her eyes, looking at Hope.

"It's just a stupid theory, Ethan." He shook his head.

"It's not stupid," he retorted. His head turned to look at Hope. "I think we're here because of our brains."

"Yeah, that's what the test looks at," Hope replied slowly. "I know that." Ethan chuckled quietly.

"That's not what I mean. I mean that we're dangerous. As in dangerously smart. There's something in our brain that's different from other people. We have the capacity for crazy intelligence. The government knows it, too. That's why we're all here." He paused, studying Hope's reaction. "It's because we are so smart that the government thinks we pose a threat. Then maybe all the psychos on this island can take care of us and do their job for them."

"There's no way to know that, though," Hope hesitatingly said. "We could have the potential to be dangerous, too."

"When I took my test, I saw it," Ethan said in a dramatically quiet tone. "I saw the paper that rated us from one to ten. Except it wasn't from one to ten. It was from one to 11. They had circled 11 for me."

They could have just lied about the scale, Hope was about to say, but then she stopped. Why would the government lie about something so pointless? If there was an 11, why didn't people know that?

"Well, it's a good theory," said Hope finally, "but it's impossible. Trust me, there's no way that I'm that smart." Ethan looked at her, his eyes glinting.

"Well, Hopie, then why are you on this island? Clearly you aren't dangerous." Hope shrugged.

"I don't know. Maybe the results are wrong."

"Were the results wrong, or were you just too smart? Obviously they wouldn't tell you that."

"I don't think so," Hope stated. "You might actually be dangerous."

"Yes," he answered ominously. "I love to murder people and throw their body in the ocean."

"Ethan, shut up," Cassidy snapped, but she was laughing.

"So, are there any more of you?" asked Hope. "I mean, there can't be only this amount of you guys. Shouldn't there be more?" Cassidy nodded, and Hope noticed her gaze move to the floor.

"Yeah, there were others," she said simply.

"How many?"

"Believe it or not, there were over 40 of us here. In the past year, they've all been murdered by creeps, like those men back there. Us six are the only young people left," Cassidy explained, fiddling with her nail.

"That's… horrible," Hope said, shaking her head. She suddenly felt worse than she had a minute ago. If all those people were killed, then she didn't stand a chance. Cassidy's chocolate eyes got the tiniest bit larger.

"I have to go," she said suddenly, running out of the worn door. The whole group of people stared at Hope as she felt her face turn hot. The boy, Ethan, came back over to her.

"Well, looks like you already know who I am!" Hope awkwardly nodded, her eyes sizing him up. "Anyway, Cassidy hates to talk about the other people who died," he told her. "Her boyfriend was one of the guys who ended up getting captured and killed by some psycho. Don't take it personally." Hope felt her body freeze.

"Captured?" Ethan's grin fell a fraction.

"Yeah, there are some different people here, Hopie."

"How did he die?"

"That's another story. One you aren't ready for. She's not really over it yet, as you can see. You better be careful, you might be next." His small smirk returned. "Want to meet the other smarties here?" Hope shrugged.

"Sure."

"Ok then!"

One by one, Ethan introduced each of the group. The first person Hope met was a boy called Aiden. He grinned, making her feel more comfortable. It was almost like she could feel her awkward feelings evaporate as he smiled. His golden-brown hair brought out the light flecks in his hazel eyes. He shook Hope's hand.

"It's nice to meet you, Hope," he said kindly. Hope returned the smile, feeling more at ease than she had a minute ago.

She gasped as a person ran through the door.

"That," said Ethan, "is Martha. She's like 60 years old. She's been on this island since she was 18. She's like our mom, but better."

"I'm only 45," she laughed through short breaths. "Sorry, I just ran 5 miles."

"From a criminal?" Hope asked in sudden fear. Martha gave a chuckle.

"No, I do it for fun. I've always loved to run."

She stopped speaking when she noticed that she didn't recognize the blonde girl in front of her.

"And who's this beauty?" Martha asked Ethan.

"I'm Hope," she said. "I just got here." Without warning, Martha grabbed her in a tight hug.

"Well, it's nice to meet you," she said in a light voice. "Call me Mom!" She pulled away, smoothing out her wavy hair. Hope didn't know whether she was kidding or not, so she just smiled.

"It's great to meet you as well," she stated. Ethan grinned.

"Now then, Hopie, let's get back to our little introductions." He gestured toward a tan girl leaning against the wall. She walked over with a shy smile.

"Hello, Hope," she said, twirling her hair around her index finger.

"This is Blisse," he told her. Blisse had kind of a pointed jaw, with large, beautiful brown eyes. Her long, stick-straight hair was ebony black. "This girl here is crazy. After all that happened to her, she is still the nicest person in the world. I've never seen her get mad before. Never." Ethan looked at her with a small amount of pride.

"Ready for another?" Hope nodded. He waved over the smallest, thinnest girl Hope had ever seen. She pushed Ethan out of the way and aggressively grabbed Hope's hand.

"Hello, hola, what's up, whatever. I'm Fire." Hope chuckled awkwardly.

"Uh, what?"

"Her real name's Sapphire," said Ethan, earning a death glare from her. "Well it is!" he said in defense. "She doesn't exactly like her name."

"I can speak for myself, Ethan," she retorted. He grinned. Ignoring her, he said, "If I were you, Hopie, I wouldn't get on her bad side. Trust me, I've done it before, and it's not pretty."

"He's right," said Fire. "I think the name Fire is pretty great, don't you?"

Hope nodded, smiling. "I like it." Fire looked at Hope oddly, her eyes staring her up and down.

"I guess that's everyone," said Ethan. "There's only seven of us in this sad little building. I guess you're number eight." He gave her a slight smirk, sweeping his hands across the room.

"Welcome to the club, Hopie."

5

The first thing Hope felt was panic. She clawed furiously at the hand covering her mouth as her screams were muffled. She relaxed immediately when she saw Ethan's grin above her in the darkness.

"Sorry to disturb you, Hopie, but I wanna show you something." She yawned and looked around. Everyone else was sound asleep.

"What time is it?" she asked tiredly. Ethan shrugged his shoulders.

"Who knows? It's not like we have clocks around here." That made Hope's eyes grow larger, despite her groggy state.

"What do you mean you don't have clocks?" Ethan shrugged his shoulders.

"I think I made myself pretty clear. We don't know the time. It's not a big deal." Hope thought this through as she slipped a hair tie off her wrist.

"Yeah, I guess so." She brought her tired muscles up to tie her hair into a loose ponytail. They stood in silence for a moment.

"Anyway, follow me. And be quiet." She could see his face light up, even under the night sky. He sprinted into the dense jungle. *Oh, not the jungle,* she thought anxiously. *At night?* She followed him anyway.

For the second time, Hope was completely out of breath. She had run for at least 10 minutes. Ethan wasn't even breathing hard.

"Alrighty Hopie, see this tree?" She nodded. "Climb it." Hope's mouth fell open.

"What if I fall?" she inquired, nervously looking up at the tree he wanted her to climb. Ethan shrugged.

"Well then, I guess you'll die," he stated simply. She looked at him like he was crazy. He smirked and raised his eyebrows. "Yes, Hopie?" Hope rolled her eyes.

"Forget it," she muttered. She held on the branch, testing to see if it would hold her weight.

"Having fun there?"

"I'm only making sure the branch won't snap," Hope said, blushing. "Hold on a second." Once she was sure the branch was sturdy, she reached for the next lowest branch. Hope continued to move slowly up the tree. After a while, the branches were getting dangerously thin. She thought about her body crashing to the ground below, which didn't help at all. "Ethan, I'm stopping now," she declared.

"Whatever makes you happy." His voice sounded from right behind her, making her jump. The adult climbed up a little more until he was right next to her. "Now, whatever you do, don't look down," he said mischievously. Hope sighed, knowing that was exactly what he wanted her to do. She gripped the branch extra hard as she peered over the edge. It was hard to see, but the stars provided a small amount of light. She stopped breathing when she saw just how high they were.

"No way!" she gasped, fighting to keep her voice from shaking. Ethan nodded his head.

"I know," he said, fighting the grin that was about to break out over his face. Hope let out a breath that she had been holding.

"How are you not afraid of being this high?" she practically yelled. Her breathing began to rapidly increase. He shrugged his shoulders.

"I guess I'm just superman." Ethan pulled both of his hands off of the tree, his grin illuminated in the starlight. A wave of fear passed through her body.

"Why do you come up here, anyway? What's so fun about feeling like you're going to fall?" Ethan shook his head.

"Oh, I don't know. I don't feel like I'm going to fall," he replied. "I just like being under the stars by myself sometimes." Her mouth opened when a glimpse of the stars caught her eye. From up here, it seemed as though she could see every star in the sky. Hope temporarily forgot she was on an island filled with criminals. She was breathless.

"Back in New York, you couldn't see a single star. This is incredible." She said all of this in an awed voice, forgetting about her deathly fear of heights. Ethan was smiling, gazing up at the glimmering stars, looking like a little kid. For once, his smirk was gone, and she saw only a boy who was fascinated by stars. She felt calm, thinking that underneath his smug expression, he was just a normal person who loved to look at the sky.

"I think incredible is an understatement," he said.

"Yeah, you're right."

Ethan looked back at her, but his eyes were oddly wide. Hope felt her heart speed up in an unknown fear at his expression.

"Ethan, are you alright?"

"Listen," he whispered, putting his finger over his mouth. She stopped immediately when she faintly heard laughing from far away. There was something about it that sent chills down her spine. It sounded insane. She felt the blood drain from her face. Hope looked at Ethan, her eyes wide.

"Don't worry about it Hopie, it's fine." Although his voice was steady, she could see that his green eyes were full of worry. "Just stay still," he whispered. She nodded, afraid that any movement would somehow bring the mad people to them. *Quit being ridiculous.*

Hope tensed up her body, holding her breath in terror. After a couple of minutes, the laughter finally subsided. Hope dared to speak.

"Do you think they're gone?" Her voice came out embarrassingly shaky.

"I think so," he whispered. "Start climbing, very, very, slowly." Hope climbed down as quietly as she could. She almost screamed when she lost her grip on a thin branch, but her hands closed around it just in time. Finally, she made it to the ground.

Ethan dropped down behind her, making her flinch. "Ok, walk slowly and quietly. After a bit, we can sprint the rest of the way."

Hope shook her head yes. She had only taken five steps when something moved in the bushes a few feet in front of her. She yelped in spite of herself. She looked behind her at Ethan's glare. *Sorry,* she mouthed. The girl kept an eye on the bush. *I must be paranoid. Either that or I'm going crazy.*

A couple of seconds later, she looked back at Ethan, unsure of where to go next. There was a problem, however.

Ethan wasn't there.

Hope felt like fainting. *I'm gonna die, I'm gonna get killed out here.* She could feel her panic rising when she felt a jolt on her shoulder. She shrieked, jumping back. Ethan's smile was from ear to ear, hiding the subsiding fear in his eyes.

"Got you!"

Hope felt water begin to form in her eyes. She turned away, furious and humiliated. He noticed something was wrong as he took a few careful steps her way. "Hope, I was just trying to-"

He was interrupted by Hope's fist smashing into his jaw. She groaned, her teeth smashing together at the pain. His stupid jaw had hurt her hand. Ethan automatically put his hand over his bruising mouth. He grimaced.

"Yeah, I guess I deserved that," he said through gritted teeth. "Geez, Hopie, did anyone ever tell you that you're a strong girl?" Hope could feel the tears about to spill over her lashes.

No, don't cry. Not now. Hope, no. Her warnings didn't help her at all. The water in her eyes overflowed. She couldn't stop, and embarrassment was the only thing on her mind. Ethan put one arm around her, his other hand rubbing his sore jaw.

"Hope, I'm sorry, I thought you would take it as a joke, I was just trying to lighten the mood." Hope put her back to him as she stared at the stars. "I think we should head back," Ethan said after a while.

"Lead the way," Hope snapped at him. He looked at her for a second, shrugged, then started running back to the building, Hope on his tail. They finally made it back to the building's doors unharmed.

"Can I ask you a favor?" Ethan asked as he held the door open for her. Hope shrugged, still incredibly mad and embarrassed.

Wow Hope, great first impression. She silently stepped through the doorway. "Just please don't tell anyone else I went with you out here," he told her. "That place is kind of, you know, private, and I don't want them to know about it. I know you're still mad, but can you at least promise me?" His eyebrows were raised in an expected expression. Hope stared daggers at him until weariness overpowered her.

"Sure," she finally said. He grabbed her wrist, pulled her back, and looked into her eyes with urgency.

"I want you to promise."

"Let go!" Hope struggled against his iron grip, but it was clear that he wasn't going to let go until she promised him. "Fine, I promise." Ethan didn't even attempt to hide his relief.

"Thank you Hopie. I'm sorry for scaring you," he added. "Hopefully the stars made up for that. Goodnight." Hope bit her lip in anger and embarrassment, still staring in his direction. Then she laid down, rolled over to her side, and fell asleep until morning.

Hope awoke to Cassidy prodding her hip with her foot.

"Good morning, Hope!" She had changed into a milk-chocolate tee-shirt covered in stains, bringing out the golden flecks in her brown eyes.

Hope sat up, her face stretching into a huge yawn. Ethan was up as well, and Hope noticed his eyes flit to her.

"Hey, Ethan!" Cassidy called, her eyes darting toward him. "Quit staring. I know I'm cute." Ethan picked up a small stone and chucked it at her. She swiftly brought up her hand and caught it, laughing.

"Oh, stop," he said through a chuckle.

A loud *smack* pierced the air. Hope's head quickly turned to the doorway. Standing there was Maya, holding something. Hope realized she had never had a formal introduction to her as she had with all the others. A small jolt of hurt made its way through her. As Maya stood menacingly in the doorway, Hope studied her. She had dark emerald green eyes with a steely look, curly red hair, and a glare on her face that Hope didn't think would ever go away. The three knives she had sticking out of an obviously self-made belt caught Hope's eye. Maya caught her staring, and Hope saw a small smirk make its way onto her face. There was what looked like paint dripping all over her hands. Hope gagged when she realized that it was blood.

"I'm back!" she called eerily. Upon further inspection, Hope could tell that she was holding small lizards tightly in her hands. The redhead eyed Ethan's bruised jaw.

"Ethan, did you fall on your chin in the middle of the night?" Maya wiped the blood off onto her torn-up jeans. Ethan was about to answer when he noticed Hope's look of begging and embarrassment.

"I guess I just had a bad dream or something," he answered, with a look at Hope. A look of anger quickly flashed across Maya's face, almost too quickly to be noticed.

"Got us our breakfast!" she said, a smile coming back to her face. "One lizard for Blisse, one for Cassidy, one for mother Martha, a lizard for Aiden, one for Ethan, a lizard for Fire, and one for me! Let's eat!"

"Uhh, Cassidy, I, well, I'm kind of hungry," Hope whispered to her new friend. She had always felt uncomfortable asking for anything, much less people she just met.

"I'll ask her," Cassidy whispered back.

"No, no, it's ok," Hope reassured quickly.

"Hey, Maya, Hope here is starving and she doesn't have any breakfast," Cassidy declared to her, ignoring Hope's plea. Hope's face turned bright red and her gaze moved to the ground. Maya's radiant eyes flashed.

"Oh, no, of course! How could I have possibly missed our little guest?" Hope could tell Maya didn't mean any of what she was saying; the fake smile plastered across her face was enough of a clue. "Come with me Hope, let's go get you some food!" She grinned and motioned for Hope to come follow her out of the building. She hesitated before giving in to her hungry stomach. Hope gently pushed open the old door. Maya was already running at top speed toward the edge of the green jungle. Hope finally caught up to her, taking huge breaths.

"Wow, thanks for helping me, Maya," she said. Maya shot her a dirty look as she glanced around. Fear and anger filled Hope's mind.

Finally, her glare settled on Hope. Without warning, she reared back her fist and slammed it into Hope's cheek.

Hope shouted, her hand flying up to cover her face. Maya's eyebrows contorted with rage.

"You're going to ruin everything," the fierce redhead snarled. "We were fine before, and you almost got us killed by those men. They will search until they find you, I know what they do. I should hand you over to them before they kill us all. Like they did last time," she muttered. Hope stared at her, shocked.

"I didn't mean for them to find me!" Maya darkly chuckled.

"Well, they did. You can get your own food." She stalked back off, then started running to the building, leaving Hope alone.

Hope chased after her. She finally could see her curly hair bounding through the trees. Maya reached the doors of the building. Her grin turned into a snarl when she realized Hope had been able to keep up with her. Hope smiled smugly despite her immense fear of the girl in front of her.

Cassidy looked over for a second, smiling at their return. Her kind eyes grew alarmed when she noticed Hope's swelling cheek.

"Hope, what happened?" she practically shouted. She bounded over, carefully inspecting her face. Hope narrowed her eyes, angrily looking at Maya.

"I got punched." Cassidy's look slowly transformed into irritation. She threw her hands up into the air, exasperated.

"Maya, what possessed you to punch her? She just about arrived on this island, and she hasn't done anything to you." Maya came right up to Cassidy. Maya was much taller than Cassidy, but the brunette didn't seem afraid.

"Getting punched isn't fun, is it Hopie?" Ethan asked in amusement as he came over.

Maya sneered at Cassidy.

"You know, I really don't like you all that much."

With striking speed, her leg shot out, hitting Cassidy's kneecap. She fell over, her face contorted in pain. Blisse opened her mouth, appalled.

"Maya?" she asked in a timid voice. Maya's blazing eyes whipped around. "Maybe you shouldn't kick her. She's really nice and… important." Blisse said the last word in a scared, quiet voice.

That was the wrong thing to say.

Maya's eyes filled with fire. Her mouth slowly lowered open, too scary to be comical.

"Is she now? Is it her kindness that makes you like her? You think that makes her a leader?" Maya's voice was rising to a shout. Hope slouched back, filled with unease. Her anger was rising to the level that she wanted no part of. Cassidy squinted her eyes in confusion and pain. "You think she's your leader?" Maya asked again. "*I* am. I am!!"

"I didn't say anything about a damn leader," Cassidy gasped out. Maya walked away from Cassidy and came up to Blisse.

"Maya!" Martha yelled, getting up from the floor. Blisse's body was literally shaking in terror. Before Maya could do anything worse, Ethan sprung into action. He took a stone from a corner and threw it, hard, at Maya's head. His aim was perfect, causing her to slump down onto the floor. Ethan flipped his head to the side.

"I didn't think I could actually do that," he smirked, winking. Blisse slowly let out a breath.

"What was that about?" she asked. Fire shrugged.

"I don't know, hormones?"

Ethan chuckled, walking over to the unconscious Maya. A small bump was forming on her temple.

"Will she be ok?" Blisse inquired, coming over to look at her friend.

"Let's pray she isn't," Cassidy said darkly. Hope knitted her eyebrows together.

"Ok, I'm sorry, I didn't mean that. My knee just hurts really bad right now, and Maya just isn't the type of person I like."

Hope took steps toward Cassidy. She gingerly rested her hand on her injured leg.

"Do you think you can walk?" Hope asked her. Cassidy smiled, but it didn't reach her eyes.

"I think so." Hope grabbed her hand and began to pull. Cassidy winced. "Ouch, ouch, ouch. Hope, you are *not* gentle." Finally, Cassidy had stood up. She took one step, and then another. "My knee seriously hurts. That girl has muscle. I think I need to sit down again." She limped over to a corner and slid her back down the wall. Cassidy gently put her scratched up hand on her knee. Sapphire's eyebrows were raised and Aiden was yawning, staring at the scene before him with wide eyes. He looked up at Hope, almost apologetic.

"Hope, what the hell did you get yourself into?"

6

An hour passed. Then two. Everyone was terrified at what Maya would do when she woke up, but no one wanted to spoil the peace.

"Hey, Hope, can I talk to you?" Blisse asked quietly. She was surprised that Blisse was speaking to her, but she nodded. Blisse gestured toward the door. Understanding the message, she got up, glancing around the room. Hope walked out of the door with the kind girl in front of her.

"I'm sorry about Maya," she began in her soft voice. "You shouldn't have had to see her in one of her moods. Normally, she's alright. I just wanted to apologize for your first day." Hope smiled.

"Well, thanks Blisse. It's not your fault, but I appreciate it just the same." Hope turned to go back inside, but she was stopped by Blisse's gentle grip on her arm.

"Hope, are you ok?" she asked, concerned.

"Yeah, I'm fine," she responded automatically. Blisse kept her gaze on her.

"Are you sure?"

"Yeah, I'm ok."

"Ok then, let's go back inside," Blisse stated. She turned to go back into the building.

More hours went by. The time passed uneventfully, just the way everyone liked. Hope could tell that Fire was agitated that they all had to stay inside for so long. Finally, she jumped up.

"Can't we do something?!" she asked. "I'm so bored!" She sounded just like a little kid who was forced to sit still. Ethan looked up, exasperated.

"What do you propose we do, Fire?" he asked. She shrugged.

"I don't know, maybe…" she broke off. "Hey, guys, do you want to play our game with Hope?" She smiled mischievously.

"Um, what game exactly?" Hope asked, a bit afraid of the answer. Ethan's face lit up in excitement.

"We like to play hide-and-seek around the island, Hopie," he told her. Cassidy jumped up with a slight wince.

"Yeah, sometimes we play it in a section of the island," she added. *That's a terrible idea!* Hope thought, not daring to say it aloud.

"What about criminals! Aren't they just crawling around here?" Ethan laughed.

"Don't be such a downer. If we see or hear someone, we just run away."

You seemed terrified when we heard a criminal, she thought, but decided not to say it.

Sapphire walked over and punched Hope playfully in the arm. Her other hand pointed at Blisse.

"Come on, she even likes this game, Hope. Don't let being on this island ruin your fun. Just do it!" Hope shrugged.

"Wow, peer pressure much?" she muttered. Ethan lifted one eyebrow.

"What was that, Hopie?"

"Nothing. So, how do you play? Is this like, normal hide-and-seek, or something else?" Ethan grinned.

"With us, nothing is ever normal." He paused, waiting for a laugh. When Hope rewarded him with a blank stare, he continued. "Basically, we get into teams. Since Martha doesn't usually play, there are two people per team." Martha smiled.

"I like to stay here and keep an eye out for things. But since Maya is still... asleep, I'll play for once." She punched his arm affectionately.

"Since I'm the coolest person here, I'll make the teams," Ethan proclaimed.

"Is that so?" asked Aiden. "Because I thought that the coolest person was me. Isn't that right, Fire?" She rolled her eyes, her mouth curling into a reluctant smile.

"Oh, shut up, Aiden."

Ethan put his hand on his chin, his stare lingering on Hope. She blushed slightly and looked down, but she could still sense his gaze.

"I got it!" he exclaimed suddenly. "Cassidy, you're with Blisse. Martha, go alone. Fire, you're with Aiden, and Hopie, you're with me." Ethan grinned. "Ok, my team will hide first. Whoever finds us first will hide next. Easy-peasy." Ethan took off running, with Hope right behind him.

The pair continued sprinting until they were out of breath.

"Ok, now that they can't possibly hear us, let's pick a hiding spot," Ethan said.

"You choose," she huffed out. Hope crouched over, catching her breath. A thoughtful look was on his face. "You know, Ethan, how in the world do you not get tired?" He smiled proudly.

"I used to be on a cross country team," he said, as if that explained everything.

"So, where are we going to hide?"

"Well, I was only worried about getting far away," he said, looking around at the trees. "I wasn't worried about where we would actually go." He gave a wide smile as he shrugged. Hope put her hand on her hip.

"Well, then where are we going now?"

"We could go in a tree again," suggested Ethan. "Or, we could go.." he broke off, an idea flying across his face. "I know where we can hide! It's about two minutes from here. Let's go!" They ran some more, Hope becoming more tired by the minute.

"Are we.. there.. yet?" Hope huffed, being out of breath for yet another time. Ethan shook his finger mockingly.

"Now now Hopie, we mustn't rush."

"I'm stopping," she proclaimed, putting all her weight onto a tree trunk. Ethan pretended to give an annoyed sigh.

"You big baby." Hope put her hands over her head.

"Excuse me if I'm not some buff cross country guy," she said in defense. Ethan puffed out his chest.

"You think I'm buff?" Hope could feel her face turn red.

"No." She pulled herself off of the tree. "I'm ready now." Ethan gave a nod of his head as he again took off sprinting. Hope followed, her lungs burning. A short time later, they came to a clearing in the jungle. A large tree sat in the middle of the open land.

"It's somewhere around this tree," Ethan stated. He walked around, kicking the ground.

"I found it when I was running here one time. I nearly fell in, just so you know. I covered it back up with leaves and all that fun stuff so nobody else could find it. I stashed emergency food in it. Ah, here it is." He started picking up leaves and throwing them until he came to a slab of concrete.

Hope's eyebrows knitted together.

"Is that a hole?"

"I thought that would be clear," he responded, "but yes."

"You want me to hide in an underground hole?"

"I got this from the town," he explained, ignoring her. "Yep, this is it!" He walked back over to Hope and grabbed her hand.

"I can walk by myself," she said, pulling her hand away in embarrassment. He gave a small grin as he walked her over to the hole.

"Be careful, Hopie," he warned.

"Wait, you want me to jump in!?" She gulped, looking down at the ground far below. He nodded, his eyebrows raising. "What if I land wrong and break my ankle?" Ethan smirked and shook his head.

"Man, Hopie, you've got a lot of anxiety in that body of yours. You'll be fine. Probably." She was still scared of injuring herself. "You might want to hurry up, there." Hope sat down, put both of her legs in the hole, and jumped into the earth.

"OW!" she exclaimed when Ethan fell right on top of her. He snickered.

"Oops." He pressed his hands into the rough dirt and pulled himself off of her.

"I guess it'll be a while before they find us," he stated. Hope nodded, but there were other things on her mind.

"Hey Ethan, I have a question." He shrugged.

"Let's hear it." She braced herself to ask it.

"Why were you so eager to play this game when you got so freaked out about the people we heard last night?" She asked her question very quickly. Ethan's smug expression faded away. He averted his gaze to the ground.

"No reason. Just forget about it," he commanded. Hope was confused.

"Why?" Ethan grabbed her arm, cutting her off.

"Just don't." His tone was firm, clearly closing the subject. Hope heaved a heavy sigh.

"Fine, I have a different question," she said.

"Can't wait."

"Well, why do you trust me so much? You showed me your little tree and this hiding spot, and you just met me. Why?" Ethan stayed silent for a while. Hope even had the thought that he didn't even hear her when he said, "I actually don't know. That's a first. I guess it's because you seem trustworthy. I'm pretty good at reading people." Hope thought there was more to his reasoning, but she kept quiet.

"One more question," she said. Ethan nodded his head. "Why does Maya hate me so much? She hit me." Ethan smirked.

"You mean like how you hit me?" He lightly tapped his bruise while Hope's face burned in embarrassment.

"I was upset, ok? I'm sorry." Ethan winked at her.

"I accept your apology, Hopie." She chewed the inside of her cheek.

"So why does she hate me?" Ethan's smile seemed to shrink a little.

"Well, think of it this way: when you punched me, you felt sad, right? Maybe even humiliated?" Hope nodded uncomfortably. "Well, maybe Maya was feeling especially angry or annoyed at that moment. Who knew what she was thinking?"

"Yeah, but you didn't see the way she looked at me," Hope told him. Ethan nodded thoughtfully. "It was like I had killed her family or something."

"True, true, but Maya isn't normally like that. Sure, she's fierce and even scary, but she must have been feeling upset." Hope raised her eyebrows.

"Ok, I guess so. How long have you been on this island?" Ethan opened his mouth to answer when he heard a scraping noise from up above. His eyes darted to the ceiling made of dirt.

The concrete slab was pushed away, revealing a smirking Fire and Aiden.

"Found you!" she shouted, with Aiden right behind her.

You couldn't have waited longer? Hope thought to herself.

"Watch out!" Aiden yelled as he leaped in without a worry. Sapphire's tiny body landed on him, her face breaking out in a grin.

"Would you twits keep it down?" Ethan snapped. Sapphire laughed and threw a handful of dirt at Ethan's face. His stern look melted off as he threw an even bigger pile, making her laugh even harder.

"How did you guys find us?" Hope asked, hoping that she only sounded curious. Fire grinned as she wiggled her eyebrows.

"I knew about this hole all along. I knew he would go here." Hope noticed Ethan's eyes fill with surprise, but it went away as quickly as it came.

"How did you know, Fire?" he asked.

"I hide in the shadows every night, stalking you as you got up from the building and left," she said ominously, making Aiden chuckle. They were interrupted by yet another two faces.

"Man you guys, I could hear you from a mile away!" Cassidy exclaimed, with Blisse smiling behind her. They both hopped down gracefully and sat with everyone else. Fire's shrill laugh seemed to echo off the walls. Hope slightly grinned, wondering if her other friends would find them easily because of the loud noise. Cassidy sure had heard them.

Hope froze.

Ethan looked at her, his massive grin slightly dwindling.

"What happened, Hopie?" Goosebumps started to creep up Hope's skin.

"If Cassidy could hear us from a mile away, so could somebody else."

"I was just exaggerating," Cassidy clarified. "It wasn't really a mile away, I just followed Fire."

"But still," Hope pressed, her breath coming out in short bursts. "There could be a criminal right above us."

"Oh, chill out," Fire said, rubbing the dirt off of her arm. "Quit being so paranoid."

"I'm just trying to be safe," Hope retorted. She could feel a blush making its way up her burning cheeks. It left her face as soon as a snap pierced the air.

"Martha!" Fire called. She was silenced by Cassidy's hand hastily covering her mouth.

"It might not be her," Cassidy whispered.

"Dude, you worry too much," Fire said loudly, taking her hand away from her mouth.

"Everybody shut up," Ethan snapped quietly. Fire shot him an annoyed look, but she shut her mouth. There was another snap, which sounded just like a step. Hope's body was frozen. Her breathing seemed to slow.

The footsteps were faster now, and it was clear that there were multiple people above them.

The noise stopped. Fire looked around oddly, ideas running through her eyes. Hope opened her mouth to speak when she heard deep voices. Judging from the tone, the sounds belonged to men. The words they were saying were hard to make out. Ethan craned his neck, trying to listen better.

What's going on? Hope mouthed to Cassidy. She shrugged, and her shoulders were slightly trembling as well. Soon, the words became clearer, making her cower even harder.

"I thought I heard them," a gruff voice said. More silence.

"That one girl, the blonde one, I'm going to find her. She caused this." No one could see what he was referring to, but she guessed it was an injury. With terror, Hope realized that the voice belonged to the same man she had first met when she arrived.

"Yeah, and she got away," another man responded.

"No one ever gets away," the first man replied, anger evident in his voice. Hope looked at Ethan for comfort, but she turned away as she saw his poorly hidden expression.

"Oh, don't worry," the man continued. "We'll find her. You'll see."

Everyone waited in complete silence. The voices seemed to fade away. Ethan was the first one to speak.

"Well, wasn't that something?" he asked, attempting to break the ice. Hope just shook her head. Everyone had surprised and scared looks on their faces, except for Fire. She was staring at Hope in anger.

"Looks like our group is now going to be hunted," she said in an accusatory tone. Hope's eyes widened.

"I didn't do anything!"

"In the two years I've been here, I've never seen them hunt for a specific person before," Blisse whispered. The ground seemed to shake in Hope's vision.

Oh man, they're gonna find me, they're gonna kill me, I might as well be dead. The fear she had been holding back was seeping into her mind, turning her blood to ice. Ethan put an arm around her, ending the sudden panic.

"It's ok, Hopie, we won't let them hurt you," he said softly. Hope smiled a weak smile.

"Let's hope you're right."

7

"So," said Aiden, "how do we get out of this hole anyway?" Ethan looked up, his eyes turning annoyed.

"I forgot to make a rope," he told them. Hope looked at him in fear.

"So we're just stuck down here?"

"No. If you fellows work together, you can lift me up. I'll make a rope out of vines and save the day."

Aiden grabbed Ethan's ankle while Blisse and Fire grabbed the other one. Ethan turned his head to Hope, who was standing back.

"Come on Hopie, don't be shy!" he called. With blood rushing to her face, she stepped forward and helped Aiden support his friend. They all pushed up their hands so Ethan could grab onto the dry earth above. As soon as he was out, Aiden dropped back. Hope copied his actions.

A moment later, a thin but firm rope made of vines was lowered down. Fire dashed to the front, jokingly pushing Aiden out of the way. Hope was somehow pushed to the back of the line. She looked up above her to see Ethan's face with his normal grin. She could hear other people's voices echoing down into the hole. He let the bottom of the vine fall to her. She felt the thick skin of the dark green plant. She grabbed hold of it, and felt it begin to lift her up. Instinctively, she put her feet on the dirt wall and began to walk up.

A pang hit her heart when she remembered doing the exact same motions when she used to go rock climbing with her dad. She hadn't done it since he had left. She could feel her eyes burn when she thought of him now. Hope had never even gotten to say goodbye to her father. She sniffed just before she reached the top. Ethan reached for her hand, pulling her above the earth. Quickening footsteps alerted them of Martha's presence.

"I see I lost," Martha exclaimed, pretending to look sad. Ethan laughed, throwing his head back.

"Whatever. I think we should head back to our place now. I want to take a nap." Aiden murmured in agreement. They began to trudge through the jungle, back to their home. Suddenly, Ethan got a look of kid-like excitement on his face. "Race you!" he called. He took off at lightning speed. Martha shook her head, laughing.

"Ethan's such a child," she said happily, taking off as well. Fire grinned and sprinted after the two. They ran for about a minute until they reached the edge of the green jungle. She caught her breath as she looked at each of the gasping people she now called her friends.

Cassidy's expression confused her. She looked as though she was heartbroken. Ethan was staring into the distance toward the town, his green eyes full of grief. With seeping dread, Hope looked far ahead of her. A bright orange light caught her eye.

Their entire building was aflame.

Hope was at a loss for words. Everything the young group had owned was in the building that Hope had first met them in. Now, their belongings had to be nothing but ash.

"Not to be insensitive, but where will we sleep tonight?" she asked. Ethan slowly turned and looked at her. His vulnerable look broke her heart. Suddenly, Fire gasped. Ethan looked at her, startled.

"What?"

"Did Maya ever wake up?" she asked, her face alarmed. Hope slowly understood that unless Maya had woken up, which wasn't likely, she would be dead.

"I guess we need to figure out where we will sleep," Cassidy brought up sadly. "Anyone have any ideas?" Hope thought for a moment.

"Ethan, couldn't we stay at the place you…" He sent her a look, cutting her off. She forgot nobody else knew about his high tree deep in the jungle. "I mean, we could stay in a tree. I saw it when Ethan and I were finding a spot to hide in," Hope explained, covering up her mistake.

"Yeah, I guess," Fire choked out, her eyes still locked on the sight of her burning home.

"Well, at least there's some good news," Cassidy brought up. Ethan looked at her curiously. "We don't have to worry about Maya anymore."

"Are you saying that you're glad she died?" Blisse gasped out, her eyebrows together.

"No," Cassidy slowly said. "I'm just saying that we aren't exactly threatened by her anymore." Fire scoffed.

"We were never threatened by her in the first place, Cassidy."

"Well," interrupted Aiden, "I guess we might as well go in a tree. We can watch out for people too."

"Lead the way, Hope," Martha said, grief evident in her voice. Hope looked at Ethan, telling him with her eyes to go first. He started to walk back into the jungle, not looking back once, leaving behind the place they all called home.

Hope tried to be as quiet as possible. Her mind had started to imagine people in the bushes, waiting for the right moment to attack. She could vividly picture some creep with an ax, ready to strike. She remembered the man's look, pure sadism in his eyes. *Hope, stop,* she told herself firmly. *Calm down. No one's there.*

"Ok, we need two people to keep watch," said Ethan. "Any volunteers?" Fire's hand shot up immediately. Ethan grinned weakly at her enthusiasm. "Ok, anyone else?" Martha stood up.

"I will," she proclaimed proudly. He pointed up to the top of the tree.

"Alrighty, ladies first," he said, a hint of himself back. He gave a large sweep with his hand.

"Such chivalry," Cassidy sneered slightly, punching his arm playfully. Hope and Cassidy began climbing to the top of the tall tree, with Blisse right behind them.

Hope couldn't believe she had touched these branches only the night before. It seemed much longer than that to her. Her hands started to ache as she reached the top of the tree. Cassidy was showing some obvious strain as well.

"We'd better stop here. The branches are getting too thin," Hope whispered. The brunette nodded. Cassidy looked down at the other two and waved her hands to tell them to stop. She could hear Ethan and Aiden make their way up the tree as well.

"We're lucky that this tree has so many branches," Cassidy whispered to Hope. She nodded. Cassidy said something else, but Hope didn't catch what it was, as she had already made herself comfortable. The vision of the engulfed building was stuck in her mind. Of course, it was only a small wooden house, but it was the only thing they could call their own on an island where they might not live to see another day. Luckily, Hope didn't have time to think about her own home as she felt herself drift off.

Cassidy weakly tapped on Hope's shoulders a few hours later.

"Hope, wake up," she said sleepily. Hope was confused, as the sky was still pitch black.

"What?" Hope asked, tired and slightly grouchy.

"Ethan told me to tell you that you and him are going to keep watch now," Cassidy explained, slurring her words. Hope didn't think that the idea of her staying up when blood-thirsty men were after her was a good idea.

"But I'm tired," she complained. Cassidy smacked Hope's leg weakly.

"Quit complaining and just go," she said, a twinge of annoyance in her voice. Hope sighed and began descending down the tree, accidentally stepping on Blisse's hand and Aiden's leg. Ethan was now on the ground, talking to Martha and Fire. He gave her a sly smile when he saw Hope jump to the ground. She was hungry, tired, and cold, and staying up for a while was not her idea of fun. "How long do I have to stay up?" she mumbled. Ethan laughed.

"Three hours," he replied. Hope felt her eyes widen in anger.

"WHAT?!

"Would you two shut up?" Aiden shouted from up in the tree.

"Hopie, shut up. And yes, three hours. That's how long they stayed up for. Shut your yap and quit complaining." Hope glared at him for a moment, but she kept quiet.

"I'm really sorry about your...house," Hope finally whispered to him. Ethan gave a small sigh.

"Yeah, me too. You know, I kind of liked that place. Then again, it sucked. So many bad memories." He gave a quiet chuckle. "Oh well, variety is the spice of life, as they say." Hope nodded, bringing her eyes up to look at the sky.

"Three hours is a long time," Ethan said a few minutes later. "So, what do you want to talk about?" Hope shrugged. The only thing on her mind were terrible, power-hungry criminals, but she didn't think that would make a great conversation.

"Tell me about your family, Hopie," he told her. "What are they like?" She was about to reply when she heard a voice from above.

"Would you two lovebirds keep it down?" The voice belonged to an annoyed and tired Sapphire. Hope blushed deeply, but Ethan didn't even look the least bit embarrassed.

"How about you go to sleep, element!" Hope heard her snicker, and then she fell silent. She looked at Ethan, confused.

"Element?" Hope asked him. Ethan raised his eyebrows, grinning.

"What's that?"

"Why did you call her element?" He laughed quietly.

"Her name's Fire, and if you weren't informed, fire is an element. You know, air, fire, earth, water." Hope rolled her eyes with a small grin.

"Yes Ethan, I got it." Ethan smiled.

"So, answer my question. Please," he added quickly. "What's your family like?"

She cleared her mind for a second, trying to think of the words that would describe the people she loved most in the world.

"Well, I remember going to parks and tiny shops with my mom and dad when I was seven years old. I was an only child. When I was eight years old, they got into a huge fight over money or something like that." Hope paused, looking at Ethan's expression. He looked so intrigued by her story, a sight that made her feel warm inside.

"They ended up splitting," she continued, "when I was nine. Mom met some guy at her work a few months later. They started dating and got married much sooner than I thought was right. He had a daughter named Haylee, who is only a week younger than I am. At first, we hated each other. We fought over petty things like who got the remote, what movies to watch, all that fun stuff. A couple of months later, we started school again. Since we were put into the same class, we always had to work with each other. We became super close as the year went on. By the end of the school year, we were somehow best friends. I love her more than anything. She was my best friend." Hope winced when she heard herself use past-tense. "She *is* my best friend. I promised her I wouldn't be dangerous. I never even said any final words to her. I just can't believe I'll never see her again."

Hope hadn't realized she had started to cry until she had finished her story. Ethan was looking at her, full of sympathy and curiosity. She could feel her lip tremble as Ethan pulled her into a hug.

"I'm so sorry, Hopie," he said sincerely. This time, she didn't push him away. She needed someone's comfort.

"It's not your fault," she said, wiping her eyes with the back of her hand. She pushed away the thought of Haylee, sniffing. Her entire life had just been spilled out to a stranger. Oddly enough, Hope knew that he really was trustworthy. He wouldn't tell anyone, it was obvious in his expression."Tell me about your family now." She leaned in slightly, ready to listen. Ethan quietly cleared his throat and began to talk.

"Ok, where do I start? Well, let me tell you where I lived. I was born in Alaska, about 20 years ago. My earliest memory is watching the northern lights." *So that's why he loves the sky so much,* she realized silently.

"I had a brother, who was related to me by blood. His name was Carter, and he was 2 years older than me. We were really close, just like you and your sister. Everybody always told us that we were much closer than most brothers. One day, we were outside, throwing a football. I think I was eleven then. I threw the ball to him and it sailed over his head. We lived by one of the busiest roads in the entire state, by the way."

Ethan paused, looking at Hope. "Why am I telling you all this again?"

Hope grinned, tapping her head.

"Because you trust me, remember?" Ethan nodded, smiling.

"Right. Anyway, he ran into the road to get the ball just as a car sped by. I watched him get hit. The car just kept going. They didn't even stop to see the person they had killed. To them, he was just a boy in the way. To me, he was my best friend, just like Haylee was to you." Ethan took a deep breath, and she was surprised that he wasn't crying, though she couldn't see his face very well in the dark. "My mom blamed me for pushing him out in the road. It was clear she loved him more. She said I should've died instead." Hope's eyes grew wide in shock.

"She said that to you?" She could never imagine her mom saying something that despicable to her. Ethan nodded.

"Yeah. That messed me up pretty bad. After we found him, she called 911. The police sped him to the hospital. That was the first and only time I've ever been in an ambulance. While we were riding in it, I talked to him, telling him how much I loved him and that I was sorry for being such a horrible thrower. I thought if I made him laugh, he would forgive me. You don't understand the guilt I felt, Hope. The doctors made me leave when we got there. I remember that I went crazy and punched a nurse in the face. They had to calm me down while they wheeled him into a room. They wouldn't let anyone see him. He died a few hours later. I never even got to say goodbye to him."

"I'm so sorry," Hope whispered. He shrugged indifferently.

"That night, when we got home, my mom threw her hairbrush at me as hard as she could. She hit me and cussed me out for a long time. The worst part was, my dad just stood and watched. He didn't even make an effort to stop her. That hurt me the most." Hope had never heard anyone talk like this. It was truly, truly awful to hear.

"I started to get bullied a lot at school," he continued. "I went from being popular to a person that everyone pitied. I fell behind in my classes, and I even stopped eating for a while. In hindsight, I probably should have seen a therapist, but my parents wouldn't even consider taking me. My life was horrible, Hope. Really, really sucky.

"I couldn't wait until I graduated. I got so mad one Christmas that I robbed a *Best Buy*. I was almost 17. I went to jail for only a week, since I didn't use a weapon and I wasn't an adult. My life was awful until a couple weeks after I was let out of jail. I saw a job offer, and I ended up applying so I could be away from home most of the day. I met a girl, Amanda, who also worked there, and we started dating. She looked just like you, Hopie. Her hair was the exact same shade. I almost thought you were her when I saw you with all those men. She was so beautiful and nice, just like you." Hope felt herself blushing, thankful that her face was hidden by the darkness.

"My life was great for the next year or so. We got serious, and I was even thinking of moving in with her. She said I could after I told her about my parents. Then, before you know it, the test came. I wasn't even sweating it. I knew I wasn't dangerous. When I robbed the store, it's not like I threatened anyone. My results were dangerous, as you know. When I came to this island, the only person here was Maya. She had gotten there only a few days earlier than I had. Right off the start, we hated each other. She was so mean and hard compared to me. We ended up starting a kind of alliance together, even though we couldn't stand the sight of each other. I did want to survive, though. That's when we met the other people on this island who were our age. Lots of girls," he smirked.

"I didn't want to date anyone, because I still missed Amanda so much it hurt. Maya, however, met her boyfriend. She finally became more bearable. It's kind of funny, actually, to see how love can change a person, especially someone like her. Cassidy arrived a few weeks later. After her came Blisse, all almost exactly a month apart. That's when all 40 of our group was here. Cassidy met some guy named Brandon about a week after she got here. We all were fine because we had so many people. We felt safe, in a way." He chortled.

"Yeah, safe on an island full of danger. Anyway, Aiden got here almost a year after I got here. Fire came a couple weeks after him. She's been here for the least amount of time, besides you of course."

He stopped speaking for a moment. "Here's where things get bad," he warned. Hope shook her head kindly.

"You can tell me."

"One day, about 20 of us were walking through the woods, including me. We were ambushed by the same guy who is looking for you. When we were in the hole, I recognized his voice. The last thing we all heard was his voice saying, "Now." About 30 people had swords, glass, and knives, and they killed everyone except Fire and me. I survived by hiding under my friend's body." Hope couldn't imagine how traumatizing it must have been to watch 18 of your friends die.

"Apparently, the other 20 were ambushed as well. Half of them were captured, and most of the others were killed. Luckily, Cassidy, Aiden, Maya, and Blisse were smart, and they ran into the jungle without getting caught. Cassidy told me something awful. I probably shouldn't tell you." She sighed, looking at Ethan with annoyance in her eyes.

"Ethan, just tell me. I can handle it." She could see Ethan smile through the darkness.

"Ok, Hope, I guess. So she said that one day she was going for a walk, alone, to clear her mind. About a mile out, she saw her boyfriend, hanging by his neck, with a vine wrapped around it. There was a message scratched into the dirt. I definitely won't tell you that, so don't even ask," he added, responding to Hope's curious look.

"Cassidy ran home that day, hyperventilating. She had nightmares for weeks. For the next few days, we would see the bodies of our friends, all in different places. That's why I won't let them get you, Hopie. I don't want to see you like that." Hope oddly felt safe with Ethan. He really did seem like he would go to the ends of the earth to protect her. With a surprising feeling of hurt, she wondered if he only wanted to help her because she reminded him of his old girlfriend. But looking at his eyes in the dark, she didn't think that he was the type of guy to chase nothing but a memory.

"Well, thanks for telling me that stuff. That is truly terrifying," she said, patting his wrist. Hope yawned, a wave of sleepiness rushing over her. Ethan noticed, and said, "You can go to sleep if you want. I won't tell anyone."

"Wait, really?"

"Of course," he confirmed. "Goodnight, Hopie." She shot him a thankful grin.

"Thanks, Ethan. Really, thank you." She smiled softly one last time, then felt darkness take her over.

Hope felt a hand on her arm. She peeled open her eyes in alarm. Hope sighed exasperatedly when she realized it was Ethan again.

"Can't I just wake up without being startled to death?"

"Just thought you might want to get back in the tree. Cassidy and Aiden are gonna keep watch." It was still dark out, but the shimmering stars provided some light.

"Ok, are you coming up too?" He nodded and gestured for her to start climbing. She grabbed hold of the branch and began to climb up. It was hard to see, causing her to almost slip a couple times. She made it back up to Cassidy, who was sound asleep. Hope tried to make herself comfortable but without any luck. Five minutes went by, then ten. 30 minutes had gone by when Hope finally felt sleep take her once more.

8

She woke up, the bright light of the sun shining through her eyelids. Hope yawned and stretched, rubbing the sleepiness from her eyes. The fatigue was washed away when she heard a horrified scream from below. She could see Ethan's silhouette practically leap out the bottom of the tree.

"Get away from here," she heard him growl to something that she couldn't see. Hope quietly climbed down the tree, waking Blisse. She made her way down until she reached the ground. Ethan was in a defensive stance, a knife out in front of him. She walked slowly behind him, careful not to make him jump. Hope gasped, looking at the sight in front of them. Martha was there, shaking. Hope realized why she had screamed; there was a man holding a knife to her neck.

"Let her go," Ethan said, full of fury. The man laughed, a sound that sent chills down Hope's body.

Once he saw the fearful blonde adult behind Ethan, his pupils dilated with excitement. His knife pressed closer to Martha's throat. The poor woman was shaking, her large eyes looking up in pure terror. Ethan unnoticeably shot a glance Hope's way.

"I've been sent to take blondie," the man began in a guttural voice. "My friend wants to have a little chat with her." Hope knew right away that he was referring to the terrifying man who had been the first to talk to her. Ethan smirked without any humor.

"Yeah, I think your plan is foiled. You're not taking anyone." The man had a queer look on his face, as if he was surprised someone dared to stand up to him.

"I believe I am," he said calmly. "So move." Ethan laughed.

"Over my dead body." The man's mouth moved up in smug gesture.

"If that's the way it has to be done."

He dropped Martha, pushing himself toward Ethan.

"ETHAN!" Fire screamed. Her small body lunged toward her friend. The man was on top of him immediately. They struggled, and Hope knew she should help. She also knew that she could be injured or even killed if she got in the man's way. She was the one he was after.

Hope watched helplessly as the man pinned Ethan's wrists with his knees. Martha was shouting for help, but she didn't make a move. Fire's eyes grew alarmed as she grabbed a stray branch. She bashed the man's back as hard as she could, but her attempted strength didn't make a difference. Aiden was searching frantically for any sort of weapon to use. He clearly knew that his hands would do nothing but get him killed. One of the man's hands held down Ethan's head while the other held a sharp silver knife.

Ethan unsuccessfully tried to buck him off while Fire continued to slam his back. With an angry grunt, the man's elbow bashed into Fire's jaw. She groaned, throwing her hand over her mouth.

"I'm getting blondie," he growled. His knife pressed onto Ethan's throat. Ethan's eyes were wide with fury and fear as his body moved and moved.

A shape flashed in front of Hope's vision. She gasped, jumping back. The large shape threw its body at the violent stranger. A boy, Hope realized, knocked him over. The man's shock was clear as the young stranger put his hands around his throat. Hope looked away, fighting tears. Although the man's intent was awful, she couldn't stand to watch him die. Ethan stood up, and Martha was wiping the tears from her aged eyes, still in shock. He walked over to Hope, his face a mask of embarrassment and anger.

"Sorry," she mumbled. She could hear the gurgling sounds coming from the man, making her face wrinkle in disgust. *Let him die already!* Hope thought, absolutely hating his awful sounds.

"He's dead now," Ethan whispered to her. Hope slowly turned her head, looking at the scene. The man's face was a deep shade of purple, and it was obvious that Ethan was right. The boy's hands were still clamped tightly around the man's throat. Ethan cleared his throat loudly. "He's dead now," he repeated louder to the boy. The stranger took a dramatic breath as he rose and turned toward them.

"Well then!" he declared, puffing out his chest. "My name's Gabe. You owe me for that little stunt right there." Hope started to step toward him but was stopped from Ethan's firm grip on her arm.

"You don't know him," he muttered into her ear. "He could be dangerous." Hope didn't believe that.

"When did you become the safety man?" This earned an annoyed but amused glance from Ethan.

"Come on now," the stranger cooed. "I won't bite!"

"Why does everyone say that?" Aiden asked, his eyes looking suspiciously at Gabe. "Why are you here?"

"I just saved your friend's life," Gabe said in a suddenly dark tone. "What else do you want?" His light eyes darted back to Hope. She looked at Ethan.

"He's right," she admitted, whispering. "He did save your life. It's not like he's going to murder me. Now let me go." He hesitantly took his hand away. Hope began to walk to him. He looked at her, sizing her up. His face broke into an even larger smile.

"Well hi there, gorgeous! It's a pleasure to make your acquaintance." He bowed theatrically then grinned. Hope smiled awkwardly.

"Um, hi. Thanks for saving Ethan." She pointed to her friend, surprised at his intense glare towards Gabe.

"No problemo, gorgeous," stated Gabe. He flashed a grin Ethan's way. His smile showed all of his surprisingly white teeth, making him look manic. "Saving lives is my forte." Hope flushed.

"Please don't call me that," she stated. "I have a name." Gabe flipped his long brown hair.

"Well then, I can't wait to hear it." Hope's eyes squinted. Ethan huffed a huge sigh, clearly displaying his disapproval.

I don't like him, he thought, his eyes narrowing. He hated the gleam hidden away in Gabe's eyes. He had seen that same look in his mother's blazing eyes, right before she had hit him.

"My name is Hope, not gorgeous," Hope clarified. "Let's get that out of the way right now. And what are you doing here anyway?" Fire pursed her lips, her eyes narrowing in realization.

"Wait, why *are* you here?" she asked suspiciously. "Isn't it crazy that you happened to appear just when we needed help?" She looked at him, expecting him to explain. Gabe just shook his head, his joyful laughter filling the air.

"Please just answer the question," Hope told him.

"Well aren't you just curious! And yes, it is a strange coincidence. I wonder why." He leaned into her, touching his nose to hers. "I wonder why," he repeated quietly. She jumped back, feeling Ethan's hand pulling on her shoulder.

"Just leave her and us alone," he snapped. "Thanks for saving my life and all, but you can go now." Gabe shook his finger, infuriating Ethan even more. Ethan's glare turned shockingly angry. "I said leave," Ethan said, pronouncing each word slowly. Gabe shook his head.

"I don't think I will."

"What do you mean, you twit?" Ethan asked angrily, moving toward him like a lion. Martha had calmed down enough to stand in between the adults.

"Enough." Although she said it calmly, both boys stopped instantly. "OK, Gabe you can stay," Martha said, receiving an incredulous look from Ethan. Gabe's expression turned smug, his mouth perking up in victory. "Yes, that's right, Ethan," Martha said, raising her eyebrows as well. "He's the one who saved both of us. But Gabe, you need to listen to us. If you cause any trouble *at all,* you will be kicked out of the group. Understand?" Gabe nodded his head stiffly, but Hope saw something flicker in his light brown eyes.

"I have a question," Fire piped up. Gabe nodded, his body turning toward her. His arms crossed as an impatient look flying across his face.

"Well, I can't wait to hear it, tiny." Fire's eyes narrowed at the word tiny, but she didn't comment back.

"When did you get on this island?" she questioned. He made a show of thinking about his answer. Ethan looked at Hope, his mouth opened in disbelief. *Oh, quit,* she mouthed back with a smile.

"I was here last year," he finally said.

"How come you didn't find us until now?"

"How come you didn't find me?" he asked simply. Fire nodded, realizing she didn't know anything else about this stranger.

"Tell us about yourself, *handsome,"* she snickered, putting in as much sarcasm as she could. He seemed unfazed by her language.

"I don't know. I took a test, I was dangerous. What else is there, tiny?" Fire raised her eyebrows.

"You got a problem?" she asked him suddenly, putting her skinny arms up. "Let's go right now." Her cold eyes were set on him. "Come on!" Gabe laughed out loud.

"Clearly, you don't realize how utterly stupid you look right now. Look at your size compared to mine. I could beat you to the ground." He laughed at her attempts to look threatening. Fire stared daggers at Gabe.

"Look, I don't know who you think you are," she said angrily. He smirked.

"Looks like someone has anger issues."

"I don't have anger issues," she snapped. "I'm just telling you that I want to fight you."

"Yeah, right pipsqueak," he sneered in her face. "You wouldn't scare a toddler." With that sentence, he reached out and struck her lightly in the jaw. She let out a gasp, more from surprise than pain.

Ethan swung a fist at Gabe's head, not aiming, just trying to hit him hard. Gabe ducked out of the way, smacking Ethan on the shoulder when he missed.

"ENOUGH!" Martha shouted. "I will not tolerate fighting." A crack sounded above Hope's head, making everyone look up. The noise belonged to Blisse, finally climbing down. Ethan reached over and helped her when she got far enough. Her face opened in a yawn. Her previous straight hair was now all knotted and tangled.

"Who are you?" she asked, noticing Gabe. He looked at her, his eyes raking her up and down.

"Eight," he said finally. She cocked her head, confused.

"Excuse me?" He heaved a sigh.

"On a scale from one to ten, you're an eight," he explained, as though that was clear as a bell. She scrunched up her face.

"Well, that's not super nice," she said. "I don't enjoy being ranked." He rolled his eyes, his mouth in a smug grin.

"Oh, are you the little daisy of the group?" She looked at him, her caramel eyes narrowing just the tiniest bit. She didn't comment back, clamping her mouth shut. Ethan glared at Gabe.

"I don't trust him," he told Hope, not exactly hiding his voice. *Me either,* she mouthed back.

"So," Hope began, "what's the plan for today?" Ethan shrugged.

"It's so strange that you guys survived on your own!" Gabe said, feigning surprise. Fire's eyes flashed.

"And what exactly do you mean by that?"

"Because," he answered, "your group is mostly female."

"I'm aware," Fire snapped. "And that has to do with…?"

"Well, girls can't fight, we all know that," Gabe said, looking down at her. Fire's eyes squinted.

"I don't know about that," she said through her teeth. "I'm strong enough to carry your corpse into the ocean."

"Fire!" Aiden exclaimed, but he was grinning hugely. She looked up at him and smiled smugly as well.

"We could go to the beach if you want," Hope suggested. Everyone looked blankly at her. "Well it's better than watching you two hurl insults back and forth," she said in defense. "I haven't really seen the ocean here yet anyway." Cassidy ran up to Hope, grateful for the distraction.

"That's a great idea!" she exclaimed happily. "Let's go!" She bounded off into a small but clear trail in the trees. Ethan grinned at her rush of excitement. He rushed after them, but not before shooting Gabe a dark look. Gabe yelled something not so nice to him, causing Martha's eyes to narrow. Aiden laughed, beginning to follow his friends.

"The ocean is one of the only good things about this island," Cassidy told Hope.

"Second to me," they heard Ethan call from ahead. They crossed the line separating the dark green and the golden sand.

Hope was astounded as she looked at the sight in front of her. The sea looked beautiful. It was a crystal blue, almost like glass.

The two girls stared out into the ocean, Hope loving the beautiful peace. Fire ruined that moment when she ran laughing into the water with splashes to make the stillness disappear. Aiden followed, chuckling with delight. Hope jumped when she felt a strong hand touch her arm.

"Come on, gorgeous, let's go back to the tree." Hope felt her heart speed up in anger when she recognized Gabe's arrogant voice. "Just you and me. We can spend the whole day together, if you know what I mean." Gabe winked his brown eye.

"I thought I said to not call me gorgeous anymore," Hope said, raising her eyebrows. Gabe shrugged.

"You did," he said matter-a-factly. "But I didn't listen." He moved closer, putting his hands on her waist. Hope's eyebrows moved together as she prodded him hard in the chest. He clamped his hands tighter, not letting go.

"Get *off*," Hope snarled, this time pushing him roughly away. He slightly stumbled, his eyes getting a sudden look of anger. He threw his body at her, grabbing her face in his hands.

"Gabe!" she yelled, her hands attempting to peel him off of her. "GABE!" His face moved into Hope's, touching his lips with hers.

"Stop!" Hope shrieked. She could faintly hear someone bounding over in the pounding of her ears. Hope aggressively shoved him away. "Why in the world did you kiss me?" Gabe tilted his head, seeming genuinely confused.

"I wanted to," he stated, shrugging. "Though I thought it would be better than that." Hope's face turned red, full of fury. She suddenly smacked his cheek as hard as she could, causing his face to turn the same shade as her.

"Don't *ever* touch me again," she growled. "If you do, I swear I will hit you harder. Leave me alone." Hope stalked off, hitting Ethan with her shoulder on accident. He tensed his body, staring at Gabe.

"What in the world were you thinking?" he asked angrily. Gabe looked at him, confused.

"I don't see why that's any of your business," he simply said. Ethan threw up his hands in annoyance and rage.

"Yes it is! She said no!" A smug smile flew across Gabe's face.

"Are you jealous?" He chuckled as Ethan's face grew redder and redder. He raised his eyebrows at him.

"Of course not, you imbecile," Ethan snapped. "I'm telling you to be a rational human being." Gabe smirked.

"Yeah, ok."

"What's your guys' problem?" The voice belonged to a curious and soaking wet Fire. Aiden was looking at Ethan, concerned.

"This twit right here," he coldly replied. With one last icy glare at Gabe, Ethan sprinted away to follow Hope into the jungle.

9

Hope didn't know where she was. She had made a mistake, but she didn't care. In some part of her mind, she knew that she was overreacting, but that didn't stop her. All she wanted was away from Gabe. She *hated* him, and she hadn't even known him for an hour.

A *crunch* caused her to jump, making her forget about the incident. *You're just imagining things.* Every time her mind had formed that theory, however, something had happened. Something bad. She looked intently at the plants, her mind full of the panic she so often felt. Her palms began to sweat profusely. *Calm down, Hope. You're just worrying for no reason. Chill.*

She heard the same noise again. It didn't sound like an animal; it sounded like human footsteps.

"Hello?" Hope called, feeling stupid. Who would answer to that? "I know you're there," she hesitantly said. Ethan's previous scare popped into her mind. She shook her head, slightly grinning, when realized that it could just be one of Ethan's pranks.

"Ethan, I know it's you. You can't scare me anymore." Nobody had emerged from the trees yet. "Ethan, stop." She heard more rustling, so she turned in the direction of the sound. Her blood turned to ice when she saw that it wasn't Ethan. It was a blonde man who had blood all over the front of his shirt. The part that made her forget to breathe was the pointed knife in his large, scarred hand.

Hope's breath caught in her throat. The man's face lit up in a smile. It was a smile that told her his intentions were bad. *Oh Lord,* she thought, terrified. *Lord, help me.* She backed up, although she knew he would follow.

"I'm here to do the task that my little friend failed to do," he said, grinning. "He was weak. Do you know what my task is, princess?" He cocked his head to the side, his mouth perked up in a twisted smile. She couldn't speak. She had had two other encounters with criminals, but this was the scariest one. She was lost, alone, with no one to help her this time. Hope shook her head no, but she knew the answer.

"I'm here to bring my leader a blonde girl. You look very much like his description. Do you know what he wants to do?" Hope shook her head again, dreading the answer.

"He wants to kill you. Not immediately, though. No no, not quickly at all. He wants to take his sweet time with the girl who got away. Now, I can take you the easy way or the hard way. It's your choice, princess."

Hope decided she would stall as much time as she could. She knew for sure that she wasn't going with this man. At least, there was absolutely no way that she would go willingly. *Get away from me,* she thought nervously. Her breathing had become shaky, although she was trying her best to hide it. Cowering hard, she found her voice.

"Why does he want to kill me?" Hope asked innocently. The man shook his head, slowly chuckling.

"I know what you're trying to do. I'm not wasting any time. Let's go." He walked forward, ready to grab her arm. She gulped, looking at all of the scars on his hand. Hope didn't even consider trying to fight him; she knew she didn't stand a chance. Instead, she called Ethan's name as loud as she could.

"ETHAN!" she shrieked. "CASSI-" she was cut off by the man's large hand around her throat.

"Shut up," he growled. "I would just kill you myself, but my boss wants the honors to himself. Personally, I don't see why he wants to kill you. But oh well, I have my orders. Now walk." He took his hand off her neck. She gasped for breath and grudgingly began to move. She chomped her lip when her ankle rolled to the side. Hope couldn't see any other way of escaping. She was terrified. *If this guy is scared of his boss, then this boss has got to be much, much worse.* She gulped at her horrifying realization.

"Please stop," Hope begged, wishing that she had stayed back with Gabe. The man didn't even look her way as he trudged on and on.

The man stopped moving.

Hope felt that she could die of relief.

Martha was there, with Ethan by her side. Hope's eyes lit up with happiness. She was saved.

"Let her go," Ethan said in a low voice, even scaring her. The man shook his head daintily.

"No, I don't think so. I will not fail this." Ethan gave him a questioning look, his eyes still as dark as the night sky.

"What do you mean fail this?" The stranger snickered. Hope got a view of his neck, which was covered in pink and white scars as well. *Please don't let me die,* she pleaded silently.

"I have orders to bring this girl back to my boss," the man said. "Even if I do fail, my leader will send out men until he gets this disappointment of a girl. You will lose her, no matter how hard you try." Ethan shook his head, laughing darkly.

"No, we won't." The man chuckled again, and Hope could feel him tensing up. She noticed him grip his knife tighter.

"ETHAN, LOOK-" she had barely given her warning when the man released her. He lunged at Ethan, his knife ready to kill him.

Not again, Hope thought in dismay. Ethan was like a deer in headlights, his eyes wide and confused. Hope closed her eyes sadly, feeling the familiar sensation of a crushing weight in her chest. Ethan would die, and then the man would then turn around and take her to this master that wanted nothing more than to hurt her.

A grunt pierced the air. Hope opened her eyes, alarmed.

She felt a flutter in her gut; Ethan was unharmed. But his expression looked so shocked and pained that Hope's head looked over at Martha.

The pieces then clicked together. It was painfully obvious why Ethan looked sadder than she had ever seen him. Martha had jumped in front of Ethan, into the path of the deadly weapon. *She sacrificed herself for him*, Hope thought in horror.

The knife was embedded in her abdomen, and a red stain was slowly spreading over her spring green t-shirt. Hope went white, her hands covering her opening mouth. *Oh my god.*

"No, no, no! Martha, why did you do that?!" Ethan shouted at her, tears pooling in his eyes. He sat down next to her. The man was grinning wickedly as he watched Ethan fall to the ground. Martha's breathing had become heavy, and Hope knew right away that she couldn't be saved. Her injury was too severe for anyone to heal. Ethan looked up at Hope. She shook her head sadly, trying to tell him with her eyes that there was nothing they could do. Martha understood.

"Ethan," Martha gasped. He turned his head quickly, desperately telling her to hold on. "Even though I'm not your real mom, I love you." Ethan shook his head, glistening tears beginning to fall. Hope hated the defeat in her voice. It was as though she had already accepted her death.

"You're better than my real mom. Way better. I love you," he told her, his voice trembling. Ethan put his hand on her pulse, desperate to keep the blood pumping inside of her. Martha weakly turned her head to Hope.

"Although I haven't known you nearly as long, you seem like a great kid. I wish I could've learned more about you." The light in Martha's kind eyes flickered. She took one final breath and looked around, as if saying goodbye to the Earth. Her face turned as white as chalk, and Hope saw her eyes glaze over.

They both knew she was gone, although no one dared to say it. Ethan's face turned to pure anger. He clenched his shaking fists as he took them off of the woman he loved.

"Hope, you might want to look away," he snarled, getting to his feet. He tore the knife from Martha's body and aggressively put it into his hand. He turned his body, facing the man head-on. Hope gasped when she knew what he was going to do. She looked away, her green eyes brimming with tears. Although it made no sense, she felt as if Martha's death was her fault. She closed her eyes as she heard Ethan's defiant scream.

Hope could imagine the man's shocked look as Ethan lunged at him with the weapon, ready to end his life. She heard shuffling and the man's yell. Ethan screamed again, the sound of pain and fury racking his body. The man's shouts gradually became quieter and quieter until they broke off completely. Hope heaved a heavy sigh and felt Ethan's hand on her shoulder.

"I had to do it," he said, without any emotion. "I'm sorry." Hope just nodded. He dropped the knife, and Hope got a quick glimpse of it. The whole surface was the wet color of new blood. She shut her eyes tightly, trying to control the bile rising in her throat.

"Yeah, I know," she finally said, her voice strained. "I get it." They stood in silence, looking at Martha's body.

"I guess we should go find the others. They'll sure be happy to hear the news," Ethan said after a few minutes of quiet.

"I don't want this to sound, well, bad, but where do we put her body?" She winced when she realized how insensitive her statement sounded. Ethan simply shrugged, his stare moving to the ground.

"Whatever we do, we aren't... keeping it. Let's just put it behind a plant or something." Hope nodded in agreement, and she grabbed Martha's arms. She looked up at Ethan.

"Are you gonna help me or what?" she jokingly asked him. Even her attempt at lightening up the situation was pathetic. Her voice sounded weak and Ethan's expression was sadder than she thought could be possible. He shook his head, ashamed.

"I'm sorry, Hope, but I can't do it. It's too much. I can't look at her body." Hope understood. She panted as she dragged the woman's body behind a flowering plant. "Thanks," Ethan told her when the job was done. Hope nodded and playfully punched his shoulder, attempting to break the stiffness between them.

"Anytime," she said weakly. Ethan pointed to the front. "Well, let's go." The pair began to walk back to the ocean shore.

"Hey, Ethan, I was curious about something," she said a few moments later.

"What?" Ethan asked wearily.

"How did you and Martha find me? I was lost."

"I was coming up to talk to you. I saw what happened with you and Gabe." Heat rose to her face when she realized that he had seen Gabe's hands slide on her hips.

"Don't worry, I hate him. Nothing was going on, I promise," she told him, a hint of urgency in her voice. He chuckled slightly.

"Yeah, I could tell. You looked pretty mad. Anyway, I just found you when I saw that man. I got Martha as fast as I could. You know what happened after that." He looked down, and Hope knew he didn't want to look upset in front of her.

"You know, you can cry with me, Ethan," she said suddenly. Ethan had stopped walking, so she figured that her statement hadn't come out too harshly. "Don't be stupid enough to think that I'll judge you."

Before she knew it, Ethan's arms wrapped around her in a tight hug. She heard him sniff and she squeezed him back. "I'm sorry. I really am. I didn't even know her that well and I could tell she was a great person," Hope said into his ear. She felt him nod.

The two stood like this for a while, in each other's arms. Ethan released her, and she was greatly surprised to not see a trace of sadness in his face.

"Let's go," he finally said. His voice wasn't shaky anymore, and Hope was oddly glad. They continued their stroll to the yellow sand on the shore. Their eyes both cautiously flickered around for danger. Hope didn't know if she could take it if they saw another criminal. Cassidy ran up to them as soon as they got past the dense jungle.

"Geez guys, you were gone a long time!" she said to them. She then cocked her head, confused. Her eyes squinted in thought. "Wasn't Martha with you?" Hope noticed Ethan stiffen. She tried to communicate with her eyes, begging Cassidy to change the subject. The peppy girl clearly didn't notice. "Yeah, I'm sure she was with you, Ethan! Where is she?" Hope urgently shook her head, but Cassidy didn't understand. "What's wrong? Why are you looking at me like that?" Ethan suddenly snapped out of his current state.

"She's dead!" he yelled at her. "She was stabbed by a man who wanted to kidnap Hope. Do you understand now, you *idiot*?" Cassidy took a step back, her expression full of hurt. It then turned to anger.

"Fine." She narrowed her eyes at him, then turned and sprinted into the jungle. Ethan's face slowly transformed into a look of horror.

"I can't believe I just said that to her. Now she'll hate me. I-" Ethan suddenly turned away, dashing down the shore. Hope watched him run, feeling incredibly sorry for him. He had lost his close sibling and his mom figure, something Hope could never fathom happening to herself. She jumped when she felt someone breathe in her ear. To her disgust, Gabe was next to her.

Hope snarled at him, pushing him firmly away with her hand. Gabe merely smiled. He *smiled*.

"Your boyfriend doesn't seem too happy now, huh gorgeous?" Hope blushed deeply.

"We're not a couple, Gabe. And even if we were, which we're *not*, it's none of your business." Gabe raised his eyebrows.

"Feisty. I like that." Hope rolled her eyes, pushing him away even more. Fire came rushing up to Hope, a small amount of worry in her eyes.

"What happened? Why did Cassidy run away? Where's Ethan?" Hope looked at her, dreading the answers.

"Um, Fire, something happened. Something bad. You're going to be sad when you hear what I have to say." Fire tilted her head, confused. Aiden had come over, wanting to hear the news as well. Blisse was still gazing out at the ocean, but Hope knew she was interested as well.

"Well, tell us Hope," Fire announced. "We're ready." She crossed her arms, her eyes looking at her with curiosity. With an uncomfortable expression, Hope told them everything.

She told them what it was like when she met the man, and what it was like when she saw Ethan and Martha in her path. She tried to make it less graphic when she described Martha's fate, but she saw that she had not succeeded. Aiden's warm eyes were rounded in shock. When Hope was done speaking, she looked at Fire. Her blue eyes were still electric, but it looked as though something had dimmed. She suddenly looked fragile and vulnerable, contrary to her normal self.

"Really? Martha's gone?" she asked, her voice fighting to keep steady. Hope nodded sadly. Gabe tapped his wrist as though he was looking at a watch.

"This is taking a long time," he said, his voice quick and angry. Fire turned her icy eyes on him.

"Shut it." Gabe rolled his brown eyes, his hip jutting out to the side.

"Did tiny just tell me to shut it? Does she think that I'll listen to her? And who the hell is Martha?" He grinned. "Oh, she was the old lady." His statement caused Hope to glare at him.

"Gabe, *shut up*. And Fire, I'm so so sorry." The girl's sad look turned into an expression of anger. She sniffed almost aggressively and pointed her finger at Hope accusingly.

"It's your fault, Hope!" Hope's mouth dropped open in shock. Before she had the chance to speak, Fire continued. "If you hadn't stalked off, we wouldn't even be in this mess. You killed one of the people I loved most in this world." Fire's lip wobbled.

"Now tell me where Ethan went," she demanded. Hope just pointed in his direction, shocked at her outburst. Fire shoved her to the side and sprinted down the shore. Blisse walked up and put her hand on her shoulder.

"Don't worry Hope, it's not your fault," she said, tears forming in her big, brown eyes. "It's just that we grew really close to her, and she took us in when we arrived. It's just a shock for her, that's all." Hope turned her head, tears pooling in her eyes as well.

"Yeah, but Fire's right. I did run off, and that was why she came to help me in the first place. It is my fault."

"It's not!" Blisse said, her voice close to a snap. "It's not your fault that some lunatic decided to capture you. If anything, you helped us get rid of him quicker. If you didn't, he could've snuck up on us when we were sleeping. You would've been taken, and I bet that he would have killed the rest of us for the fun of it. Sapphire is just in a bad mood. I think it will be a while when she truly gets over it. I mean, it will take a long time for all of us. But don't worry, Hope. Please don't think that it's your fault, because it's not." Hope smiled weakly.

"Thanks, Blisse. I really needed that." Hope snapped her head over when she heard Gabe mutter something. "What?" she snarled. Gabe grinned, pretending to zip his lips shut.

"I heard it," Aiden said, looking at Gabe with disgust. "I'm not saying it." Hope walked over to him, putting her face close to his. Hope shook her head repulsively.

"Next time you say something under your breath, you will regret it." She pulled herself away from him before he could kiss her again. Hope turned to the ocean, hating herself more than she thought possible. She felt Blisse walk up next to her.

"The sea is really beautiful, huh?" she asked. Hope nodded.

"Yeah, it is." She peered out into it, wishing that she could just go home. Her eyes squinted when she noticed something white, far out into the distance. She nudged Blisse's arm. Blisse's caramel eyes turned toward her.

"Yes?"

"Is it just me, or does the ocean look, well, different?" Hope asked. Blisse looked out at the glittering sea. Hope looked at the shore as well, sensing that something was odd. She could've sworn that the sand looked different for some reason. *Larger* was the word that popped into her head.

"What do you mean?" Blisse asked. Hope didn't know what to say.

"I don't know. I mean, wasn't the sand area smaller or something?" She felt ridiculous, but she was sure there was a difference. Blisse looked out, her eyes squinted in confusion as well. All of a sudden, her large eyes got even bigger.

"Hope, you're right. It is different. Look out in the distance." Blisse pointed far out. Hope squinted her green eyes, trying to get a clearer look. *That's strange,* she thought. *Why does it look so different?* She felt a spike of fear when she realized what it was.

"Blisse," Hope said, trying but failing to keep her voice steady. She put her arm on Blisse's wrist. "I think that's a tsunami." Hope read about it in books, but she had never actually experienced the event for herself. She felt her stomach sink.

"We have to go," she said loudly. "Now!" Blisse nodded, grabbing Aiden.

"Guys, come on! There's a huge wave out there!" Hope suddenly had a thought that sent a surge of panic throughout her entire body.

"Blisse! What about Fire?" Hope had an even worse realization. "What about Cassidy and Ethan?! They don't know! Oh my god Blisse, what if they die?" Blisse looked into Hope's scared eyes, and Hope noticed that Blisse's eyes had hardened. She didn't look so fragile anymore. She looked like a soldier.

"Hope, listen to me. I'm worried about them too, but if we don't leave now, we will all die. We can think about it later, ok? But now, we need to get as far inland as we possibly can. Come on!" Blisse ran off, and Hope made sure Aiden and Gabe were following her as well. Hope nervously glanced at the ocean one last time, noticing that the wall of water was getting closer and closer.

Oh god, this is all my fault.

Hope sprinted after them into the dark jungle, wondering if anyone had ever messed up this badly.

10

Fire's lungs were burning as she sprinted down the sand. All she could think of was Martha. Her loving mom figure was now dead. She would never come back.

Fire screamed as loud as she could, not caring if anyone heard her. She ran some more, her lungs aching for air. Finally, she tripped over her own feet.

She let out another shrill sound as she dropped to her knees and began punching the sand. She shouted until her voice was hoarse while her hands tore through her knotted hair. Fire opened her mouth wider, letting all of her emotions erupt. Her mouth tasted salty from all of her tears, but she continued to yell. She couldn't see anything with her blue eyes blurry with water.

The despaired girl finally stood up, rolling her shoulders back.

Fire took a deep breath and wiped her eyes. She looked out into the sea, her fists clenched tightly. The small girl wiped her puffy eyes once more and sniffed. She squinted her eyes in confusion, thinking that the white wall in front of her was an illusion from her tears. But when her eyes were clear, the strange thing was still in her vision.

Fire finally focused, clearing her mind of the sadness that threatened to consume her. *What the hell?* she thought, brushing the wet hair out of her eyes.

A wall of water was coming.

Fire's gut dropped, immobilizing her from terror. She knew right away that she was much too close to the water.

I'm not gonna make it, she repeated in her mind. Her previous thoughts of despair melted away as she faced the realization that she could be dead in a minute. She dashed into the jungle as fast as she could, not looking back.

Cassidy was out of breath. She had run for 20 minutes, non-stop, with her dark brown eyes full of tears. Ethan's comment had hurt her, but there was no way she would cry in front of him. She leaned against a tree, feeling as though she would collapse any second. Everything was turning black at the edges, and she was wondering if maybe she pushed herself a little too hard. *Focus, Cassidy.* She stayed against the tree, filling her lungs with oxygen. *Martha...*

A moment later, she felt her bottom lip start to tremble. *No,* she thought firmly. *Don't think of that. Think of something else.* The next thing that came to her mind was Brandon. A single tear trickled down her cheek. She slapped herself quickly, begging herself to think of something else. Instead of thinking of somebody, she chose to take in her surroundings. Cassidy felt a jolt of panic when she realized she had no idea where she was. She also noticed that everything was eerily quiet. Normally, there were always birds or some other animal making noise.

"Hi there, Cass," said a voice right behind her.

Oh my god.

Her heart skipped a beat.

She spun around, instinctively putting up her fists. The girl's teary eyes grew wide at the sight before her.

Maya.

Cassidy's mouth hung open. Her shaking hand slowly moved over her mouth in astonishment.

"Maya?" she said softly. Her old friend smirked weakly, her hand covering her neck. Cassidy really looked at Maya, now that her shock was calming. She gasped when she saw how bad of a condition Maya was in.

Her face was covered in bruises and cuts. There was a large burn on her forearm, and her ankle was twisted at a strange angle; obviously she was somehow injured. Her once beautiful red hair had been jaggedly chopped off at her ears. The biggest difference, however, was her expression. Her face looked hesitant and soft, much different from the tough look she always wore. Cassidy also noticed that she was shaking slightly.

"Maya?" she repeated in a disbelieving tone. Maya nodded grimly.

"You said that already." Cassidy shook her head, not understanding how she could have woken up.

"I thought you were, well-"

"Dead?" Maya asked, emotion gone from her tone. Cassidy nodded, her eyes focused on the dirt-packed ground. "Well, I'm about as alive as I can get. As you can see, I'm perfectly healthy." Maya gestured to her injuries sarcastically. *I can't believe she's alive,* Cassidy thought in wonder. She didn't know if that was a good or bad thing.

"What happened to you? We thought you had died in the fire!" Maya glared at her, a hint of herself back.

"Yep, I could tell. You guys didn't come back for me," she said, causing Cassidy's face to turn red. Maya's look turned slightly smug at her discomfort. "After our little fight, something hit me in the head. I assume you know what it was?" She raised her eyebrows while she crossed her scarred arms. Cassidy nodded once more.

"Ethan threw a rock at your head," she simply stated. Maya chuckled without humor.

"I guess I'll have to have a little talk with that, as he would say, twit." Her gaze turned to the sky. Cassidy bit her lip awkwardly as the minutes passed. Maya's eyes were still gazing at the azure skies above.

"You were saying…"

Maya's stare snapped back to reality. "Oh, right. So after that, I woke up. You can imagine my surprise when the entire building was on fire and all of you were gone. I thought it was you guys who set the fire to kill me. No, no, I'm not done," she said, responding to Cassidy's look of horror.

"I ran to the door, but it was stuck. I finally pried it open, but by then I was burnt." Maya showed Cassidy her arm. "I walked down the road a bit, and I was jumped. Apparently, some guys recognized me from when we were saving Hope. They beat me up, as you can see, and then dragged me by my hair off into another building. I snuck a knife from a guy's jacket and cut my hair so they couldn't drag me again. I know they were planning to make me tell them where you were. I obviously wasn't going to do that, so I escaped the next day. I killed a guy who tried to stop me." Maya's sad look turned into a victorious grin. "You should have seen it, all the blood. Anyway, I pretty much stayed in that tree over there." She pointed to a tree, covered with many plants. "I have stayed there for the past few days until I saw you. And now, we're here. You're all caught up."

"Who started the fire?"

"How would I know?" she asked darkly. "I was unconscious, remember?" Cassidy scratched her arm.

"Wow, Maya. I'm sorry." Maya shook her head.

"Don't lie to me, old friend. I know you were glad to get rid of me." Cassidy didn't respond.

"Anyway, where were you while I was hurt?" *She's making me feel bad,* Cassidy thought guilty. *And it's working.*

"Well," she began, "when you were… out, we played our game." She said the last part in a mumbled tone, feeling worse by the minute. Maya raised her eyebrows in an amused look.

"Is that so?"

"Yes," Cassidy answered. She then told her everything about the game, about the man who wanted Hope, and the arrival of Gabe. Maya nodded thoughtfully.

"Seems like you guys had a blast," she said. "Tell me about this Gabe." Cassidy loudly snorted before she could help it.

"He's someone who you would want to kill."

Maya nodded once more. The thoughtful look disappeared from her face, a look of confusion replacing it. "Hey, do you hear that?" Cassidy bit her cheek in thought, tasting blood.

"Hear what, exactly?" Maya cocked her head, her eyes looking around in thought.

"That's just it. The jungle is too quiet, don't you think?" Cassidy nervously nodded.

"Yes, you're right! I thought that earlier. I wonder why." Maya's head snapped to the side in a look of pure terror.

"Cassidy!"

Cassidy's chocolate eyes met Maya's green, green ones for a split second. Then, they were swept off their feet from a huge wall of water.

Ethan was still running. He was conditioned for this, so he was only the least bit tired. He wasn't crying, contrary to his other friends. He was numb; he didn't feel any emotions. It was like his mind had just shut down.

He looked at the tall trees, seeing a plain, disgusting green. Ethan just didn't want to stop moving. He felt as if he ran enough, he would just collapse and never get up again. Maybe if he ran and ran and ran, his lungs would fail. Martha was one of the only people he had ever loved.

She was his family.

And she had died, right in front of him. He could remember the chill that went down his spine when he saw the knife in there, right in her body. He remembered the crimson blood staining her shirt, her dead eyes glazing over...

Stop it, he told himself. His mind still wouldn't forget the image. He slapped himself, hard. He was stunned by the pain, but it didn't help. He ran some more, but he was stopped when he tripped over a root. Ethan didn't get back up.

A sound became louder and louder in his ears. He shook his head, trying to get rid of it, but it didn't go away. He looked to his right. *What the?*

There was a clear substance coming for him. He wondered if he was just imagining it, in temporary insanity from his grief.

Am I already losing it? He smiled softly at his situation, grimly finding humor in it all. *What a great day.* He chuckled without humor as he closed his eyes, letting the water pound into his body.

"Blisse, keep going!" Hope shouted to the exhausted girl in front of her. Although she could tell that Blisse was trying, she was going to collapse from exhaustion any second. "Guys, stop!" Gabe turned around and looked at Hope like she was crazy.

"We can't stop now! Are you serious?" Hope looked him in the eye.

"Yes, I am serious. Blisse, no offense, but it looks like you are about to die. Just come over here, and climb this tree. Get as high as you can, ok? Go, go!" Gabe ran in front of everyone and began to grab the branches to the tall tree. "Gabe, can you make it up the tree before Christmas?" Hope asked him with panic creeping into her tone. He ignored her, or didn't hear her. A few minutes later, everyone had gone up but Hope. Blisse looked down at her.

"Hope, come on! The wave will catch us soon!" she said urgently. Hope started to climb up the tree faster than she had ever done before. She was up only seven branches when she saw the water rushing at her. Hope's eyes grew wide, and now she really had to face the thought of death.

"Guys, hold on!" she yelled to them. *Ok Hope, you can make it.* She hugged the branches with all her might and closed her eyes. She took a deep breath, then felt the force of the water tear into her body.

Cassidy's lungs were filled with liquid. She didn't have any warning of the dangerous water. She felt her arms smack hard against trees, and she could only pray that she would survive. She didn't know which way was up, or which way was down. Cassidy roughly kicked to the surface.

At least, she thought it was the surface.

The last thing she remembered was her head smacking against a hard object. Cassidy fell unconscious.

Fire heard the water behind her. She didn't dare look back. If she did, she wouldn't be able to move. Her lungs seemed to explode any moment now.

This is it. I'm gonna drown. She had to stop running. The small girl mustered up the courage to look back.

Fire felt the water swallow her up. She was thrown this way and that, her small frame thrown around in the liquid monstrosity. She tried to swim to the top of the rushing water. Her hand popped out of the water, and then her head. Her small body was surviving.

Fire twisted herself around, looking for anything to hold on to. She panicked as more of the forceful water came crashing over her head. She had only taken a small breath. Her lungs couldn't hold out much longer without any air. She pushed her arms up, feeling the air once more. Finally, she felt her head pop up out of the liquid. She gulped in a huge amount of air, desperate to do so before more water came over her head.

Fire blindly reached for anything that she could find. She felt her hand grasp something, but the water snatched her away. With all of her strength, she grabbed and held onto the next thing she could reach, which was a thick branch. She knew she was weak from all of her running.

If the water's force didn't ease up soon, she knew that she would be swept away to her death. For now, all she could do was hold on and pray to survive.

Ethan felt the tough force of the water, and his body went completely numb for a couple of seconds. His mind processed that this was a wave and that he was going to die. This sent a surge of panic through him.

He formed a simple thought. *I don't want to die.*

He became more urgent with each time the wave threw him around.

I don't want to die!

Ethan tried to kick to the surface. He had to take a breath soon, or it would be all over. He had a problem; there was no way to tell which way to go.

His head was pounding harder than ever. He gave one final kick and dimly felt the air on his head. He *had* to keep his head above the water. The liquid was so strong, it felt just like knives were stabbing him everywhere. Ethan pondered whether he should just give up. It would be so much easier to let the water fill his lungs.

He felt his body slam against a tree. The impact knocked the wind out of him, and he excruciatingly resisted the urge to gulp in a huge amount of air. Ethan hated having to take small, quick breaths. He reached for a vine just before another portion of the wave slammed into him. Ethan closed his eyes, his will to survive growing stronger.

Hope managed to hold onto her branch. She could only wish that the others had done the same. The water rushed over her head, and she was glad that she had taken a deep breath. The water pounded her mind. That and the deprived oxygen had given her a raging headache. One minute passed, and now Hope was feeling the burn in her lungs. She had never held her breath this long, and the roaring water made it even harder for her to not gulp in a huge amount of air. Her lungs were aching, and she knew she would have to breathe oxygen soon. The other option was to inhale the water.

The force of the wave eased up a bit, but her head was still entirely submerged. Hope's lungs were about to burst. She realized that she had to try to climb up to the next branch. She gripped her branch more firmly, knowing that she would be swept away to her death if she let go. With all of her strength, she reached for the branch above her. Just as she was going to breathe no matter what, she felt her head reach the surface. She took a deep breath, and she felt her head clear a little.

She gasped for air. Hope tilted up her chin, making sure that her head could be as far up as possible. *I almost died.* This thought sent a chill through her body. *I could be dead right now.* Hope looked up. She could faintly see Blisse, high up in the tree. She could imagine her clinging desperately to a branch.

"Blisse!" Hope yelled. At least, she had intended to yell it. Her voice came out raspy and whispery. She loudly cleared her throat. Hope looked down again, feeling a jolt of happiness. The raging water had now lowered to her sternum. Of course, anyone would still be knocked right off of their feet if they made one little slip, but it encouraged Hope when she knew that the water was slowly but surely lowering. "Blisse!" Hope called again. Her voice was louder and clearer. *Wait,* Hope thought, a feeling of dread making its way into her system. *Cassidy and Ethan are still out there. They could be dead. They most likely are dead.*

"Blisse!" screamed Hope. Finally, Blisse looked down. Hope could barely see that her black hair was thrown all over her face.

"Are you ok?" she called down in a raspy voice to Hope. She nodded but then realized it was hard for Blisse to see.

"Yeah, I'm fine! What do we do about Ethan?"

Blisse was silent for a moment.

"I don't know! If it makes you feel any better, Gabe is still here." She pointed to a figure high above her head that Hope could barely make out.

"Hello gorgeous!" he called down sweetly. "I'm here!" Hope rolled her eyes, and she found herself wishing that he would have been swept away.

"I'm ok too!" Aiden called down. Hope knew that he must be on the other side of the tree.

More minutes passed. By now, the forceful water was level with her waist. Hope nearly had a heart attack when her hand almost lost its grip on the soaked branch. Five minutes went by. The water lowered to her femur, her knees, and then her ankles. Of course, she knew that there was no way she could possibly get on the ground safely.

"I'm bored!" Gabe called to them.

"Aren't we all?" Aiden replied. Hope sighed quietly.

"We can go in a moment!" she screamed back up to them. "The water is lowering. The wave was pretty small!"

Everyone held tightly onto the tree, waiting for Hope's signal. About 10 minutes later, Hope decided it was safe for them to climb down.

"Hey, Blisse! I think it's ok to go to the ground!" Blisse glanced in her direction and then began to slowly descend down.

"Let's go Gabe! Come on!" Hope heard her yell to him. She slowly climbed down, careful not to slip on the wet branches. She hopped down onto the soaked ground, hearing the other three softly land behind her.

"So Ethan, Sapphire, and Cassidy could really be dead?" Hope asked, knowing the answer. Blisse's eyes grew large as she looked at the ground.

"Yes Hope, they could be." Blisse sniffed.

Come on Hope, she thought. *Do something. Comfort them, if that's all you can do.*

"Well, I guess we should keep going then, huh? They could still be alive." Blisse sadly nodded, blinking away tears.

"Yeah, good idea Hope." Blisse put up her hand. Any other time, Hope would've thought that was just a bit too over-the-top. But now, it made her sad to watch Blisse's shaking hand raise to the sky. Gabe snorted, visibly rolling his eyes.

"Why did we get stuck with you?" Aiden snapped. Gabe shrugged.

"Ah, who knows. But you know you love me!" Aiden mumbled something not-so-nice to him while Blisse put her hand down. Gabe looked around impatiently, heaving audible sighs. Blisse suddenly contorted her face into a forced smile.

"Ok, let's put that thought behind us. At least we're all safe, right?" Hope nodded, but didn't feel like she agreed. "Alright," Blisse said, stretching out her legs. She shot one last glance at the tree they had grabbed onto. Hope's light eyes locked with hers. "Let's go find our friends."

Cassidy opened her eyes. She saw a blurred, large shape. Her lungs burned. At first, she didn't even try to take a breath, still under the thought that she was underwater. The girl noticed the green ground and realized with joy that the wave had passed. She had no idea how long it had gone on. She opened her mouth to breathe, but no air could get through. She began to panic, her throat clawing for air. That was all ended, though, when she started coughing. All the water she had inhaled was now coming out. She took a breath and coughed at the same time, making her choke. Finally, she took a few deep breaths, and her coughing fit was finished. She found Maya in front of her, a weak smirk on her face.

"You know, Cassidy, you're not supposed to inhale the water," she stated, wringing out her short hair. Cassidy grinned wryly and nodded.

"Thanks for the tip." The two girls sat in silence, their large eyes locked. "Maya, listen. I'm sorry that you were captured. I really mean it. Trust me, none of us were glad that you were dead. I promise." Maya put two thumbs up.

"Thanks, that really means a lot." Although it was clearly sarcastic, Cassidy smiled.

"How long was I out?"

"About 5 minutes," Maya replied. "To be honest with you, I thought you drowned."

There they stayed for a long, long time. Cassidy's legs were too shaky to support her weight, and it was clear that Maya couldn't handle running into another criminal anytime soon.

"I'm so sorry," Cassidy stated, over and over again.

Before Maya could reply, something caught her attention. She stared at something behind Cassidy, her emerald eyes growing wide. Cassidy turned around, interested in what had intrigued Maya.

There was a girl behind a tree, staring at them. She would've been hidden, but her bright red hair was unmissable against the soaked trees. Cassidy opened her mouth to speak, but shut it when she saw what Maya was alarmed about. One of the girl's eyes were covered, a leaf taped to it in place of an eye patch. Maya was the first one to speak.

"Hey honey, how are you not dead?"

"*Maya!*" Cassidy snapped. Maya looked startled and annoyed.

"What? I wanna know how this little girl didn't drown. You know, in the huge wave we were sucked into?"

"I'm a good swimmer," the stranger shyly replied.

"Hey! Have you come to join the party?" Maya called to her. She gestured for the girl to come sit. "Well, come on now, don't be shy!" The stranger opened her mouth but shut it. She just gawked at them, frightened. Maya heaved an annoyed sigh.

"Get over here, now." The stranger looked at them cautiously, but she hesitantly took a step forward. Maya looked at her impatiently. "So, little red, what's your name?"

"I'm Katherine," she said timidly, in a voice that reminded Cassidy of Blisse. She was extremely curious about what had happened to her other eye, but she didn't want to be rude. "So, who are you? Where did you come from?" Katherine asked. Maya chuckled.

"No, I want to hear about you first. Where are you from?" The girl shook her head in protest. Maya grinned humorlessly. "Listen sweetie, I could hurt you and make you tell us, or you can tell me and we all can smile uninjured. Now, I assume your ears work properly, yes?" Katherine quickly nodded."Alrighty then. Answer the question," the adult commanded. Katherine cleared her throat and began her story.

"Ok, well, I came here about a month ago."

"Where did you stay?" Cassidy interrupted. Katherine looked at her.

"I hid in an abandoned building for a really long time. I stole some food from some men who lived right by me. They had no idea I was there. One time, I was watching the night sky when I heard one of the men yell. He was accusing some guy of stealing all his food. He-" Katherine's voice cracked, and Cassidy was surprised to see a glistening tear trickling down her face.

"He broke the other guy's neck, I saw him. The next night, I gathered everything I had, which wasn't much. I didn't want to stay there anymore. If I was caught, who knows what that man would've done? I was in the jungle, and I began to fish from the ocean. I was actually pretty happy." Cassidy nodded, but she couldn't tear her eyes away from the large hole in Katherine's face. "About two weeks later, I'd say, I met Gabe, a guy who had just arrived. He-"

"Wait!" Cassidy yelled, cutting her off. Katherine's body jumped back.

"What?"

"Does this Gabe dude have brown eyes, a horrible ego, and long brown hair?" Cassidy chuckled. "Sort of like a mop." Katherine's jaw was slowly dropping open with each word.

"Yes! You just described him perfectly!" Cassidy nodded. "Yeah, it does look like a mop," Katherine said, grinning.

"Hold on a second," Cassidy said, realizing what was off. "How do you know him? He told us he was here last year." Katherine roughly shook her head, her wet hair flying off her face.

"Oh, no, I'm positive he had just gotten here. I saw him get off the helicopter." Cassidy shook her head.

"Why would he lie to us? That doesn't even make any sense." Katherine shrugged, her mouth suddenly dropping open.

"How do *you* know him? I saw him jump off a cliff. He died!" she explained, her eye filled with growing suspicion. Cassidy squinted her eyes.

"He's not dead! He's in my, well, our group," she said, responding to Maya's glare. "I swear, I met him just an hour ago!" Katherine's eye grew wide.

"Wait, he's alive?" Her voice shook as she spoke. Impossibly, her face turned even whiter. Cassidy nodded, her teeth biting her lip.

"Yeah, he is. Why do you seem so nervous?" Katherine gulped. Maya made a show of looking at her wrist.

"Come on, little red. We don't have all day. Why are you scared?" Katherine's shaking hand pointed to her covered eye.

"He did this to me."

11

Fire finally opened her eyes.

She was still glued to the tree, and it seemed as though she couldn't find the strength to take her arms off. Or maybe the will to. Her friends were all gone, most likely floating dead in the water.

For a while, all the tiny girl did was stare up at the deep blue sky. *Shock* was the word that seemed to linger in her mind.

"I'm alive," she whispered to the air. "I did it. I'm alive."

She suddenly pried her arms from the branch and fell, tumbling to the ground. "I'm alive!" she screeched maniacally. "I'm alive!"

A dull ache lingered in her numb arms. She moved her arms in a circular motion, attempting to wake her body back up. *You must look ridiculous,* Fire grimly thought, laughing. She *laughed.*

"Oh my god, you are insane," she muttered to herself. She could almost feel as her mind slipped into a bad mood.

"Ethan!" she called. "Hey!"

Click-click.

Fire turned around suddenly, scared out of her wits. "Who are you?" she asked, embarrassed by her scared-sounding voice. She covered her mouth immediately, realizing that she had made a mistake in her previous shouts. There could be a man watching her at this very moment.

A thought then came to her that made her relax. The tsunami! It must have killed a lot of crazies. Fire smiled a sick smile. She loved to think of the men struggling for air as the water slowly but surely filled their lungs.

The strange click sounded again.

"I said, who are you?" Her voice became louder. She spun around in the other direction.

For one terrifying moment, Fire wondered if she really *had* gone insane. If it was her own mind, she was screwed up beyond help.

She heard the noise once more behind her, much closer this time.

"Who the hell are you?!" she shrieked this time. The click pierced the air again, right next to her.

She screamed in terror before she could help it. Standing before her was the largest beetle she had ever seen. Its face was around an inch taller than her, and its shell was the disgusting color of mud. Fire felt her heart skip a beat.

The most horrifying thing about this bug was its jet black eyes, looking more like empty holes in the bug's face. She waved mockingly at it, her dark eyes wide in fear.

"What's up?" she told it, slowly backing away. "You alright there?"

The thing clicked its mandibles and crawled a little closer to her. Fire quickly hopped back. Although she knew that no god could possibly exist on this hell of an island, she prayed to anything her mind would think of. *Let me be ok,* she begged to no one.

Begged.

This wasn't her. She never acted so vulnerable, not anymore.

Oh Fire, she thought to herself miserably. *You're nothing without your friends.* If Ethan were here, he would think of a plan. Aiden would protect her and fight this monster. Cassidy would figure out this scientific impossibility. But now, it was only she.

Fire slowly backed up some more. The two locked eyes for a while, neither of them moving an inch. The bug's eyes looked strangely human. This thing's size was just impossible, there was no other way to say it. Thinking about it made her head hurt.

Without warning, the bug scurried toward her. Fire screamed and dove to the side. She quickly jumped up and began to sprint off into the jungle.

She took a look back and wished she didn't. The bug was chasing after her. It was a predator. Fear took hold of her as she ran away, knowing that she was its prey. She ran and ran until she couldn't.

She snuck a look behind her again. She could faintly see the bug in the distance, not letting its prey go free. As she ran some more, the ground gradually changed to rock. *That's weird,* she thought. *I don't remember ever seeing this before.*

She took more steps, and saw what she had never seen before; a chasm. She gazed at it, mesmerized.

Woah. Very carefully, she peered over the edge. She felt chills when she saw how far down the water was.

If she and Ethan had found this on a normal day, they would most likely be cliff jumping right now. *I wish Ethan was here.*

She heard the familiar clicking noise behind her. Fire felt a pang of fear when she looked behind her, worrying that she had stared into the water for too long.

It was there, coming still. Fire didn't know where to go. *Oh god, what do I do, what do I do?* The chasm went as far to the side as she could see. She looked down at the water again. She looked back, and then realized what she had to do. She closed her eyes briefly and prayed to air.

Please be deep, please be deep, please be deep, she pleaded.

She screamed a shriek of fear and defiance as she leaped into the water far, far below, right before the beetle snatched her.

Cassidy put her hand over her mouth in horror.

"Gabe did that to your eye?"

"Yeah, he did," Katherine said sadly. "We got into a fight over food one time. He got so angry, I really thought he was gonna kill me. He took a stick and he was just about to hit me with it. Somehow, I moved weirdly, and he jutted the point out, and well, he stabbed my eye. It was damaged beyond repair, so I had to, you know, cut-"

"I got it," Maya said quickly. "I don't need the details, sweetheart." Cassidy winced, imagining it.

"Did it hurt?"

"No Cassidy, I bet it felt great," Maya muttered. Cassidy stared at her.

"He was a terrible human being," Katherine added. "He said so many awful things. I never should have shown emotions to him." Cassidy shook her head in disgust.

"That's so horrible. I'm so sorry about your eye, Katherine. Truly. It should have been his eye." Katherine nodded.

"Yeah, I know. But there's nothing I can do." They all sat in awkward silence for a few minutes. Cassidy suddenly jumped up, startling the other two.

"Guys! Why are we just sitting here? We need to find our friends! Come on!" She looked around, desperate for any clear trail. She felt a jolt of happiness when she finally spotted an almost hidden trail, nestled in the tall thick trees. "Well, come on!" She began to walk over to the trail. Cassidy looked over and found Maya right next to her.

"Do you trust her?" Maya asked her softly after they were out of Katherine's hearing range. Cassidy paused for a moment.

"Yes, I think I do. I mean, she got her eye poked out, for heaven's sake. It looks like she was telling the truth, don't you think?" Maya nodded hesitantly

"Yeah, I guess. I just think we shouldn't trust someone so quickly." Cassidy nodded at her observation. Maya abruptly stopped, causing the girl to almost fall right into her.

"What the-" Maya covered Cassidy's mouth with her hand and pointed. There was a woman close to them with her back turned. Her head was down, and Cassidy felt a spike of fear.

"Why is there a person there?" Cassidy whispered. "She should be dead from the tsunami."

"She should be," Maya replied, "but she's not."

"Guys, why did you stop?" Katherine said loudly. Maya quickly put her other hand over the girl's mouth, but it was too late. The stranger slowly got up from her kneeling position and turned towards them. Her expression was amused, a shark-like grin spread across her mangled face. Her mouth was covered in the blood from the thing she was eating. Cassidy looked at the shape that had been torn apart, and she gasped.

Oh god oh god oh god.

She turned toward Maya, who was scared as well but trying not to show it.

"Maya," she whispered. Maya's head turned in her direction, her eyes never wavering from the threat in front of them. "I swear that's a person. Lord forgive me." Cassidy took a deep breath, attempting to control the rising bile in her throat. "Doesn't it look like it?" Maya's eyes filled with realization, terror, and disgust. Cassidy could only hold onto the hope that the person was dead.

"We have to go," she whispered back. "Now." The girls began to back up slowly, Katherine now realizing the kind of danger she was in.

"Stay, friends," the woman cackled. "I want to introduce myself. Come here. Be my friend!" Cassidy noticed the gleam of madness in the wild woman's eye. The stranger's brown frizzy hair was tossed around her face, some strands sticking to her forehead by the blood.

This is straight out of a horror movie, the terrified girl thought. The trio backed up even more, but the lady was up and moving now, her bloody lips pulled back in a smile. "If you won't be my friend by choice, you will be my friend by force." The lady pulled out a dagger from her torn leather boot.

"Hey red, what happened to your eye?" she asked Katherine, cocking her head. "Did it fall out? Did you eat it? " Maya pulled Cassidy's arm to the side.

"This lady has got some serious mental issues," she whispered in her ear. Cassidy nodded and wished that her feisty friend would do something about this woman. With an almost tangible pain, Cassidy realized that something inside Maya had broken. She used to be the one Cassidy would look up to in conflict. Now, Maya was just as confused and terrified as she.

"How about I take out your other eye?" the woman asked, inching closer. "Oh yes, oh yes, I'd like that. Can I?" Katherine backed up, but she was blocked by the thick trunk of a tree.

"No," she said, her voice shakier than Cassidy would've thought possible. The lady whimpered, the sound more like an animal.

"Yes." She dashed toward Katherine, making the redhead screech. Katherine ducked quickly as the woman stabbed the dagger, aiming for her face. She grabbed her by her long hair. She brought the knife up to her throat, ready to make a swift movement with her hand, ending Katherine's life. The small girl was cowering, making the knife slide against her neck.

"Please don't kill me!" Katherine begged. The lady pouted.

"But I'm hungry, little red. I'm so very hungry." The young adult's eye grew wide as she realized what the stranger was implying. The woman brought back the knife.

"Wait!" Maya shouted. The woman stopped, looking like an angry little kid.

"What?" she whined. Maya glanced quickly at Cassidy, then back at the scene before her. Cassidy knew Maya was about to do something. But when she saw the look in her eye, she knew it was something bad.

"Kill me instead," the redhead declared. Cassidy's mouth fell open.

"What? No!" she yelled urgently, rushing forward. Maya gently but firmly pushed her aside.

"Yes, Cassidy. It'll be ok." The brunette girl shook her head.

"No Maya. I already lost you. I'm not losing you again."

"Cassidy, can't you see that I want this?"

"But Maya," she said sadly, "you've survived this long. Don't do this."

"That's just it," she replied. "I've only been surviving, not living. What's the point, Cassidy? What if I don't want to be here anymore?"

Maya shook her head slowly and began to walk to her killer.

"Release her and take me," she demanded. The woman looked at her, confused. She suddenly let Katherine go, and she dropped to the ground, shaking.

"You will be my friend instead." She grabbed a handful of her bright red hair and pulled her to her chest. She grabbed the knife, and Maya's emerald eyes were dimming, as though she was already dead. She gave a mocking salute and pushed the curly hair out of her face.

"Goodbye, old friend," she whispered to Cassidy. "I'm sorry for kicking you," she added, with the saddest chuckle Cassidy had ever heard. "Now get out of here. You don't want to watch this."

The woman plunged the knife into Maya's chest, but Cassidy never saw it happen. She was gone, tears blinding her. She could faintly sense Katherine behind her, running at top speed.

"Goodbye, Maya," she whispered to the wind.

12

"Hope? Cassidy?" Ethan called out. He wouldn't believe that his friends were dead. They weren't. "Hope!" he called again.

Ethan roughly pushed past large leaves connected to soaking trees.

He had survived.

Martha hadn't.

The thought of her made his eyes burn. Martha was dead. He kept repeating the phrase over and over as if that would ingrain it in his mind. If he could accept it, it might not be like a knife in his heart any longer. He pushed through more dense green leaves.

Finally, he came to a tree that had branches attached to it. With a sigh of relief, Ethan put his hands on the soaking wet branches. They were slippery, but it was better than the ground. He effortlessly climbed up the tree, gripping the branches tightly.

Martha's dead, Ethan. She's dead and she's not coming back.

"Hey!" a voice called from down below. "Hey, you in the tree!" Ethan froze, not looking down. That voice didn't belong to Hope, Cassidy, Fire, or Blisse. It sounded stronger and deeper. However, the sound was clearly from a girl. "You, in the tree! Come down here!"

"What do you want?" Ethan called, still not looking at her. How this stranger had survived the awful tsunami was beyond him.

"I want to talk to you!"

"What? No!"

"I won't kill you." Her voice sounded exasperated and annoyed now. Ethan finally found the nerve to turn his head. Looking down, he was much higher than he realized. He wasn't afraid of heights, but he was nervous that he could slip and fall from this high up. In his line of vision, he saw a woman peering up at him. He locked eyes with her large ones, and he could immediately tell that she wasn't insane. At least, not beyond help. She seemed to slouch her curvy frame a little bit, and her strawberry-blonde hair cascaded over her shoulders.

Ethan ever so slowly put his foot down on the next soaking branch. He gripped it tighter, willing to stop the shaking of his hands. Quivering would mean slipping, which would mean paralyzation or death.

He finally reached the wet earth. He planted his feet firmly, turning to look at the stranger. She gave him a sly smile, showing him a perfect line of yellow teeth.

"Well," said Ethan, "I'm here. What do you want?"

She chuckled, a sound full of bitter amusement.

"Well, my intent is not to kill, for one thing. How did you survive that wave, pretty boy?"

"Listen," he said hesitantly, backing away. His hand unconsciously drifted toward the knife in his belt. "I need to find some people, and if you won't help, you can get lost."

"What's your name?" She completely ignored his statement as she circled around him. "Come on buddy, I don't have all day."

"You first," Ethan demanded, bringing up his knife. "I've dealt with enough crap today, and I won't play games with you." She twirled her long hair around her finger, smirking.

"I'll tell you my name. I'm Isabelle, but call me Belle."

"Ethan," he curtly replied. She circled around him, putting her hand on his shoulder. He slapped it away.

"So, Ethan, why are you here?"

"I just told you, I got separated from some friends. Are you here to help or hurt me?"

"I'll help you," she replied, looking at him slyly. Clearly, she was just toying around with him; Ethan could see the spark in her eyes that told him so. "So, Ethan, do you love these friends? Do they comfort you when you're hurting deep inside?" Ethan's exasperated eyes looked at her strangely.

"You're crazy."

"What's your point? Now, where do you suppose we go?"

"I don't know," he confessed. "I was just going to walk until I found something." Belle snorted.

"Wow, you sure are a real Sherlock." She started to walk while Ethan followed her hesitantly.

"So," the girl began, after they had traveled for a few minutes, "are you a newcomer to this island?" Ethan snorted.

"I wish, but no."

"You see any criminals yet?"

"Definitely," Ethan said, nodding vigorously. "One of my good… friends was killed by one of them," he told her, referring to Martha. He didn't want to tell this girl about that horrible death that still made his eyes burn. It was ridiculous, but it seemed like only something that he and Hope should be burdened with. Belle's face looked sympathetic, but her hazel eyes told a different story.

"That's not very fun," she replied, looking straight ahead. "If it makes you feel better, my sister was killed too."

"I'm sorry, Belle."

"Oh, don't be," she responded, chuckling. "She was a real piece of work, not anything special, let me tell you that. Actually, I was the one who ended up killing her."

Ethan did a double-take.

"Sorry, what?"

"You heard me. I don't need people with me, Ethan, it just doesn't work out." She sighed. "People just end up getting hurt."

Ethan looked at her blankly, his face reddening. How was he supposed to reply to that?

"Well, that's not good."

"You aren't the best at small talk."

"Ok, please," Ethan almost snapped, "let's just not talk then."

She tilted her head, her light hazel eyes taking in his appearance. Her stare lingered on his eyes. Finally, she let out an annoyed breath.

"Fine, I'll stay with you. Your intentions are good," she snapped.

"How can you tell?" Ethan asked. "For all you know, I could be a serial killer, waiting to earn your trust before I murder you and hide your body in the jungle." Belle nodded approvingly.

"Well, I like the way you think, friend. I can read people easily, it's one of my powers. One might even call it sorcery." Ethan snorted.

"Yeah. You read me right, alright. There's no way I could ever kill you." He raised an eyebrow slyly. She laughed, and the sound somehow made him like her more.

"So, where shall our adventure begin?"

"Well," he said, "the jungle might be a good place to start."

"Like I said, a real Sherlock." He rolled his eyes, a smirk impossibly making its way across his face.

"Just help me find my friends."

"How much longer?" Gabe complained. "I'm tired!" Hope put a finger to her lips. "Gabe, shut up!"

"But I don't want to. This walking is getting ridiculously tedious."

"Gabe, you are really inspiring my inner serial killer."

"And you, gorgeous, are inspiring my inner beast." Gabe's eyes locked with her as he grinned his infamous grin.

"I swear, if you make another noise, I'm turning you over to the criminals," Hope threatened, tearing her gaze from his greedy smile.

Blisse hesitantly nodded, looking at the floor.

"You do need to be quieter," she mumbled. He looked at her disapprovingly.

"You just went from an eight to a five in my book," he told her. Aiden rolled his eyes, patting Blisse kindly on the back.

"Gabe, you really are a jerk." Gabe shrugged, looking back at Hope.

"It's ok, I'm gorgeous's jerk." Hope gritted her teeth.

"Dude, for the last time, *I don't like you!* Get that through the thing that you call a brain!"

"Oh come on, you know I give you butterflies," he said, much louder than was needed. She automatically slapped her hand over his mouth.

"Shut your mouth," she hissed. He made a shrugging gesture. She squinted her eyes at him, the urge to punch him growing stronger and stronger. A minute went by. Aiden peered around the trees, making sure that they hadn't attracted anyone's attention. Blisse looked nervously around as well. Without warning, Gabe took her hand off of his mouth and laced it with his. Hope quickly tried pulling away, but he wouldn't release his hand.

"Hey, let go! Now!" she demanded in surprise. Gabe completely ignored her as his lips traveled toward her. Hope brought up her other hand and slapped him roughly. "Gabe! Do you know what no means?" Gabe smiled and nodded his head.

"Of course, gorgeous." Hope finally pulled away from him. She looked at him hopelessly.

"Gabe, what is your issue?" Gabe took a few more steps closer to her.

"Whatever do you mean?" He laughed and looked around in amusement. Aiden and Blisse greeted him with blank stares.

"You know what I mean," Hope snapped back. She set her jaw. "Gabe, what was your life like before you were sent here?" Gabe put his hand on his chin theatrically.

"I was the coolest guy you wish you met, gorgeous."

"You are an awful person," Hope said, shaking her head. "You know that, right?" He chuckled, and grabbed her arm again, pulling her closer to him. Hope smacked his arm. "Geez, you are impossible! Can't you get it through your head that I don't like you?"

Gabe continued on his rant, unfazed by Hope's language.

"Maybe little five here wants to date me instead," he stated, making a grab for Blisse.

"Leave her alone," Aiden suddenly said with a fierce tone. Gabe looked at him in genuine shock. At least, Hope thought it was genuine. Who knew what Gabe could be thinking?

"Hey gorgeous," Gabe said, grinning again. "Look, he's mad. What makes you angry?" She gave him a look.

"Your goddamn self, Gabe."

Hope attempted to control her breathing. *It's ok, Hope. Chill out.* Gabe grinned, watching Hope try to keep calm.

"Well," he said, especially looking at Hope, "it's not a surprise you're getting so worked up. You know what they say about girls and their emotions." A laugh that scared her came out of Hope's mouth.

No, calm down.

However, her firm thinking didn't help her at all this time. Before she knew what was happening, her hand had already smashed into Gabe's nose. She faintly felt the tingling pain in her hand, but her rage and adrenaline overpowered it.

"Really?" she shouted at him, not caring if any criminals heard her at this point. She noticed Blisse put her hand on her shoulder to calm her down, but she shook it off. Gabe took a few steps back, shocked but still amused by her rage. She felt a sick pleasure at all the blood rushing from his nose. Aiden chuckled.

"Hey Gabe, why are you backing up? Don't you think that girls are weak?" she taunted him. Hope found what he said next unbelievable.

"Well," Gabe started, "they are."

Hope saw red cloud her vision, and before she knew it, she was on top of him. Her knees held him down as she gave him all she had. She punched him as hard as she could, no longer caring about what anyone thought.

"I AM STRONG!" she screamed like a maniac. She dimly noticed Blisse firmly grab her arm; she was only focused on causing Gabe as much misery as possible. Hope was lifted up by Aiden and Blisse. The kind girl looked directly in her eyes.

"Hope, calm down. Take a deep breath, ok? Calm down." Hope stopped struggling and fell limp in their arms. Although she was now breathing steadily, she felt pleasure at how Gabe was lying on the ground, his front covered in blood. That feeling went away as soon as she looked at all of the blood covering her shaking hands.

Oh my god, she thought in horror. *I did that.* She looked at Blisse for comfort. Aiden was attempting to conceal a smile, his warm eyes now focused on an angry Gabe. "I did that," Hope whispered to Blisse. "I... I made him bleed."

Maybe I am dangerous after all.

"AHHHHH!" Fire screeched as she fell down. *This is it. I'm gonna die.* Sheer panic filled her mind as the water became nearer and nearer.

She slammed into the water that reminded her of a wooden floor. The wind was knocked right out of the small adult. The liquid held her down, and this brought back horrific memories of the tsunami that had almost ended her life just earlier that day. All she could hope for was that the bug didn't jump. If it did, she would definitely be crushed.

She kicked to the top, determined to reach the surface. Finally, her head reached the oxygen. Immediately, she looked up at the bug. She could practically see it making its decision. Fire hoped it chose to go away. *That's weird*, she thought to herself. *It shouldn't be this intelligent.* She saw it begin to back up.

"Thank you!" she called to it with a smirk. That was a mistake. The beetle came back to the edge, and although the insect was very high up, the two locked eyes. Her blue eyes suddenly widened in surprise.

Shit.

Before she knew it, the bug stepped off the edge. Fire screamed and began to swim as fast as she could. She felt a flood of water pour into her mouth. She gagged on it, but her energy never ceased. The bug couldn't land on her. If it did, she would die.

She swam quickly away from the insect's landing spot. She glanced behind her for a split second, seeing if she was far enough. The bug was just about to hit the water. She breathed a huge sigh of relief. She wasn't going to get crushed! What startled her, though, was the splash that the huge beetle had produced. The small wave carried her a safe distance. Now, it was time to see if it could swim. If it could, it would be all over. Fire would die. She held her breath, more nervous than she had ever been. She watched it float closer, and her heart skipped a beat.

But instead of continuing, she noticed that the large bug had begun to sink. It flailed all around, trying to get closer to its prey. Soon, it's terrifying face was the only thing that wasn't submerged.

"Ha, you stupid bug!" She treaded water until she was sure it had gone underwater. She waited a few extra minutes, until she was positive it wouldn't come back up. She chuckled to herself as she began to swim forward, looking for something she could climb up.

A few minutes had gone by when she began to worry. The sun was beginning to sink in the sky and there was no sign of anything that she could grab onto. She knew that there was no way in the world that she could keep swimming much longer. *What if there's nothing that I can climb up on?*

This thought brought a small pang of panic. *You did what you had to do,* she reassured herself. *You would be dead otherwise.*

"Help!" she called, hoping anybody could hear here. Fire swam on, becoming more worried with each tiring stroke.

13

"So Ethan," Belle asked, as they walked to nowhere in particular. "What would mentally destroy you?"

Her tone was so casual that her statement didn't even register in Ethan's brain. He stopped walking abruptly.

"Did I hear you correctly?" She chuckled.

"Well, I hope so."

"What kind of a question is that?" he asked, a little disturbed with this girl who kept telling him things that he didn't want to know. She smirked.

"I want to get to know you better."

"And asking me for my favorite color wouldn't have sufficed?" She grinned at his obvious discomfort.

"Ok green eyes, what's your favorite color?" He looked at her, slightly grinning.

"Have you ever heard of the *aurora borealis?*" Belle looked at him smugly.

"Yes, I have. And you don't need to impress me. Just say the northern lights." Ethan grinned.

"Caught me there. Anyway, that's a mix of my favorite colors. Whenever I think of green, a picture of the northern lights in the starry sky come to mind. I grew up with those lights, so I guess that's why it's my favorite color."

"Well, you sure went into detail on that one!" Ethan just shook his head, but there was a smile on his face.

"What's yours?"

"Red," Belle said, without any hesitation. He nodded.

"Why red?"

"It's the color of blood." He looked at her blankly, disgust evident on his face. She snorted, a sound that for some reason made her more likable.

"I'm kidding! I like it because my boyfriend first proposed to me during a total lunar eclipse. I always associate that color when I think of him." Ethan looked at her curiously.

"I take it he's not on this island with you?"

She looked at him as though he was the biggest idiot on the planet.

"If he was, do you really think that I'd be wasting my time with you? I'm joking," she added, noticing the look on his face. "His name was Keegan."

Ethan smiled uncomfortably. Belle started to walk again, swinging her arms as she whistled an unfamiliar tune. Ethan was just about to whistle back when he heard a sound. It sounded like a scream, but not from terror. *Frustration* was the word that came to mind.

"Belle, stop!" Ethan called to her. She turned around, her face tinged with annoyance.

"What, man?" Ethan put his finger to his lips.

"Shh. I swear I just heard someone's voice. Listen." The two waited in silence for a moment.

"I don't hear anything," Belle stated. "You're tired; you're probably just hallucinating. We should go to bed now anyway." Ethan shook his head in protest.

"But, I could've sworn-" he stopped abruptly. "See, there it is again! Didn't you just hear it?" Belle shook her head, but he could see in her eyes that she was lying. "It sounds like someone's in danger! Let's go help them!" He began to walk in the other direction, but Belle stopped him.

"Ethan, look. That's sweet and all, but you're not Batman. Whoever that is can deal with it on their own. It's time you get some sleep." Ethan tore his arm out of her grasp.

"Fine, Belle. You can stay here, but I'm going. If that were me, I would want someone to help me." The scream sounded again. "Bye." He began to run again.

"Boys," she whispered softly to herself, rolling her eyes. "Always tryin' to be the hero." With a dramatic sigh, Belle jogged after him.

"I've never come across this before," Ethan said a few minutes later. He was standing on the edge of a cliff, gazing down at the water below. Belle was beside him in a moment.

"Why do you sound amazed? It's just a stupid chasm," she said, clearly annoyed. Ethan was looking around curiously.

"I swear, didn't the voice come from this direction?" Belle shook her head and rolled her eyes again.

"Ethan, let's go. Look how dark it is. Come on," she begged him. Ethan was just about to turn around when he heard it again.

"Someone help!" the terrified voice called. He spun around, and looked down.

"Belle, look!" he exclaimed. "Someone's down there!" Belle snickered.

"Yeah right. Like anyone could be in the water, you idiot." But the girl looked over the edge.

"Hey!" Ethan shouted, startling Belle. "Can you hear me?" The person in the water was silent for a little bit.

"Yes!" he heard them call.

"Ok, I'll help you in a second, alright?"

"Sure, I'll just wait here!" the voice shouted back. Ethan worked at lightning speed.

"Ok, Belle, grab as many vines as you can. And do it quick, because the sun's nearly gone." Belle nodded, and began to rip some vines. Ethan carefully walked back over to the edge. "Hang on, I'm almost there!" he called. A minute later, Belle had grudgingly ripped out numerous vines. Ethan quickly tied the vines together. "I hope these hold," he said softly. Belle gave him an incredulous look.

"Wait a second, you're making a rope?!" Ethan nodded.

"Yes, why do you sound so shocked?" The girl gave an exasperated sigh.

"It won't work, Ethan. Don't get your hopes up." He punched her playfully in the arm.

"Anything is possible if you believe!" He grinned. Belle rolled her eyes and went to sit down under a tree. A few moments later, the vine was long enough to reach the water. "Do you think it'll hold, Belle?" he asked her. She gave another sigh.

"Ethan, you already know what I think. But you might as well go ahead and give it a try. Clearly nothing I say will pull you away from this crap." Ethan looked over the edge, squinting to find the silhouette of the person below. It was becoming much harder to see in the dimming light.

"Hey, are you still there?" he yelled below him.

"Yup!"

"Ok, I have a rope that I'm gonna let down. Grab onto it and you can spiderman up the wall. Got it?"

"Yes!" they shouted back. Ethan began to slowly lower down the self-made rope. *Come on now. Don't break on me.* If he couldn't save Martha, he would at least save the poor soul trapped in the deep chasm.

"Tug on it when you have it!" He felt the slight tug and knew he succeeded. "Alright, swim close to the wall!" He faintly saw the person's silhouette moving toward the wall made of rock. "Alright, I'll start pulling it up now! Put your feet in front of you and start walking up. And hurry, it's getting really dark!" Belle was getting up now, interested in what was happening, although she tried not to show it.

"Ethan…" He cut her off.

"It's going to work, trust me!" Ethan peered back over the edge. "I said you can climb up now!" he called down, a bit annoyed that they were taking so long.

"I am!" the voice called, much closer than last time. Ethan could now distinguish that the voice belonged to a girl.

"Oh, sorry! I didn't even notice. You're really light!"

"Oh, I didn't notice," the girl said, her voice dripping with sarcasm. Something jolted in Ethan when he heard the voice up close. He felt his hopes rise. *No,* he thought. *It can't be Sapphire.* Ethan's happiness faltered when he heard a *riip!* His panic grew.

"What was that?" the voice called. The person was obviously trying to keep their voice steady. Belle was looking over, an amused look in her eyes.

"Nothing!" Ethan called. "On a completely different subject, you might want to hurry up!" He felt the girl climb faster than she had previously. Ethan turned to talk to Belle. "See, Belle, I was right, it does work." He wasn't paying attention when the rope slipped a little from his hand. He heard the girl shriek. "Sorry!" he yelled. Ethan looked at the rope in his hand. The vine was becoming thinner and thinner.

If she didn't hurry up soon, she would fall back into the water, which was a long way down. The sky was darkening, and Ethan felt a few sprinkles of rain on his arm.

"Ok, don't freak out, but the rope is breaking. So hurry!" he shouted once more. He looked down to see how much distance the girl had left. Ethan had a pleasant surprise when she wasn't far below him. With rain and the setting sun clouding his vision, he couldn't get a clear picture of the girl below him. Ethan gulped when he looked at the rope; the girl was hanging on by a thread. "Give me your hand!" Ethan urgently told her. She climbed up a bit more. The girl made a grab for his hand, but she couldn't reach. He wished he could see her face in the dark.

"I...I can't!" she gasped to him. "I'm too short!" Ethan's eyes grew wide at the voice.

"I knew it! It is you!" She stopped climbing for a moment.

"Ethan?" she asked excitedly. He was filled with joy.

"Fire! It is you! Oh my gosh! I found you! I thought you drowned!" Ethan stopped breathing for a second when he glanced at the rope. "Fire, you have to grab my hand *now*. You can do it. Just reach for my hand!" With one last final burst of energy, Fire's hand shot up. Ethan grasped her hand just as the rope completely snapped. Fire screamed as she dangled in the air. "Ok, I can just pull you up now. You can relax." She panted as he pulled her up with minimal effort. He pulled her into a tight hug when she reached the edge.

"Ethan! I can't believe it's you. I thought you were dead too!" she said into his chest. Belle cleared her throat, causing Fire to let go. She raised her eyebrows as she looked her up and down.

"Um Ethan, who's this?" Fire asked with a tight-lipped smile. Belle moved closer to Ethan.

"I'm Belle. Who are you?" the girl replied in the same tone. Fire squinted her eyes and smirked.

"Oh, I'm Ethan's best friend." Belle didn't blink.

"Fire, calm down," Ethan warned. By now, the rain was coming down in sheets. Belle barely concealed a snicker.

"Did he just call you fire?" She nodded, showing that this was obvious. "That's your name?" Belle asked. The small girl glared at her.

"My real name is Sapphire. I go by Fire. You got a problem with that?" Belle put her hands out in front of her.

"Calm down lady. Don't get so worked up." Fire stared daggers at her until Belle looked away.

"Anyway, Ethan, what happened while we were split up?" she questioned. Ethan was relieved that they had changed the subject.

He told her everything that had happened to him. Belle was braiding her long hair, looking bored, but Fire knew she was interested as well. "Well, I'm so glad you're ok." Ethan looked at her, curious about what she went through. "Ok, I want to know about you, but let's get under some shelter first. I'm getting soaked." Belle nodded, as though she had been thinking about this all along. The trio walked until they got under a tree with massive leaves. "Alright Fire, I'm listening." Belle smirked.

"This will be good," she muttered under her breath. Fire told him everything about the tsunami. She tried to make the bug as detailed as possible. She noticed Ethan's eyes grow wide at the statements she had made.

"But, that's impossible! There's no way there could be a bug that big!" he said. Belle looked at the girl with disgust.

"Ethan, don't be so naive. Clearly, she's making it up. There's human nature for you." Fire glared at her, extremely annoyed.

"Ethan, I'm not making this up. What would be the point?" Fire rolled her eyes. "And Belle, if there wasn't a bug, as you say, then why would I have been in the chasm in the first place? I wasn't there to chill in the water, you know." Belle blushed as Fire grinned. "Yeah. That's what I thought." Belle's red face went away.

"You know, *Fire*, I really, really, really don't like you." Fire dramatically rolled her blue eyes.

"I really couldn't find a damn to give."

"You know, you girls shouldn't fight over me," Ethan said, attempting to break the ice. Both girls weren't amused. He grinned awkwardly. "Sorry."

"Anyway, have you found Cassidy or Hope yet?" Fire asked him. Ethan sadly shook his head.

"No, not yet." The small girl frowned.

"Hope had better still be alive. I yelled at her right after you left," said Fire. Ethan raised his eyebrows.

"Why'd you yell?"

Fire grinned sheepishly. "Well, I kinda sorta told her that Martha's death was her fault. Then I shoved her and ran after you." He was appalled.

"Fire..." he said, shaking his head.

"Knowing me, you shouldn't be so surprised," she retorted. Belle was watching the two with disgust plastered all over her face.

"Um, guys, if you don't mind, I'm going to sleep." She seemed to rethink her last statement. "Actually, I don't even care if you do mind. I haven't slept in like, two days. Too busy fleeing for my life from creeps and all that. Night." Belle made herself comfortable on the wet ground. Fire gave Ethan a look.

"Can I sleep too?" she asked him. Ethan gave a soft smile, nodding. Her eyelids shut as she fell into darkness, the sound of rain soothing her mind.

"Cassidy, hold up!" Katherine called, her voice in obvious strain. Cassidy didn't turn around. She had only one thought on her mind: Maya. "Cassidy, please!" She turned around, and Katherine's face filled with surprise at the sight before her. The girl's face was red and blotchy. Cassidy's eyes were filled with tears, but she was not ashamed to show them. "Cassidy, I am so sorry," Katherine began, but she put a finger to her lips.

"Katherine, do you know Maya?" Katherine tilted her head, confused.

"Yeah, of course." Cassidy shook her head.

"I mean, do you really know her? Do you know her likes, dislikes, favorite things, and what bothers her?" Katherine slowly shook her head.

"No." Cassidy heaved a sigh that was almost a sob.

"Well, I did. A few days ago, my friends were all in a building together. Maya was rude and she kicked me very hard. My friend, Ethan, was forced to knock her unconscious. We went to play a game, but when we returned, the building was on fire. We all were positive that she had died. Now, this is going to sound horrible, but we were kind of, well, glad that she was dead." Katherine gasped. "Yeah, yeah, I know," she said, without emotion.

"When I found her today, I wasn't glad. But as I talked to her, I was happy that she had survived. She's intimidating, but believe it or not, she has her good moments. She was a lot of fun before her boyfriend died. You don't understand how crazy it is that she was willing to die. Just like that. I never knew that she thought her life wasn't worth living. I guess that's the depressing part. She just wanted to get out of this crazy thing we call life. So Katherine, please don't act like you understand this, ok? Because you don't, and you never will." Katherine nodded, astounded at her story.

"So, what's the plan now?" she asked curiously. Cassidy shrugged helplessly.

"I want to find my friends. I just don't know where the hell they are." Katherine looked at her with admiration.

"You really love these friends, don't you?"

"They are my family," she simply said. The two walked in silence.

"Um, I know we need to find them, but do you think we can go to sleep? It's pretty dark right now," Katherine said nervously. Cassidy smiled weakly.

"Sure. We need sleep. Actually, you do. I'll stay up for a while and keep watch." The young adult gave her an incredulous look.

"Aren't you tired?" she questioned. Cassidy shook her head grimly.

"No, not really. I'm fine, I promise." Words had never felt so empty. "Goodnight, Katherine." She smiled.

"Goodnight, Cassidy."

As the darkness settled around them, Cassidy set her back up against the tree. The image of the bloody knife wouldn't leave her mind, and she knew for certain that it would star in her dreams.

"Maya," she whispered. She sniffed, and her hand went to the knife in her belt. She slowly pulled it out as tears welled in her eyes. Cassidy's eyes stayed glued to the small blade nestled in her hand. Unconsciously, it floated to her own skin.

Gabe put his hand to his nose. He pulled it back, and it was covered in a deep shade of red.

"I'm sorry," Hope said quietly, looking at the ground. "I don't know what came over me."

"Wow, gorgeous," Gabe said through gritted teeth. "And you wondered why you're on this island." He groaned dramatically. "People with temper issues belong on this island full of psychos, blondie. People like you."

Hope sniffed, covering her wet eyes with her hand. His eyes lingered on Hope's distressed trembling, and he felt his body heat up with pleasure.

"Gabe, it wasn't that bad," said Aiden. "I mean, no offense Hope, you have some muscle, but he's fine."

"Aiden," Hope said in an ashamed voice. "I belong on this island. I hurt him."

"No. Hope, believe me, you are good." Aiden's eyes looked down. "None of us belong here."

"He's wrong," Gabe declared. "That's violence if I've ever seen it."

Blisse looked at him angrily.

"Hope, don't feel bad for this creep," she said suddenly. "He's just trying to make you angry. You don't belong here, I promise." Hope gave her a small smile. Gabe leaped up, his nose bleed only a small trickle now,

"It's ok gorgeous, I'm all right now!" Hope glared at him; she had never felt such hatred for a person before. She wanted him dead.

Don't think that way. You don't want him dead. The girl took a few deep breaths.

"Blisse, we have to find our friends now. I'm sick of waiting," she told her. Blisse nodded.

"Yeah, I know. But it's getting really dark now. I think it'll be unsafe."

"Oh, screw our safety," Hope exclaimed. "I want to find them. If you won't come with me, that's fine, but I'm going. I can't stand this!" Aiden nodded in agreement at her statement.

"Yeah Blisse, I think we should do what Hope says. She already showed us what she is capable of," he said, pointing toward Gabe's minor injuries. Hope squinted her eyes.

"I said I was sorry, Aiden." He nudged her arm playfully.

"I know. I'm just kidding. I'm acting like Ethan, aren't I?" She nodded. "I miss that twit," he said, looking at the ground. Hope looked over at Gabe, a look of disgust on her face.

"Hey, Gabe. Are you coming or not?" He nodded.

"If that's what you want, gorgeous." She rolled her eyes.

"Ok, Blisse, what direction should we go?" She bit her lower lip and looked around.

"Well, they probably are inland, considering the tsunami. I say we just go straight and see what we find," Blisse proposed. Hope nodded.

"Are you sure you're not tired, Blisse? If you really are, we can stay." She shook her head, smiling.

"No, no, you have me all hyped up. Good pep talk, by the way." She laughed. "Let's go on an adventure!"

14

Fire woke up before dawn. She looked over at Ethan, who was sound asleep. She chuckled softly to herself at the sight of Belle, who was sleeping with her mouth wide open. Fire rose up and walked to the edge of the chasm. She looked down at the water with a disgusted face. *I'm never swimming again.*

All of a sudden, she felt a hand on her shoulder. She shrieked, louder than she had ever done before. She spun around, terrified. The small adult felt ridiculous when she saw Ethan standing there, laughing harder than ever.

"I got you so good!" he declared. Fire scoffed.

"Let's see who's laughing when I push you into the chasm," she said as she advanced toward him. He chuckled.

"If anyone's going down there, we all know it'll be you." She reached for his arm, but he grabbed both of her wrists. His eyes glinted as he threw her over his shoulder swiftly. He laughed when he heard her scream. "Let's go to the water," he called, as he slowly walked to the edge. When he was as close as he could get with falling, he turned around so Fire could see.

"Ethan, put me down!" she shouted. "You're too close! ETHAN!" She fiercely clawed at his back. He was laughing as he gently set her down.

"Man, you are so easy to scare." She rolled her blue eyes.

"Shut up." Ethan poked her in the shoulder.

"Look who's waking up," he whispered. He pointed to Belle. Fire had to hold back a laugh. Belle's hair was in every direction, she had drool on her chin, and she had dark bags under her tired eyes.

"Morning, Belle," she sneered. "Looks like you had a great sleep."

"Ethan, I feel really sick," Belle said in between multiple yawns. Fire smirked.

"If it makes you feel any better, I feel great!" she stated happily. Belle glared at her.

"I'm serious, I feel like I…" Suddenly, her face contorted. "Hold on!" She quickly ran into the trees and vomited. Fire scrunched up her face.

"Well, that's nice," she said in disgust. Ethan nodded.

"Just the thing to start off my morning." They were interrupted from a noise on the other side of the river. Fire looked at him, a small portion of fear in her eyes.

"Ethan, who's that?" she whispered to him.

"I don't know, just don't move. We don't want to call attention to ourselves." Her neck twitched to the side, and he assumed that was her attempt at a nod.

"Hey!" they heard a voice yell. "Who are you?" Fire gasped as she realized they were speaking to her. She grabbed her friend's arm. He began to move forward to the edge.

"Ethan, why are you moving? Stay here!" she whispered urgently. He shook his head.

"What's the point?" he asked, his voice becoming louder than a whisper. "They already see us, and it's not like they can exactly cross the chasm or anything." Ethan walked carefully, gulping at how far below the water was. "Who are you?" he questioned back to the people on the other side.

"My name's Blisse, and I come in peace!" Ethan and Fire looked at each other, not believing their ears. Fire's face lit up in joy.

"Blisse! It's Ethan and Fire!" He watched her walk to the edge of her side as well.

"Ethan?!" she yelled back in disbelief.

"Yes, Blisse, it's me! Are you alone?" he asked her.

"No!" she replied back. "Gabe, Aiden, and Hope are with me!" Ethan felt his heart jump.

"Can you bring them to the edge too?" he called.

"Yes!" He watched her disappear for a few moments.

"Fire, I can't believe they found us!" he exclaimed. "That was so much easier than I thought it would be." Fire nodded happily, then stopped, her eyes full of worry.

"How will they get over to our side?" she asked him. "The chasm looks like it goes a far way down." She pointed to their right and left. Ethan felt his hopes falter.

"You're right, I didn't think of that," he said nervously. Blisse appeared back onto the edge, followed by her friends. Right away, he noticed Hope's golden hair blowing in the slight breeze.

"Ok," Blisse called to him. "Just come over here!" Ethan laughed awkwardly.

"Well, you see Blisse, we have a small problem," he said to her.

"What is it?"

"We don't exactly know how to get across the water."

"Then what do you propose we do?" Aiden piped up from behind Blisse. Ethan shrugged and looked at Fire for help.

"Don't ask me!" she whispered to him. Suddenly, she had an idea. "Ethan, I have a plan!" He raised his eyebrows.

"Is it a good plan?" Ethan asked. Fire laughed nervously.

"Well, it's a plan." Ethan prepared himself for whatever crazy plan Fire had devised.

"Let's hear it." She nodded.

"Ok, so you know how I jumped into the water last night?" He nodded, not especially liking where this was going. "You made a rope out of vines, right? And it held long enough. Just make four of those vines!" Ethan bit his lower lip.

"Yeah, but you weigh practically nothing. The rope will probably snap much earlier for them, especially Aiden and Gabe," he warned her. Fire shrugged.

"I guess, but I think we should take our chances. The worst thing that can happen to them is that they fall back in the water. That won't kill them. I think." Ethan slowly nodded.

"Ok, Fire, I hope you're right." He turned back to the other four on the opposite side. "Ok guys, this is going to sound insane!" he yelled to them. "I'm gonna make a rope out of vines! After that's done, jump into the water and grab onto the vine. I'll pull you up and you'll be fine!" The other side was silent.

"There's a lot of things that could go wrong with that plan," Blisse warned him. Ethan nodded.

"Yeah, I know. But it's the only plan we got, even if it sounds absurd. I'm gonna start making the rope now, ok?"

"Ok!" he heard her call. By now, Belle was just emerging from the trees, her face in pain.

"Oh man, I feel horrible," she complained.

"I'm sorry Belle, but I need you to pull more vines, like you did last night. Actually, we need four times the vines that you had last night. And hurry, this is urgent!" She heaved an exasperated sigh.

"Really?" she whined. Ethan nodded.

"Fire and I will tie all the knots together when you're done. Please hurry!" She began weakly ripping the plants. "Blisse, who's going first?" he called to her. Ethan saw everyone huddle together.

"Hope said she'll go first!" she yelled. Ethan grinned.

"Ok, hold on a sec!" A few minutes later, the sick girl had pulled many vines off, and Fire had begun to secure them together. "Fire, make sure they are really tight, ok?" She nodded, and handed him the large rope. "Belle, keep pulling more vines!" he said urgently. She coughed once and went back to her task. "Blisse, Hope needs to jump off!" He saw Hope walk closer to the edge.

"Ethan, what if I die!" she called, clearly nervous. Ethan shrugged, remembering when she had asked him that on the first night.

"Then you'll be dead! Now jump!" Hope glanced down, terrified, now starting to regret that she had volunteered to go first. She backed up and began to run.

"AHHHHHH!" she shrieked as she leapt off the cliff. The girl looked down at where she would land. She hit the water with a loud *smack!* For a second, Ethan thought that she had drowned, feeling panic erupt inside him. A moment later, her head popped up. "It's so c-c-cold!" she shouted to him, her teeth chattering. Ethan nodded.

"Yes, water usually is. Swim to the wall and I'll lower the vine!" He held onto it tightly, and began to let it down. Hope grabbed onto it, and he pulled her up, just like Fire. She made it to the top without the rope thinning too greatly. He was relieved that the rope seemed to be much stronger than the night before.

Hope gave him a grateful smile as Belle walked out from the trees.

"He wasn't gone for a long time, you know." She stopped talking, her eyes taking in Hope's appearance.

"Hi!" Hope said brightly. Belle pursed her lips in a line, staring at the girl in front of her. Awkwardly, the blonde adult turned to Fire.

"I didn't mean to yell at you, Hope," she admitted, rubbing her arm uncomfortably.

"Thanks, Sapphire. I'm sorry for making you mad."

"Fire," she muttered. He continued making ropes for Blisse and Aiden. "Here, Ethan, I'll help you," Hope offered. They both lowered the rope as Blisse jumped into the chasm. After they pulled her up, Aiden did the same. His weight was harder to lug up, but it was much easier with three people helping instead of Ethan himself. Gabe was the only one left.

"Come on, Gabe, you have to jump!" Ethan yelled to him. He shook his head.

"No!" Ethan looked at Hope, annoyed.

"I can't believe you had to deal with this twit for a day," he whispered to her. Hope nodded.

"I know, I almost didn't." Ethan held a grin.

"Gabe, let's go!" he shouted impatiently.

"I don't want to!"

"Gabe, do it now or we'll just leave you there." He watched the adult walk up to the edge.

"Fine. Here I goooooo!"

"Belle, give me the rope!" Ethan said to her. She threw the rope at his chest, hard. He grabbed it and lowered it down to Gabe. He held onto it and began to climb up. Ethan was struggling to lift him.

"I hope the rope snaps," Fire muttered. It began to become thinner.

"Gabe, we're throwing over another rope. Grab onto that!" Ethan said to him. They let it over the edge, and he felt Gabe hold onto it. Finally, he reached the edge. "Geez Gabe, how much do you weigh?" Ethan asked, catching his breath.

"210 pounds of pure muscle," he bragged. Fire stared at him.

"Would you like an award?" Hope yawned.

"Ethan, can we take a nap? We were up all night trying to find you guys." Ethan shot her a kind smile.

"You stayed up all night to find me, Hopie?" She nodded. "Yeah, you can rest." The group of four made themselves comfortable under a tree and eventually drifted off.

"Katherine, wake up," Cassidy whispered while gently poking her. The redhead groggily sat up.

"Why?" she asked, her voice sleepy.

"We have to keep looking for them," Cassidy said. Katherine yawned.

"Fine." The girls sat up, stretching. "Where are we going to go?" Cassidy shrugged.

"I don't know. Let's just see where we end up," she said tiredly. They both began to walk. "So, Katherine, I don't know much about you. Tell me about yourself."

"Um, well, I guess I'm just your average girl," Katherine simply said. "Why?"

"Just trying to start a conversation," said Cassidy. It took everything in her not to sigh.

"Alright, but what's one thing that not many, if any, people know about you? There's gotta be something!" Katherine stopped moving, thinking about her answer.

"I can't think of anything!" she exclaimed. Cassidy took a deep breath.

"Listen, Katherine, what's one interesting fact about you?"

"Um, well, I guess I can run really fast." Cassidy nodded, exasperated.

"Will you tell me something about you?" Katherine inquired.

"Well," she began, "I love to write." Katherine gave a slight thumbs up. Cassidy slightly clenched her fist. *So much for small talk.*

"So, tell me more about Gabe," Cassidy requested. "What else did he say to you?" Katherine bit her lip as her hand unconsciously flew to her empty eye socket.

"Well, he gave me every line in the book. He told me he would take a bullet for me, that I wasn't like the other girls, all that stuff. I genuinely thought he cared about me. Just after a few days, he asked me out. I told him that I was flattered and everything, but I think we should wait a while and make sure we're alive. His kind face turned so dark that I thought he was going to kill me then and there. Anyway, he started throwing little insults at me for the next few days. Then we had that fight, and you know what happened after that," she explained, pointing at her socket. Cassidy bit her lower lip.

"So, you never answered my question." Katherine looked surprised.

"What question?"

"I believe I asked you if it hurt a while ago," Cassidy feebly joked. The redhead laughed weakly.

"It was a pain that I never felt before. That's the only way I can explain it. Just hope that you never have to endure that." The girl nodded.

"Let's hope."

The pair continued to walk in silence, looking for a sign of their friends. Cassidy turned the corner and stopped in her tracks.

There was a girl, right in front of her. For a moment, nobody moved or spoke. Cassidy was completely frozen. The stranger put her hands up immediately as her eyes dilated with terror.

"Please don't hurt me!" she cried out. Cassidy studied her, still catching her breath. Katherine's eye was wide.

"Who are you?" Cassidy asked. The girl was wearing an army green tee-shirt with short jean shorts. Her large, amber eyes were full of fear. Her most notable feature was her bright blonde hair.

"I come in peace, I promise. Please don't harm me," she pleaded. Cassidy was slowly becoming agitated.

"That's not what I asked. I want to know who you are and how long you've been here. Speak." The girl nodded, her hands shaking. Cassidy slowly breathed in deeply, attempting to calm her racing heartbeat.

"I just got here about 10 minutes ago," she explained quietly. "My name's Haylee."

"Well, nice to meet you, I guess, Haylee. I'm Cassidy, and this is Katherine," she said, pointing to the peppy redhead. Haylee flinched slightly at the sight of Katherine's one eye. "So you said that you just arrived here?" The blonde girl nodded.

"Yes, I did. I almost got seen by a group of men, but I hid behind a tree." Cassidy felt a stab of fear.

"They're close by?" she asked, trying to keep her nervous voice from shaking. Haylee slowly nodded, sensing that something was wrong.

"Yes," she timidly confirmed, realizing that they were in deep trouble. Cassidy knew she was on the verge of having a panic attack. She took deep, calm breaths.

"We need to get out of here, *now*. Haylee, what direction are they in?" The girl pointed behind her. "Ok, run the other way, right now. Come on!" she whispered. The three girls sprinted like their lives depended on it. Cassidy had to stop after five minutes of running at top speed.

"I think… I think we're ok now," said a gasping Haylee. Katherine couldn't speak, so she nodded.

"That could've been much worse, you know," the brunette began. "Luckily you were there, Haylee. If we didn't have the warning, they could've found us." Haylee smiled weakly.

"What's their problem, anyway?" she asked.

"Well, they're hunting my friend, Hope. She got away and-"

"Wait!" Haylee almost shouted, her eyes growing wide. "What's your friend's name?" Cassidy raised her eyebrows.

"Her name is Hope. Why?" Haylee felt her heart quicken in excitement.

"Does she have bright green eyes, blonde hair, and she came about a week ago?" Cassidy looked at her strangely and shook her head yes.

"That about captures her. I assume you know who she is?" Haylee nodded as a grin made its way across her face.

"I know her better than anyone. I'm her sister."

15

Cassidy's mouth dropped open

"You're her sister?"

"Well, technically, we're stepsisters, but same thing, right?" Haylee smiled. "So, where is she?" she asked excitedly. Cassidy bit her lower lip sympathetically.

"Um, well, you see, that's why we were walking in the first place. She and some other of my friends were separated from us recently. I'm trying to find them. I met Katherine here along the way." Haylee's grin fell slightly.

"Oh. Anyway, how is Hope? Do you guys like her?" Cassidy smiled.

"Yeah, Hope is great. I like her a lot."

"I haven't even met her yet," Katherine piped up.

"Yeah, she's a sweet girl. I hope she's still alive," Cassidy added. That killed Haylee's good mood immediately. Her delighted face fell as she realized that her sister could very well be gone. Cassidy must've noticed her comment, because she said, "Oh, crap. I'm sorry Haylee. Really, I am. It's just that this island's pretty dangerous." Haylee shook her head yes, beginning to become sadder and sadder.

"Uh huh, I understand." She cleared her throat. "Do you have any idea where they could be? I mean, you must know Hope a bit, right?" The girl became more confident as she went on. "And you know your other friends really well! You must have a guess where they are!" Cassidy honestly had no idea what her good friends could be thinking, but she didn't want to see the young girl break.

"Yeah, maybe. Follow me." She started leading the other two through the jungle, wishing desperately that they happened to stumble upon their friends.

Gabe slowly opened his eyes. The sound of a million crickets filled the air with the starry sky providing enough light for the world to be visible. His eyes slid over to look at Ethan. He was asleep with his hands spread out and mouth open. Gabe snorted quietly as he pulled himself off of the damp ground. Careful not to wake anyone, he slowly tip-toed over to the beginning of the jungle. Belle was curled up right by the trail that he needed to go on.

Ugh, damn it. Quieter than ever, he put his right foot over her, his face scrunched up tight. She didn't stir. With a triumphant grin, he stepped onto the trail. He slowly and silently walked until he was far enough away. Then, he began to sprint through the trees.

He continued bounding for about 10 minutes, his breathing beginning to quicken. Finally, he reached his destination. Grinning smugly, he walked through the door of his boss's building.

"Gabriel."

Gabe turned at the gruff voice that spoke his name. Gabe mockingly gave a tip of his nonexistent hat. "Have you got them, Gabriel?"

"Yes," Gabe answered proudly. "They will be delivered tomorrow. I will bring them to you in the morning."

Gabe was answered with a prideful sharky smile that shone through the darkness. The deep voice spoke again, this time with evident delight.

"Perfect, boy. Perfect."

The large shape of the man walked back into the dirty hallway. "Gabriel, I applaud your loyalty. I will get everything ready for tomorrow."

Gabe smiled victoriously as he took his steps into the warm muggy air.

"Pleasure doing business with you, Grayson."

He ran back into the night, his joy plastered across his face. His plan was going to work. He was going to prevail. He was going to do what he was made to do.

The first thing Gabe felt was a sharp pain in his side. He groggily turned over at what had caused it. A grinning Ethan came into view as his vision cleared. He soon noticed everyone else looking down at him.

"Why the hell did you do that?" he asked angrily, getting to his feet. Ethan's smirk became larger.

"Well, we needed to wake you up, huh Gabe?" Gabe dramatically glanced around.

"I'd be willing to bet one hundred dollars that you didn't wake up these hooligans by kicking them," he accused. Ethan shook his head.

"Oh, that? Well, you see, I don't necessarily like you!" Gabe smiled without humor.

"Thanks, pal. The feeling's mutual." Belle glared at Gabe as she tied her strawberry-blonde hair into a ponytail.

"So, who are you?" she questioned in her naturally snippy tone. Gabe looked her up and down, a smile growing on his face.

"I'm a man who has just set his eyes on a hot lady." She looked at him as though he couldn't be real.

"That's not what I asked. I take it your name is Gabe, yes?" He nodded, although he clearly wasn't paying attention to anything that she was saying. "Hey!" she called as he answered in silence. "I'm speaking to you! Quit looking at me like a dog!" Gabe moved his head again.

"Yes," he replied. Belle rolled her eyes and walked up to him.

"I don't know why you can't get it through your head, but I'm not into you. I told you to stop. Next time you don't answer me, I'll punch you so hard that your nose will come out on the other side of your head. Do you understand me?" She brought her fists up, showing them off.

"It's ok," Gabe said. "I like pain if it's from a hot girl." She raised her eyebrows.

"Well then, maybe you are psychotic," she said. He nodded, licking his lips. Ethan pushed Belle out of the way, his hard eyes glaring into Gabe's.

"Last time I checked, you were practically drooling over Hope," he stated, pointing to his beet red friend. "What happened to that obsession?" Gabe chuckled.

"Oh, her? I'm over it. She's not very gorgeous anymore." Ethan gave him his meanest look he could form, and Hope squinted her green eyes in hatred.

"Shut it," she said simply. Gabe shrugged, smiling, as he blinked his eyes.

"Ethan, we really should go look for Cassidy," Hope told him. Ethan nodded, still keeping his gaze on Gabe.

"Yeah, ok," he finally said. As Hope turned to look into the jungle, she felt pressure growing on her arm. Without a doubt, she knew it was Gabe as she quickly spun around.

"*Off,*" she growled.

Fire heaved a sigh as she got up and walked over to a nearby tree. She aggressively pushed all of her weight onto the trunk, which wasn't much. Fire watched Ethan, his face in an expression of anger. She looked at Hope, whose eyes were boring into Gabe.

Fire's blue eyes gazed at Aiden. She watched the way he threw his head back in laughter, the way his eyes shone like emeralds in the blazing sun.

She jumped when she felt a small touch on her shoulder. Her head spun angrily around, revealing a snickering Belle.

"Can I help you?" Fire asked snarkily. Belle's hazel eyes shot over to Aiden.

"You like him, don't you?" She raised one eyebrow in a knowing smirk. Fire felt her face become hot, so she decided to narrow her eyes.

"No, I don't. And I don't see why it's your business, Isabelle." Belle scoffed.

"If you expect for me to call you Fire, you had better call me Belle." Fire's head gave a stiff, reluctant nod. Amusement flooded back into Belle's face. "Don't lie to me, Fire. I see the way you stare at him, I'm not an imbecile. Just admit it."

Fire crossed her arms. She could tell that her face was a deep shade of red. Belle chuckled. "See, you're blushing."

"I'm blushing because you're making me uncomfortable, you idiot," Fire snapped back. Belle's mouth perked up.

"Whatever you say. You haven't got a chance with him anyway," she added. Fire fumed.

"I do too have a chance with him!"

"And there it is," Belle said, laughing. *Damn,* Fire thought, clenching her fists. "There's nothing wrong with liking someone, you know." Fire didn't reply back. "Why don't you just tell him?" Belle asked.

"Keep it down," Fire said through gritted teeth. Belle smirked.

"What, you don't want him to hear us?" She paused, waiting for her nod. Fire stubbornly kept her head still, her eyes angrily focused on the ground. "Oh, you have it bad, my friend," Belle snickered. Fire glared at her.

"I'm not your friend." Belle flipped her long hair.

"Yeah, I figured as much."

Fire rolled her eyes as she got up away from Belle.

Gabe was pacing around, his mind now off of Ethan. He needed a way to bring everyone with him.

Well, Sapphire won't go with you! Ethan won't either, and Hope definitely won't. Gabe put his hand on his chin, panic beginning to seep into his mind. What if he couldn't get Hope? What if she absolutely refused to go with him? Clearly, she was stubborn, and she had stupid Ethan as her own little protector. There's no way that Ethan would ever let Hope go alone with Gabe, he knew that for sure. Letting Grayson down, though, was a million times worse than facing Ethan. With a swallow, Gabe put on the nicest expression he owned. Though from Hope's view, he looked much too fake to be true.

"Hey, Hopie, come with me for a second. I want to show you something," he said slyly. Hope stood where she was, unmoving.

"Don't call me that," she ordered. He cocked his head in fake confusion at her statement.

"Isn't that what your boyfriend calls you?" he asked innocently. Hope glared at him.

"Obviously I won't go with you." Gabe shook his head, beginning to genuinely become nervous.

"Please!" He put out his hands in a pleading gesture, giving the most pitiful expression he owned. He hated that he had to do this in front of everyone else, especially Fire, but it had to be done. Hope's face softened. She was shocked at Gabe's change in emotion.

"Well…," she began hesitantly. "Um, I guess it couldn't hurt." Ethan gave her a surprised look. Hope performed the look back mockingly. "Ethan, it's not like Gabe will kill me in the jungle, Right?" Gabe gave her a sly smile, and she raised her eyebrows. "Right?" she asked again. He nodded, his smirk returning to his face. "Sure, Gabe, I'll go with you for a moment. What do you want to talk to me about?" He shook his head mockingly.

"Now, now, gorgeous, let's not rush. You'll see." He gestured for her to follow him. Ethan grabbed her arm, causing an annoyed Gabe to turn around. "Well, are you coming or what?"

"I'm going with her," Ethan said defiantly. Gabe laughed and shook his head.

"Sure, let golden boy come with us. Why not?" Ethan stopped in his tracks.

"Wait, you actually want me to come with you?" he asked, incredulous. Gabe smirked.

"Well, I do believe that's what I just said." Ethan rolled his eyes.

"Let's go, Gabe."

"Your wish is my command," he sneered. Gabe led the other two through the jungle, getting closer to his destination with each step. Hope kept her suspicious eyes on Ethan. She didn't realize they had stopped walking until her face hit Gabe's shoulder.

"So, Hope, did it hurt?" he asked her casually.

"Did what hurt?"

"When you fell from Heaven." He smirked as she rolled her green eyes.

"Did you really take me all this way to *flirt* with me?" she questioned. "Besides Gabe, that has got to be the most used line in history." Gabe grinned.

"Don't worry, gorgeous.That line's only plan A." She looked at him, confused.

"Well then, what's plan B?" His grin grew wider.

"To kidnap you."

Hope froze for a moment, not really comprehending what he had just said. Ethan gasped as he realized what Gabe had just stated. He reached for Hope's arm.

"Hope, come on. We have to leave," he whispered to her urgently. Gabe brushed his light brown hair to the side.

"Guards!" he yelled into the air. Ominously, a group of men gathered around them, their movements all perfectly synchronized. Ethan thought about running through the gaps between them, but that was before he noticed the sunlight glinting off their weapons. He saw a variety of knives, maces, and spears spread out among them.

"Yeah, about that," Gabe said to Ethan. "You see, you can't leave. Well, I guess you can. But that would mean getting severely injured, and we wouldn't want that, now would we?" He chuckled humorlessly. Hope forced herself to speak through her building fear.

"Wow Gabe, that's such a funny joke. Ok, you can call off these men now. Great job. You got us, all right," she said. He rolled his eyes, laughing.

"Oh, Hope. Gorgeous, gorgeous Hope. You wouldn't understand." He laughed to himself. "Now, follow me." Ethan raised his eyebrows, clenching his fists tighter.

"No, Gabe. We won't follow you," he stated simply. The boy turned around and gave Ethan a dark look. It made him really look like he belonged on this island.

"Oh no, Ethan. I think you will. Would you like my friends here to make you come? Just a heads up, I'd come willingly if I were you. The second option involves a lot more blood and pain. Now, let's go. This is the last time I ask you." Ethan stared him down, but made no move to escape. He could see that there was nothing he could do against Gabe's guards. Gabe cocked his head, looking for any sign of defiance in Ethan's clouding eyes. Hope felt herself give up any hope of escaping when she saw that spark leave his eyes; it was as though he had accepted defeat already. She felt her walls of resistance crumble as well.

"Go on, Gabe," she said without emotion. "Lead the way." Gabe smirked, ecstatic.

"I wouldn't have it any other way." He began to stroll along a narrow trail in the dense jungle. The two friends followed him grudgingly, glancing helplessly at each other. The men followed behind them, weapons ready for any sign of escaping. Gabe looked back and smiled in victory.

Everything was finally going as planned.

16

"Gabe, where are you taking us?" Hope asked after they had been moving for 15 minutes. He looked back and motioned for his guards to stop.

"Funny you should ask that, gorgeous. We're already there." He pointed to more trees.

"Gabe, you've lost it already," Ethan said while shaking his head. "All those things right there are trees. Do you know what trees are, Gabe?" Hope had to hold back a massive laugh at Gabe's expression. She knew she should be worried, but his look was so angry, it was comical.

"Ethan," he said calmly. "If you make another smart remark again, my guards will injure you. Oh, and might I add, if you attempt to hurt or kill me, guess what will happen to you?" Ethan shrugged.

"I don't know, but I bet it has nothing to do with the guards." Gabe gave him back the same look. Ethan sneered, his eyes filling with amusement. "You know, Gabe, I bet you think a lot of me and Hope here. Look at all those weapons! The funny part is, we have none, and there are…," he stopped to quickly count the men. "There are seven guards here!" Gabe's brown eyes squinted in anger. Hope knew that expression; something bad was about to happen.

"Oh, Ethan," he smirked. "You really shouldn't have said that." The two boys made eye contact for a second. Ethan saw his eyes grow in pleasure. He only said three simple words, but they were chilling all on their own.

"Guards? Kill him."

Fire sighed dramatically.

"Shouldn't they be back by now? It's been, like, 20 minutes! What the hell are they doing in there?" she asked as she paced around. Belle nodded.

"Yeah, I know. I wish they would just come back. You know what? Gabe probably got lost. He seems slow." Blisse was chewing on her lower lip, causing it to bleed.

"Do you think we should look for them?" Blisse questioned.

"Let's wait for a few more minutes," Aiden proposed. "If they aren't back soon, we can go look for them, ok?" Blisse nodded worriedly.

"It'll only be a minute," Aiden started to say when he saw the look in Belle's eye.

Soon, ten minutes had gone by. Blisse brushed her black hair out of her face.

"You know what? I vote we go check on them now. This is getting ridiculous. They should be back," she said. Aiden nodded.

"Ok then, let's go!" He began to stroll along the trail that Hope and Ethan had gone on. Blisse shook her head.

"No. I'll check first, with someone else. For all we know, it could be a trap. If we all go, we could all get killed."

"Yeah, you're right," Aiden admitted. "Fire and I will stay here for now. Belle, go with Blisse." The girl flipped her hair with her hand.

"Ok Blisse, let's get a move on." The two girls walked on the path where their friends had gone.

"So, Belle, I really don't know much about you," Blisse began, after they had strolled along a trail for a few minutes. Belle held up her hand.

"Save the small talk. I really couldn't care less, ok? I only want to find Ethan. He's the only person I sorta-kinda like. And even then, that's not saying much." Blisse looked down, surprised at her attitude.

"I'm sorry." Belle glared at her.

"Shut up, Blisse," she said simply. The friendly girl ceased speaking at once. "This sucks," she muttered under her breath. Blisse kept silent as the two walked on.

"How much farther?" Katherine complained. The trio had been walking for an hour and they hadn't stumbled uponany clues yet.

"Katherine, she's trying her best," Haylee said. Cassidy turned around, a small smile forming at the corners of her lips.

"Thank you, Haylee. And yes, I am trying. I want to find them just as much as you do Katherine." The redhead smiled sheepishly.

"Sorry," she muttered. Haylee began walking again.

"So, Cassidy, how long have you been here?" she asked.

"Um, I don't know exactly. A smidge more than a year, I know that." The blonde adult nodded in awe.

"That's crazy."

"Help me," a deep voice murmured.

Cassidy gasped. She knew that voice didn't belong to Katherine or Haylee. She closed her eyes, prayed, and slowly turned around.

Standing before them was a man. Cassidy was hit with the familiar bullet of fear when she was face to face with a criminal. Even a year could never dilute the terror. She looked out of the corner of her eye at the other girls cowering behind her. *Great. Now I have to take charge.*

"Hi there," said Cassidy, growing stronger with every breath. "Don't take this the wrong way, but you are blocking us." She thought that the tough-girl approach was the best way to go. There wasn't any other choice; cowering in fear had gotten them nowhere.

The man didn't move. His dark, large eyes were darting back and forth. There was something... off about him. His black hair was in all directions, as if he had rolled around on the ground for hours. "Alrighty then, if you don't move, we are going to pass you." Cassidy nodded slowly, looking for any sign of recognition or sanity in his eyes.

The stranger locked eyes with her, but he didn't get out of the way. The brunette sighed shakily. Idiots like this had always given her the creeps. "Haylee, Katherine, come-" she cut off abruptly when she noticed the man's mouth open.

He took a step closer, which caused her to gasp slightly. He took another step, and this time she saw that he had a limp. She quickly looked behind her at her two friends. Haylee was shaking and Katherine was completely frozen, her terrified eye wide. The strange adult opened his mouth once more, but this time, a word came out. It was only one word, but it sent chills down her spine. The word made absolutely no sense.

"Grayson."

Cassidy cocked her head.

"Um, who's Grayson?" she asked, now positive this man wasn't right in the head. However, before the man could answer, he dropped to the ground. It was so sudden that Katherine yelped.

"Do you think we should, you know, check his pulse?" Haylee whispered from behind her. Cassidy nodded, but didn't move. Katherine bit her lip and nodded quickly, but she didn't make a move as well. It was quite possible that this odd man could be a trap for them. What crazy criminal man wouldn't want to kidnap three young girls?

Five minutes passed in silence, and still the man hadn't moved an inch. Cassidy let out a huge breath as she bent down and picked up a small stick. She looked at the man as she softly threw the stick at him. The girl was almost sure that this would startle him, making him jump back up. She was wrong, though, when he stayed as still as a statue. She looked behind her at the two girls.

"I think it's safe to check now," she whispered. Haylee nodded slightly, and Katherine still didn't move. Cassidy slowly took a step toward the body. After there wasn't a response, she moved again. She continued to do this until she was right in front of him. She glanced back one last time, making sure she was choosing the right decision. The other two nodded.

She reached for his wrist as she held her breath. She softly poked his wrist, not daring to breathe. Cassidy finally grabbed hold of his wrist and picked it up. Still, the man was unresponsive. This was the moment of truth; she put two fingers on his wrist. She pressed down as she bit her lip, hard. Cassidy was becoming more worried as his pulse would not come. After three minutes of terror, she stood up. She walked back to the girls, their eyes wide. Haylee was the first to speak.

"Well?" she asked. Cassidy's eyes fell.

"He's dead."

Hope stopped breathing. Ethan's eyes grew in surprise as well. No one was expecting Gabe to say those words. The boy grinned at their shock.

"What's the matter, lovebirds? Cat got your tongue?" He chuckled. One of the guards stepped forward. Hope shook her head, and she knew tears of fear were falling down her face. Ethan was frozen as the guard advanced toward him. He pulled out a dagger, and Hope knew what would happen.

"Gabe, please don't kill him, he didn't do anything, please!" she begged, stumbling over her words as more tears fell. Gabe raised his eyebrows.

"Why, gorgeous? Why do you care?" She shook her head.

"I-I don't know, Gabe. Please, Gabe, just don't kill him!" she begged again, now hiccupping from all of her stress. She shrieked when the guard put the weapon up to his neck. Hope knew that she wouldn't survive a day alone in Gabe's clutches. She needed Ethan to stay alive. Gabe sighed a dramatic sigh.

"Wait," he demanded. "Alright, gorgeous, I'll make a deal with you." She wiped her eyes as she slowly nodded. "Ok, I won't kill him. But there's one thing I want you to do."

"Ok, fine," she said. "What is it?" She knew this wouldn't be good as she saw a grin make its way across his face.

"I want you to kiss me, Hope. Willingly, this time."

Her eyes grew wide. Ethan's shocked face turned blank.

"No!" Hope replied, her face turning red. "Of course not!" Gabe shook his head.

"Oh, that's too bad. Guard, you know what to do." The man brought the knife closer to Ethan's neck, drawing blood. He winced slightly, making Hope gasp. Gabe shook his finger mockingly. "Time is running out, gorgeous. Kiss me or he dies." Hope gave a helpless look toward Ethan. He gestured for her to do it. Hope gave Gabe the darkest look she owned.

"Gabe, I despise you. I despise you more than I think it's possible," she snapped at him. He grinned.

"So, is that a yes?" he asked her. Hope put on an expression of pain.

"Yes, *Gabe*." She walked up to him. Her face burned in preparation of the awful humiliation she would feel. The girl shut her eyes tightly as she felt his lips on hers. All she felt was extreme hatred at this boy who had ruined her life on this island. Ethan watched with a controlled angry expression, his short nails digging into his palm. As she felt his grip lesson, she pulled away quickly as her body shivered and gagged in disgust. Gabe's triumphant grin did nothing to lessen the painful embarrassment that would not leave her mind.

"Ok, release him," he told the guard. The man threw Ethan to the ground none too gently. Hope wiped her lips roughly with her hand. "Well, Hopie, wasn't that nice?"

She rolled her eyes as she said, "I thought I told you not to call me Hopie. Why can't you listen to me?"

"Well, the place is right through these trees," Gabe stated, ignoring her question. Ethan squinted his eyes.

"What place, Gabe? Just tell us where we are going!" he demanded. Gabe chuckled while he shook his head.

"Ah, you don't make demands my friend," he replied. He began to walk through the trees. The guards grabbed Hope and Ethan's hand and put them behind their backs.

"I'm not your friend," Ethan muttered as the man pushed him along. Hope prayed that she wouldn't get hurt or threatened by a guard as well. She was scratched by branches that jutted out, making her grimace. Hope was biting her lip out of nerves, causing her to taste blood. The two continued to move through the sharp branches until they came to a small wooden shack. She glanced at Ethan, who looked surprised.

"I swear, I've never ever seen this building before," he whispered. Hope looked it up and down, not really seeing anything special.

"Uhh, Gabe?" she asked timidly. He twirled around theatrically.

"Yes, gorgeous?"

"It's just a shack," she said simply. Gabe's eyes widened in fake surprise.

"Oh really? I hadn't noticed!" It took all of her self control to not roll her eyes in annoyance.

"Well," she said, "why are we here exactly?" Ethan nodded, wanting to know the answer as well. Gabe grinned.

"Oh, you shall see, gorgeous. Now, follow me." Hope really didn't want to. If they were to be moved into the shack, they would be trapped. They could be captured and never seen from again. Suddenly, Hope had a horrible feeling in her gut. They had to get out of there before they would never have the chance to.

"Blisse!" Hope screamed at the top of her lungs. "Aiden! Fire!" Gabe angrily spun around.

"Oh gorgeous," he snarled. "You're going to regret that." Hope was ecstatic, though, when she heard someone reply to her call.

"Hope?" a voice yelled back. She and Ethan locked eyes in joy. Gabe's face turned dark.

"Well this is just great," he said sarcastically. Suddenly, a smile began to grow. "Wait. This is great!" Hope pressed on her lip harder, knowing that his pleasure wasn't good. "Guards, go get them," he commanded. The girl shook her head quickly.

"Gabe, no! Please don't!" she begged him. He shook his head mockingly.

"Oh Hope, that worked before." She knew what she should do, but she really didn't want to suggest it. She decided she would when the guards began to walk toward the source of the noise.

"Gabe, wait! I'll kiss you again!" she told him. She was sure this would work. Her breath caught in her throat when his head moved from side to side.

"No, that's ok, gorgeous. But I'm glad you enjoyed it so much!" He skipped to the front where two other guards stood. "Well, they should be here at any time," Gabe said as he brushed his hair with his fingers. Hope slumped to the ground in defeat. Her friends were almost already captured, and it was all her fault for shouting for them in the first place. Ethan looked at her, his once bright eyes now filled with sadness.

"Hope," he whispered, reading her thoughts. "It's not your fault." She just shook her head as she felt her eyes brimming with tears. All she could do was wait until she saw her friends again. A few moments later, the guards came back. One of them was holding Blisse tightly, making her wince whenever she moved. Belle was there as well, the same annoyed look on her face that she always wore.

"What's the big idea?" she asked, trying to get her arms out of the man's hands. Belle's eyes narrowed. "So, Gabe, what *are* you doing?" He just grinned at her question.

He motioned for the guards to keep going. Hope's plan had failed. They weren't saved, and she had gotten her friends mixed up in the mess. She now knew she would be forced into the shack, and who knows how long she might be in there? With one look at the ecstatic expression on Gabe's face, she knew it wasn't good at all.

"Alrighty then children, follow Gabe!" he said, laughing at his sick sense of humor. Hope was pushed roughly by the guards behind her. *Well, this is it.* She grabbed Ethan's wrist for comfort as they were led into the wooden building.

"Oh come on! How the hell are they not back yet? This is insane!" Fire was pacing around, worried. She put her hands through her brown hair, exasperated. Aiden was biting his nails.

"Honestly, I think I'm right. I'm pretty sure it's a trap. I mean, Blisse knows how worried we are." The girl nodded slowly.

"You're right! It's gotta be a trap! We need to go look for them! No, no, wait, let me finish," she said, responding to Aiden's look of disapproval. "Whoever is trapping them probably won't have any idea that we are coming. Since we know it's a trap, we'll keep super quiet. I bet Blisse was stomping through the trees." Fire's eyes grew wide as she snapped her fingers. "You know what?! I bet Gabe did something!" Aiden was confused.

"That's a pretty serious accusation, Sapphire," he stated. She narrowed her eyes.

"It's Fire. And I know it's serious, but I think it's true. Ok, listen to me. Everyone hates him. Actually, I think everyone wants to kill him, I know I do. He called Hope gorgeous, even though she asked him to stop multiple times. He-"

"Fire," Aiden cut her off. "I know. I was there. I know he's a jerk. But that has nothing to do with what you're saying. What's your point?" he asked. Her eyes grew wide in annoyance.

"I know, I know, I'm getting there. Anyway, he probably got mad or something. But here, listen to this; remember when we first met him? Remember when Hope told him that it was such a coincidence that he showed up just when we needed help? I think that he didn't show up by chance. Something is up. There's no way he just happened to be in that exact spot." Aiden bit his lip as he thought about her evidence.

"Yeah, there's something sketchy with that," he said. "But still, accusing him of capturing Hope, Ethan, Blisse, and Belle? All by himself? That's honestly pretty far-fetched." Fire put her hands up.

"Aiden, no! Why do you always try to see the best in people? He's a jerk, like you said! Is it really that hard to understand that he is behind this? I'm sure he is!" Fire exclaimed, becoming more sure that her statement about Gabe was correct. Aiden shook his head. "We don't know if he's alone. We learned nothing about him."

"Fire, are you sure?" She walked right up to him, her light eyes full of fire.

"Aiden, I've never been more sure of anything in my entire life. Now, let's go find our friends and get them back!" She took off into the trees, following the path that Gabe had taken. Aiden, shaking his head but smiling, followed her into the dark jungle.

Fire ran and ran until she felt her lungs would burst. She glanced behind her, almost expecting to see nothing but air. She felt a warm feeling in her stomach when she saw him bounding after her. The girl stopped, panting hard.

"Girl, for your size, you are impossibly fast," Aiden proclaimed, gasping. Fire grinned in pride.

"Yeah, I know, tell me about it later. Right now we have to find them. Aiden, be as quiet as you can." He nodded, pretending to zip his mouth shut. The two creeped around as stealthily as possible. A few minutes passed by and still they discovered nothing.

"Fire…," Aiden began with a trace of doubt in his voice. She put her finger to her small lip as she gave him a sharp glare. *Shut up,* she mouthed. Fire then took her finger away from her face and pointed. Aiden looked in the direction, and his hazel eyes grew wide in surprise. Fire hadn't been wrong about her guess that something was off. There was a building in front of them.

"Well, doesn't this just look like a five-star hotel?" Aiden asked. The structure in front of them was anything but that. This was a wooden shack with one single door. It looked as though it would fall apart if they did so much as touch it.

"Yes Aiden, definitely a luxurious place," she replied in the same tone. "I wonder what this is." Her eyes raked the structure, not finding anything odd about it.

"It just looks like an abandoned building," Aiden remarked, voicing her thoughts. Fire's head jerked to the side when a noise startled her. Aiden looked over in alarm.

"Must be another stupid bug," she muttered to herself with seeping fear. The noise came from behind a tree. "Do you think we should look?" she asked. Aiden slowly moved his head up and down.

"Yeah, we might as well check. We're just scared for no reason. A stick probably just fell or something," he guessed. "Ok Fire, get behind me." She padded to his side.

"No," she whispered. "I'll go first. We all know I'm braver." Aiden chuckled quietly.

"Ok girl, lead the way." With her eyes set on the tree, she began to take slow, large steps. Fire held her breath as her head looked around the corner of the thick truck. She breathed a huge sigh of relief when she saw nothing.

"Look, Aiden. There's nothing there." She clenched her fists, humiliation sinking into her system.

She stopped when she noticed something was wrong. Fire realized that she couldn't feel him breathing over her shoulder. With a bad feeling in her gut, she turned around. Her mouth dropped open when she saw what had happened to him. A large man had his hand around Aiden's neck. His hazel eyes were full of terrible fear. Fire sent her icy blue eyes toward him.

"Ok, dude. What do you want?" she asked wearily, getting straight to the point. The man's answer surprised her.

His chapped lips went up in a smile.

"I want you."

"Gabe, where are you taking us?!" Hope practically snarled at him. He gave her a slight smirk as he turned around.

"Oh, gorgeous, all in good time." Gabe opened the door for himself and let it go. Hope winced when the door came back and hit her face. Hope gasped as she looked all around the inside of the building. Although it looked incredibly breakable and small from the outside, it was anything but that. The floor was made of metal, and the ceiling was high above them. There was a hallway in front of them, which would lead them to more doors.

"How is this even possible?" Ethan asked in awe. Gabe winked.

"My master is a genius; he'd rip your mind to shreds, old pal. He can do anything he wants. He didn't want anyone to find his lair." Hope choked on air.

"What do you mean master?" she asked. Gabe gazed at her, his chocolate eyes full of amusement.

"You'll see," he simply said.

All of a sudden, Hope heard an awful scream outside. It reminded her of Martha, and she knew that whoever had made that sound was in deep trouble. Her eyes grew large before she could help it. Gabe's eyes lit up. "I see my master has arrived."

"Who screamed?" she practically yelled, frantically struggling in the guard's arms.

"Probably a girl, by the way it sounded," Gabe replied, stating the obvious. She bit back a sarcastic reply. A moment later, the doors flew open. Hope's eyes grew even wider at the sight before her.

Aiden was desperately clawing at the large hand around his throat. Fire was clearly the one who had screamed. She was held by a man as well. For the first time, her eyes had fear evident in them.

"Are you ok?" Hope asked out of habit.

"Oh yeah, we're just fine and dandy," Aiden replied surprisingly snarkily, gasping for breath.

"Release them," Gabe stated with a lazy flick of his hand. Aiden dropped to the ground as the man let him go. "So, Grayson, I see you've returned." The man nodded, his eyes filling up with delight at the sight of Hope.

"I see you've brought my friend," the man said sinisterly. "How… *perfect*." His happy eyes raked her up and down. "You know, girly, it's quite rude for you to have taken this long to come to me, don't you think?" She gulped loudly. Ethan protectively put his hand on her shoulder.

"You won't touch her," he said, his voice in the low tone he had once used. It still greatly scared Hope how he could talk that way.

"Oh. Is that so, boy?" The man asked him eerily. Ethan's hard eyes were set directly on his. "I believe we will have more guests later today," he said suddenly. Hope narrowed her eyes despite her growing fear.

"What guests?" The man just grinned.

"You'll see," he said simply. Hope was fuming.

"Why does everyone keep saying that?" she exclaimed. The stranger shook his head mockingly.

"Now now, let's not get ahead of ourselves, girly. Don't forget that I'm in charge of what happens to you now." He winked his eye at her.

"Cassidy," Ethan whispered aloud. The man suspicious eyes darted over him.

"What did you say, green eyes?"

"That's who you are talking about," he realized. "She's going to be your guest." Their captor's lips went up in a sick, disgusting smile.

"I do believe I have heard that name somewhere," he said. "Would she be the brown haired chick?"

"Don't call her a chick," Fire snarled at him. Aiden roughly nudged her with his toe, warning her that her tone was going too far.

"Yes," Gabe chimed in excitedly. "She'll be an easy target, she's nothing special."

"She's better than you'll ever be," Aiden said darkly. Gabe shrugged casually.

"We'll see about that. She's just like me on the inside. She has no clue what she'll do to survive." Gabe's eyes glinted. "You know, you think you know someone before they are confronted with death. Never underestimate someone's will to survive, Aiden."

"Gabe, Cassidy is kind," Hope snapped at him. "You have no right to say otherwise."

"It's true," Gabe's voice rang out. "Just wait until she kills someone."

"Oh, she won't kill anyone," Fire growled out, "but I will."

"*I* will be the one doing the killing here," Grayson interrupted. "Now come with me."

Belle snickered, blinking her eyes.

"And why the hell would we do that exactly?"

"Because if you don't, I will take you forcefully and hurt you in a way you won't even begin to understand. Now *let's go.*" He cleared his throat. "Oh, and Gabriel?" Gabe's head eagerly spun around. "Go get our guest."

17

"What *is* this island?" Haylee choked out. Her heart was beating fast in the horror of seeing somebody die. The way his body had just slumped was beyond terrible.

"Somewhere we don't want to be," Cassidy said grimly. "Just hope that you won't have to kill anyone."

"Wait, you have killed someone before?"

"No," Cassidy shortly replied, "but I've seen it happen. I haven't killed anyone and I never will. On this island though, you never know what people you will come across."

"People like Gabe," said Katherine darkly. Cassidy reluctantly nodded.

"Like who?" Haylee asked, confused. Cassidy dryly chuckled.

"Somebody who you don't want to meet, that's for sure."

"I beg to differ, Cassidy," said a voice.

Cassidy's pulse boiled in hatred at the sound of the arrogant voice behind her. Katherine let out an audible gasp, her hand unconsciously moving to her good eye.

"Gabe." Cassidy's voice came out as a cold statement. Gabe bowed, grabbing Haylee's hand. She looked at it uncomfortably.

"How are you here?" Katherine asked, her tone growing to a high pitched scream.

"You were with Hope," Cassidy accused, pointing a finger at his chest. "Blisse and Aiden too. Where are they?"

"Well, they aren't dead yet," Gabe said casually. "I came to find you."

"I don't believe you," Cassidy said, her tone growing suspicious. "If that were really true, Aiden wouldn't have sent you."

"I'm not lying Cassidy, I did come to find you."

"Who's Grayson?" Katherine suddenly shouted, with tears in her eyes. "Who is that!?"

Gabe's smug face seemed to falter for a moment.

"How do you know about him?"

"So you know him," Cassidy realized aloud. Gabe roughly released Haylee as he lunged to tightly grab Katherine's arm. She shrieked, batting him away, but he was much stronger than she was.

"*How do you know about him*?" Gabe's demeanor had completely changed. He had gone from an annoying cocky jerk to someone who looked as though he could snap someone's neck in a heartbeat. Cassidy wasn't so sure that she prefered this side of him.

"Let go!" Katherine cried out, thrashing around in his iron grip.

"Gabe," Cassidy snapped. "She won't tell you if you hurt her like that." She pointed her finger toward the dead man who was still slumped on the ground. "That man said it just before he died. I don't know how he randomly just dropped, but he yelled the word, well, I guess the name, Grayson." Gabe's hysterical grip seemed to lessen the tiniest bit. He gruffly cleared his throat.

"How did he die?" Haylee frightfully asked. Seeing Gabe wig out gave her the shivers. The way he had seemed to just completely snap terrified her.

"He died from fear," Gabe said. His tone almost sounded… cheerful. "Grayson gave him a syringe that fed him nightmares for days. He never slept."

"That's why he looked so tired," Cassidy realized aloud, disturbed. "He was scared to sleep."

"Wait," Haylee stated. All heads turned to look at her surprisingly aggressive tone of voice. "How did you know that?"

Cassidy had a terribly suspicious feeling in her gut as her head slowly turned around.

"Gabe…" she trailed off, studying his poker-face. "How did you know?"

"You're a liar!" Katherine screamed, ripping off her self-made eye patch. "You are evil! You did this to me!" She angrily pointed at her eye. Cassidy dry heaved, seeing the mangled hole in her face on clear display. Sticky, dark blood was spread out all over the inside of the patch, and some repulsive goo mixed with red covered the blank space.

"Put the patch back on, darling," Gabe said smoothly. He didn't look the least bit bothered by the disgusting sight. "Nobody wants to see that hole in your pretty little face."

"I will not!" Katherine's voice took on a tone of hysteria. "You didn't come to find us, you came to kill us! You are an evil man!"

"Gabe," Cassidy hesitatingly began, "why are you here?" Gabe's mouth went up in a dark smile.

"I was never lying, I did come to find you guys. Just not for the reason you may think." Cassidy tensed up, slowly clenching her fists.

"We are not going with you. Please leave."

"Guess where we are going," Gabe demanded. He circled around the three girls dangerously. "We're going to Grayson's place. It's time we have a little chat."

"No!" Haylee gasped out, her hands squeezing in fear.

"You're lying," Cassidy accused, but her eyes looked worried. Gabe daintily shook his head.

"You see, I've never been a liar," Gabe stated. "I prefer to call it… not telling the whole truth. Now follow me, girls."

"No," Katherine said, tears streaming down her face. "Make me!" Without warning, Gabe was right in front of Katherine's face in two steps.

"Do you want me to make you?" he whispered to the frightened girl. "I will make you. Or you can say goodbye to your other pretty little eye as well." Katherine's body shook.

"And you," he said, moving his threatening stare to Haylee. "We can see how pretty you'll be without the skin on your face." He pulled out a knife that had been hidden under his shirt and placed gently on Haylee's shaking cheek.

"And you," he murmured, coming closer and closer to the furious Cassidy. "You'll be first. You will feel the most pain. Believe me, sweetheart, I can make it last. I've had plenty of practice. You will follow me now, or I will do this and more. I will not wait any longer." Cassidy held his stare, her glare not wavering. Gabe rolled back his shoulders. "Your choice. We'll go the easy way or the hard way."

"We'll do it," Katherine choked out from behind her. "I can't lose my other eye." A low snarl made its way out of Cassidy's throat.

"I can outrun you, Gabe. You may be stronger, but I'm quicker."

"That's true," he admitted, "but your friends can't. How would you like to know that you saved yourself? How would you like to live with the knowledge that you're a dirty little coward?" The resistance crumbled from Cassidy's watering eyes. Gabe snickered, his dark eyes shooting holes through her. "Exactly. Now follow me. If any of you try to run, I will not hesitate to cripple you. Grayson said he needed you alive, but he didn't say that your bodies couldn't be broken."

"You are a terrible human being," Cassidy said through gritted teeth. "You deserve to burn in hell."

"Oh little Cassidy, we all do. Do you know nothing about human nature? At the end of the day, we're just a bunch of selfish lowlives who are anything but a clean slate. Why are you on this island?"

"I am not evil, Gabe. I am anything but evil," she hissed. Gabe looked at her oddly.

"You don't strike me as especially intelligent, I wonder what your ability is," he muttered to himself. Cassidy stopped moving at once.

"Ability?"

Gabe's body tensed up.

"Nothing."

Cassidy planted her feet on the ground as she stubbornly crossed her arms over her chest.

"Why did you say that you didn't think I was smart? What did that have to do with how evil you think I am?" Cassidy paused, her eyes growing wider. "Ethan's theory!"

"What theory?" Gabe spat out. Cassidy shut her lips tightly, sending him a glare. He angrily stomped right up to her body, putting the sharp tip of the knife on her wrist. "Do it," she dared him, staring right into his hard eyes. "Slide your hand, slice my vein. I want you to do it. I *dare* you." For a moment, it looked as though Gabe really would glide the silver knife over her skin. He then took a deep breath, pulling himself together.

"I don't give a damn about your stupid theories," he muttered to himself. "Now walk." Cassidy reluctantly obeyed, but she couldn't get his words out of her mind.

I wonder what your ability is.

Katherine was hysterically crying in the background, her pitiful hiccups loudly sounding through the air. Haylee was trying but failing to steadily control her breathing. Gabe repeatedly checked behind him, making sure his victims were still following his lead. He mentally grinned when he saw how depressed their facial expressions were. They looked completely and utterly *hopeless.* Gabe snickered aloud.

Oh, Grayson will have fun with them alright, he thought smugly. *And it's all because of me.* He continued their walk of despair through the dark, dark jungle.

18

"*Ouch,*" Belle growled. The metal chains weighed painfully on her wrist. She said some other words that made Fire nod her head in agreement.

"My apologies," Grayson said, his lips up in a smug smile. "I can't have you getting away."

"That would be a pity," Ethan muttered, staring at Grayson with a disgusted expression. They were in the center of the impossibly built shack, all lined up in a row.

I feel like a prisoner, Hope grimly thought. With the depressing line and the rusted chains, Hope couldn't help letting out a dry chuckle. She especially missed her mom and Haylee at this time, but there was no way she would allow herself to look vulnerable to this messed up man. *Don't think about them,* she chided herself, *and you'll be fine.*

Fire winced as Grayson mechanically tightened up her handcuffs to fit her tiny wrists. Her lips were pressed together in a straight line; it was obvious that she did not want to show any vulnerability.

"At least Cassidy's ok," Blisse told herself aloud. "She's not captured." She had spoken louder than she had realized. Grayson's eyebrows wiggled as he glanced at her. His lips suddenly pursed together, as though he was in thought.

"I remember you!" he suddenly announced loudly, making her jump. He walked right up to her face, and it took everything in Blisse to not shut her eyes. "Do you remember causing me this?" He pointed to the bright mark of a scratch on his upper arm. He aggressively turned to Hope.

"This is because you got away!" he shouted in her face with spit flying from his lips. Hope flinched back, watching the menacing man come closer and closer. It was horrifying, staring into those small, cold, beady eyes as he shouted at her, blaming her for injuries that she nowhere near caused. "You're going to pay for that," he snarled softly. "And I'm going to enjoy every minute of it."

Now was the moment when Hope could tangibly feel the panic enter her mind. She could now process that this man, however mentally messed up he could be, wanted to hurt her. Badly. His darting eyes showed her everything she needed to know.

Deep breaths, Hope. Deep breaths.

Grayson still stared at Hope angrily, his fists dangerously clenching and unclenching.

A noise echoed through the air.

Grayson quickly moved his head around, angry yet curious at what the sound could have been.

Gabe came triumphantly marching in, with three girls behind him.

The first one was clearly Cassidy, Hope knew. Her wavy hair was thrown messily around her face, and some strands stuck to her face from tears.

The second girl was a freckled girl with piercing red hair, who was unfamiliar to Hope. She had some leaf or object stuck to her eye, and her visible eye was puffy and large in fear.

And the third girl…

No.

It couldn't be.

There was no way that could be her.

There was no way that the girl could be Haylee.

Hope shook her head, refusing to believe it. Haylee could not be here. Haylee could not have been proclaimed dangerous.

Or could she have been?

Hope mentally counted the amount of days she had been on the island. Haylee's birthday was roughly a week after her own, give or take a few days. Was there even the slightest chance that the sweet little blonde girl could be Haylee?

When the small girl turned her head Hope's way, Hope knew that nobody else could replicate that stare. That was the Haylee she knew.

The same Haylee who had stared at her with those loving auburn eyes that she had always adored.

And suddenly, Hope could do nothing to contain the pure joy.

"Haylee!"

"Hope!" she shrieked. Without thinking, Haylee tore herself away from the line of people and wrapped herself around Hope. Hope wished more than anything that she could squeeze her back, but the chains prevented her from doing as much as lifting her hands.

"Haylee, I love you," Hope murmured, forgetting about showing weakness as tears of happiness trickled down her cheeks.

"I thought you were dead," Haylee whispered back, crying softly as well. After what seemed like a mere few seconds, Haylee was roughly pulled away by Grayson. His old hand gripped her shoulder tightly as he threw her back in line. Gabe was leaning on the back wall, looking at Hope with an odd expression. He didn't exactly look happy, but he didn't look angry or smug either. His arms were crossed as his curious stare didn't let up.

"Gabe, get the chains," Grayson demanded. Gabe was still looking at Hope with that strange look. "Gabriel!" Grayson snapped. Gabe's head whipped around suddenly. "Get their chains." The look of smug happiness appeared back on his face.

"Well, I would just love to!" He winked at Hope victoriously as he went to fetch the restraints for his new prisoners.

"Please don't tie me up!" Katherine begged, more tears falling from her eye. Grayson shot her an annoyed glare, but he didn't comment back.

A minute later, Gabe pranced through the doorway, showing off more of the old metal handcuffs.

"Hands out," he commanded Cassidy. Her face burned in humiliation as she stared him down.

"No."

"Hands out!" he yelled. Cassidy winced, limply putting up her hands. Grayson none too gently dragged her over to her spot in the line of prisoners. He threw her against the hard wall, attached her chain to a spot in it. He did the same for Katherine and Haylee. Hope eagerly stretched her neck out to peer at Haylee. At the moment, she was scared like everyone else, but she didn't look hurt physically.

Soon after, everyone was pressed against the wall in their restraints. Grayson walked to the middle of the center. Hope suppressed a gulp, keeping her eyes locked on him.

I'm dead.

Fire was angry.

Although she was never going to admit it out loud, she knew it was her fault she and Aiden were in this mess. Now, they were tied up and gagged. If she had just stayed back by the chasm like Aiden had suggested, then they wouldn't have been ambushed. She tried to communicate her apology with her eyes to him, but he was avoiding her gaze. He was angry as well, and he had a right to be. His eyes stayed stubbornly on Grayson, and she couldn't blame him. Fire craned her neck to look at Hope, and she saw that her face had lost all color. Of course, who wouldn't be terrified of some crazy old bald man who wanted to hurt them?

Grayson cleared his throat dramatically.

"Well hi there, friends!" His icy gray eyes looked at everyone almost greedily. "You don't know how long I've been waiting to see all of your faces!" Strangely, no one spoke as Grayson paused. Maybe it was because of the way his stare somehow seemed to claim them all. He looked like a madman. "For those of you who don't know, my name is Grayson," he explained. "I own this island. And when someone escapes from me, I'm not the happiest person you'll meet." Ethan glared at him.

"Give me a break man, you don't own this island. You got sent here because of some serious mental issues."

"Ethan, shut it," Belle hissed. Ethan paid no attention to her snap.

"And you're right," he continued, "you're not the happiest person. You are the most psychotic person I have ever met, and that's coming from a boy who grew up with some not-so-snazzy parents. 'Not the happiest' is quite an understatement." Grayson grinned.

"That was very bold, young man!" Grayson snickered at Ethan's dark look. "And yes, it could be considered an understatement."

"What I want to know is *why* you're doing this," Aiden piped up. "What's the point? Does this make you happy or something?"

"You escaped from me," he said simply. "People don't escape from me."

"But why do you care so much?" Aiden persisted. "Who cares if we escaped you?"

"Forget that," Belle chimed in. "What is your plan? What is it that you want to do with us?"

"We're gonna kill you," Gabe said, walking up next to Grayson.

Belle looked at them oddly.

"When?"

"Soon," Grayson replied. "First, I want to have some fun with you guys."

"But why not just shoot us now?" Belle retorted. "It'd be easier. There's also the possibility that we could escape."

"You won't escape."

"But we could."

"Belle!" Fire hissed. "Shut the hell up! What, do you want to get shot on the spot or something? How do we know you aren't working for this freak too?"

"I just want all of the details, Sapphire. If they are waiting to kill us, they must have something better in mind. I mean, better for them, but worse for us."

"You are smart," Gabe observed. "And correct."

"Oh yes, she is," Grayson said with his cheshire cat grin. "It's funny that you asked that, darling. I think it's time for our first experiment."

In the silence, it was possible to hear a pin drop. Nobody wanted to be the first test subject of the psychotic man who had abducted them.

Grayson's dark eyes slowly moved over everyone's faces. Hope could feel the blood rush to her cheeks as she looked down. His small eyes stopped on Blisse, who was shaking harder than ever.

"Good choice," Gabe whispered, watching her with cheerful eyes. "She's one of the nicer ones, too. She's perfect for this." Grayson put his hand on his chin, nodding with more and more joy.

"What's your name?"

"B-B-Blisse," she stuttered. Grayson smirked.

"The 'B' is a bit redundant if you ask me."

"My name is Blisse," she stated, her voice stronger this time. "With one 'B'. Now what is it that you would like from me?"

"Blisse, I am going to take off your chains, ok? And if you attempt to fight or escape, I promise I will kill you right now. Do you understand?" She nodded, her dark eyes growing wide. "Very good." He walked over to her while he fished a key out of the large pocket in his khaki shorts. Hope heard the *click* of the lock opening. Blisse rubbed her sore wrists, her head looking up in terror. "Now, girly, come here," he demanded.

She hesitantly shot a worried glance toward Ethan. He sadly nodded, telling her with his eyes that she had no choice. She bit her lip hard as she slowly walked to Grayson. He watched, grinning in horrible delight. Hope gave her friend the best sympathetic look she had. Blisse was cowering as he put his rough hand on her shaking shoulder.

"See this needle?" he questioned her. She took a small breath as she shook her head yes. "I am going to stick it in your neck."

Grayson suddenly let out a delightful chuckle. Hope noticed a look of disgust plastered over Ethan's face. She was repulsed at this man's sick sense of humor as well. Hope's eyes wandered to all of the tied up people. Katherine's face was as white as a ghost, and Haylee was pale as well. Fire was shaking, but it wasn't in fear; it was in pure rage.

"So, what's it gonna do to her anyway?" Fire snarled. "Is it heroin or something?" Grayson looked at her with a knowing smile.

"Oh, you'll see." He gripped Blisse's shoulder tighter, making her gasp in surprise. Hope saw him slyly slip something into her pocket. It was so fast that she didn't even know if she had imagined it or not. Blisse's pale palms were sweating like crazy as her eyes focused on the dark liquid inside. The man wiggled his eyebrows as he plunged the needle into her neck.

19

Hope stopped breathing, horrified at what the outcome would be. Who knew what this man was capable of? Who knew how smart he could be? Although she was ashamed to admit it to herself, she was extremely curious at what effect this fluid would have. Blisse yelped in pain at the sharp prick. She closed her eyes, and Grayson's aged eyes were full of curiosity and madness. The silence that followed was the worst part.

A minute later, Blisse's big eyes opened. Fire let out a huge gasp before she could help it, and understandably so. It was impossible to miss what was so alarming about Blisse.

Her once warm caramel eyes were now a cold, jet black.

"Blisse..." Fire said in fear. She scrunched her eyebrows together in shock. Blisse's horrible eyes were quite familiar, but she couldn't put her finger on it.

"Oh, she's not Blisse anymore," Grayson said mischievously. "This liquid changed her mind." Belle blinked, her eyes growing slighter larger.

"Dude, how do you even come up with this stuff?" Grayson laughed, a gruff sound that sounded anything but amusing to Hope's ears.

"Now, let the fun begin."

Blisse's mouth turned up in a smirk. Hope was praying that Grayson had just been lying, that it only affected her eyes.

"Hello, old friends," Blisse said in a voice that was so unlike hers, Hope wanted to scream. It was deep and dark and downright *scary*. Haylee was terrified; nothing ever like this had happened, especially to her. The government officials never mentioned that something like this was brewing on the island.

"Blisse," Ethan said, in a gentle tone. "Listen to me. I-" he was cut off by Blisse shooting up her hand.

"Speak one more time, and I swear I will slice your throat." He stopped immediately.

"Um, excuse me?" Haylee piped up from the other side. Blisse shot her a glare so terrifying it could've turned anyone to ice. "N-n-never mind," she squeaked. Blisse slithered over to her. Haylee was cowering so much that she looked like she was being electrocuted.

"No, girly, what is it that you were going to say? I'm sure we'd all love to know!" Blisse told her, her voice sounding like it was from a horror movie.

"No, I-I promise, i-it's nothing," Haylee said, nodding her head. The girl's black eyes were full of delight.

"Oh, you want to be silent? Fine, I'll make you silent!" Blisse strolled over slowly. Grayson nodded, letting her do whatever she pleased. Blisse picked up a piece of cement from the corner. Haylee's eyes grew so wide, it looked like they would pop out of her skull. It dawned on her what the possessed girl was going to do. Ethan desperately wanted to say something, but he remembered what Blisse had told him earlier.

"Next time, you'll regret not answering me. Now, let's make you silent," Blisse said, her mouth curving into a terrible smile. It was like there was a scarier girl version of Grayson and Gabe combined. Haylee struggled against her bonds with all her might.

"I'm sorry! Please, I'm sorry!" Haylee pleaded as tears fell down her face. It was painful for Hope to watch her best friend beg for her safety. Blisse just grinned, ignoring her pleading. The girl brought the cement up in her hands as Haylee screamed. It was an awful, awful sound.

"Hasta luego, girly," Blisse sneered. She smashed the square of cement on the top of her head. Haylee screamed before she fell unconscious. Hope's mouth opened wide, tears falling from her big eyes. Blisse hit with such force that no one would be surprised if Haylee died. Hope couldn't face the realization that her best friend was dead. She knew she would wake up, she knew it. Ethan now was filled with fear, knowing that his old friend wasn't kidding when she threatened him. Any rational thinking went down the drain.

"Now," Blisse began, "anyone that doesn't listen to me will get hurt, just like this girl here." The corner of her mouth went up in a smile.

"Holy crap!" Fire shouted out of nowhere. Grayson gave her a look.

"What do you want?"

"I thought Blisse's eyes looked familiar. I just remembered where I saw them! The bug!" she exclaimed. Grayson gave her a look of surprise, but his eyes were amused.

"What bug, child?" Fire gave him a slight glare.

"You know what bug. I bet you were testing your serum out on it! I remember, its eyes were black, just like hers! No wonder it was trying to kill me!" The man grinned humorlessly.

"Then how do you explain its size?"

"I don't know, I'm not a scientist, I-" she cut off abruptly. "Wait a minute," she said, narrowing her eyes. "How do you know that there was something wrong with the size of it?" Grayson's smile faltered.

"Wait, what bug?" Katherine asked. Grayson gave her a look so evil, she fell silent at once. Fire ignored his glare, and said, "When I was alone, after the tsunami, I was walking through the jungle. I saw a bug, and I'm not kidding when I say it was larger than me. I almost had a heart attack when it lunged at me. This stupid beetle chased me. Obviously, something was wrong with it. As you all know, bugs aren't intelligent. I jumped into a chasm to escape it. Can you guess what happened to it?" She gave Belle a glance. "Hey, Belle, do you know what happened to the beetle?" The blonde girl rolled her eyes, fuming when she saw everyone look at her.

"It drowned, Sapphire," she said, in the most condescending tone she could muster. "Isn't that obvious?" Fire looked at her with a repulsed expression. "Don't look at me like that," Belle snapped.

"Anyway, it drowned, as Belle here so lovingly told us." This statement earned an angry look from Belle. "There was no way it should have gone after me for that long," Fire continued. "Grayson, I think that you had something to do with it. And by something, I mean everything. So tell me." The man looked at her with interest.

"Wow girly, you gotta lot of nerve to talk to me that way. It's almost like you want to feel pain," he said. Fire stopped ranting, but the spark in her bright eyes didn't go out.

"What can I say? That's just who I am." Grayson walked up to her face. Although he towered over the tiny adult, she didn't break eye contact. She stared into his hard gray eyes with fury.

"You know what? I would actually like you as a second assistant. It's a pity we can't do anything about your size…." All of a sudden, his dull eyes lit up with an idea. "I can use the serum on you! I can make you bigger, just like the bug! How about it, kid?" he asked her. Fire shook her head before he had finished.

"Absolutely *not*," she stated firmly. Grayson shook his head with fake sadness.

"Oh, how sad. I guess I'll just leave you to your fun little death." He looked at Gabe. "Gabriel, stay here," he demanded. "I'm going to go look at the plans you left me. Let's let our guests… get to know the new Blisse." Gabe nodded, shooting a smug glare at Fire.

Blisse walked around, her stare boring into everyone's horrified eyes. She swiftly pulled out a gun from her pocket, a sight which filled Hope with dread. *So that's what Grayson put in her pocket.* She was going to use the gun on somebody, Hope could feel it. *Don't let it be me,* she begged silently. *I don't want to die.*

Blisse stopped directly in front of Ethan. Hope felt her heart stop. His eyes were trying to stay focused on the ground instead of Blisse's evil eyes. She chuckled creepily.

"Nah, I won't kill you right now," she said, a twinkle in her impossibly dark eyes. Ethan stopped himself from letting out a sigh of relief. Blisse continued her stroll around the room, savoring the fear in the air. Katherine made the dreadful mistake of locking her eye with Blisse's eyes. Blisse's face lit up in a grin. Katherine seemed to shrink back against the wall. Blisse walked slowly, holding the gun higher and higher.

She's going to shoot her, Hope thought in horror.

"We might as well kick this party off with a little entertainment!" Blisse said happily. Ethan looked at her furiously, but luckily her stare was focused on the shaking Katherine. She walked up closer and closer, until her nose was almost touching hers. Blisse suddenly pulled up the gun, pointing it straight at Katherine. Her freckled face was as white as a ghost. Hope looked at the scene with horror, but she knew that there was nothing she could do.

"Now," Blisse started in her newly amused voice, "I am going to shoot this gun, and nobody can stop me. If no one volunteers to save her, we'll see if this girl's blood matches the shade of her hair."

Katherine's face contorted as she clenched her fists. She had been threatened by someone once before, and she remembered that all too clearly. But this time, there was a difference. When the psycho woman had held a knife to her throat, she had been plain crazy, there was no doubting that. However, this time, Blisse knew exactly what she was doing. Gabe looked on, his face amused.

"Is anyone gonna help me?" Katherine asked in a trembling voice. Tears threatened to overflow her copper eye. Cassidy was staring at the floor, guilt flooding her mind. Although everyone liked Katherine, nobody loved her enough to sacrifice their life for her. Even Fire looked awfully sad, but there was absolutely no way she would die for her. Katherine's big eye locked with Cassidy. "Please..." she begged helplessly. Blisse raised her eyebrows.

"So, that's it then?" she asked, clearly knowing the answer. Everyone's choice was plastered across their face. Blisse shrugged. "Ok then. Time to die," she stated casually. Katherine's breaths came out in small, quick gasps.

"Gabe," she whispered. Her voice wobbled as tears blurred her vision. "You can change your mind. Please don't let her do this."

"Oh darling," he mused, "can't you see that I've betrayed you?"

With Blisse's mouth twisting into a smile, she pulled the trigger of the small gun.

Katherine's blood spattered on the concrete wall behind her. She slowly dared to look at the gaping wound in her abdomen. Gabe's eye gave an almost imperceptible twitch. He walked stiffly over to her still-standing body. His hand reached out, but she flinched away. Katherine screamed in pain as her legs went out from under her.

"Don't touch me," she gasped. Her arms were painfully still held up by the chains. Gabe's dark eyes narrowed. His almost non-existent look of pain went away. He bent down, looking at her wound.

"Hey, Kathy, remember when I said that I would take a bullet for you?" She nodded, her eyes growing with anticipation. She looked almost... happy that he was reminding her of the time that made her happy. It made Hope sick.

"Well," he began, "I lied." Her breath caught in her throat. Katherine's light eye glistened with tears.

"And to think that I would've taken one for you," she said sadly, as pain ebbed through her body. He shrugged, turning away. "How can you be so horrible, Gabe?" Her words were slurring together; she knew her death was right around the corner.

"Oh Kathy, you should know that by now," he stated. "Goodbye." Her teary eye darted over to Hope. *I'm so sorry,* Hope mouthed. Her sparkling green eyes were now blinded by tears. Katherine took one final breath. Gabe watched with amusement as her body went slack. Cassidy pursed her lips, but she didn't dare say anything in front of Blisse.

"Well, wasn't that some entertainment!" Blisse exclaimed.

"Why did you do that?" Belle asked, scarily calm. Blisse had gone from threatening to actually killing now. Too scary to be comical, Blisse's head slowly turned toward her.

"Shut up," she hissed. Belle stopped speaking at once. Normally, she would've snapped back with some sarcastic comment. Now, she did exactly as she was told.

Belle, what did you get yourself into? she thought bitterly.

Grayson was smirking as he walked back into the room, beyond pleased that his syringe had worked. He now had his own personal assistant who could kill his hostages for him.

"Gabe, escort these young adults to their rooms," he commanded.

"Of course," Gabe told him. "Who should I take first?" Grayson put his hand on his chin.

"Take blondie. You might as well kill her first. We wouldn't want her to escape my clutches again, now would we?" He shot Hope a delighted glance. "Oh, and take green eyes too. Let's get rid of him as well." Gabe nodded as he gave Ethan a smirk.

"Looks like I'm in charge now, huh?" he asked, chuckling. "I chose deaths just for you! I can't wait!" Hope stared at him, devoid of any emotion.

"Let's just go, Gabe," she told him in a robotic voice. She looked at Haylee once more, her eyes full of pain. Ethan looked at her and patted Hope's shoulder.

"She'll be ok, Hope. Whoever is above us won't let her die."

"Yeah, I guess. Thanks for trying to make me feel better." Gabe's grin was a bullet to her eyes.

"Follow me to your room." Hope opened her mouth to say something, but closed it after Gabe raised his eyebrows. She heaved an exasperated sigh as she began to walk after her enemy. Ethan was behind her, his hand on her back, steadying her. He bit down hard on his lip. *If only I hadn't run away,* he thought. *This never would have happened.* He sighed as well. Grayson smirked once more. Ethan grudgingly followed Hope. It looked like her time on this island would be much shorter than she had thought.

20

Gabe threw Hope into a dim room. The walls were made of cement, clearly unbreakable.

"Well, this is a nice change of scenery," Ethan observed. Hope shot him a look, not finding his statement funny.

"It's a prison cell, Ethan."

"I was being sarcastic, Hopie."

"I hope you like prison cells, because this is where you'll be spending quite a lot of time," Gabe said cheerfully. "That's not true, actually. You won't be alive much longer."

He turned to walk out of the door, but stopped for a moment. "Oh, and gorgeous, don't worry. I'll have plenty of fun with your little friend!" She felt her pulse rage with terrible hatred. She made a not-so-kind gesture with her finger. With Gabe's light eyes sparkling, he shut the door. Hope heard the *click* of the lock that sealed them in.

When Hope turned around, her heart almost jumped out of her throat.

A small shape was moving in the corner. Hope could see that it was the size of an animal.

"That's it," she whispered to Ethan. "Gabe locked us in with some animal that's gonna eat us." Hope's arm began to shake. Ethan peered closer to the corner.

"It's not an animal," he finally said. "That right there is a human."

"Is it insane?" Hope whispered frightfully. "Is that why Gabe put us here? Is it going to kill us?"

"Let's go and see," was Ethan's grim reply. He stepped in front of Hope, putting out his hand in a gesture that was both kind and a warning.

"Um, hi," Hope said hesitantly, her voice trembling so much it even surprised her. "My name's Hope," she told the person, speaking more firm this time. "Who are you?" Still, the stranger didn't respond. Hope lightly bit her lip, frustrated that her attempts to make conversation were failing. "Listen, I don't know what happened to you, but will you please talk to me?" She desperately tried to keep the impatience out of her voice. When the stranger wasn't showing any sign of speaking, she looked at Ethan helplessly. With a weary sigh, he spoke to the person for the first time.

"Listen, we aren't going to hurt you," he said. Hope did a double take. His voice was gentler than Hope even thought was possible. Hope had never heard anyone speak that kind before. "We really want to talk to you," he continued in the voice that made Hope melt. "Trust me, we're just like you. I promise I won't hurt you. I give you my word. Will you please talk with us?" There was a moment of suspenseful silence. Finally, the pitiful human gave in.

She slowly lifted her head, revealing a mane of wavy chestnut hair. Hope's mouth fell open in surprise; she was sure the stranger wouldn't cooperate with them. She had freckles covering her nose and long, thick eyelashes framing her amber eyes. The most noticeable thing, however, wasn't her natural beauty. The look in her huge eyes was absolute terror. Hope also noticed that the girl's hands were shaking like crazy. Ethan smiled a warm smile. "Thank you," he said kindly. The girl's upper lip was trembling, giving her the appearance of a small child. "Will you tell us your name?" The girl looked up from her dark lashes. Hope saw that her eyes were glistening.

"My-my name is Sum-mer," the girl stuttered, speaking in a voice that belonged to an angel. In a small way, Hope had to admit that she was a bit jealous of this stranger's beauty. She wasn't envious of what she would've had to endure to have that terrified look in her eyes.

"What a lovely name," Ethan stated in his silvery tone. He had no trace of his smirk that he so often wore.

"So, Summer, will you tell us why you are here?" he asked gently. Summer froze, her glistening eyes growing impossibly large. Hope was extremely curious at what had happened, but she didn't want to speak and cause the girl to go back to being quiet. Minutes passed without a word. Ethan patiently stayed silent, his sympathetic gaze completely focused on her. At last, the girl took a shaky breath.

"I was captured by Grayson a couple weeks ago," she whispered, her amber eyes filling with a strange urgency. "Some of my friends had f-found some alcohol s-stashedd, and I thought they were being too loud." Summer's frame was starting to shake as bad as her hands. "I was out alone, taking a walk to clear my mind. Someone jumped- someone jumped out at me, and I was knocked unconscious. I-" she cut off, her voice cracking. A single tear fell as she quietly cleared her throat. "Next thing I knew, I w-was in a room. There was a keyhole, but n-no key. To get the key, I had t-to, I-I," she cut off again, tears falling freely at the memory. Ethan kindly put his hand on her wrist.

"It's ok," he reassured her. "Take your time." She looked at him, hyperventilating.

"I had to go into a room that was filled with b-bugs," Summer choked out. "It was h-horrible.There w-were insects covering the walls, they were scuttling all over the floor. They, they were in my ears and I- I can't get rid of the feeling of beetles scurrying all o-over me, the-"

"Stop!" Hope yelled suddenly. Chills were all up and down her body. She couldn't stand to hear another word of her awful story. Summer was sobbing, now in Ethan's arms, the memory tearing at her brain. Ethan had goosebumps all over his arms as well.

"I can't express how sorry I am," Ethan told her, stroking her hair. "Grayson is a psychopath. This should never happen to anyone, much less you. I am so, so, so sorry that this happened to you."

She cried out against his chest, her body heaving with sobs. Hope simply sat there, hugging her legs. She couldn't imagine having to go through that. And she thought three mosquitos were a nightmare.

"I'm sorry too," Hope stated, sounding pathetic compared to Ethan's enrapturing tone. Time passed, Summer still enclosed in Ethan's loving grasp. Hope was staring at the ground, the chills not disappearing.

"I think we need to go to sleep," Ethan suggested. The blonde girl nodded gratefully. However, Summer shook her head, the fastest movement she had done since they had met her.

"I don't think I-I can," the girl admitted. "I-I've had awful nightmares the past few weeks. I think I'll just s-stay up for a while."

"I'll sleep right by you," Ethan told her softly. "I'll keep the nightmares away." The brunette girl looked at him, her small lips forming a smile.

"Really?" she questioned in awe. A corner of Ethan's mouth went up into a smile.

"Really." Summer slowly laid down on the hard surface.

"I guess I'll just sleep over here then," Hope said, her voice tinged with annoyance and hurt. Ethan noticed right away.

"If you want, you can sleep over here too, Hopie," he stated. She shook her head.

"No, I'm fine. Goodnight." Hope knew guiltily that she shouldn't be acting this way, not at all. She closed her eyes, thinking of her friends outside of her prison. The last thought she formed was about Haylee. Then, her breathing became heavy as the darkness took her.

Blisse was happier than she had ever been. The thought of Haylee's unconscious head dropping brought her immense joy. The terrified faces of her prisoners made her ecstatic.

"Now, Grayson, what shall we do with these guys?" she asked creepily. He smiled his awful smile.

"I think it's time to show them their fate," he replied. Fire felt her pulse race in anticipation. All of a sudden, she snorted loudly, feeling stupid. Why did she feel such an adrenaline rush? Blisse snarled at her, shutting her up.

"Let's start with feisty here," she said happily. "What's gonna happen to her?" Grayson smirked.

"I'll take her to her room. But first, I need to attach something to you, girly." Fire raised her eyebrows.

"Attach?" she repeated, not liking at all where this was going. He reached into his pocket and pulled out a piece of fabric. It looked almost like a patch. Grayson flipped it over, showing the other side of it, which was covered in a dozen small but menacing needles. Fire felt her heart race as he made his way toward her.

"I made this special… thing just for you. I hope you like it!" She narrowed her eyes as he put his finger on her arm.

"Don't touch me," she snapped. He ignored her statement as he positioned the item over her arm. Fire struggled, afraid of what he would do, but her chains kept her from getting away. He sneered sadistically at her attempts of escape as he plunged it into her forearm.

"Ahhhh!" she shrieked, stunned by the piercing pain of the needles embedded in her skin. A purple stain was spreading where her arm had been punctured. She took a deep breath. "Ow," she repeated calmly, her blue eyes watering but not overflowing. "What will this do?" Fire asked Grayson in the same dangerously calm voice. He just smiled a sharky grin at her.

"Ah, you'll see girly. You'll just have to wait and see. Oh, but don't worry; you will know its effects soon enough." Her icy eyes narrowed in anger. "Now, Gabe," he began, responding to his assistant walking back through the hallway. "Take this young thing into her room." Gabe's eyes filled with delight as his mouth opened in a wide smile.

"It's about time," he said happily. Grayson unlocked her chains as Gabe grabbed her arm roughly. He made sure to press extra hard on the spot where the patch was. She flinched at his touch, biting hard on her lip. "Oops, my bad," he sneered. She jutted her elbow into his gut, making him grunt. She smiled mockingly.

"Oops, my bad!"

He pushed her none too gently down the haunting hallway. A minute later, he forced her into a cold room with a hard, wooden floor. He kicked her in her small back, and she sprawled across the floor into a tangled mess.

"Sweet dreams!" Gabe called her as he walked out of the room. He stopped for a moment, and then turned back around. "Actually, scratch that; you won't be dreaming tonight, my dear Sapphire." He spun back around and started to stroll down the hallway.

"Wait!" Fire called in desperation. This resulted in Gabe comically poking his head in.

"You called?"

"What do you mean?" she questioned, confused. He made the motion of zipping his lips shut.

"Oh no, I can't tell you that. Just consider it as a…a hint if you will. Now, goodnight!" With his mouth turned up at the corners, he slammed her door shut, sealing her in. He walked daintily down the hall.

Finally, he was doing what he was meant to do.

Belle winced. Her nails felt like they would break off any minute now. Oh well. That's what attempting to pick a lock with your bare hands will do to you. She tried not to make her straining obvious; possessed Blisse's black eyes were darting around. Belle made the mistake of locking eyes with her. An evil smile made its way across her face.

"Well well well, if it isn't the girl who treated me so well in the woods," she stated, taking small steps toward her. Belle gasped.

"Wait, you remember that?" she asked. Blisse nodded, her eyes squinting. "Hold on; that means that you must remember who you really are!" Belle realized aloud. The evil girl laughed, although there was no trace of humor in the horrible sound.

"No, honey," she sneered, getting closer and closer. "This is who I really am, girl. And I really hate you. You made the mistake of getting on my bad side, and that's not what you want. Don't forget that I have much more power than you do." Belle narrowed her eyes. Suddenly, Blisse's hand flew across her face, making her eyes water.

"Don't narrow your eyes at me," she demanded. "Next time you do that, I'll replace my hand with a hammer. Understand?" Belle wasn't going to give her the satisfaction of nodding. Blisse raised her eyebrows. "Ok then, I'll just go get the hammer."

"No!" the girl shouted in spite of herself. Blisse's mouth went up.

"What was that?"

"Yes, I understand," Belle told her grudgingly. The black-eyed girl nodded in approval.

"Although, you'll probably wish you chose the hammer when you find out what I have planned for you," Blisse said under her breath. Belle's mouth dropped open.

"What do you mean by that?" she asked, beginning to feel a trace of fear in her system. The girl just grinned and walked away. A moment later, Gabe came skipping in.

"Sapphire is in her room for the night!" he exclaimed. Grayson nodded.

"Good job, boy." Gabe smiled like a little kid.

"You know, you are such a genius! How do you do it?" he asked. Grayson just grinned smugly. It made Belle want to punch him.

"Now, for the rest of you; you'll find out what will happen to you tomorrow. For now, you can just sleep peacefully in your chains. Oh, and if I hear any chatter, I *will* kill you. Night!" He flicked off the lights, leaving the young adults in their restraints. Aiden was the first to close his eyes. He wanted to let everyone know that it was ok to sleep; who knew when they would sleep next? Cassidy noticed, and she did the same. Finally, everyone's eyes were shut.

Nobody fell asleep.

21

Fire yawned. She made herself comfortable on the floor. Well, as comfortable as she could get on hardwood. She stretched out and closed her eyes, feeling herself beginning to drift off despite the terrifying circumstances.

Suddenly, a huge shock racked through her body.

She screamed in pain and leaped up. Her pulse was racing like crazy and chills covered her body. *What the hell?!* She took a couple deep breaths. *Maybe I just imagined it.* She knew that there was no way she imagined the horrible pain she felt, but that was the best explanation she had.

For 10 minutes, Fire stayed up, sitting against the wall. Her eyes were darting all around, looking for any source of the electricity that hurt her. As the time ticked on, the startling shock wore off, and she was feeling more and more tired. She decided to go to sleep; she was probably just hallucinating. After all, she had been moving all day and she was super stressed out.

The girl hesitantly laid down on the rough floor. Fire tensed up like a rubber band. Five minutes later, she closed her eyes and her breathing became heavy. At that moment, the awful shock went through her again. It felt as though someone was mercilessly giving her electric shocks.

"What's the big idea?!" she shouted, extremely frustrated. She sat up fast, a wave of dizziness flooding her mind. Her whole body was tingling from the attacks she had received. She knew one thing for sure; there was no way that she was going back to sleep again. "Gabe!" she yelled. He didn't come, which wasn't surprising. Obviously, there had to be a reason that she was getting shocked. *Come on, Sapphire. Use your brain; think. Why are you getting shocked?* Fire thought hard about anything Grayson had said. She knew that she was onto something, but she couldn't put her finger on it. *Come on, Fire! I bet the answer is right in front of your face!* She thought about what Gabe had said.

'*Think of it as a...a hint if you will.*' Gabe's words rang in her mind. *Come on Sapphire! What else did he say?* Fire put her hand on her chin. Suddenly, it dawned on her. She realized what he had been implying when he had said that she wouldn't be dreaming that night. Fire's body tensed up as her mouth dropped open.

"Oh, that little…," she knew now why she was getting shocked. Stupid Grayson wouldn't let her sleep! Fire's arms broke out in goosebumps. She knew what happened when a person was deprived of sleep. She remembered learning about it in school, forever ago. First, you would become crabby and moody. Then, the headaches would come. Afterwards, you could suffer severe paranoia. The hallucinations could make you crazy, and there was absolutely no way she would do that to herself. "Gabe!" she called again, her voice rising to a higher pitch. "GABE!" she shrieked, straining her vocal cords. Finally, the door creaked open to reveal a content Gabe.

"How may I help you, Sapphire?" he asked, talking through a yawn. The adult ran his fingers through his messy dark brown hair. His brown fur slippers padded into the doorway.

"Why the hell is it that I get shocked when I try to sleep?" she inquired in a suspicious and accusatory tone. Gabe shrugged comically, making the fierce girl's eyes darken. "Don't you dare shrug at me," she snapped. "You're the person who chose this for me; you said it yourself, you moron." Fire rubbed the sore skin around the patch. Her skin was turning a threatening shade of purple. She gagged when she noticed that some of it was even starting to turn black.

"Did you think of pulling it out?" Gabe asked, his twinkling eyes showing through the darkness. Fire narrowed her eyes.

"No."

He cocked a smile at her. "Well, maybe you should try that."

With her eyes dead set on Gabe, she started to put her finger under the edge of the patch on the inside of her arm. Bracing herself for the pain that would surely come, she began to lift the edge. She scrunched up her face slightly, but not taking her eyes off of Gabe's amused ones. Fire gasped in pain before she could help it. The needles weren't even coming out of her skin, but she already felt horrible pain. It felt like her arm was submerged in acid, burning her skin. She kept trying to rip it out.

Gabe watched, a smug grin making its way across his face. Finally, Fire stopped. The agony in her arm became stronger and stronger each time she even slightly lifted the fabric up. She let it go. The girl noticed that her eyes were watering. She hastily wiped them with the back of her palm, not daring to let Gabe see weakness inside her. He stared at her, his eyes a little squinted. He didn't have a smug look or even a glare; he just looked at her. A moment later, he nodded his head approvingly.

"You know, Sapphire, you actually endured it a lot more than I thought you would. I'm surprised." She shot him a glare, her mind slowly trying to rid itself of the excruciating sensation of slowly pulling out the needles.

"What, did you expect me to scream in pain or something? If you did, you're an idiot," she snapped. He slowly shook his head, his light eyes full of amusement.

"Yeah, you're right, I guess I didn't. You're actually pretty tough, I'll give you that," he stated. She stared at him, her mouth gaping open.

"Wait a minute, did you just compliment me? Did the infamous Gabe-" she broke off. "Wait, what's your last name?"

"I don't have one," he said coldly. "That was taken away from me." Fire gave him an odd look as she continued.

"Did the infamous Gabe just give me praise? What next, the end of the world?" Although she was being dramatic, she was actually a little surprised. Gabe's face was turning a deep shade of red. He hoped it didn't show in the dim lighting.

Her face took on a more serious expression. "Now tell me how to get this patch off me," she demanded. Gabe chortled.

"Hmm, looks like you aren't so high and mighty when I'm in control of you." She rolled her eyes, exasperated. "I've already told you how to get it off, Sapphire."

"I mean, is there another way I can get it off? You know, an option where it doesn't feel like my arm is being burned off?"

"Actually, there is," Gabe said. Fire felt her hopes grow, although she knew that she shouldn't get too excited.

"There is?" Gabe looked her dead in the eyes, no trace of humor on his face.

"No. I lied." A moment of silence passed, Fire's eyes growing wider and angrier.

"I really hate you," she growled through gritted teeth. "If you had a bigger ego, you wouldn't be able to fit through that door."

"And if you were any shorter, you'd probably flicker out of existence," he said smoothly. Fire rolled back her shoulders.

"Fight me, Gabe." Gabe sighed, rolling his eyes.

"Listen, little girl, I am over 210 pounds of nothing but muscle, and you couldn't even pass for five feet tall. There's no point in you threatening people all the time, it makes you look incredibly stupid."

Fire stomped up to him.

"Fight me anyways!" She flexed her thin arm, mentally wincing at the sharp pain from her patch. Gabe smirked, prodding her away with his finger.

"Well, goodnight, Sapphire. Dream of me!" He took a few steps out into the hall. "Oh, wait. You can't!" He slammed the door shut, and Fire somehow knew he wouldn't come back, no matter how much she shouted. She could still hear him chuckling as he skipped down the hallway.

"Well Sapphire, I guess you'll be pulling an all-nighter tonight," she muttered bitterly. She sat upright against the hard wall. Fire was super drowsy, and she felt her eyelids become heavy. She snapped up right away, knowing that she was a second away from being shocked yet again. In jumping up, she smacked her head against the wooden wall. She swore while she gently rubbed her head, cursing Gabe for leaving her here.

She took a deep breath, preparing for the night to come. *Well this'll be a fun eight hours*, she thought dryly. All she could do was think about her friends, still in their chains. *At least they can sleep.* She was surprised to feel a single tear sliding softly down her cheek. Fire rested her head on the wall with a moan.

"Belle," whispered Aiden, as loud as he dared. She didn't respond. "Belle," he repeated, slightly louder this time. *Don't let Grayson hear,* he begged to no one. "Belle!" This time, the girl's eyes opened a fraction. Aiden held his breath, looking to see if Grayson had heard. It was impossible to see anything clearly in the darkness that the night brought.

"What do you want?" she asked, her words slurring together. "The night is meant for sleeping, idiot." Aiden ignored her insult.

"Let's try to escape," he whispered. "This is our only chance." He heard the rattle of Belle's chains as she stretched.

"Yeah, ok," she said through a yawn. "What you propose we do, Aiden?" He shrugged. When he realized she couldn't see him, he said, "I don't really know. Try to pick the lock or something." He heard Belle's exasperated sigh.

"Aiden, there's no way that I can pick this lock. I already tried, so there's no use to suggest useless solutions," she said groggily. Aiden shook his hands, trying to slide down the metal circle on his hand.

"Well, I can't wiggle out of them, Belle."

"No dip, Captain Obvious," said an annoyed girl. "Let me sleep."

"I don't know what else to do." Aiden struggled half-heartedly. "I can't believe that you just want to give up." Belle's head snapped up.

"I'm not giving up," she retorted. "There's nothing we can do to get out of these stupid chains."

"Well, you could at least be a bit helpful," he muttered.

"I'm not a freaking optimist!" she practically yelled. "There's nothing we can do, Aiden!" He was about to reply when he heard the sound of an opening door.

"Quick, pretend you're sleeping," he said, despite his feelings toward Belle. He heard her chains go slack as she leaned against the wall. Aiden did the same, but he kept his eyelids squinted open. It was just in time, as he saw Grayson stomp in.

"Who the *hell* is talking here?" he asked dangerously. Aiden pretended to breathe deeply, greatly hoping that the man would buy his act. "Answer me now," he commanded. "I'm not in a good mood during the day, and I'm a billion times worse when my sleep is disrupted." His eyes moved slowly around, hoping to catch the person who was talking. "I know you're listening," he said eerily. "Next time you talk, I will beat you all severely. Don't ever let it happen again."

Aiden saw his silhouette turn around and walk out of the room. He limply held up his middle finger while Grayson's back was turned. *Oh Aiden,* he thought sadly. *You're dead. You're so dead.*

"No Haylee," I say firmly, stealing nervous glances at the ground far below through the smudged window. "I am not jumping out of this plane. Do you hear me?"

126

Haylee's jumping up and down in excitement, not even attempting to hide the massive smile spread across her face.

"C'mon Hope!" she says to me, reaching for my shaking wrist. She has a twinkle in her amber eyes that makes my face break out in a smile, when really I want to look tough. "It'll be fun!"

"But what if my parachute doesn't open!" I exclaim, desperately trying to stall what I know is inevitable. I mean, I know I'm going to jump out of the stupid plane; it's Haylee's birthday, and this is what she's been dreaming of doing. She's told me over and over that if she's dangerous, she'll never get the chance to do it. I've told her over and over that she won't be harmful, but she doesn't care. She keeps pulling the 'but what if I'm dangerous?' card on my mom and I. We all know that she knows she won't be dangerous either; that's just a way of pressuring me into going skydiving with her. There's no way that my innocent step-sister could even harm a fly, much less survive on an island filled with murderers.

"Hope, your parachute will be fine," she reassures me, slightly rolling her eyes. I still don't believe her, but I take a few small steps forward. "Now," says Haylee, her grin getting wider, "let's jump out of this thing." She forcefully grabs my wrist and pulls me to the door of the plane.

"Why did I agree to this?" I wonder aloud. Haylee chuckles.

"I was surprised when you agreed too, Hope. You're such a scaredy-cat; you never do anything." Now, that made me mad. If there's one thing I hate, it's people underestimating or doubting me.

"Oh yeah?" I say, crossing my arms in annoyance. "Watch me jump like no one's business." Haylee laughs a joyful laugh.

"Let's see what you got, sista." With one determined look her way, I prepare myself for the jump. The view of the ground scares me to death, but I'm anything but a quitter.

"Ready to jump!" a man says, signaling for me to leap. I glance at Haylee once more. She's giving me the thumbs up sign as she mentally prepares herself as well.

"Let's do this thing," I mutter to myself. I take a small step. Then one more. My foot hits the air. The blue sky is a blur to me as I give a shriek of fear and delight. I take a look at the ground, so far yet so close. Finally, I completely let go of my worries as I fall through the sky.

Hope sat up. She didn't gasp or jump up; she just sat. She was surprised to notice that her eyes were wet with tears. She sniffed, remembering the time when she was on the plane with Haylee. It seemed like a distant memory that had happened to someone else, not her.

"Haylee," she whispered sadly. Her moist eyes darted over to Ethan. Summer was laying on his arms, her tiny frame curled up. Despite her bittersweet memories, she felt a small spark of jealousy. She sniffed some more, looking helplessly at the door that sealed her in. Hope slowly stood up, stretching. She scrunched up her blotchy face when she noticed how stiff her muscles were. *Well, that's what you get when you sleep on a cement floor, Hope,* she told herself.

She walked quietly over to the sleeping Ethan. She knelt down, taking in his features. Hope noticed the way that the lines of stress and worry were gone from his face, the way his eyelids were so gently closed, the way his chestnut hair was sprawled across the hard floor. *He looks so peaceful.*

She almost regretted wanting to wake him. Hope poked his arm gently. "Ethan," she whispered. His breathing was steady, and he made no move of stirring. She scratched him lightly, not wanting to accidentally wake Summer. She scratched him harder. His still eyelids lightly fluttered open, revealing his sleepy green eyes.

"What, Hopie? Did you want a piece of me too?" He chuckled, exhausted. Hope grinned weakly.

"I just want you to sleep with me, Ethan," she said. He raised his eyebrows. Hope quickly shook her flustered face. "No, not like that," she exclaimed. "I just had a really… sad dream, and I just want some company."

"Whatever pleases you, Hopie," he told her, lightly grinning. Without warning, he grabbed her arm and pulled her to him. He lightly but firmly nudged Summer over to the other side of him. "Now," he began, "what was your dream about?" Hope took a calming breath.

"Well, I dreamed about Haylee," she said. She slightly felt Ethan tense up under her. "Why did you just freeze?"

"I just wish you would stop thinking about Haylee," he explained. "It makes you sad."

"My dream was an exact memory. It's like I was there, thinking and feeling everything, but I knew that it was a dream. I don't know, it was weird. I was in a plane, about to go skydiving for her birthday. I didn't want to go, but Haylee's expression made me know that I would do it anyway. She was really happy, and that made me happy. I guess I'm just sad that I realize that Haylee can bring me happiness, sometimes when no one else can. And she might not wake up again, Ethan. The sun in my life might not shine anymore." His gaze was entirely focused on hers, absorbing every word that she had to say. She loved the look in his eyes, the way he yearned to listen to her every word.

"I don't know what to say, Hope," he finally whispered. "I'm so sorry."

"It's ok," she said, bringing up her hand to wipe her watering eyes. "I'll be fine soon. Just help me fall asleep again." She rested her head on his chest, finding comfort in the soothing sound of his heartbeat. He brought up his hand and gently stroked her golden hair.

"Don't worry Hope, I'll chase the sad dreams away." She snorted before she could help herself. "What's so funny?" he asked. "Is it my feeble attempt to make you feel better?"

"Don't be so cliche," she said jokingly. He pushed her hair out of her face.

"Well, what do you want me to say?" He laughed.

"Nevermind," said Hope. "Just go to sleep, Ethan." She shifted her body, making herself comfortable.

"Goodnight, Hope," he said, chuckling. The last sound she heard was Ethan's racing heartbeat as she drifted off to sleep.

Fire softly hit her head again and again against the wall. The room seemed to become fuzzier and darker. Sitting still made her body desperately want to close its eyes. *I freaking hate this!*

Fire angrily stood up, becoming dizzy. *Well Sapphire,* she thought, *might as well get you awake.* She started groggily doing weak jumping jacks, her eyelids falling down. *Screw you, Grayson.* She looked down at her arm. She forced her eyelids open, as it was hard to see in the dark. What she saw next sent a wave of nausea throughout her whole body. Her skin around the patch was dark purple and swollen. Little flecks of blood were visible as well. She could only imagine what her actual punctured skin looked like.

"I hate Grayson so much," she growled under her breath, staring at the door. "When I see you, I'm going to kill you." Fire thought about screaming, but she realized that Grayson would probably not like that very much. *No point in making him angry, I guess.*

Just to check, she pulled one corner of the patch. Immediately, a bullet of pain raced down her arm. She loudly swore through her teeth, fighting back tears. Clearly the patch wouldn't come off without a fight, if it could come off at all. This thought sent a wave of fear through her mind. What if it couldn't come off? What would she do then? Was it possible to die from sleep deprivation?

Fire started to jog around the room, set on getting herself awake. She forced herself to not again look at her repulsive arm. As she jogged, she automatically started to move her arms, as she had done whenever she ran. Each time her arm moved, she felt a sharp pain where her patch was. Finally, Fire couldn't take it anymore. She sat down hard, her legs slamming onto the concrete.

I just want to get off this place. She gently touched the patch, wincing at the quick pain that she couldn't stop. It was almost like pressing down aggressively on a bruise, but it felt a million times worse. *I would take my dad over this.* She took a deep breath.

Wow, has it really come to this? I would rather live with my dad then deal with Grayson? She ran her hands through her greasy hair. "Wow," she said aloud. "This sucks."

She remembered the time when her dad had once locked her in a closet because she accidently broke his hockey trophy.

"This is what you deserve," he had said, as he slammed the door shut. She had been sealed in there for three hours, her little legs tired and her face blotchy. That was her first memory of him. Fire remembered when his favorite football team lost. He had thrown his beer can at her face, and the sharp edge cut her cheek. Her mom had to take her to the hospital for six stitches, and her dad had been angry about the cost.

"Just leave it," he had told her mom angrily. "Sapphire isn't worth the money." She had been strong then, her eyes not shedding tears.

Fire remembered when he had killed her pet hamster while she was at school. He lied, telling her that it had died by itself. She could still feel the painful sadness she had felt when he laughed and told her that he had strangled it.

"Bad girls don't get pets," he had told her. "Bad girls like you, Sapphire." With a pain that stung worse than the patch, she finally allowed herself to relive the worst day of her life, so many years ago.

22

Fire was twelve years old. She was walking to class, her head down and headphones shielding her mind from the world. She walked up to her locker, forcefully shoving her old backpack in. The edges ripped. Of course, it ripped because her dad had never felt the need to buy her new school supplies. He said he didn't have enough money, but somehow he always had a new pack of beer every three days.

"Sapphire!" her friend Charlotte called. Fire took out her headphones, smiling.

"Charlotte,, hi!" Charlotte's honey eyes looked at her in concern. "Sapphire, what happened to your eye?" Fire gently touched her swollen black eye.

"Oh, I hit it on my counter," she lied. Charlotte touched it softly.

"Wow, it must've hurt, huh?"

The memory of her dad hitting her rang in her mind.

"Yeah, it hurt a lot." Fire shut her locker and began walking to the school bathroom. Charlotte followed her.

"Holy crap, my eye looks horrible!" Fire exclaimed, staring sadly at her reflection. Charlotte poked her shoulder playfully.

"No, you look fine! Besides, if anyone asks, you can just tell them that you hit it on your counter. No one will judge!"

"Yeah, I guess," Fire said halfheartedly. *If only Charlotte knew the truth. Then she would judge me.*

Fire walked out of the door with her friend at her heels. They both walked into their classroom. Right away, her teacher, Mrs. Dominique, looked at her sympathetically.

"Miss Sapphire, what happened?" she asked with her heavy accent. Fire shrugged, looking at the floor.

"I hit it, but I'm fine." Mrs. Dominique looked at her worriedly, but she didn't say anything else. Fire strolled over to her seat. The first hour went by fine, but then her teacher called her up to the desk.

"Sapphire, honey, are you telling me the truth about your eye?" Fire's vibrant eyes avoided eye contact.

"Yes. I hit it."

Mrs. Dominique's gray eyes were full of understanding.

"Sapphire, your eye wouldn't look like that if you had just hit it. That type of bruise comes from a fist. Is everything ok at home?"

"No, no, I'm honestly fine," Fire said hastily. She knew how angry her dad would be if he found out that she had told somebody about her eye. Her teacher's tone became more firm.

"Sapphire, I'd like you to tell me the truth. It'll just be between you and me, alright? I won't tell the class anything."

Fire gulped, chewing roughly on her lip.

"Um, well," she said hesitantly. Mrs. Dominique's smile was kind, but her eyes were knowing. "Yes," Fire finally said. "My dad hit me. But I'm fine, I promise," she added quickly.

"He hit you?" the voice belonged to Fire's classmate, Sage. Mrs. Dominique's face went pale.

"Sage, you had no business hearing that. Go sit down."

"She heard me?" Fire whispered in horror. Her teacher looked at her, her face in an expression of sadness.

"Yes Sapphire, she did."

"But you said no one would hear."

"I know I did." Mrs. Dominique's old eyes were pained. "I didn't mean for that to happen." Fire nodded firmly as she walked quickly back to her seat. Sage and her friend Emma were looking at her, whispering. Fire used her long, dark hair to hide her burning face.

An hour of class passed. It seemed as though Mrs. Dominique was purposely avoiding Fire's eye contact. Finally, after what seemed like much too long, the bell rang, signaling the end of school. Fire rushed out.

"Sapphire, wait up!" Charlotte called. Fire stopped, waiting for her. They both walked together to the bus.

The bus ride to Fire's house was only three minutes. The principal had told her dad over and over that it would make more sense for him to just pick her up from school, but of course he hadn't listened.

"See ya tomorrow!" Charlotte happily called. Fire nodded once, but her mind was on something else; her dad. She was beyond positive that her teacher had called him about the incident.

As soon as she walked in, she heard heavy footsteps.

"Dad?" she asked in a small voice. Her father's blue eyes were aflame as he stared her down.

"I got a call from your teacher today. It was about your eye. Did you tell her about your eye?" He brought his face dangerously close to hers. Gulping, Fire nodded. His lip curled into a snarl. "That was a mistake, Sapphire."

Without warning, his fist smashed into her shoulder. Her eyes burned. His hand hit her other shoulder with the same force. Fire fell to the ground, tears falling from her eyes. "Never speak of this," her father said lowly. Fire nodded as she ran to her small room. She threw herself onto her bed, sobbing into the pillows. At some point, she fell asleep.

The next day, Fire woke up, wincing. She couldn't move her shoulders without feeling a stiff pain. She didn't even change her clothes from the previous day. She threw on a worn sweatshirt, hiding her bruises on her arm. She forced herself to walk down the stairs without the hurt showing on her face. Fire breathed a sigh of relief when she realized that her dad had already left for work.

The girl grabbed an old banana from her fridge. On her way out the door, she saw a piece of paper on the counter.

Not a word, said the note. Fire grabbed the note from her dad and chucked it in the garbage. She walked out to wait for her bus. As soon as she got on, all of the kids stared at her. Her face turned red as she sat in the seat, alone.

The bus ride seemed to go as quick as a wink. She got off the bus and went to her locker like she did everyday. All of her classmates didn't bother to hide their stares.

"Hey Sapphire!" Charlotte exclaimed, as bright as ever. Sapphire gave a limp wave as she took off her backpack. She felt herself wince. "Sapphire, what's wrong?" asked Charlotte, having seen the pain in her eyes. Fire shook her head, her eyes focused on the floor.

"Nothing. I'm fine." Her friend nodded her head.

"Ok, good." They both walked to class, Fire secretly dreading when they would walk through the door. As soon as she walked in, everyone's head snapped over to her.

"Can I help you with something?" Charlotte asked, obviously annoyed at the attention. Sage kept her eyes on Fire as Charlotte and Fire went to their seats. Mrs. Dominique walked in later, still not looking at Fire. The day went by, full of whispering and stares. Fire deeply regretted having said the truth. Finally, the bell rang. Before she could run out the door, Sage stopped her.

"What did your dad do this time?" she asked, looking at Fire's slouched posture. "Did he hit you again?"

"What the heck are you talking about?" asked an annoyed Charlotte. Sage looked surprised.

"Wait, you don't know?" Charlotte flipped her light hair in anger.

"Know what?"

"That Sapphire's dad hit her." Charlotte rolled her eyes.

"Come on, that's not true. Tell her, Sapphire." Fire looked at the floor, water pooling in her eyes. Charlotte slightly opened her mouth. "Sapphire, tell her that your dad didn't hit you," she said urgently. Fire let a tear fall.

"If I did, I'd be lying," she whispered. Charlotte's mouth dropped all the way open.

"Wait, your dad caused your black eye?!" Fire nodded, ashamed. Her friend squinted her eyes. "Why didn't you tell me?"

"I didn't want anyone to know," Fire mumbled. Charlotte looked at her angrily.

"But we're best friends! You can tell me anything! Why in the world didn't you tell me that *your dad abuses you!?*"

A crowd of people came over, intrigued by her yelling.

"So it's true!" one boy yelled. "Sapphire's dad hits her!"

"Someone call the protective services!" another girl yelled. Fire couldn't stop her tears anymore. Suddenly, she aggressively pushed past everyone as she sprinted out of the door. Charlotte did the same.

"Sapphire!" she yelled desperately. "I didn't mean to say it loud! Sapphire, come back!"

Fire angrily turned around.

"Don't call me that," she demanded. Charlotte looked confused.

"But Sapphire's your name." Fire put her hand on her hip.

"My dad uses that name against me," she snapped, holding tears. "He screams it as he hits me." She felt pleasure at the shocked look on Charlotte's face.

"Don't talk to me ever again, Charlotte. Don't text me, don't look at me, don't even think about me. Our friendship is done. And don't ever call me that name again." Charlotte's face looked horrified and hurt. Fire's face was a mix of smugness and humiliation as she ran out of the door and past the bus.

Fire didn't even realize she was sobbing until she realized her hand was blurry beyond recognition. She hadn't had the chance to truly cry in years. She had a reputation to hold, which was the tough leader of the group. She had never allowed herself to cry in front of anyone, especially Ethan or Maya. There was absolutely no way she would ever show weakness. Everything she had been holding back, she let go.

You know what? she thought. *I lied. I wouldn't take my dad over Grayson.*

"Hopie!" Ethan exclaimed. "Hopie, wake up!"

Sighing tiredly, Hope opened her eyes, revealing Ethan and Summer looking down at her.

"Hi, Hope," Summer said, a trace of happiness in her voice. Her large eyes were no longer full of tears and her hair was tied back.

"Good morning, Summer," Hope said in a yawn. She felt ashamed and stupid for being jealous over Ethan the previous night. Summer deserved Ethan's attention and love much more than she did. "You know," said Hope, "I don't know much about you. If we're stuck in here, we might as well make the most of it."

"What do you want to know?" Summer's shy voice asked. Hope shrugged.

"Um, what's your favorite color?"

"Yellow," she said immediately. "Like the sun."

"That's really nice," Ethan said brightly. "I like yellow too. I wish there was more yellow in this room."

Summer smiled slightly. Hope right away wished that she was as pretty as Summer. She felt shame at thinking such a thing in the conditions they were in. But it was impossible to wish the thought away. It was as though Summer's small smile could light up the whole room.

"What did you like to do for fun? You know, before the psychotic government sent us to this hell," Ethan said through a perked grin. Summer smiled a sad, longing smile.

"I loved history," she said, looking down. "It was like an escape for me. I always adored the past. I wish I was still in school." She gave a strange chuckle. "Huh, I never thought I'd miss school."

"That's really interesting!" Ethan told her. "Since I'm a big tough jock, obviously, my favorite subject was gym."

"Mine was math," Hope piped up. "I just find everything so fascinating about numbers. It's so cool to see how things work."

"I didn't know that," Ethan said. "You struck me as more of a reader. I didn't think you'd be into math."

"Because girls can't excel at math?" Hope said jokingly. Summer's golden eyes were lit up, absorbing every word.

"That's not what I meant," he said through a laugh.

"Well, I do like to read too. I tried writing once, but I just can't. It's really hard to make the words flow for me."

"Same with me!" Summer stated. An ounce of enthusiasm had crept its way into her voice. "I absolutely loved reading, too! Reading is so interesting to me!"

"You see," said Ethan, "I never liked reading. To me, staring at a dead piece of wood just didn't seem like my idea of fun." Hope snorted.

"That's not what reading is, Ethan." Ethan shrugged, his grin wide.

"C'mon Hopie, you gotta admit I'm funny."

"So Summer, where did you come from?" Hope asked. Her face turned into a look of longing.

"Colorado," she said. Her eyes looked up. "I loved the way the snow looked on the mountains. I loved the way the sunset was purple and orange and pink."

"That sounds gorgeous," Ethan told her. Hope dramatically winced.

"Don't say that," Hope told him, chuckling. Ethan looked at her curiously.

"Say what?"

"Gorgeous," she replied. "Gabe ruined that word for me. I just don't like it anymore." Summer looked at her kindly.

"Well, thanks for talking with me, Hope. You seem like a very nice person." Hope smiled back, her jealousy evaporating.

"Thank you Summer. You are so sweet, too. Has anyone ever told you how pretty you are?"

Summer's face turned red.

"You think I'm pretty?"

"Oh, definitely!" Hope exclaimed. "Has no one ever said that?" Summer awkwardly smiled.

"No, actually. I've never been called pretty in my life." She looked at Hope gratefully. "And Hope, you are so beautiful too. I always wished I could be born with naturally blonde hair." Hope snickered.

"Yeah, it's great. Until everyone calls you a dumb blonde each time you get a question wrong." Summer laughed, then put her hand over her mouth.

"Sorry, was I not supposed to laugh?" Hope's face broke out in a genuine smile. "And Ethan," Summer said almost shyly, "you are very handsome."

Before she could help it, Hope burst out laughing. Each time she looked at Ethan's shocked and amused expression, she laughed even harder.

"What Hopie? You don't think my muscles are hot enough? Does my face not seduce you?" He struck a pose, showing off his bulging biceps.

"Oh gosh Ethan, shut up," Hope said through a grin. Summer shrugged, smiling.

"Well, I thought he should get a compliment too. He's been really nice to me. You too, Hope," she added. Hope grinned, wiping her eyes.

"Well thank you, Summer."

"In a strange way, I'm glad you guys are here," Summer said. "But listen, I don't mean it in a mean way. Honestly, if you guys hadn't come, I might've just… ended my misery. This is the first time I've talked to someone in awhile. Thank you for that."

Ethan's bright eyes shone.

"I'm glad," Ethan said, patting her wrist. "You're a strong girl, you know that?" Summer's eyes went to the ground in embarrassment.

"Thank you, Ethan."

"Hi friends!" Gabe bellowed. Aiden groggily peeled open his eyes. Gabe walked right up to his face. "WAKE UP!" he yelled. Aiden jumped, feeling his hatred pulse.

"Was that really necessary, Gabe?"

"No," Gabe said, his smirk coming to his face. "It wasn't necessary. But it was entertaining watching you jump!"

Suddenly, Blisse walked through. Aiden begged that the whole evil Blisse had just been his imagination, but that thought died when her pitch black eyes pierced his. Her hair was ominously thrown over her face, making her look like some sort of demon from a horror movie. Following his infected friend was Grayson, with an old, chipped mug full of some brown liquid in his hand.

"Did you all sleep well?" he asked in his booming voice. He was greeted with blank stares and silence. Grayson smirked. "Oh well, if that's how you want to be. I have an announcement to make."

Cassidy gulped. She felt insanely uncomfortable as Blisse's judgemental eyes seemed to look her up and down. It made her feel ten times worse when Grayson's hard gray eyes lingered on her.

"The announcement," he said, a smile growing on his face, "is that the first people will die today."

Belle willed herself to not make eye contact with anyone. There was no way in the world that Grayson could choose her to die. He couldn't. Belle was not ready to die, but she dreaded whoever did. Although she'd only known Grayson for less than a day, she knew that his intentions would be horrible.

"I created it!" Gabe exclaimed before he could help it. "I created your death!"

"Well, aren't you just a little ball of sunshine?" Belle muttered. Grayson looked at Gabe in approval.

"Yes Gabriel, you did. Would you like to say who will be chosen for this little idea of yours?" Gabe nodded happily. Everyone chained up against the wall held their breath. Cassidy's pulse quickened, and pure dread seemed to swallow her up.

"I want to kill..." his eyes looked up, going to Cassidy. She opened her quivering mouth in terror, causing Gabe to delightfully nod. "Cassidy and Aiden."

23

Cassidy let a gasp escape from her mouth. His statement triggered tears to fall from her eyes onto her cheek. *Not me. It can't be me.*

Aiden's body froze. In some way, he had been expecting his name to be called. He hadn't been the nicest to Gabe back when they had first met. However, hearing his name officially be said made his mind go blank. He was going to die.

"Follow me folks," Gabe told them slyly. Grayson walked over with the keys to their chains, a smile on his face.

"Oh, don't look so scared!" he exclaimed to the pale Cassidy. "One of you will survive!"

This made Aiden feel much worse. He already knew that he would die to save Cassidy. He wouldn't accept her death. He gave one last look toward Belle as he walked to his death room with his best friend.

Gabe stopped at a room far down the hallway. He over-the-top swept his hand through the doorway.

"Right this way, children!"

Cassidy didn't even shoot him a glare. She couldn't contort her face into something so evil when she was this terrified. Aiden followed, wiping his clammy hands on his shorts. Gabe gave him a peppy slap on the back as he walked through.

The first thing Cassidy did was nervously look around. There were two thick brown ropes hanging from the ceiling, and the floor was made of glistening metal. She would have to jump to grab onto the ropes. The word that popped into her mind was *noose.* Aiden's eyes darted all around as well. Gabe grinned at their nerves.

"What is this?" Cassidy asked. Her voice came out sounding weak and raspy.

"Well, I'd love to tell you!" Gabe said brightly. "See these ropes right here? Go on, feel them." Cautiously, Aiden walked over to the rope, his eyes glancing back at Gabe. "C'mon Aiden, touch the rope already. It won't bite you." With a glare, Aiden grabbed the rope. It fit perfectly in his hand. Gabe nodded.

"Very good! You see, you will have to grab onto the ropes." He prodded Cassidy in the back. She got the message, and she went grudgingly to hold the rope as well. "Ok, make sure to hold them quite tightly."

Cassidy noticed that Gabe was moving backward as he spoke. Backward. Toward the door.

"Gabe?" she said hesitatingly. "Why do we need to hold onto the ropes?" He rewarded her with a mysterious grin. Gabe continued to move back, his eyes locked on his ropes. As soon as he stepped out of the doorway, Aiden got a horrible feeling in his gut. He knew that he should have acted sooner. Cassidy allowed the fear inside her to show on her face despite herself. Gabe swiftly slid a clear wall between him and the door. Aiden knew that the wall was trapping them in.

"Better get to the rope!" Gabe called to them. Aiden shot him a glare, but he listened. Cassidy did the same. Gabe smirked, touching something on the outside wall that they couldn't see.

Suddenly, Cassidy felt the floor begin to shake. She shot a terrified glare to Aiden, who was grabbing onto his rope desperately.

"Hold on tight!" Gabe yelled through the clear barrier. "This is my little death trap for you! You'd best hold on, because if you fall, you die!"

Cassidy couldn't believe how cheerful his tone was. Aiden shot her a robotic look.

"What do you mean fall!?"

"I mean fall," Gabe declared. "So grab on tight!"

"Do you mean onto the floor?!" Aiden practically shouted. Gabe's eyes lit up.

"Something like that, Aiden. And if I were you, I wouldn't want to let go!"

"It's just the stupid floor," Cassidy muttered to Aiden. "Why the hell would I care if I fall?"

The ground on the other side of the room began to *move.* It was sliding in their direction, leaving a large space where it was previously. Cassidy couldn't see what the floor was uncovering, but she knew with dread that she would find out soon enough.

"I'll do it," Aiden stated. Cassidy gave him an astonished look.

"What do you mean?"

"I'm going to fall. Obviously the floor is going to disappear, and we will have to hold onto these ropes."

"No," she told him firmly. "You are not going to let go. Do you hear me?" Aiden's eyes glistened. Gabe chuckled, watching them argue about their dreadful ending. The floor's shaking got rougher. Cassidy had to tightly grab onto her thick rope to keep from falling over.

"Put both hands on!" Aiden demanded loudly. Cassidy obeyed him, wrapping her hands tightly around. Gabe's smug face was peering at them.

"When the weight is entirely off the rope, that's when the other person will be let down," Gabe explained, having to yell over the loud rumbling. Tears of fear began trickling down Cassidy's face. Gabe smiled. What he said next sent chills down Cassidy's shaking arms.

"Let the best win."

Suddenly, the floor's shaking stopped. Cassidy and Aiden both gripped it much tighter, knowing that their game was about to begin. The ground began to split apart much faster. Cassidy screeched, practically throwing herself on the rope. Aiden felt his pulse race. *This is it. I'm going to fall.*

"Hold on Cass!" Aiden yelled. The floor was just about to slide out from under her feet. Cassidy mentally screamed as she tightly grasped her rope.

Soon, the entire ground was completely gone. Cassidy and Aiden were dangling above a threatening looking green liquid, held up only by the strength of their arms.

Cassidy's lip quivered uncontrollably. She looked down, shrieking at how high they were. The green substance below her seemed to be bubbling. The rope was digging into her palm, but she didn't dare move her grip.

"How is this even possible?" she asked, tears falling down her face. Aiden looked at her helplessly.

"I think that's acid below us. Cassidy, whatever you do, don't let go."

"I can't hold on forever!" she cried out. "I have to let go soon!"

"No Cassidy! We have to think of something!" Aiden said desperately. Cassidy was freely sobbing now, her gaze on the bright acid below.

"Aiden, we can't, Gabe created this, we're gonna die!"

"No!" Aiden yelled. "I will. I'm not going to let you fall!"

"Aiden… " Cassidy could feel her hands getting sweaty. She pulled up her legs, trying to make herself more secure on the rope. She couldn't let Aiden die for her.

"Maybe we can get out!" Aiden suggested. Cassidy shook her head pitifully.

"There's no place to go! The entire ground is *gone!* Aiden, I can't hold on much longer! I'm going to die!" She gulped, her face contorted in fear and pain. Aiden gripped tighter on his rope as well.

What can you do, Aiden? You are smart. Come on.

Cassidy's rope swayed. She shrieked, digging her nails into the rough material.

"Aiden, I'm going to fall!" she sobbed.

"No you won't!" he responded in the same tone.

"Aiden, my rope is swaying! I have to let go!"

Her vision was blurry, but she couldn't move her hand to wipe her eyes. There was no doubt in her mind that she would fall into the menacing acid below.

Something clicked in Aiden's mind. His teary eyes widened.

"Cassidy, say that again!"

Her terrified expression turned toward him with confusion.

"Huh?"

"What did you just say?"

"I said that my rope was swaying!"

"I have an idea!" Aiden exclaimed excitedly. Cassidy sniffed, and her eyes were covered by her messy dark hair. She would never find the courage to remove one hand and brush it away.

"What's your idea?" Cassidy's hands slid down an inch, making her scream. "And hurry!"

"You know how the ground will come back if the weight on a rope goes away?"

Cassidy nodded, her mouth opening wide in a scream. The acid stayed sizzling below her, and her arms were beginning to ache. "Cassidy, rock your body, then throw yourself onto my rope! I'll catch you, and we'll be safe!" Cassidy looked at him, shocked, through her tears.

"Are you insane!?"

"Well, I'm on this island, aren't I?"

"Aiden, I can't do this!" Her words were slurring now. Aiden looked at her roughly.

"Yes you can Cassidy!"

"Aiden!" she screamed. Her grip was slowly but surely sliding down. Her sobs echoed through the large room. "Gabe, come back!"

Gabe had left for good. He had left them there to die on their own.

"Cassidy!" Aiden bellowed. "Do what I said! One of us is going to die anyway, so we might as well try it!"

"I can't! If I swing, I'm going to fall! My arms are too tired!"

"Cassidy, this is not who you are!" Aiden yelled. "You are a strong person who will do anything to survive! Please just think rationally, ok? I'll grab you when you jump, I promise!"

Cassidy's shaking arms were barely holding on. Her hands were getting much too sweaty, and she knew that she had seconds left.

"Cassidy, now!"

Oh God, please let this work. I don't want to die.

"Aiden," she said softly, her lip trembling. "I'll try. But I'm going to fall. I'm saying goodbye now."

She began to sway her body back and forth, desperately trying to tighten her grip. "Ready?!"

"Yes!" Aiden yelled back. With her eyes set on Aiden, she began to rock harder. Her hands stung, and her legs were trying to grasp the rope.

"I'm going to jump!" she cried out. "Please let this work, Aiden!"

Aiden nodded, his eyes hardening. Cassidy took one single breath before she let herself fly over the acid below.

She shrieked in terror as she put her hands out to grab Aiden's rope.

"Aiden!" She felt her hands wrap around the thick material. Her grip wasn't firm enough, and she began to slide down. Aiden's legs tried to support her, but he couldn't without weakening his grip. He strained as hard as he could to help his friend from dying. Cassidy desperately held onto the rope, the bubbling acid still simmering below.

"Aiden, nothing's happening!"

"I know!" he replied angrily. "I don't know why!" Cassidy's cries became louder and more helpless. Sweat was pouring down her face as she still slid down more.

"AIDEN!" Her voice was hysterical, and the tears blinded her vision. Her fingers were shaking. Her hands slid down. Her mouth opened in a shriek. And she let go.

24

"Cassidy!" Aiden screamed. Cassidy let out an inhuman sound as she fell through the air.

She hit the hard metal ground with a thud. It took her a second to process that the ground had moved as she was falling. With a sob, she let her head drop.

Aiden was breathing deeply as he stared at the ground, his face full of sadness and horror. He was in utter shock that he had survived. He was alive. Cassidy was on the ground in shock. He had never seen her break down like this before.

"Cass?" he asked quietly, walking over to her. Her shoulders were shaking, and he could hear the sounds of despair coming from her mouth.

"T-t-thank you!" she almost yelled. "Your plan worked!"

Aiden weakly struck a pose with his hand on his hip. A smile went across his face.

"Well, I guess I'm smart." He then looked at the floor, realizing something. "Cassidy, we are literally standing on top of the acid. I don't like that." Cassidy nodded, her face growing dark. Her shoulders were now rolling back, and her eyes were drying.

"Neither do I. We need to get out of here."

It was almost as though Gabe could hear them from far away. He slid away the clear wall that he had put in the doorway. It was almost comical the way his face turned as white as a sheet.

"How the *hell* are you two still alive?" His voice didn't come out as a snarl, but rather a shocked whisper. Aiden folded his arms triumphantly.

"We outsmarted you, Gabe." A shadow passed over Gabe's face, causing Aiden to smirk. His arrogant expression had been wiped clean off his pale face.

"That was a one time trap," he whispered to himself fearfully. "I don't know how to make it work again." Gabe stared at the floor with angrily wide eyes. "Grayson," he murmured.

"What, are you afraid of Grayson or something?" Aiden asked.

"I would be. If I failed him, I'd run for the hills," Cassidy told him, beginning to breathe calmly again.

"I will kill you tomorrow," Gabe choked out. "No more contests. I'll just shoot you, I can't fail at that. I don't know how on earth you two brats survived together, but it won't happen again." He took a shallow breath. It was almost disturbing to see Gabe this way. His normally smug eyes were nervously darting to the door. "Let's go back to your chains." He weakly held a piece of metal up, making them walk by force. Aiden grabbed Cassidy protectively as they both walked back proudly to their shackles.

"Ahh!" Hope screamed, startled by Grayson violently swinging open the wooden door.

"I hate to interrupt this little chat," he said mockingly, "but I need Winter."

"Her name's Summer," Ethan piped up, annoyed. Grayson shrugged.

"Yeah, the thing is, I don't really give a damn, boy." He walked stiffly over to the three adults. Summer naturally grabbed tightly onto Ethan's arm. "Oh, and blondie, your friends are in a bit of trouble right now."

"What do you mean?" Hope asked suspiciously. She pushed herself off of the ground roughly. Grayson's mouth went up.

"Yeah, and one of them will die," he said casually. Hope's body seemed to flood with ice.

"What?" Her body was frozen in horror. Her eyes urgently darted to Ethan. *Did you hear him?* she mouthed. Ethan rewarded her with a sad and angry nod. Summer's body pressed up against Ethan's nervously. "Oh, I don't think he'll be able to protect you," said the amused man. "Get up or I will force you to. Your choice."

Summer gulped as she stood up, grudgingly releasing her tight grip. Ethan slightly winced, looking at the large nail marks she left on his wrist. Hope automatically tensed up her body.

"No no blondie, you stay here." Grayson paused, seeming to think better of what he said. "Actually, I want you to come as well. You too, green eyes," he stated happily. Ethan glared at him, his light eyes full of suspicion.

"Why do you want us to come?" he asked. Grayson stared at him, his head tilted.

"Don't question me. Come, or you'll receive the same fate as Winter here." This statement made Summer's eyes grow so large, it looked as though they would fall out.

"W-what do you mean the same fate as me?" she asked, her small hands beginning to quiver. Her previous terrified and helpless state was coming back. Grayson gave her an amused glance, but didn't answer her question.

"Come, children. Follow me." He began to walk out of the depressing room.

"Should we go?" Hope whispered to Ethan. She knew that whatever Grayson wanted, it couldn't be good. He looked at her as he supported the cowering Summer.

"We have to," he whispered back. "You heard him; something bad will happen to us if we don't." Summer looked at the doorway uneasily.

"He's gonna kill me," she choked out. "I just know it. He's gonna kill me." Ethan turned toward her.

"No he won't, Summer." Although his tone was reassuring, his eyes told a different story. He knew that Grayson's happiness meant bad things were coming. Summer couldn't even smile back. Her face had gone white. Her eyes were darting back and forth, and Hope felt stuck to the ground. *At least it's not me,* she thought.

Hope gave a tiny gasp when she realized what she had been thinking. She hated herself for even thinking such a selfish thought.

"You ok there, Hope?" Ethan asked, noticing her movement.

"Yeah, I'm fine," she replied guiltily. A moment later, Grayson's head popped through the doorway.

"You think being slow will keep you alive?" he asked dangerously. "Stop taking so long." Ethan stared at him, fake sadness plastered all over his face.

"Oh, I'm sorry that we are causing so much trouble for you. I mean, we're the ones being threatened and all, but I can see why you're so annoyed."

"Ethan!" Hope gasped. "Don't say that."

"Your girlfriend's right, boy," said Grayson. "I suggest you follow me this time, kids. I won't give you a second chance." He walked out once more. This time, the three of them followed grudgingly. Ethan half led and half dragged Summer forward. He could see it in her eyes that she was already accepting that she was going to die. She could only hope that her death would be quick and painless. Knowing Grayson, though, things were never peaceful.

They all walked down the impossibly large hallway. Hope glanced at the different rooms to the side of her. Although she felt horrible for her friends, it was oddly reassuring to know that they were so close by, even if they were captured against their will. Finally, Grayson slowed down. He came to a stop in front of a big bronze door.

"And we're here," he stated mischievously. Summer gulped nervously as she surveyed the entrance.

"What's behind the door?" Ethan inquired, greatly dreading the answer. Hope slightly bit her lip out of nerves. Even though she knew that this door didn't concern her, she felt terrified looking at Grayson's repulsive grin.

"I want you to guess what's behind it, boy," said the man. "Look at the door, green eyes. What do *you* think could be behind it?" Ethan squinted his eyes, taking in every part of it. He was about to comment when he saw a small swirl. Upon closer inspection, he made it out to be a flame. Ethan gasped when he put two-and-two together.

"Grayson...," he slowly began.

"Yes?" he replied. Grayson's eyes were becoming amused when he saw the answer click in Ethan's brain. Ethan didn't want to say what he knew was behind the door in front of poor Summer, but she deserved to know her fate.

"Is there- is there fire behind the door, Grayson?" he asked. Summer gasped at his question.

"Y-you think there's f-fire behind the door?" she questioned nervously. He sadly nodded his head.

"Yeah. I mean, the door's gold and there's a tiny flame right here," he said, pointing toward the small squiggles engraved on the door.

"Is that your final guess, boy?" asked Grayson, a knowing smile coming to his lips.

Ethan stayed silent, his lips in a thin line.

"Smart boy. Yes, there is something related to fire on the other side of the door. Technically, the flame symbol is representing heat, but same thing, right? On the other side, there's a sauna. But there's a catch! I rigged it so it can go up to deadly heats. Basically, it kills people. It's one of my favorite inventions," he explained. "Think of it as a death sauna, if you will." Summer's round eyes filled with horror as his intentions dawned on her.

"No," she whispered, but she knew he would force her into the room. She helplessly glanced up at Ethan. Glistening tears were pooling in her eyes. Grayson snickered, enjoying her fear.

"Well, Winter, it seems like you know what I'm gonna do. So, go ahead kid. Step inside the room." Without warning, Summer took off down the other end of the hallway. Grayson cursed under his breath as he sprinted after her.

"Oh my god, oh my god," Hope said aloud. "Ethan, he's going to cook her alive." This realization was too disturbing to comprehend. She could feel panic brewing in her system. He calmly put his hand on her shoulder.

"I know, Hope," he said sadly. "But there's nothing we can do. If I try to fight back, he'll put me in there too."

"Ethan?" she asked a minute later.

"Yes?"

"I feel horrible," she admitted. Suddenly, the words began pouring out of the distressed girl. "When we were in the room, I thought about how lucky I was that it wasn't me who was going to die. It was the most selfish thought ever and I feel terrible and guilty and bad and now Summer is going to die in the worst way possible and I-" she broke off, taking a quick breath. Before she could continue, Ethan put his finger to her bloody lip.

"Hope," he whispered. "I had that thought too, ok? I know it seems selfish, and in a way, it is. But it's fine. Anyone would be beyond relieved if they found out that they weren't going to die. Any sane person would be overjoyed that someone else was going to do it instead, and that's ok. You're not a selfish person, Hope," he reassured her. She heaved a heavy sigh as she buried her face in her hands.

They were interrupted by Grayson full-on dragging Summer to the room. She was struggling and screaming, "Please don't let me die! Please!" Ignoring her pleas to survive, Grayson kicked open the door and threw the shouting girl inside. Before she could get out, he quickly slammed the door shut, locking it. Hope could hear her desperately banging on the door, begging to be let out. Hope grabbed Ethan's hand for support. He intertwined his fingers with hers, staring at the floor in pain. Grayson took a few steps over to a thermostat on the wall. He snickered at the two adults gripping onto each other.

"Let's not set it high right now," said an amused Grayson. "Let's make her death slow. You guys make such a great couple when you suffer together." Ethan tore his gaze away from the floor and glared at him.

"Grayson, do you even know how sick and twisted you are? You belong in, like, a mental asylum or something." The man grinned.

"Well, I didn't get put on this island because of my knitting skills." At that moment, Summer's dreadful screams cut off for a second. Grayson looked up happily. "I believe that the heat has kicked in now." The trapped girl's banging had become louder and louder. She knew that she was facing death.

"HELP!" Summer shrieked. The scream was so piercing that it surely must have torn her throat. Hope looked sadly at the sadistic man.

"Grayson, I honestly can't believe what a psycho you are," she said, devoid of emotion. He shrugged.

"Well, what can you do?" He twisted a knob, turning the heat up another notch. Impossibly, the beating against the door became louder. Ethan's expression was more pained that Hope would've thought was possible. Grayson's delighted face soon turned dull.

"Ah, I'm bored of this. Let's make it hotter, shall we?" He twisted the knob far to the right. Hope could only wait for Summer's screams to become louder. Grayson turned his body toward the two friends. "Come on children, let's go back to your prison now," he said happily.

"But Summer…," Hope said half-heartedly. She knew that there was nothing they could do to stop Grayson's sadistic ways. He pointed to the direction of their room.

"Walk," he demanded. He turned back to the thermostat that controlled Summer's life. With a wink in Hope's direction, he savagely turned the knob as far right as it could go. Ethan gasped before he could help it. "Well, she's a goner," Grayson said casually. Hope's mouth fell open in astonishment at his tone. She opened her mouth to speak, but she was stopped by Ethan's firm grip on her arm.

"It's not worth it," he whispered, his eyes shining. Hope sadly nodded. The two slowly took steps away. All they could do was listen to Summer's agonized screams as they walked hand in hand back to their cell.

Hope felt tears pooling in her eyes. Ethan rubbed her shoulder gently.

"It's ok," he reassured softly. Hope shook her head.

"No, it's not. Nothing is ever ok anymore."

Grayson popped his head in joyfully.

"My my, wasn't that just some quality entertainment?" he asked. Hope looked at him, anger taking over her features. His eyes suddenly lit up. His face spread into a smile. "I'll be right back," he said mysteriously. He skipped away making sure to lock the door. Ethan and Hope both locked eyes.

"He looks really excited," Hope observed nervously. Ethan grimly nodded.

"Yeah. I really hope he won't do to us what he did to Summer." Hope tensed up.

The doorknob rattled, causing their eyes to both dart that way. Grayson's face appeared, followed by his large body. He was holding something behind his back, but Hope couldn't see what it was.

"What's that?" Ethan asked, eyeing his back as well. Grayson snickered.

"Something for blondie," he stated. Hope went white. She could feel her heart race faster and faster. Ethan protectively put his hand on her shoulder.

"Nah, I don't think so," he said. Grayson's eyes narrowed dangerously.

"Excuse me? I don't believe I asked you, green eyes. Watch yourself."

"Yeah Ethan, chill," Hope whispered to him. He looked down at her. *Sorry,* he mouthed. Grayson suddenly pulled out his hand from behind him.

Hope's eyes widened. In his hand was a metal baseball bat, the handle wrapped with duct tape.

"What's that for?" she squeaked. Grayson's eyebrow perked up.

"Why don't I show you," he said. Hope's eyes looked desperately back at Ethan. Grayson took a few steps her way. He put the bat tighter in his hand. "Get out of the way, green eyes," he commanded. Ethan shook his head.

"No."

Grayson sighed.

"Whatever. I'll make you leave then."

"Ethan, no!" Hope yelled. She aggressively pulled his hand off her and pushed him to the side with a strength she didn't know she had. He looked at her in surprise.

"Hope, what the hell?!" he exclaimed. She took a deep breath, staring at Grayson.

"He was going to hurt you," she said, as if that explained everything. She gulped at the menacing bat he held so tightly in his hand. "Is that going to kill me?" she asked anxiously. Grayson surprised her as he shook his head.

"Nah, *this* won't kill you," he said.

"Are you implying that something else will?" Ethan yelled from the ground. Grayson pretended to swing the bat, making Ethan flinch in spite of himself. The man laughed joyfully. Hope gulped.

"Is that a yes?"

"We'll see," answered Grayson. "Now blondie, come here." Hope shakily took a few steps towards him.

"What are you doing?" she asked, wiping her sweaty palms on her stained shirt.

"Stand still," he commanded, ignoring her question. She glanced at Ethan on the floor behind her. He was looking at her desperately, knowing that trying to stop Grayson would result in a horrible punishment. He gripped the bat tighter, getting ready to swing.

"Wait!" Hope shouted. Grayson stopped, annoyed.

"*What?!*"

"Well, won't the bat kill me if you swing it hard?" she asked, trying to stall. Grayson shook his head.

"It will only knock you unconscious for a bit," he explained.

"Why do you want me knocked out?" she asked nervously. Grayson grinned an evil smile.

"So I can put you in your death machine."

Hope's mouth dropped open in horror before she could help it.

"No!" Ethan shouted from behind her. Grayson put the bat behind his head. Before Hope could dive to the side, he swung the bat. She felt a crashing pain at the top of her head. It felt like a million hammers were being dropped onto her head. The bat caused a loud *smack* to echo throughout the room.

"Hope!" Ethan yelled. She was still standing, the pounding in her head about to envelop her in darkness. The ground seemed to move below her. Her body swayed, and she collapsed. Ethan lunged toward her.

"No," Grayson snapped. He pointed the bat toward Ethan, making him tense up. "You move, and I swear I will beat you until you die," he growled. "Now back away from her body." Ethan glared at him, but he moved away from the unconscious girl. Grayson smirked. "Very good."

He grabbed Hope's ankles, keeping the bat tightly locked in his hand.

"Where are you taking her?!" Ethan yelled. Grayson's face looked up at him.

"Say bye bye to your friend." He dragged her out into the hallway. Ethan snapped out of his frozen state and lunged at the door. Grayson snorted at his attempt to save Hope. Ethan pulled his hand away just in time to avoid it getting slammed.

"Hope, no," he said feebly, feeling his heart drop to his knees. "Hope."

25

Fire rubbed her temples with her fingers. She had a major headache and her forearm was throbbing crazily. She forced herself to look away from the disgusting sight of it. Swearing had become her number one source of entertainment now.

She was startled by a loud knock on her door.

"What?" she asked viciously. She forced her body off of the ground, curious to see what Gabe or Grayson could want.

"Hello, Sapphire," Gabe cooed as he walked into the doorway. "Sleep well?" Fire felt her blood boil.

"Gabe, just tell me what you want or get out. I'm tired of your crap." Gabe raised his eyebrows in a smirk.

"I can see why you'd be tired. I actually have someone who wants to meet you." Fire looked at him hesitantly.

"Who?"

Gabe pointed behind him, and Blisse walked through. A chill went throughout Fire's body. "What does she want?"

Gabe's light eyes twinkled.

"She only wants to talk to you, Sapphire. Surely you won't deny her such a little request." Fire huffed a sigh as she crossed her arms.

"Fine."

"Well, I wasn't exactly asking for your permission," Gabe said condescendingly. Fire rolled her eyes. Blisse's eyes looked around as she walked into Fire's prison.

"So, Blisse, what do you want?" Fire wasn't exactly in a terrified state at the moment. Her headache was raging and she wanted to punch Grayson more than anything. Blisse's eyes looked like deep pits as she sat down across from Fire.

"I want to talk to you." Blisse's voice was so calm that it really was unsettling. Fire put her head into her hands.

"Well, just talk. It hurts my head when I talk." From the corner of her eye, Fire saw Blisse hold back a grin.

"Oh, is your sleep deprivation getting to you? My sincerest apologies." Fire was in such a mood that she didn't even snarkily reply back. Her pounding mind just wanted to fall asleep.

"What do you want Blisse? Why are you here?"

"I want to talk about your dad," she answered. Fire felt her body tense up. Her arms went rigid at her side. She momentarily ignored her pain as her head snapped up.

"What about him?"

"What was it like?" Blisse asked mischievously. "What was it like to be terrified of your own home each day?"

"Shut up," Fire snapped. Her breathing seemed to speed up in anger. Blisse just chuckled.

"What was it like when your mom died? What was it like when you watched the knife enter her throat?"

"Stop it." Fire's voice came out as more of a growl than actual words. "I know what you're trying to do, and it won't work."

"What am I trying to do?" Blisse asked innocently. Fire just stared at her.

"If you're not going to have an actual conversation with me, you can get out."

"That was quite bold, little gemstone. I think I will leave. I have better things to do. Have fun staying awake!" Blisse got up effortlessly and walked out the door. Gabe was leaning against the wall, smirking.

"Wow Sapphire, something happened to your mom? Tell me about it!"

"OUT!" Fire screamed. Her shriek made a wave of pain erupt in her head. Gabe put his hand through his hair.

"No, I don't think I will."

Without thinking, Fire angrily got up. She stomped over to the smugly grinning Gabe with fury.

"Get out of here, *now*. Or I swear, I will kill you." Gabe raised his eyebrows.

"Do you swear on your mother's grave?" Fire gave him a look that was full of pure fury. Laughing, Gabe stepped out and shut the door. For no reason, tears gathered in her eyes. She sat down on the ground, sniffing. Fire was plain miserable. With a sniff, she rested her head on the wall.

Haylee's eyes opened. Dark spots filled her vision and everything was fuzzy. Painfully, she moved her head to the side. She saw a beautiful girl with brown hair crying, chained up next to her. She saw a blonde girl with her fingers in the hole of a lock. Her features were rough with anger and desperation. Worst of all, she saw a girl with black eyes. Her hair matched in an incredible but awful way.

Where am I? Who is she? A small sigh escaped her mouth. The pretty brunette girl's head turned in her direction. Her rich brown eyes seemed to grow.

"Haylee?"

She didn't know who she was talking to. Her auburn eyes grew wide as to say *who, me?* The brown haired girl nodded, her teary eyes looking confused.

"Haylee, you're ok!" Her voice came out in a whisper. She was probably whispering because of the scary black eyed girl. "Oh, Hope's going to be so happy!"

Haylee's eyebrows scrunched up.

"Who?"

The stranger's face seemed to fall all at once. Her bloody lips opened in horror.

"No. No, no, no." Her eyes opened wide in urgency. "What's your name?"

Haylee shrugged, still taking in the room that she seemed to be trapped in. She realized that she was chained up as well, and a horrible pain filled her head. The brunette girl's breathing seemed to speed up. "You don't remember, do you?"

"Remember what?" Before the dark haired girl could reply, the darkness claimed Haylee again.

Ethan pounded against his door. He could only imagine what crazy contraption Grayson had created for Hope.

"Let me out!" he screamed hysterically. "Somebody help!" He knew that his shouts were pointless. None of his friends could get free with the freaky new Blisse watching them with those ebony eyes. He kicked the door angrily, swearing at the pain in his foot. "Get me out of here!"

Hope couldn't die. She couldn't. She couldn't die without saying goodbye to Haylee. If he hadn't said goodbye to Carter, he would've gone crazy. He slapped the wall, angry tears blurring his vision.

"No, no, no!" He grabbed the knob aggressively, turning it back and forth. He heard a click. "What the hell?" he wondered aloud. He pulled the knob. The door swung open.

That's not possible. That's not possible.

There's no way Grayson would have forgotten to lock the door.

Or did he?

After all, he was dragging Hope. Could he have forgotten to lock Ethan in? No, there's gotta be some guard watching me right now. Grayson wouldn't be that idiotic.

Hesitantly, Ethan took a step out into the hall. His head whipped around nervously, looking for any source of some guard. Nobody was there. This is impossible.

Well, was it really that impossible? Was it possible that Grayson could have forgotten him just this one time? Ethan looked around once more. Then, he took off sprinting down the long hallway.

He thought about screaming Hope's name. Ethan was just about to when he remembered that she was knocked out. And if Grayson heard him, he would never have this chance again. He walked past Summer's death sauna and felt acid rise from his stomach. He walked past door after door, realizing that his friends could be held captive in any one of these rooms. One of the doors was cracked open. Huh, that's odd. He continued on his way.

Ethan almost slapped himself for being so stupid. It was open! That's where Hope had to be! As quiet as a cat, he tiptoed to the door. Silently, his eye peeked through the crack. He saw Grayson there, tying Hope up. That was enough for him. Ethan debated whether he should just storm in or not.

Come on Ethan, think rationally! he firmly told himself. If he just ran in there, he didn't think he could overpower Grayson, especially when his dangerous bat was just out of reach from him. Angrily, Ethan backed up. He needed to figure out a plan! At least Hope was safe for now.

Come on Ethan, what can you do? The word *gun* popped into his mind. A gun! That's what he needed! Grayson's bat was no match for a bullet.

"Ok, where can you find a gun?" Ethan asked himself aloud. He continued along, quietly testing each door's knob. He knew where Grayson was at the moment, so he wasn't worried about him. If Gabe found him, he could probably take him in a fight. It was the thought of Blisse that almost made him freeze. She was a demon now.

No Ethan, don't worry about that right now. Hope is your number one priority, not Blisse. Where can you get a gun? He kept testing the doors, looking for anything that would help him keep Hope alive.

He couldn't believe his luck. A flutter of joy went through his veins. A large supply closet of weapons wasn't locked. For a moment, he wondered if this was Grayson's punishment for him. Maybe he was still locked in his room in some sort of coma, dreaming all of this.

No, that's not true. This is real. You need to play the hero this time, Ethan.

Ethan slowly walked in, his eyes still darting around, making sure that he was in fact still alone. Quickly, he scouted around. *Ok, gun, gun, gun, where are you?* He found a large butcher knife, multiple nail bombs, and even some old fashioned muskets. *Come on, where is a pistol?*

A pile of small daggers caught his eye. He slid a couple into his pockets for safekeeping.

Finally, he found a small pistol. It was a perfect fit in his hand. Ethan couldn't stop the smile of triumph that spread across his face.

Gotcha, Grayson.

26

Hope slowly opened her eyes. The first thing she felt was a horrible throbbing pain in her head. A million knives were in her brain, they had to be. With a groan, she tried to look around, but her vision was too fuzzy to see anything right.

Bracing for the pain that she knew would come, she went to sit up. Hope was pulled back down to the ground. Her already pounding head smacked against the concrete floor. Her pain-filled mind faintly comprehended that she was tied down. Hope had no idea why she was restrained, but she knew that it couldn't be good. The girl pulled as hard as she could, trying to release her hands. Hope wouldn't accept the fact that her efforts would get her nowhere.

"Somebody help me!" she yelled, not really knowing what was going on. Her eyes were desperately darting all around, hoping to see anything that would get her out of her restraints. Hope's struggling coasted to a stop when she noticed a shape on the ceiling. A feeling of dread was slowly but surely seeping through her veins. If she squinted her eyes, she could faintly tell that the shape was directly over her middle. Her thoughts were interrupted when she heard the slow creak of an opening door. She quickly moved her eyes to the source of the sound. Hope felt her heart speed up in anger when Gabe walked through.

"Well hi there, gorgeous. Having fun there?" he asked. She gave him her best glare, her vision finally coming into focus. She remembered that the awful pain in her head was given to her by Grayson's bat. "I see that you're a bit tied down for the moment!" He laughed crazily at his own joke, his brown eyes looking at her up and down.

"Gabe," she said flatly. "You are a sick, sick person." He shook his head.

"Nah, don't call me sick," he said. "There's not a cure for me." Hope raised her eyebrows. She swore she heard the smallest, smallest change in his voice. It wasn't much, but it was something.

"Gabe?" she asked, her tone slightly suspicious. "Is there something you want to talk about?" He looked at her as though she was the most stupid person on the Earth.

"You know, you are a very idiotic person, gorgeous."

"Then what do you want?" He gave her that same expression.

"Is it that hard to put two-and-two together?" He pointed toward the threatening shape above her. Hope gave him an odd look.

"Well, Gabe, I don't know what that thing is. You see, my head is very sore from a bat." She tried to keep her tone under control, but it was hard when Gabe's smug expression wouldn't leave her eyes. He wiggled his eyebrows.

"It's a saw, gorgeous. Are my hints enough for your meager brain?" She gulped, her eyes looking nervously back up.

What the…

Suddenly, it clicked in her pulsing mind.

Oh my god oh my god oh my god, she thought in hysterical, crazy-making fear. *This is not happening. This is not happening.*

He nodded his head when he saw the realization dawn in her eyes. Hope's face went whiter than it had ever been. She was more scared than the countless times that she had seen needles, more scared than when Haylee had forced her to go skydiving, more scared than anything she had ever done. When those times had happened, she always knew she would survive. But this, this she couldn't survive.

"Gabe… please don't do this," she begged him, her voice soft. He shook his head, a terrible smile coming to his face.

"No Hope, I don't think I will listen to you." Hope could feel her heart race as she waited for the saw to start. She could only hope that her death wouldn't be as painful as he wanted it to be.

"Hey, Gabe, why do you even want to kill me?" she asked, making any attempt to stall. "I'm just a girl, and I haven't done anything to you." He put his finger to his chin.

"This is my challenge," he said finally. Now she was confused.

"What do you mean challenge?"

"Well, Grayson wanted me to do this for a while now," he stated, thinking that this was clearly implied. Hope squinted her eyes.

"What do you mean for a while now?" she asked, genuinely curious.

"Well, since you're going to die anyway, I guess it couldn't hurt to let you know." He grinned mischievously. "I've been forced to keep silent all my life. Screw that."

Gabe leaned on the wall with one shoulder.

"Ever since I was a kid, I was trained in self-defense. I guess my parents knew I would be considered dangerous. I mean, it wasn't that hard to tell. I bullied kids and was out of school more than I was in it. Anyway, I guess the government somehow found me. I honestly have no idea how. I guess it isn't too hard for them to find a way to spy on you. When I was 10, they asked me to train with them. I learned how to take down anyone. I also learned how to find people's weaknesses. I know your weakness, gorgeous." She was savagely biting on her lip.

"What's my weakness, then?" she inquired. He chuckled as he shook his head.

"If you know what it is, you could change it, and then where would I be? The government liked me, and they knew I would test as dangerous. Guess what they did, Hope," he commanded. She laid there in silence, looking at the ceiling."They implanted a metal chip in my ear." He raised his eyebrows, turning to the side. "They've been talking to me, gorgeous, telling me who the smarties I gotta kill are. You are one of them."

Hope forgot to be angry for a moment. She was a target? Why Hope? She wasn't dangerous, was she?

"But why? I'm not even special!"

"Yeah, that's what I thought too, when I first met you. But I guess they know what they're doing. Can you guess who else is on my nice little kill list?" She was about to speak when he put up his hand. "Ethan," he stated with a smirk. Hope gasped.

"It's funny, because almost everyone else in your little group are targets too. When I found you, I couldn't believe that all of you were in one place. It was a jackpot, gorgeous. I-"

"Wait," Hope cut him off.

"What do you want?"

"Well, if you were meant to 'get rid of us' then why didn't you just do it? I mean, if you were trained, as you say, then surely you could've just taken one of us by surprise."

"Yeah, I thought of that," he replied. "But if one of you were somehow excellent at combat, you might've been able to fight me. And then you would kill me. I had to earn your trust first." Now it was Hope's turn to snort.

"Yeah, well, you didn't do a good job of that. We all couldn't stand you, Gabe." She stopped immediately, realizing too late that he was the one in charge of her death. If he was offended by her comment, he could start the weapon right away. Luckily, he didn't seem to notice her insult.

"Yup, don't worry, I couldn't stand any of you either. But it was my mission, I had to get you guys to trust me. After a while, though, it was clear that no one was exactly fighting to like me."

Maybe it's because you're an annoying son of a gun who degrades people, Hope thought silently.

"I decided that it was time for plan b," Gabe continued. "While you idiots were asleep, I came over to this shack to talk to Grayson about what we needed to do. He agreed, obviously. And now, here we are. I'm all caught up. Can you guess what the next part of the plan is?"

Hope knew what it was, but there was no way she would say it out loud; that would be like accepting her death, and she *wasn't* ready to die. She clamped her mouth shut, and Gabe knew what she was thinking.

"Yes, Hope, you are going to die. You might as well accept it. It's gonna happen. The best part is, I get to watch. I get to watch the light leave your eyes. Not Grayson, not Blisse, *me.* Now, Hope, I'll just go pull on the lever. Are you ready to die, pretty?" Hope shook her head, tears pooling in her radiant eyes. He got up and began to walk to the saw's lever.

"Hold on, Gabe!" she called desperately. He snapped his head around.

"*What?*" He crossed his arms impatiently.

"Well," she said, "doesn't it seem wrong to you?" Gabe narrowed his eyes.

"What seems wrong?"

"Well, just the whole thing. I mean, the idea of an island full of psychos is just… terrifying! What makes you want to do this? Does it bring you joy? Does it make you happy when other people suffer? If it does, you are far beyond help, Gabe. I hope you know that." Gabe sighed theatrically.

"No gorgeous, it's not terrifying. What better way to get rid of a threat than to send them off to get killed? It's better to execute the smart people so they don't start an uprising. If you think about it, it makes perfect sense." Hope's mouth hung open, not believing that he could be serious.

"Gabe, you're not listening to me! Basically, what you're doing is showing that killing is wrong… by killing. It does not make perfect sense. Actually, it's quite twisted and horrible. Just think about how many people you have killed. Doesn't that get under your skin at all? Or do you just think '*Oh, there goes another life!*'? I mean, seriously, the whole concept of it is just creepy." Hope was beginning to feel afraid that his mind was completely clouded by logic. He shrugged.

"No Hope, you're not listening to me. The island plan is perfectly sensible and logical. In a way, I'm actually protecting the world by getting rid of threats. You are the one who's twisted if you think that threats should just roam around out there freely. Really gorgeous, have a brain." Gabe started to walk again. "It makes me a hero, Hope. Something you'll never be." He snorted. "And I think it's great to watch you guys suffer. That's an added bonus."

"That's so sad," she observed. Gabe paused his movement.

"What's so sad?" he asked. Hope gave him a look full of sympathy.

"It's sad that you think what you're doing is ok. It's sad that to us, you're a villain, but in your mind, you're a hero." He looked at her blankly.

"Your point is?"

"My point is that you used to stand a chance. Now, you're a lost cause, Gabe." She half-heartedly struggled. "And that's the sad part. You had potential." He glared at her.

"I don't remember hiring a therapist," he snapped. "Now gorgeous, *shut up.*" Hope began to hyperventilate in fear. There was nothing to say that would convince Gabe of anything. Her eyes looked into his with urgency.

"Gabe, please, please, I'll do anything for you!" she pleaded. He raised one side of his mouth.

"You are a coward, gorgeous. You beg so pitifully. It's quite funny, actually."

"So, Gabe, how will the saw work?" she questioned, desperately clinging to any source of stalling her death. He rolled his eyes.

"Well, Hope, the saw will start spinning. Then, it will begin to lower," he explained in an obvious voice. "I'd say that in 60 seconds, it will reach your body." He reached for the lever, but pulled his hand back. "And just so you know, gorgeous, this will hurt. A lot." He winked his light brown eye at her as he dramatically pulled down on the lever.

Hope's breath caught in her throat as the saw made a grinding noise. The fear that she was feeling was threatening to make her absolutely insane. Then, it started to spin. She saw it drop a few centimeters each second. Gabe walked over to her, savoring the fear that was surely all over her face.

"Now, we wait." He made himself comfortable as he stared into her terrified eyes. "You know, Hope, you really are hot. It's a shame that you have to die." Hope struggled against her bonds, causing her wrists to burn from the tight rope.

"ETHAN!" she shrieked, bordering on hysteria. "ETHAN, CASSIDY, FIRE, HELP!" She screamed, her mind filling with panic. Gabe chuckled, moving his dark hair with his hand.

"Oh, Hope, they can't help you. They are dying in their own ways. In fact, I chose the way each of them will die. Would you like to know your friend's fates? They're not at all pleasant." Hope gave him a glare full of all the hatred she owned.

"I'd say you have about 30 seconds left. You know, the funny thing is that if I wanted to, I could just flip the lever, and you could live. But do you wanna know the even funnier thing? I won't!" He laughed sadistically. "Anything you'd like to say before you are sliced open?" Hope was now blinded by tears.

"Gabe, please," she begged helplessly. She knew he wouldn't budge. Gabe moved closer and pushed a strand of blonde hair out of her face.

"20 seconds," he whispered.

All of a sudden, she heard the door fly open. Hope tried to blink away the tears as Gabe shot up. Finally, she could see clearer than she had a few seconds ago. She looked over, and her heart stopped with joy. Ethan was standing there, a weary expression on his face.

"No," Gabe whispered in terrifying fury. Hope's friend grinned in relief.

"Yes." Ethan whipped out a pistol from his back pocket. "Now move or I'll shoot." His green eyes were set on the lever. Gabe's eyes darkened.

"No, I won't move. Hope is going to die no matter what," he said dangerously. Ethan just shook his head.

"If you say so, Gabe." Without another breath, Ethan shot the adult in his leg. Gabe screamed as he fell, covering the wound with his hand. Hope looked up, and her heart stopped again, but for a different reason. The saw was almost against her skin.

"ETHAN, HURRY!" she shrieked. He looked at her for a split second and dashed to the lever. He pulled it up, but it wouldn't budge. Her tears were coming back.

"Ethan..." With one final effort, he yanked up the lever. This time, his sudden strength worked, and the saw stopped just above her skin. Gabe was on the ground, his face turning whiter by the second. Ethan was panting hard from the effort it took. Hope was crying again, this time out of pure happiness.

"Ethan, thank you so much, thank you!" She stumbled over her words, trying to stop the flow of her tears. He put his hand on his hip.

"No problemo, Hopie. Now, let's get you out of these restraints, shall we?" She nodded as he walked over, kicking Gabe hard in the shoulder. Hope knew she looked like a total mess. She was sniffing as he pulled a dagger from his pocket and cut through the ropes. First, he freed her hands. Then, he moved on to her ankles. Finally, Hope was free to move again. The only thing she did was pull Ethan into a tight hug.

"Thank you," she said into his ear. He replied with something that she couldn't make out, but she swore that she heard the word love.

"Now," he said. "Let's go get our friends back." Hope was still shaking as she took her first step. Regardless of the inhumane thing Gabe had just tried to do to her, Hope felt a jolt of guilt as she looked at him writhing on the floor. For a moment, they locked eyes. Hope noticed a tiny tear trickling down his cheek.

"I'm sorry, Gabe," she whispered. "I'm sorry for what you've become."

Hope turned to Ethan and they rushed out of the door, leaving Gabe to bleed on the floor.

All Gabe could feel was pain. He didn't think he'd ever be able to use that leg again. He touched it gently and winced at the sudden shock it sent through his body.

"Grayson!" he called. Nobody appeared at the doorway. "Oh, for the love of...," he muttered. "GRAYSON!" he screamed again, as loud as his voice allowed. He heard the sound of rushing footsteps in the hallway. Grayson stood in the room, an expression of annoyment on his face.

"What?" he whined. He took a few small steps forward.

"Ethan shot me in the leg," Gabe said, attempting to keep his voice steady through the pain. The glow in Grayson's face turned ominous. His eyes narrowed dangerously as he took another step.

"What do you mean he shot you?" he growled. "I thought that you were executing Hope with the saw, not playing games with green eyes." Gabe laughed weakly.

"Hope was almost dead, but he barged in and shot my leg," he explained. "I wasn't playing games." The only person that Gabe would never dare talk back to was Grayson. He hadn't even scraped the surface of all the horrible things this man was capable of. "I'm sorry," he apologized. Grayson was standing like a statue in the doorway.

"And where did they go?" he asked, taking yet another step. Gabe shrugged and winced at any movement in his body. Grayson chuckled, but it was far from amused. "Oh Gabe, you'll be sorry alright. You better pray to your god that they don't escape from this shack. If I don't find them, I'll put you right under this saw." Gabe gulped, beginning to feel a growing amount of fear. "Now," he said, "let's go see where they're hiding." Grayson turned to walk out of the door.

"Wait!" Gabe called desperately. "My leg!" The man turned around.

"Walk it off," he sneered. He dashed out the doorway and turned to the right.

"But… but my leg," he said feebly. Gabe looked down and felt a large wave of nausea pass over him. He could see part of his bone through the dark, maroon blood that was spilling out of his wound. Gabe knew that he would never be able to use his right leg again. He decided to test the ability of his other leg. Slightly trembling, the adult rose to his single knee.

Ok Gabe, you are going to stand up.

Taking a deep breath, he moved his uninjured leg to take a step.

"Ahh!" he screeched, falling right back to the ground. He swore up a storm. Gabe decided against calling for Grayson; after all, he had promised to saw him in half. The muscles in his face tensed up. *No Gabe, you are not going to cry,* he commanded himself. *You're not weak.* He glanced at his bloody limb once more. The concrete walls blurred together as he felt the water in his eyes overflow.

Oh god, he thought. *What have you done?*

In a matter of minutes, he was weeping freely. The injury in his leg was only a small part of his incomprehensible sadness. A lifetime of holding back tears was finally, finally letting go.

He screamed, letting out his anger in a shrill sound of pure pain. The blood was pooling in a terrible puddle on the rough floor. Gabe was unable to stop the sobs racking through his body, his breaths coming out in short gasps. His blotchy face was scrunched up as his leg was losing a deadly amount of blood.

His body swayed.

The room was becoming more blurry and dark by the minute. Gabe touched his hand to his leg, gagging when he pulled it back. His entire hand was covered in the awful shade of crimson blood. He began to shiver, his body becoming covered in goosebumps. His damaged mind formed four simple words: *I want to die.*

Gabe heard the faint sound of footsteps running in the room. He could faintly make out Grayson's shape in his blurred vision.

"Gabe," he panted, his eyes contorting into dark slits. "What have you done?"

"They got away?" he asked, surprised at the weakness in his voice. Grayson walked dangerously over to his shaking body on the floor. With one swift motion, he savagely kicked Gabe's wounded leg. He screamed, feeling a pain that he had never imagined. It felt like nails were being driven into his skin. White-hot nails that were dipped in acid and ripping his nerves apart. He swallowed, his flowing tears coming to a stop.

"I'm going to kill you," whispered Grayson. Gabe weakly shook his head. *Do it,* he thought to no one. He faintly knew that by now, his loss of blood was too much. He was beyond the point of being saved. Gulping, Gabe slammed his head on the concrete ground. He groaned, but this pain was miniscule compared to the flaring agony in his leg. Before Grayson could stop him, he brought his head back up and bashed it once more. The man roughly grabbed Gabe by his arms.

Grayson dragged him down the impossibly long hallway like a limp rag doll. In a part of his mind that was filled with pain beyond endurance, Gabe knew the route Grayson was taking. He was bringing him to the room where Summer had been burned.

"You're gonna burn me," he whispered in sudden fear. Grayson shot a glance downward.

"I don't have time for that, boy," he growled. "I have plans to be carried out."

They reached the room that could be turned into an oven. Grayson threw Gabe roughly in with his leg excruciatingly rubbing against the floor. Summer's body was there, charred to the bone. Grayson glared at him, true rage plastered across his face.

"You could have lived if you weren't so stupid, Gabriel. You could have lived."

"It's too bad your ugly face is the last thing that I'll see," Gabe weakly chuckled from the floor.

"Still sarcastic, even as you're dying," Grayson said with a roll of his eyes.

With one last final effort, Gabe strained his head to look at his injury. He saw a trail of crimson blood leading from the saw. He felt a strange sense of peace when he looked at the mangled mess that was his leg.

With one last, deep breath, Gabe threw his head on the floor. This time, he didn't bring it back up. The room was filled with darkness as Grayson closed the door for the last time.

27

"In here Hope!" Ethan exclaimed, firmly grabbing her shaking wrist. She quickly turned and practically threw herself in the closet that Ethan ran in. Hope winced, her hand scraping against the jagged edge of a door knob. Ethan slammed the door shut. "Try to control your breathing," he whispered. She nodded, gasping for air. Moments of silence went by as they carefully listened for footsteps. "Hope, are you ok?" he suddenly asked. She shrugged.

"Yeah, I'm fine," she replied quietly. "If you would've been just 5 seconds later, it would have been too late." She shivered, remembering the horror of seeing the saw directly on top of her. "Hey, Ethan, how did you get me?" she asked. "How did you escape?"

"It's a long story," he warned. She shrugged.

"I got time."

"Well, ok. So Grayson forgot to lock the door after he dragged you out. I escaped and then came into this closet. I picked up a gun and saved you." Ethan chuckled. "Well, I guess it wasn't long at all."

"Do you think we could save our other friends?" Hope couldn't stop the hopefulness that had crept into her voice. Ethan looked at her intently.

"I don't know," he finally said. "I really don't."

"Well, at least you're honest with me. So what do we do now?"

Moments of silence passed. Ethan's gaze kept snapping between Hope and the weapons located in the closet. "Ethan," Hope said, waving her hand in his face. "What do we do now?"

"Blisse!" he said suddenly. Hope shook her head.

"Nope, I'm Hope." Ethan didn't even seem to notice her comment. Hope's eager expression contorted into an odd look.

"Ethan, I'm just kidding. What about her?"

"Blisse," he said again, in the same surprised tone. Hope cocked an eyebrow.

"Ethan, tell me what's going on in your head. What's your plan?"

"This must be where Blisse gets her guns! Let's destroy these weapons so she can't!" Hope snorted before she could help it.

"Ethan, I don't think that's really possible. But maybe we can break out!"

Ethan's expression turned full of disbelief.

"Hope, the weapons idea was crazy, you're right. Your idea pretty much is insane. How in the world could we possibly break out?"

"I don't know," Hope retorted, feeling stupid. "I wish we had a key or something. Then we could get out."

Ethan's eyes suddenly got huge. Without warning, he grabbed Hope's arms in a hug.

"Hope, I could just kiss you!" he exclaimed. Hope chuckled, feeling blood rush to her face.

"Why exactly is that?"

"I saw a set of keys in here before I got you! I didn't think anything of it, but I hid them so Grayson didn't have them!" He released Hope gently as he dashed to the corner. "It's right here," he mumbled to himself. Ethan popped up, a large smile spread across his face. "These have got to be an extra set or something. I think it will work!"

Hope's face spread into a smile as well.

"Ethan, that's great!" She then had a thought that made her smile waver a fraction. "Wait, when will we do it? Grayson will find out that you escaped soon enough. What do we do?"

Ethan's twinkling eyes seemed to dim a little.

"You're right." His voice had lost some of its previous enthusiasm. "Well, maybe we can just stay in here for a while. Who knows, maybe Grayson thinks we escaped outside. That might buy us some time." There was uncertainty evident in his voice. Hope nodded encouragingly.

"Yeah, that makes sense. I guess we can stay here." She decided not to ask what would happen if Grayson found them in here. She gave him a quick smile as she began gathering daggers.

Grayson ran through the hall, feeling an anger that he had never felt before. His vision was red as he bounded into the room where his victims were being held. Belle looked up, her eyebrows scrunching together. She shot a confused look Aiden's way. Blisse's dark eyes looked up in annoyment.

"Yes?" she asked. Grayson's fists were clenched as he glared at Blisse.

"Green eyes and blondie escaped."

Aiden felt a jolt of triumph when he heard Grayson speak those words. Belle suppressed the arrogant smile that threatened to spread across her face. Blisse's look of frustration went away as quick as a wink. Her face contorted into a look of disbelief.

"No." She said the word simply as she walked to the middle. Grayson nodded roughly.

"Yes, they did. Gabe failed us." Blisse was fuming.

"He failed us," she repeated. Cassidy pursed her lips to keep from smiling. *That's right,* she thought smugly, *Ethan outsmarted you.*

"Well, what will we do now?" Blisse asked quietly. Grayson's eyes darted to Belle. She quickly moved her gaze to the ground, her face getting hot.

"Just kill that one," Grayson demanded to Blisse. Although Belle wasn't looking up at them, she just knew that his finger was pointing at her. Blisse's anger seemed to dim as she walked over and unlocked Belle's chains.

"Don!" Grayson screamed viciously. A middle aged man ran through the door with a gun in his hands.

"Grayson?" he asked. Belle knew that he must be yet another guard. "I'm going to go find green eyes," Grayson snarled. "Blondie too. Kill this girl."

"Which plan?" Don asked. Blisse grabbed Belle's wrist, digging her nails into her skin. Grayson put his hand on his chin for a moment.

"Plan X," he finally said. Don nodded thoughtfully. "Room 15."

The guard ripped Belle from Blisse and put her hands behind her back. Panic and fear filled Belle's mind as he prodded her ahead.

Ok Isabelle, what can you do? She knew that she couldn't struggle, at least right now.

"So how will I die?" she asked, making sure that her voice sounded innocent and oblivious. The man rewarded her with silence. "Come on man, I'll be dead in less than an hour. Just tell me how I'll die. It won't really make a difference."

Don sighed, using one hand to scratch his slightly gray hair.

"Ok, I guess so," he finally said reluctantly. Belle knew that he was scared of Grayson. Maybe that's why she could hear the rapid beat of his heart.

"So, child, have you ever heard of anthrax?" Belle looked at him oddly. She had read about that so many months ago.

"Yeah, I think so. Why?" She didn't remember much, but she did remember that it was a type of bacteria that did something weird to the lungs. Don paused, causing Belle to almost stumble.

"Well, that's what the room is full of," he said. "There's anthrax all over the floor. Once you breathe it in, your lungs will swell up. I think you know what happens then."

Despite her plans to run, she felt chills erupt on her skin.

"And did you come up with that?" Her voice was still sounding high pitched and ditzy.

"Gabriel actually did," Don replied. "Grayson got the bacteria. How, I don't know." He continued on his walk, pushing Belle forward roughly. They moved in silence. Finally, they neared the door located the farthest down the hallway.

"Isn't that kind of dangerous?" Belle asked. "You know, keeping deadly bacteria in a room in this house?" Don shrugged.

"That's why it's the farthest down."

Belle took a couple more steps as she looked at the door. There was a squiggly shape on the door, probably meant to show what this room contained. Belle was still held captive in the man's strong grip.

"I'm going to get the keys out now," Don told her. Belle nodded, but she was thinking of her plan. *Come on Belle, you'll be fine.* If her plan didn't work, she would inhale the anthrax and suffocate to death on her own lungs. It didn't escape her that this man was much larger and stronger than she was. Her own 5 '10 height wasn't a match for his higher than 6 feet. *No, come on Belle. If Sapphire, who's a pipsqueak, can punch someone, you can too.* Belle's body was much more filled out than Fire, so at least she had that small advantage.

Don used one hand to hold her tighter as he dug in his pocket for the key. Belle took a deep breath. *You have one shot. This is your chance.*

Suddenly, Belle's right foot slammed into Don's kneecap. He screeched in pain, his knee giving out. Belle twisted her body out of his grasp so that her face was facing his. She roughly dug her fingers into his eye, not allowing herself to listen to his screams. She kneed him in the gut and kicked his other knee angrily. Finally, Don fell onto the ground, groaning. Belle leaped down and aggressively snatched the key from his hand.

"That's what you get for messing with me," she growled. Her voice was no longer high and naive but her normal snarl. She jabbed the key once into his eye, most likely permanently blinding him. Belle almost hysterically unlocked the door, careful to gulp in a huge amount of air before it was opened. She grabbed his shoulders and pushed him into the room, part of his head smacking on the edge of door.

Don looked up at her, but this time his eyes were wide and desperate. Grimly, Belle realized that's how almost everyone she met looked when they knew they were going to die.

"Wait!" he cried out. He knew the effects of anthrax better than anyone, probably. With regret tugging at her heart, she shook her head.

"Bye, Don." She slammed the door shut, relocking the door. Belle took a breath, thankful that she hadn't breathed in any of the germs. She could still hear Don pounding on the door as she walked sadly back down the hallway.

"Blondie, get out here!" Grayson screamed viciously. He heard some pounding on the door to his right. Excitedly, he ripped open the door. Instead, he came face to face with a very angry Fire.

"What do you want?" he snapped impatiently. "I need to get green eyes, and you're wasting my time. Don't pound on the damn door again."

"Wait!" Fire screeched. She felt a dagger of pain shoot through her head when she screamed. The look in Grayson's eyes was enough to make her blood turn to ice. "I can help you! Please," she begged. "I'll help you find them if you can let me sleep, I swear I will." Grayson looked at her with confusion.

"And why should I let you when I have multiple guards?" Fire didn't have an answer to that. Grayson smirked as he said, "Exactly."

Before he could shut the door again, a man came bounding down the hall, gasping.

"Grayson, Grayson!"

"Spit it out!" Grayson demanded. The guard was catching his breath, looking up nervously.

"That one girl who was with Don... she got away."

Grayson's eyes turned as dark as a storm.

"She got away? As in... escaped?" The guard nodded cautiously. Grayson stared him down for what seemed like forever. Without warning, Grayson's hands shot out on the man's neck. With a swift twist of his hands, the man dropped dead. Grayson looked back at Fire, who was slumped against the wall tiredly.

"Come with me, girly," he snarled, grabbing her arm. "Find your friends, and I'll take off the patch. Let them escape, and I swear I will drill that damn patch into your skin. Find them. Now." He moved out of the way allowing Fire to walk out.

"Wait, don't you have Blisse with you?"

"Well, of course," Grayson said, rolling his eyes. "But she's out of the shack for the day and night. She's looking for other people to bring here; I have a lot of plans that I want carried out." Fire nodded, but the words felt like a knife to the brain. The pounding in her head seemed to turn her vision blurry. Thinking made her mind want to shut down, but Grayson had given her an offer that she couldn't refuse. She had to find Ethan.

Fire groaned loudly as she forced herself to move down the hall. Grayson had shoved some keys into her hand, and she used those on each of the doors. He had left Fire to find Hope and Ethan while Grayson was looking for the girl who escaped. Fire didn't know who the girl was, but she hoped that whoever it was was ok.

She opened up an orange door. Inside was a girl on the ground. Her skin looked... odd. It looked red and blotchy and *off*. Fire forced herself to investigate the room. The girl lying on the floor had no pulse, as Fire had to figure out the hard way. With a moan, she peeled her eyes open more. The girl on the floor's eyes were closed, and the skin on her hands looked shriveled up. The word *burn* came to mind. Her skin looked bubbly and papery up close. Thinking she was just hallucinating, Fire waved the thought away as she walked out of the room.

"Ethan, how many weapons do you need?" Hope asked jokingly. He hadn't stopped hiding the sharp daggers for the last five minutes. Ethan snickered.

"Well, you can never be too prepared, huh Hopie?" He finally stopped his frantic movement. "The door is locked, right?"

"Yep," she replied. For added effect, she jiggled the door knob. "See? We're good for now." She paused. "Unless Grayson has a key. Then we're screwed." Ethan nodded, patting the metal in his pockets.

"Well, let's pray that he doesn't have a-"

He stopped immediately when he heard the knob jiggle.

From the outside.

Hope's body froze. She was standing right in front of the door. If it really was Grayson there, she'd be dead before she could even scream. Ethan's eyes were angry and wide at the same time. "Hope," he whispered, almost too quiet to hear. "Get back here." Hope tried, but her legs wouldn't respond to her mind. *Move, Hope!* she thought, yet her words had no effect. She was literally paralyzed with fear.

The door slowly creaked open. Faster than a bullet, Ethan leaped up and ran toward Hope with a dagger in his hand.

"Grayson," he growled. However, it was not Grayson who was standing before them. Ethan's look of fury completely melted off his face.

"Sapphire!" He dropped the knife, pulling her into a big hug. He accidentally pressed his arm on her patch, making her yelp. Ethan pulled away, concerned. "What's wrong?"

"There's a patch on my arm," she said. In her mind, the words sounded perfectly clear, but to Hope and Ethan her speech was slurred.

"What?" Ethan asked nervously.

"I can't sleep," she stated. Hope couldn't even begin to understand her slurred words.

"Is she drugged?" Hope asked. Fire shook her head. She made a motion with her hands by putting them together and on the side of her head. Fire could only hope that they got what she was trying to say.

"Sleep?" Ethan inquired. Fire roughly nodded, causing yet more pain to erupt in her head. She pointed to the patch on her arm, then to her brain. Suddenly, everything clicked in Ethan's mind. "Oh! That patch has some kind of drug, doesn't it?!"

"Hmm," Fire said, moving her head up and down slightly. Ethan quickly shut the door behind her.

"Fire, stay here and rest." She shook her head.

"Buttthepatch," she said, her words still slurring badly. A light went on in Ethan's brain.

"Oh, the patch is causing it! Let me take it off of you!" A wave of nausea went through him when he looked at her arm in the dim light. It was black, blue, and purple all at once. He reached down to get it, but Fire pulled sharply away.

"It hurts," she said to him, covering her arm.

"Let me do it," Hope suggested. "Having someone else take it off quickly might work better than you self-inflicting pain. And trust me, you really need sleep. Just let me do it."

"No, no," Fire murmured, repeating it over and over. Ethan reluctantly snatched Fire over to him. He gently set her on the ground, holding her arm out to the side.

166

"Do it, Hope," he said softly. Hope looked at Fire sympathetically.

"I'm so, so sorry." She grabbed the edge of the patch and began pulling.

A pain Fire had never imagined came over her. Her arm was being submerged in acid, it had to, there was no pain like that that could exist…

Fire shrieked, starting to thrash like crazy on the floor. The patch was slowly but surely being peeled off. The sight of the skin underneath made bile rise up in Hope's throat. It was by far the most disgusting thing she had ever seen. Ethan was sadly stroking Fire's hair with pain and regret evident in his eyes.

"What if someone hears us?" Hope had to almost yell over the sound of Fire's screams.

"Then I guess we'll all die!" Ethan shouted back. By now, the patch was peeled halfway off her arm. The blood was pooling onto the floor, and Hope desperately fought the urge to throw up. Poor Fire was hysterically screaming and crying, and it took everything in Ethan not to throw his hand over his best friend's mouth. Fire's arm looked utterly *repulsive*. Sweat was pouring down Fire's face, and her face was scrunched up in tears. Hope couldn't take it anymore. One last time, she aggressively tore it off.

Fire let out an inhuman shriek. It was a miracle that Grayson or one of his guards hadn't come to check on the commotion.

The patch had finally been completely ripped from her skin. Fire was gasping and heaving on the floor, taking sniffs and deep breaths.

"Is it off?" she whispered.

"Yes," answered Ethan as he wiped the tears from her eyes. "You can sleep now, Fire."

She was about to tell them about Grayson and the girl who escaped, but she couldn't muster the strength to do so. She slumped over to the ground and fell into a pile in the corner. She half expected to be terribly shocked again, but before she could truly think, her mind belonged to the darkness.

"Don, where the hell are you!?" Grayson stomped through the hall, walking past Aiden, Cassidy, and Haylee, who were still chained up.

"What happened?" Aiden dared to ask. Grayson sent him a look of death, but he answered anyway.

"That little brat got away too! I have no idea what happened to my damn guard anyway, and you both survived your acid trip. NONE OF THIS SHOULD HAVE HAPPENED!"

"Yeah," Aiden said, making his voice as sarcastic as possible, "Nothing went as planned. It's really too bad that you didn't get to do twisted things to us. Kinda sucks, huh?" Grayson slowly stalked toward Aiden, but he didn't back down. Soon, the threatening man's nose was right up to his.

"Everything will go as planned, boy. Say something like that again and I will kill you on the spot."

"What happened to Blisse?" Cassidy suddenly asked, sounding nervous. "Where's she?"

"She's out," he answered angrily, backing up toward the hall once more. "And now I have to find that idiot girl and get her back. Anyone else escapes and I get my gun."

Belle locked herself in a room to her right. There was no possible way that she could go down the hall and run into Grayson, or even Blisse. It gave her shivers to think about Blisse's reaction when she found out about her escape.

Poor Don. Although there was no way she wanted to die, she felt terrible for forcing the guard into the room, but it had to be done. She could only imagine him breathing in the anthrax that would kill him.

Belle took a good look around her room. There was a spear attached to the other side of the room, and there was a chair in the middle. It was painfully obvious what this room's purpose was. *Wow, I hope no one has to come in here.* Just for kicks, Belle went and sat in the chair. There were leather restraints on the arms, probably meant to lock someone in. The spear was facing her, and Belle knew that if this were real, it would get closer and closer until it would pierce her heart.

Belle shivered at the thought of it. She got up and moved to the wall right by the door. If Grayson happened to find her, she wanted to be as ready as possible.

The door started to pound.

Someone started screaming behind it. Belle pressed up her ear.

The sound was from a girl. All she could hear was begging and pitiful pleading, and the firm voice of a man.

Panic erupted in Belle's chest. A guard was taking someone in here to die.

In Belle's hiding spot.

28

Selena Thorne was not happy. She would have never expected her 21st birthday party to be held under a wobbly hut on an ocean shore. Her two best friends were there, trying to make the most of it.

"Happy birthday, Selena!" exclaimed her bright-eyed, peppy friend, Genevieve. She was attempting to put up birthday decorations. Well, if you considered palm trees and mounds of sand decorations. Her other close friend, Aspyn, was pathetically creating a birthday cake. At least, that's what she called it.

"I wouldn't call some pieces of fruit and coconut cake," said Selena, only half kidding. She was genuinely bummed that her party she'd been waiting for all her life turned out to be lame. She and her boyfriend had made plans to go to the first bar that they could legally go to when they were 17. Her life had been turned upside-down when she was announced dangerous. Luckily, she had her loyal friends to keep her sane. Genevieve was a naturally model thin girl with hair that was dry and crisp from malnutrition. Her copper eyes could be beautiful, but instead they were dull and sunken into her face. Aspyn was a pretty Asian girl with dark brown roots clearly visible through her faded pink hair.

"Hey, at least I'm trying to make your birthday not as sucky," Aspyn said in defense. "You're just sitting there like a bump on a log."

"Well excuse me if I would rather be with Dan at the bar on my birthday," Selena snapped. Aspyn stopped decorating her so-called cake at once. Her startlingly gray eyes narrowed as her jaw hung open.

"Well," she began, "you're not. So quit wallowing in pity and help make your cake." Aspyn flipped her hair for effect. Selena heaved a dramatic sigh and stood up.

"I'm going for a walk," she declared, grabbing her knife that she always slept with. That was her one prized possession that she was extremely proud of. She had sharpened it to perfection, and it could cut through anything. Her affection to this knife scared her friends, although they never mentioned it. She stomped out of the self-made shelter. Genevieve jumped up quickly, accidently stepping on a small mound of sand.

"I'll come too!" she said happily. Selena smiled dryly.

"*Alone,*" she clarified. Her friend's expression fell a fraction. "Oh, and Aspyn, your cake is actually the stupidest thing I've ever seen," she sneered. Genevieve's copper eyes grew wide.

"Selena!" she gasped, appalled by her attitude.

"What you want, Gen?" Genevieve stroked her dirty-blonde hair.

"It's kind of dangerous to walk alone right now," she warned. "It's almost completely dark, and who knows what could be lurking out there?" Selena sighed.

"We've never even seen a criminal, Gen. Why would tonight be any different?" she questioned. Genevieve shrugged helplessly.

"Just because we haven't seen one yet doesn't mean we never will," she retorted. Selena waved off her comment.

"Oh, whatever. If you need me, don't look for me. I need some time to breathe."

What did we do? Aspyn mouthed to Genevieve. She shrugged, not happy with Selena. The angry girl gripped her knife in her hand, and walked into the jungle alone.

I miss Dan! she thought bitterly to herself as she cut through the vines that were in her way. Selena continued to cut through the plants in fury until she came across a large tree. There were small plants covering the ground, and a piece of red fabric. *What the?* She inched closer, carefully inspecting the plants. *Hmm,* she thought to herself. *The plants look new, almost. The leaves aren't squished.*

She got a chill when she realized that a criminal could be here, right by her shelter. Selena shrugged the thought off, as she wanted to look around. She picked up the rag using her index finger and thumb. She was disgusted at how wet it was when it touched her dark skin. She put the rag into her left hand, looking to see if there was water on her fingers. Selena peered closely, seeing a silvery substance. *That's strange, it almost looks like…* she dropped the rag in horror.

"It's covered in blood," she realized aloud. She wiped her fingers on her arm in disgust. "Holy crap!" she practically shouted. "It's new!" She kicked the rag away some more, repulsed by the feel of the blood. "What kind of sicko has a rag *covered in blood!?*"

"I wouldn't call myself a sicko," stated an amused voice behind her. "I just do what I gotta do."

Selena spun around, automatically jabbing out the point of her prized knife. In front of her was a girl, no more than 20 years of age. Her thick, black hair made her look like a demon in the eerie light.

"Now now," said the mysterious voice, "let's not get hasty. Everybody knows that you always introduce yourself before your knife."

"Who are you?" asked a cautious Selena. The stranger grinned and walked forward. "I said, who are you?" she repeated angrily. "Stop walking, or you'll get on first base with my knife."

"I am the night," the stranger said ominously. "I am all that is dark, all that is twisted, all that is evil. They call me Blisse." Selena tilted her head, noticing that something was off.

"What's wrong with your eyes?" she asked. "Step into the starlight so I can see you." The person took a few steps into the light. She put up her head, showing her eyes proudly. Selena gasped before she could help it. "Why do you have black contacts?" she inquired, faintly sensing danger. The stranger bared her teeth.

"They aren't contacts, child," she snapped.

"How do you get your eyes that way then?" Selena asked, her voice slightly accusatory. The person laughed, a sound that made Selena know that this stranger was bad. Very bad.

"Is this a prank?" Selena suddenly asked. "I swear, if you're trying to prank me, I will-"

"I have a question for you," said the black-eyed girl, interrupting her. "Have you come across a group of people recently? There's a blonde girl with them." Selena thought this question was strange, but she just shook her head.

"Nope. My friends and I just stay out of everybody's business," she stated. The strange girl nodded.

"Is that so?"

"Yes," said Selena, now beginning to genuinely worry about this girl. "Well, I should probably get going then. My friends will be worried." However, the person was standing right in front of the path that she needed to follow.

"No, they aren't waiting for you," the girl said with amusement. "They know where you went, girl."

Suddenly, she grabbed an axe off of the ground that wasn't visible in one swift motion. Selena quickly pointed her knife at her again.

"You see, the thing is, you've seen me. And I can't have you telling anyone about me," the stranger explained. "Otherwise, my little group would know where I am, and I can't have that. I'm sorry, but now I have to kill you." The black eyes focused on her scared ones. "I'm not sorry," she grinned. The person started walking toward Selena with her axe swinging. Selena snapped out of her frozen state and began to run.

"Help!" she screamed to no one. She dashed through the jungle, her adrenaline keeping her from feeling the pain of the scratching thorns. Out of nowhere, the girl jumped on her. Selena screamed in fury as she wrestled to get away from the evil girl. However, the stranger's impossible strength pinned her to the ground. The dark-eyed girl chuckled sinisterly.

"Oh, it's hilarious when people think that they can escape," she said. Selena struggled against her iron grip, but it was no use. Her crazy strength kept her from moving.

"GENEVIEVE!" she shrieked hysterically. "ASPYN!"

"Your friends can't hear you," the girl snarled. "Maybe you shouldn't have come alone. I know I wouldn't have." She positioned the sharp blade over the trembling girl's throat. Her ebony hair was draped over her shoulder, not wanting it to spoil her view. She saw the blade move slightly as Selena gulped. "Now, goodbye." She paused before sliding her hand to the right.

Selena's eyes were watering as she stared at the weapon. No matter how hard she tried, she couldn't get the knife close enough to kill the demon on top of her. Blisse pressed the blade on her throat, stopping her struggles. "Good girl," she said sweetly.

She swiftly sliced Selena's throat with the blade. The girl convulsed as the blood trickled from her mouth. Blisse watched with unfathomable joy. When she was sure that she was dead, Blisse got up to fetch her rag. She grabbed it in her hand and walked back to the corpse of the young adult. With a twisted smile, she cleaned up the wound with her trophy.

"Fire," Ethan whispered, gently stroking her dark hair with his hand. "Wake up, Sapphire." With a groggy moan, Fire pried her eyes open. For a moment, the room was all a blur. Blacks blended with grays which blended with whites...

She rubbed her eyes roughly, attempting to sit up. Ethan and Hope kindly grabbed her arms and helped pull her.

"What do you remember?" asked Hope softly. For a moment, Fire couldn't recall a single conversation she had had the time before.

Without warning, everything completely crashed in her mind. The sensation she had felt when the patch was being ripped off rushed into her brain, and suddenly she was still there and the burning feeling was still creeping up her arms...

She slapped herself. Hard. That got rid of the excruciating visions of the day before.

"My arm," she choked out. Her voice cracked as it came out. "How is my arm?" Ethan gave her a reassuring smile.

"Look for yourself."

It was like her arm had completely renewed itself. At the most, it looked like she had hit something and bruised it. The only thing left of her awful trauma was a medium-sized circular bruise on her arm. She still winced slightly when she pressed on it, but it was a colossal improvement from before.

"How did that happen?"

"I think it's because the drug is out of your system," Hope quietly answered. "Since the needles are gone, your skin could rid itself of the poison and repair itself."

Fire looked around, and she now could faintly notice that her head felt like someone had repeatedly smashed it with a hammer.

"I need water," she said, her raspy voice making that clear. "My head feels like crap and I need water."

"We'll do what we can do," Ethan told her. "I don't know how soon we can get it, though. Grayson hasn't found us yet."

"But I need it now," she whined. Her throat felt as dry as a desert, and it was impossible to believe that she had ever even tasted the cold, thirst-quenching water.

Stop it, she commanded herself. "Ethan, I'm so thirsty."

"Not now," he said firmly. "I'll do the best I can."

Fire's head contemplated that she was in a closet, but she had no clue to how she'd gotten there.

"Where the hell am I?"

"You, my friend, are in a weapon's closet," Ethan answered. "It's a wonder that we haven't been found yet."

"I hope everyone's ok," Hope said, her unconscious sister and best friend coming to mind. Ethan nodded, gently patting her knee.

"I can't believe I got to meet Haylee. It's no wonder you love her, I can see why. You know, you two have similar tendencies." Hope chuckled.

"We aren't actually related."

"Yes, I know. But when you spend a lot of time with someone you love, you sort of adopt some traits. You and Haylee have the same posture. I don't know if you realize it or not, but when you're scared or nervous, you both hold yourself the same way." Ethan snickered. "It's kind of funny, actually. It's like having a second Hopie."

"Not if she doesn't wake up," Hope said darkly, a sigh escaping her mouth. Ethan looked at her with sympathy.

"She will, Hope. She'll wake up."

Belle held her breath fearfully. The door's lock was slowly being turned. If she stayed where she was, she would be found right away. *Come on Belle, think; you can't hide, what else can you do?* Her eyes searched the room frantically, but nothing came to mind. There was nothing to fight with, except...

Except for...

The spear. The spear that was positioned to spear the heart of a potential victim. Maybe, if she could snap the stick that it was attached to, she would have a weapon in hand. Her guess was that if a guard was holding a girl outside, he probably wouldn't immediately have a weapon.

Well, it was worth a try.

As quick as lightning, Belle dashed to the wall with the spear. The stick was about as long as her arm, and she could see that much of it was hidden in a hole in the wall. It's purpose was to slowly extend out, letting the victim see the weapon that would bring them death. Belle couldn't imagine anything more horrifying than being tied up, completely helpless, being forced to watch as a spear came closer and closer until it entered your skin but wouldn't stop.

She pushed away the thought as she grabbed as much of the stick that was visible. It was much thinner than bamboo, but it still was very hard to even make a crack in the strange wood.

The door continued to shake as the keys were put in the lock.

Belle knew she didn't have much time. She frantically grabbed the stick and tried to snap it in two. Sweat began to form on her forehead, but she didn't dare try and waste precious time by wiping it off.

The door was unlocked, and it slowly creaked open.

With one last hysterical effort, Belle felt the wood break. In her hand was a spear, with the other side splintered but intact.

The girl who had screamed was Cassidy. Grayson was there, holding her roughly by her hair. Belle mentally sighed with relief when she thought about how she could've picked another room, how Cassidy would have been speared.

The way Grayson's eyes grew so large would've been comical if his intent was not to kill.

"You." His face twisted into a mask of fury. Belle smirked, covering up the amount of fear she felt.

"Me."

Cassidy looked as though she would cry in happiness. *Thank you,* she mouthed over and over again. Belle tore her glance away from Cassidy to focus on Grayson.

"Where is Don?"

"Breathing in some yummy anthrax," Belle smoothly replied. "Come on man, you should know that I wouldn't die that easily."

"Yes," Grayson snarled, "and this time it won't be easy. I made a mistake to try and make your deaths long and painful, I should have just shot you when I had the chance."

"I warned you at the beginning," Belle told him, her uncontrollable grin plastered smugly across her face. "Remember, Grayson? I said it would be easier to just shoot us, but you didn't listen. And that's your weakness, you can't listen. You only follow your rules, and that's what ruins your plans. You don't listen to Blisse, you don't listen to Gabe-"

"Gabriel is dead," Grayson replied coolly. "I locked him away with no food or water while he bled. I don't need to listen to anyone, Isabelle."

"But that's where you are wrong," she stated. "You can't always live on your own, Grayson. Trust me, I needed to find my friends to keep me sane. You need friends, Grayson."

"Friends are for the weak," he growled. "Friends hold you back, Isabelle. I don't need friends."

"But you do!" she persisted. "Grayson, why didn't you kill us right away? Answer that."

Grayson stared at her like she was the worst person on the planet, but he stayed silent. Belle dryly snickered.

"You didn't kill us because you are a psychopath, plain and simple. You've been on this island for a long, long time Grayson, and it's hurting your mind. You didn't kill us right away because once you get excited, you can't think rationally. *You are a sick man.* You get excited over causing other people pain, and it's just wrong. Would you like to know what the saddest thing is?" Belle didn't even wait for him to shake his head.

"The saddest thing is that you could have friends, but you just have a bunch of men doing your dirty work. You are insane, Grayson. You did something inhuman to Blisse. You deserve to die."

As Grayson was staring with pure fury at Belle, Cassidy saw her chance. She slipped her arm from his grasp and punched him in the neck with all her strength. He made a gurgling choking sound and Cassidy lunged toward Belle. Belle caught the crying girl and put her behind her. The spear jutted out of Belle's shaking hand threateningly.

"Now let us through." Belle quickly walked toward the doorway as Grayson was still trying to breathe normally. Angrily, Belle hit him in the head with the side of the spear. It wouldn't kill him, but it looked as though he would be smarting a huge headache later.

"Wait," Belle gasped, looking at Cassidy with large eyes. "What about Blisse?"

"Don't worry," Cassidy reassured her. "Blisse isn't here right now. Grayson said she went into the jungle for awhile." Belle audibly let out a sigh of pure relief.

"You know, we might actually make it out of here," she said. Cassidy nodded, grinning.

"Belle, that was some really sweet stuff you said about friends back there. I didn't know you felt that way."

Belle's face flushed a deep red.

"I don't mean it," she said, her normal snappy tone back. "I did it to prove Grayson wrong."

"Alright," Cassidy said. But as she looked at Belle's maroon face, she knew that she had just gotten a glimpse of a Belle that she liked.

"This is crazy," Fire muttered, holding her head in her hands. "How have we not been found yet? I mean, I don't want to be found or anything, but how has Grayson not wandered in here yet?"

"Whatever the reason may be," said Ethan, "I really couldn't be more grateful. I just wish I knew what could be going on."

"Yeah, me too," Hope chimed in. "I really hope everyone's ok."

That's when their door exploded.

Belle fell in with a crazed expression on her face with Cassidy right behind her.

"We escaped," she gasped, "and we can get out! We need to go, now!" Hope looked up in terror.

"What about Grayson and Blisse?"

"Blisse is gone and Grayson can't breathe!" Belle said all of this in a super fast tone, trying to catch her breath. Ethan and Hope locked joyful eyes with each other.

"Wait!" yelled Fire. "What about Aiden?"

"And Haylee!" Hope added.

"We can get them later, but we have to leave before Blisse comes back. Let's go!" Fire hastily pushed herself off of the ground, running out of the door.

"Ethan, grab a gun," Belle said to him as she grabbed a pistol for herself. "There might be guards somewhere." Ethan gave a quick nod before he picked up a small, movable weapon. Cassidy reached for a longer sword in the corner.

The group ran faster than they had ever run before. They dashed down the hallway, ready to help their tied up friends and get the hell out of the prison.

Grayson was now standing in front of the entrance, his breathing a bit steadier. His arms were crossed, and his eyes were like a deep thunderstorm.

"Grayson, get out of the way," Cassidy snarled. Her previous panicked eyes were now steel. The man standing there was grinning, scratching his bald head. "And I am *not* afraid to use force." She jutted out the sharp tip of her sword for effect.

"Just a second ago, you were crying in fear," Grayson laughed. "It was so pitiful, really. How embarrassing." Cassidy's face flushed red, but she kept her eyes locked on him.

"I'm going to kill you," she said quietly. Grayson let out a hysterical chuckle.

"You? You're going to kill me?" Grayson looked at Ethan. "*She's* going to kill me?" He laughed and laughed as Cassidy balled her fists. "You'll never kill me, child."

"Yeah, that's what I thought too, when I first got here," she said through gritted teeth. "When I first arrived on the island, I thought 'oh Cassidy, how will you ever survive'? But you know what I've learned since then? I've come across criminals in my time here. Some are cunning, some are evil, and some are simply insane; you're all three. I've learned that cowering in fear will never get you where you need to go, Grayson. I'm not going to beg for freedom anymore. Either you let me out willingly, or we go anyway. Your choice."

Hope really looked at her friend for the first time in a while. Her face had lines of stress that made her look ages older, and her body stood straighter than it had before. Her once friendly, energetic smile was now dark and unforgiving.

"But you'll feel really guilty after it," he cooed. "I'll be in your dreams, in your thoughts. You'll always know that you killed somebody, that you took a life."

"Oh, I thought about that," she agreed. "But here's the thing. I'm giving you a choice. I'm not just mercilessly killing you like you've done to countless innocent people. I said that I won't harm you if you move. If you choose to die, that's your choice, not mine. If you want to be stabbed, fine by me. I really don't give two shits whether you live or die. Understand that I won't feel guilty at all, Grayson." His knowing smile wavered a fraction. His big point had been a total flop. "Now, decide. If you don't choose in 30 seconds, I'll kill you, despite what your decision may be. If I were you, I'd hurry up." Her piercing glare stayed dead set on Grayson. He returned the glare, but he didn't take a step back.

"I will pound you into a pulp," he threatened, putting up his scarred fists. Cassidy rolled her eyes.

"Um, I think we all know that you could. Look at your size, you psycho." Hope suppressed a chuckle. Who would've thought that Cassidy would speak to him like that?

"But that's not the point," she continued. "I have a sharp weapon and you don't. It doesn't matter how strong you are when I can end your life." He chuckled his evil laugh.

"You can't even hold a sword right." He snickered at her incorrect grip on the weapon. She raised her eyebrows.

"That's true, Grayson. But do you wanna know something? When I was in high school, I was the best softball player there was. My throws were perfect, my catches were phenomenal, but my hits, my hits made me *me*. I could hit the ball like no one's business. I could only hit because my arms were strong. And that's exactly what I'll do with this sword. There's no way you could dream of stopping my power hit. Who cares if I can't hold it right as long as it does what I want it to?" Grayson's hopes were slowly falling. All of his points against her didn't do anything. It was clear that Cassidy had won. She smirked. The unfamiliar expression on her face made Cassidy looked oddly terrifying.

"Time's up, Grayson. Are you moving or not?" The man squinted his eyes. He stood there, not daring to move.

"No, you are my prisoners, and you are staying here. This little attempt is cute, but get back to your rooms." Cassidy sighed. Her dark eyes darted to Hope. For a moment, Hope could see part of her friend in her icy eyes. There was a look of hesitation, a look of begging. Hope knew that whatever her friend said, she really didn't want to kill Grayson. Cassidy's eyes focused back on the man in front of her.

"Whatever you say, Grayson." She paused, so unnoticeable that Hope barely saw it. With a quick breath, her hand shot forward. The front of the sword sank into his chest as he gasped. Cassidy looked shocked as well, but she kept her hand steady. She jutted the weapon further into his body. Almost carelessly, she dropped the sword, but the damage had already been done. Hope could barely see some blood in Grayson's mouth. It was astounding that he was still standing up with the large wound in his chest.

"Now," Cassidy said, deliberately avoiding to look at Grayson, "let's go get Haylee and get out of here before Blisse comes back. If she does get here, we'll never have the chance to get out. Ethan, grab the key from Grayson's pocket," she commanded. He nodded and walked over to the weakening man. He harshly snatched the key from his worn pocket. Ethan threw it to Cassidy. She walked over to the unconscious girl, Hope walking nervously behind her. Cassidy quickly bent down and unlocked the chains.

"Ethan, come help!" Hope called. He rushed over to the two girls. "Aiden, open the doors for us. Us three will carry Haylee." Ethan shook his head in protest.

"No, it's fine, I'll carry her by myself. She can't weigh that much, right?" Almost comically, he swooped her up in his arms. By now, Grayson was slowly sliding down the wall.

"Karma's a bitch!" Fire couldn't resist saying. It brought her pleasure to watch her tormentor slowly die. "When you mess with the fire, you get the flame!"

"Really?" Aiden said, rolling his eyes. "You have one cool thing to say to him before he dies, and you choose that?" Fire chuckled, playfully smacking him in his shoulder.

"It's epic." Before she could stop herself, she roughly kicked Grayson in his arm. Ethan came walking over, his strong arm supporting Haylee's head. "Aww, is Ethan carrying something for his girlfriend? How gentlemanly!" Fire said, snickering.

"I would smack the living daylights out of you Fire, but I'm holding a person," he said calmly. She mockingly contorted her lip into a pout.

"Ethan just threatened me! Abuse, abuse!" She ran around grinning, yelling, "Abuse, abuse!"

Hope forced a smile, but she didn't respond. Cassidy looked at her with sad eyes.

"Hope, I'm sorry-"

"It's not that," Hope interrupted. "You did what you had to do. I'm just sick of it all. aAl of the killing, all of the capturing, just... everything. I just want to be on my couch with a blanket at home. Good god Cassidy, I just want to be ok. I don't want to be caught in the middle of all this violence anymore. I mean, the stuff people will do to each other is downright terrifying. I'm done with it!" Hope felt the muscles in her face tense up. *No Hope, don't you dare cry right now. Don't you dare.* She blinked away the sudden tears. Ethan looked behind him.

"Are you ready, kids?" he asked. Fire grinned.

"Aye aye, captain!" she replied, giggling. He let out a groan.

"Let's go." He sighed as he held open the door with his back. Fire skipped out with Aiden right behind her. Cassidy and Hope walked side by side. Hope allowed herself one last glance into her prison. *I'm free,* she thought. *I'm actually free.* She tilted her head up to the shining sunlight above her. She gazed at the beautiful, green jungle that was so refreshing after the depressing shack. *I'm free.*

29

Blisse was on top of the world. She had killed everyone she met, and nothing made her feel the way death felt. Taking someone's life was a sign of immeasurable power, and it was a power she loved.

A corner of her mouth turned up just thinking about what she was going to do to them. She now had people that she could experiment on without consequence. She grinned as she walked over to the small outside of the shack, followed by her two guards. She ran her hand through her thick hair. She used her free hand to yank open the wooden door.

Blisse gasped before she could help herself. Grayson was lying on the floor, a bloody wound on his chest. His eyes were still open, giving him the appearance of a zombie. There was a guard next to him, looking for a pulse that he would never find.

"Grayson?" Blisse asked, almost sounding bored. She was beyond positive that he was dead; nobody could survive that severe of an injury. She suddenly had a terrifying thought.

MY PRISONERS!

She ran to Hope's execution room, faster than she had ever run before. There was nobody beneath the saw that Grayson created. Blisse screamed, a sound of pure rage. She angrily stomped out of the room to check on the others, although she knew that it would be pointless. If Hope was gone, there was no doubt that everyone else was away. Just the same, she popped her head in each of the rooms. To no surprise, all of her victims were gone. She jumped up and down, screaming in angry frustration. Minutes went by, full of screaming and punching.

With a death glare, she angrily walked down the hallway.

"What happened to them?" Blisse asked the guard in a dangerously calm tone. He shrugged, his eyes averted to the floor.

"I don't exactly know, Miss," he said. "I was out to get food, and I came back to this." Blisse's eyes darkened even more.

"Weren't you supposed to be helping Grayson watch them? You *were not* supposed to be on a walk." He looked up nervously. It was comical to watch this grown man look at her like a scared dog. "So, you disobeyed orders from me?" He chomped his lip. Blisse's lip curled into an evil smile. "Wrong choice." She bent down to his level. "Do you know what I do to people who don't listen?" she whispered.

The guard who walked with her was watching the scene unfold nervously. He knew his friend would die from the monster Grayson created. The guard sitting down shook his head no. Blisse's eyes lit up in delight.

"I kill them." The guards gray eyes grew alarmed. Before he could say anything, her hands shot out in front of her. In one swift motion, she fatally broke his neck with her incredible strength. The guard's friend winced at the loud *snap!* that sounded. Blisse turned to the other guards behind her. "You know, it's better to kill you as well. Now with Grayson gone, I really don't need you. I won't waste my time feeding you."

The other guard stood frozen, his eyes locked on Blisse's black ones. Suddenly, he took off running out of the door.

"No!" his friend yelled. With a sigh, Blisse stood up. He watched her sprint and tackle the runaway man. He could only stand there and wait for her to kill him. There was no point in running anymore. Blisse slowly walked back to the entrance, creating crazy-making suspense. She grinned when she saw him standing there.

"Well well, aren't you just my good little boy," she cooed. He watched with distaste as she got closer and closer. She came over and put her small hand on his chest. "You're scared," she observed. He raised his eyebrows in an attempt to look tough.

"No I'm not," he snapped. She chuckled.

"Yes, you are. I can feel your heartbeat. It's so, so fast." Her stare went up to his face. "Well, it was nice knowing you," she said with a smile. The last thing he saw was Blisse's twisted smile looking up at him. She heard the crack that brought another death as his body fell to the ground in a heap. Now, she needed to focus on Hope's group.

Ok, where would they have gone? she thought, frustrated. She was interrupted by footsteps behind her. She spun around.

"What?" she snarled viciously. Two other men were there, frozen. She heaved a huge sigh. One of the men quickly put his hand out.

"Wait!" he said desperately. Blisse looked at him.

"This better be good," she said, tapping on her wrist. He pleadingly put out his hands.

"Don't kill us," he begged pitifully. *I can have some fun with these guys,* Blisse thought happily. She suddenly brought up her hand, making them flinch.

"And why shouldn't I?" she asked, enjoying the fear they were trying to hide.

"We can help you," the other man stammered. Blisse nodded in approval. *I'm tired of this,* she whined in her head. *I just want Hope!*

"Yeah, ok, you won me over," she said, sounding bored. The man's huge sigh of relief was audible. "But, you have to do whatever I say. Deal?" The two men locked eyes, pondering their decision. Blisse sighed loudly, making their heads snap toward her.

"Deal," said the first man hastily. The second man nodded his head in agreement. Blisse wiggled her eyebrows.

"Alrighty then!" All of a sudden, she had a thought that brought a smile to her face.

With Grayson gone, I can be my own master! She bared her teeth, liking this realization more and more.

Nobody can control me anymore! I can do whatever I want. She grinned as she walked out of the concrete room.

I am me. I am mine. I control me now.

Blisse strolled over to the door where Grayson lied. "Did they really kill you?" she asked the corpse. "You're a lot weaker than I thought!" She kicked him aside triumphantly as she walked out of the doorway and into the light. The guards followed nervously behind her, shooting each other cautious glances. *Nobody can control you now,* Blisse thought.

Look out, Hope. Here comes Blisse.

"Guys," Ethan whispered. Hope looked over at him curiously.

"What?"

"Look," he said softly, gesturing to Haylee's head. Her eyes were slowly fluttering open with a groan. Hope stopped moving at once.

"Haylee?" She dared to wish for the best. Haylee's blonde head slowly rose up, and Ethan set her gently down on the ground.

Hope threw herself at her sister, throwing her arms around her neck tightly.

"Haylee, I thought you were dead!" Hope could feel tears of joy swimming in her eyes. Haylee's arms very hesitatingly wrapped around Hope's back. After a few minutes, Hope pulled away, looking into Haylee's eyes. Those familiar auburn eyes looked back at her with surprise, fear, and confusion. Hope looked back oddly.

"Haylee, why are you looking at me like that?" Hope felt a hand on her shoulder. Looking up, she saw Cassidy.

"Hope," she started sadly, "she doesn't remember you. She doesn't remember anyone. The cement caused her to lose her memory, I think. She briefly woke up for a moment at the shack. I'm sorry." Hope felt lead flood her veins. She slowly pushed herself off of the hard ground.

"Haylee," Hope whispered, her top lip beginning to tremble. "You really don't remember me?" Haylee shook her head sadly.

"No, I'm sorry. You seem really nice, and I wish I knew who you were," she said, her eyes wide and innocent. Hope desperately looked into them, looking for a sign of even the slightest spark of recognition. "But it's like there's a block in my memory, and I can't remember anything. I'm really sorry." Hope took a steadying breath.

"You know Hopie, she probably will remember in a day or so," Ethan said encouragingly. She weakly nodded her head. There was a moment of silence, everyone yearning for Haylee to remember.

"So guys, where are we gonna sleep tonight?" Fire asked through a yawn. Aiden's eyes grew wide as he realized something.

"You guys, what if this serum makes Blisse not have to sleep? asked Aiden fearfully. "I think that she'll spend the whole night hunting for us, Ethan. We need to find somewhere safe." Ethan nodded. There was no way he wanted to come face to face with an angry Blisse in the pitch black.

"We could climb a tree," Hope suggested. Ethan shook his head, making her raise her eyebrows.

"No no, it's a good idea," he said quickly. "But Belle told me that Blisse remembered them talking on a trail."

"He's right!" she piped up.

"If she can remember that, when she was herself, I'm willing to bet that she can remember other things," he continued. "Guys, remember when the town was on fire and we had to sleep in a tree?" He paused, waiting for his friend's heads to nod. When they did, he said, "Blisse is really smart now. I mean, she was smart before, but she's intelligent in a different way. She's looking for the best way to find us. I think that she'll know that the first place we'll look is in a tree. Your idea would work, but I'm afraid that Blisse will look up, and we don't want that. We need to go somewhere that she'd never even think of looking."

"What about that hole in the ground?!" exclaimed Aiden. Ethan shook his head.

"No, she was there too, remember?" Aiden's face turned beet red, embarrassed. Cassidy nervously raised her hand.

"I know where we can go," she said. Ethan's eyebrows went up in disbelief.

"Cass, everywhere we've gone, Blisse has been there too. There's nowhere that she hasn't seen," he reminded her. Her normally pale face was slowly turning red in a blush.

"Don't worry, no one has been here. Not even you, Ethan." Fire narrowed her ocean blue eyes.

"Cassidy, where is it?" she asked impatiently. Her face was becoming redder and redder.

"Well," she began, "when Brandon and I were dating, we… we snuck off in the middle of the night sometimes."

"You what?!" Ethan exclaimed in surprise. Cassidy smiled sheepishly.

"Yes, we did. One time, we found a cave. There was a secret entrance in it that I found by dragging my hand across the wall. I don't think Blisse will even think about looking in any cave, much less the one that I'm thinking about. I don't know where it is, but I do know that it is not too far from the town. If we can just find our old building, I can lead us from there."

"What did you guys do in the cave?" Fire asked mischievously.

"It doesn't matter what we did in the cave," Cassidy snapped, her face hot. "The point is that I know we'll be safe, assuming we get to it before Blisse gets to us. Trust me, it's pretty hidden." Ethan put his hand to his chin dramatically.

"It seems good enough. First, we need to find where our old building was."

"Hey guys, I have a question," Hope stated. "There's only one town, and your building wasn't super far from when we first met Grayson. How come they never attacked you before?"

"Hope, there were 40 of us. They wouldn't have stood a chance," Fire said, rolling her eyes slightly. "I thought you knew that."

"I forgot," Hope said in defense. "I've had a long week, ok?" Ethan started walking. "Um, Ethan, where are you going?" He shrugged his shoulders.

"Oh, I don't know. I want to see if anything looks familiar. I know every part of this island, just not this part," he explained.

"It would be faster if we split up," Aiden suggested. "Then we could meet together and say what we found." Ethan put his hands out.

"Absolutely *not*. The last time we were split up, things didn't go so well. And by so well, I mean they went terrible. We are going to stay together. I don't want to risk losing any of you." His eyes darted over to Hope before he could help himself. Aiden nodded.

"Yeah, ok, my ideas suck. I'll just stop talking now." Fire chuckled at his statement.

"Well," said Ethan, "let's go find that cave!"

"Cass, will we make it there soon?" Ethan asked. Although he hadn't meant to, his voice had come out as annoyed and impatient. The group had been moving for an hour, coming across nothing that would shield them from their evil friend. Hope's legs felt like lead.

"Ethan," Cassidy said calmly. "We'll get there. Shut the hell up." She suddenly sped up, walking far in front of everyone. Hope looked ahead, her face full of sympathy. *Poor Cassidy,* she thought. Without thinking, she picked up her pace to catch up with her friend.

"Ethan, I'm not in the-" Cassidy broke off when she saw Hope's golden hair. "Oh, sorry," she said, her voice dull. "I thought you were Ethan." Hope chuckled.

"Yeah, I noticed. Cassidy, what's wrong?" Hope firmly planted her feet in front of her friend, keeping her from running away. Cassidy flipped her dark hair angrily.

"I'm struggling a lot right now," she said quietly. "You don't understand how I feel." She spun back around and began walking. Hope quickly reached out and grabbed Cassidy's shoulder. "WHAT THE HELL DO YOU WANT!" Cassidy shouted, startling Hope.

"Why are you acting like this?" Hope asked with a little hurt in her tone.

Of course, Hope knew that everyone was on edge. How could they not be?

"I get it Cassidy," Hope said with a small smile. "You're tired and hungry and stressed." Cassidy just stared at her.

"Hope," she finally said. "Thanks for trying, but you don't understand."

For some reason, this mere sentence made Hope's blood turn to fire. She was angry for a reason she couldn't even put her finger on.

"You wanna know how I feel?" Hope practically yelled as she crossed her arms. "I feel sad, scared, confused, annoyed, and helpless. Want to know why?" Cassidy began to speak, but Hope cut her off.

"I'm sad because my best friend might never remember who I am. That's what's hurting me so bad, Cassidy. We're all tense, I know. I'm helpless because I know there is nothing I can do to jog Haylee's memory." Hope said all of this in an angry tone, her eyes locked on the girl in front of her.

Cassidy stared at her in silence.

"You've been on this sucky island a lot longer than I have," Hope said. "This is a terrible shock to me." By now, everyone else had caught up to the still-standing girls. Cassidy forced her face into an uncomfortable smile.

"Ok, I'm sorry. You're right." Hope suddenly found it tough to feel any sympathy for her friend.

"I accept your apology," she said. It came out sarcastic without her meaning to. With a shocking pang, she realized that she was sounding just like Gabe. Fire rolled her eyes, heaving a huge sigh.

"You know, this isn't getting us to a cave any faster," she said, annoyance clear in her tone. Hope felt her body turn slowly toward Fire. Her mind turned red once again.

"Shut up, Sapphire," she simply said. Fire stopped speaking at once. Shock flew across everyone's face. Fire's once ocean eyes now were as deep and dark as, ironically, a cave.

"What did you just say?" she asked dangerously. Hope snorted, humor gone from the sound.

"You heard me. Your impatient tone doesn't help one bit. In fact, you are making me crazy. So please, *for the love of god,* shut up." Aiden chuckled uncomfortably, his eyes darting between the two adults.

"Well, at least I'm not wallowing in sadness about some stupid sister who lost her memory," snapped Fire. She mockingly put on the best fake sad expression she owned. *"Oh, Haylee, how can I possibly continue without you?"* she sneered. Cassidy's mouth dropped open in astonishment.

"Fire, that's-" Sapphire's hand shot up, silencing her.

"Cassidy, stay out of it." Fire shot her glare back at Hope. The blonde adult was fuming. She couldn't remember a time when her pulse had raced this much.

"How dare you?!" she yelled. "How dare you bring Haylee into this! At least I have someone who I love!" Fire's eyes were full of anger. Ethan saw her tense up, her back parallel to the ground.

"For your information, there is someone I love," she retorted. "Don't talk about stuff you don't know, you idiot." Hope rolled her eyes.

"Please, I really doubt that you love anyone. I bet you're not even capable of love," she shot back. Fire raised her eyebrows.

"Wanna bet?" she challenged. Hope visibly took a deep breath, her hands clenched.

"Yeah, actually I do. Who in the world could you possibly love, Sapphire?"

"My mom," she snapped back. Hope was about to reply, but she slammed her mouth shut.

"Your mom?" she asked, her tone slightly gentler. Fire snorted grimly as she nodded.

"Yes, *Hopie,* my mom. Do you know why?" Hope shook her head, feeling a slight jolt of embarrassment. "Oh yes, perfect time for story telling. One time, when I was 13, I was sitting at home, watching tv. My dad, oh my dad, he was a real drinker. Every night, he came home completely drunk." Aiden took a few steps over to her, putting his hand gently on her back.

"You don't have to do this," he whispered in her ear. "I know how hard this is for you." She shook his hand off.

"I'm fine." She smoothed out her long brown hair.

"I dreaded the nights when he would come home. He always would slur his words and stay up until 2 in the morning." Hope raised a quivering hand. "What, you have a question?" Fire snarkily asked. Hope nodded, her eyes averted to the green below.

"What was he?" she asked. Fire scrunched her eyebrows together.

"What the hell are you talking about?"

"I meant," said Hope, "what job did he have?" Fire chuckled dryly.

"You didn't think he had a job, did you?" Hope frowned, scratching her arm awkwardly.

"Oh."

"Yeah, *oh*. One night, he brought three of his even drunker friends to my house. My mom tried to tell them to leave, but my dad pushed her on the floor. They all came over to me. I remember feeling dread. So Hope, picture this: a house full of booze, with a small, 13 year old girl sitting on an ugly green couch, not knowing what was happening, but scared for her life. He came over, his friends all grabbing and touching me. He said something to my mom, and she screamed. I remember his hand snaking out. I remember the feeling of his hand on my throat." Fire visibly shuddered. Hope now felt awful about confronting her a few minutes earlier. Her mouth was slowly dropping lower and lower with each awful word.

"My mom got up from the floor and came over," she continued. "She grabbed a knife, and-" she choked off.

"She grabbed a knife and killed one of his friends," she continued. "She screamed at me to call 911. I remember the shouts as I ran to the phone. The police told me they were on their way, and all I could do was wait. I came back into the living room, and-" she stopped. Her muscles in her face were clearly tensed up. She suddenly pinched herself, making her jump. She took a breath and continued.

"My dad was on the floor, a knife in his throat. My mom was covered in blood, but she was ok. She got up, and she started to walk towards me. I saw my dad get up behind her. I screamed to watch out, but it was too late. He tore the knife out and stabbed her in the neck." Her eyes clouded. "I, a 13 year old, watched as they both died on the floor, covered in blood. I love her, Hope. She sacrificed her life for me."

Hope felt her eyes pool with water.

"Is that why you were so sad when Martha died?" she asked, her voice completely gentle.

"Whatever," she snapped. Then Fire nodded, her eyes focused on the ground. "Yes," she whispered a bit more gently. "Martha was my new mom. When she died, it was like I lost my mom all over again." Aiden's mouth was set in a frown.

"Everytime I hear your story, I just feel horrible, Sapphire," he said softly. She sniffed, punching him weakly in the chest.

"It's Fire," she feebly snapped. He smiled, shaking his head.

"I think Sapphire is a unique name." He reached out his arm hesitantly. When she didn't object, he put it around her shoulders. Cassidy grinned weakly. Her eyes suddenly lit up in joy.

"We're close to the cave," she exclaimed, looking around at the familiar scenery. Fire nodded, taking a steadying breath.

"Well then, what are we waiting for?" They began walking again, Aiden's arm holding Fire close.

Cassidy's eyes were looking around in wonder.

"I haven't been here since Brandon died," she said with water in her eyes. "It's so pretty here at night." She looked up and down, marveling at the black crystal walls of the cave. Fire nodded, her eyes looking around as well.

"Yeah Cass, it seems very romantic here. I can almost imagine you and Brandon-"

"Ok, shut it," said a flustered Cassidy. Fire chuckled.

"So, you are sure that Blisse won't find us here?" Hope asked, trying to hide the nervousness from her voice. Cassidy shrugged her shoulders.

"Well, I never said that." Hope's eyes grew wide.

"What!?"

"Dude, chill," she said. "Blisse could find us. All I said was that she didn't know about this place." Hope sighed, rubbing her hands on her old blouse.

"Yeah," said Ethan. "I hate it, though. I don't know what Blisse will do if she comes back to herself."

"When," Hope corrected him.

"What?"

"When she comes back," said Hope. "She's coming back to herself, she has to. Grayson was smart, but there's no way that she will stay a monster forever. I know she'll turn into herself, no matter how long it might be." Ethan patted her hair.

"Well, looks like someone has been thinking positively," he said. She rolled her eyes.

"I'm serious, Ethan."

They were cut off by a shrill scream that pierced the air. The two adults made eye contact for a split second. They dashed to the back of the cave. The sound belonged to a stark-white Belle, pointing to a man. Her face was lit up in terror.

"What... what the hell is that *thing*?" Fire asked, looking at the man with a look mixed with fear and disgust. Hope gasped when she saw why Belle had screamed and why Fire looked so revolted. The man's bottom lip was gone, a jagged mess where it once had been. It looked as though patches of hair had been ripped out, leaving red bumps on his head. But it was his upper body that was so alarming; the man had no arms. There were two mangled holes where his arms belonged. Bits of pink flesh dangled from his body. Hope threw her hand over her open mouth as bile rose. Fire quickly slid a small dagger from her boot.

"Tell me who you are," she growled. "Now." The man was staring into space, his eyes wet. He didn't even seem to notice the group of people standing in front of him. Fire knelt down, the knife dangerously jutted out. "Yeah, here's the thing," she said. "You are freaking my friends and me out, and I want answers. Tell me, or you can come face to face with my knife." The man shook harder than Hope thought was possible.

"Kill me," the man whispered. Fire crossed her arms.

"Who are you!?" she asked, frustration overpowering her tone. Cassidy put a hand gently on her shoulder.

"You know, maybe I should talk to him," she whispered. Fire looked as though she was about to speak, but she shut her mouth. She got up grudgingly and moved to the side. Cassidy gave a kind smile, willing herself not to look at the awful remains of where his arms had been. "Ok, so will you tell us what happened? Take your time," she added. The man's eyes looked up, and Cassidy could see all the pain in his past.

"I've been abused," the man said, in his raspy voice. Hope felt horrible for him. Each time a word escaped in his croaky voice, she felt chills down her spine. Selfishly, she was beyond happy that that wasn't what had happened to her. Cassidy looked at him sympathetically. She figured that he must have been under 40 years of age. "The devil did this to me." A single tear made its way down his cheek. Cassidy smiled uncomfortably.

"What do you mean the devil?" The man sniffed. "What did it look like?"

"The devil was disguised as a child," he said, his face scrunching up. "A black eyed child." Cassidy felt her heart skip a beat.

"Did she have black hair?" she asked, dreading the answer. He weakly moved his head up and down. Cassidy looked behind her at the faces of her friends. Her hands began to quiver. "Blisse did this."

Ethan's face grew into a horrified look.

"She's beyond our help," he said sadly. Hope half heartedly shook her head, but deep down, she agreed with Ethan. Cassidy gave all of her attention on the man.

"What did she do to you?" she whispered. The man gulped.

"The devil took me. She tied me up in a room. She said no questions, but I asked who she was. She got angry, so so angry. She took my mouth." Hope gave another look at his jaggedly removed lip. He started crying, his eyes clouding at the horrific memory. Cassidy gestured to his missing arms.

"What else?" She dreaded the answer, but she was excruciatingly curious. Blisse had done this. She needed to know.

He took a shaky breath. Cassidy sensed that his mind was soon going to be pushed over the edge. "Listen, we really need to know this," said a gentle Cassidy. "Please." His sky blue eyes filled with water, but he looked up.

"There was a contest," he whispered. "A staring contest." He gulped, his blue eyes piercing into Cassidy's. "Whoever blinked first had-" he choked off, more tears sliding down his face. "They had their arms..." He put his face down, attempting to shield his tears. "I lost!" he sobbed. "I lost, and the devil punished me!" Hope gazed at him, a look full of terror and pity.

"How did she kidnap you?" Cassidy asked, her arms erupting in goosebumps. The man cried freely, his sobs echoing in the dark cave. He shook his head.

"Cassidy," said Ethan softly. "We know enough. Don't push him anymore." Cassidy shook her head yes. She got up and walked back to her group of friends.

"I hate Blisse," Fire said, clenching her fists. "Even if she comes back to herself, it will never be the same. No matter how much she does, it will never make up for this." She gestured to the weeping man. "Blisse deserves to die." Ethan put his hands out in front of him.

"Fire, that's a bit too harsh."

"It's not," Hope said suddenly. Everyone's eyes darted to her. "She gave Haylee amnesia, scarred this man's life, and has caused us all much more fear than anyone should ever have." Ethan threw up his hands, exasperated.

"So if you see her, you'll just pull out a knife and *stab* her?" Hope shook her head wearily.

"I think we all know that I can't kill anyone. So no, I can't kill her. But one of you can. Especially Fire, I know she could do it." Fire nodded.

"Yes, I will. If I see that-"

"Chill, Sapphire," Aiden interrupted. Her eyes found his.

"No."

"Guys, stop," Hope said. Fire shot a glare at her, but she stopped when she heard the man's breathing quicken. The man's light eyes were widening in horror. Hope looked at him oddly. "Um, are you ok?" she asked.

"It's coming," he whispered. The man rolled his eyes to the back of his head.

30

Cassidy opened her mouth, her body chilled to the bone.

"What's coming?"

He suddenly slumped to the ground. Fire looked up in surprise.

"I think he just died," she said softly, stating the obvious. She hesitantly took a few steps towards him. Suddenly, shouts erupted from every side of the cave. They echoed throughout the entire room, making Hope shiver.

"This is so awful," she whispered. She naturally moved closer to Ethan. He protectively wrapped his arm around her, pulling her in. Aiden did the same to Fire.

"We have to leave," Aiden said, his eyes looking all over the cave. "Now."

Laughter sounded, louder than all of the shouts. Goosebumps creeped up Ethan's skin. He and Aiden locked eyes. The word *Blisse* hung in the air, unspoken. Impossibly, the laughing got louder and closer. The group huddled together, everyone's eyes wide and alert.

All of a sudden, all the noise shut off. It was instantaneous, like a switch was turned off. Everyone looked up.

"I hate this. I hate this so much," Hope muttered. Ethan nodded.

"The feeling's mutual," he whispered back.

Footsteps filled the air. Fire put up her fists, her icy eyes looking for a fight. Cassidy shrunk back into the crowd. *We need Maya*, she thought. The sound got louder and louder.

"Maybe they're just trying to freak us out," Aiden proposed.

"Who's they?" Ethan asked as Hope said, "Well, they're doing a good job of it." Her palms were sweating, and she resisted the urge to wipe her hand on her ripped up leggings.

The footsteps got louder, louder, louder. Cassidy felt as though she would go insane from the awful suspense of waiting. Finally, a silhouette crossed the opposite wall. Fire held her breath, her grip on Aiden tightening. The shape came closer and closer. Hope bit her lip, tasting the metallic taste of blood. The shape stopped into the dim light. Hope shook, the shape confirming what they all dreaded: Blisse. She eerily waved, her fingers wiggling.

"Hi, friends," she called. "Lovely to see you again!" She walked closer, and Hope could see the shape of a guard behind her. "You know, for a little bit there, I thought you actually hid from me! What an amazing surprise when you met my little man!"

Fire's eyes narrowed in anger.

"Blisse," she said. "You are despicable." Blisse nodded, about to speak. Fire's hand shot up, her face contorted in a glare. "No, no, I'm not done." This earned a pure evil glare from Blisse. "I can't believe how horrible you are," she continued. "That man was innocent. You had absolutely no reason to torment him like that! He was terrified for his life, don't you understand that? You are nothing."

Blisse grinned, infuriating Fire even more. "How can you smile!" she screamed. "There are no words to describe you! None! I *hate* you. I loathe you! And real Blisse, if you're listening, I hate you too. If you ever come back, I will never, ever forgive you. Never." Everyone held their breath, curious about Blisse's response. Blisse cocked her head to the side.

"Is that so?" she asked innocently. Fire nodded, her glare not straying from Blisse's coal eyes. "Well, we all have our bad days, huh?" She strolled over, making Fire flinch. Blisse sneered when she saw Ethan and Hope together. "Hope, how are you two lovebirds holding out?" Her voice dripped sarcasm.

"Shut up," muttered Hope. Blisse took a step, causing Ethan to get into a fighting stance.

"Wow, judging from your anxiousness, you'd think you were fighting a serial killer!" Blisse exclaimed. Ethan snorted without humor.

"Well, let's go!" said Blisse. Aiden raised his eyebrows.

"Go where exactly?"

"To my evil lair!" she said sarcastically as she cackled, sending chills down Hope's spine. "You aren't going anywhere this time." Ethan curled his hands into fists.

"We're not going anywhere with you," he snarled. Blisse slowly shook her head.

"Oh, that wasn't what you should have said." Suddenly, the guard behind her sprang out. Another came to them.

"How many guards do you have?!" exclaimed Cassidy. The three people slowly made their way toward the group. Blisse reached into her pocket and pulled out what looked like a gun.

"This is of my own invention," she said. "I wouldn't get hit with it if I were you. I'm just forewarning you, it hurts." Ethan shook his head angrily. Blisse simply shrugged. "Whatever you say, boy."

Without warning, she pointed the gun directly at him.

"Wait, will the gun kill him?" Fire asked, trying to keep the desperation out of her voice.

"Nope," said Blisse. She held the gun, raising her eyebrows, as if asking *are you sure?* Ethan kept his death glare locked on the evil girl in front of him. Her twisted smile spread across her face.

"Wait!" Fire shouted. She ran to jump in front of him, but it was too late. Blisse pulled the trigger.

Hope saw a golden light fly from the gun and into Ethan's chest. Ethan fell on the ground without a scream. Suddenly, his body started twitching and spasming. Foam began to trickle from his mouth.

"Ethan!" Fire yelled, trying to get close to him. His eyes were bulging, focusing on nothing. Fire turned her small frame toward Blisse.

"Screw you!" she shrieked. She started sprinting toward her.

"No!" Aiden yelled. He dashed after her as well. Blisse was watching the scene with a smirk on her face.

"Looks like my gun works," she mused happily. "How grand!" Hope glared at Blisse. *How could you have been so nice?* she thought. She could only imagine how Ethan felt.

"Stop it!" Cassidy screamed. "He's had enough! Stop!" Blisse paid no attention to her pleas as she watched Ethan twitch on the floor. Finally, Ethan's eyes closed. His breathing became heavier.

"Oh, he's already unconscious," Blisse said, disappointment evident in her tone. "Ah well, I guess we should get going then." Aiden glared at her, holding a weakly struggling Fire.

"We aren't going with you," Aiden growled. Blisse pointed the gun at him, making him flinch.

"Now," she commanded. Aiden shot a look at Ethan, lying on the floor. He looked at Cassidy, her desperate stare trying to help him. He saw Hope, standing there, looking helpless. Him and Fire made eye contact together. He looked into her dark blue eyes. They were full of something that he had never seen them before; pure fear.

Just go, she mouthed. He raised his eyebrows. *Are you sure?* he mouthed back. She sadly nodded. *We don't have a choice.*

"Tick tock," said Blisse.

"Ok," Aiden said reluctantly. "We'll go." He could see Blisse's eyes light up, even in the darkness.

"Perfect."

The guards took suspenseful steps to the huddling group of friends. Hope shot multiple worried glances at Ethan, hating the way his breathing seemed to be slowing.

"Don't touch us," Fire snapped quietly to a guard. Blisse laughed.

"Well, Sapphire, I need to make sure you won't get away, don't I? Don't fret, they'll only injure you if you try to escape." Fire gave a disgusted glare toward the man who grabbed her arm. He aggressively tore her from Aiden, causing her to bite back a scream. The other men grabbed Cassidy, Belle, and Hope. The girls didn't even attempt to struggle. One strong guard effortlessly picked Ethan up, throwing him over his shoulder.

"Why are you doing this?" Cassidy softly asked the man who was restraining her. He halfheartedly shrugged, his aged eyes avoiding her gaze. "Please, don't do this. Don't kill innocent people."

"I won't kill you," the man gruffly said. Cassidy's eyes widened.

"You won't? What are you going to do, then? And why are you helping Blisse?" The man quietly sniffed.

"I didn't want to help her," he finally said, ashamed. Cassidy looked at him with loads of sympathy. She needed to be as nice and understanding as possible to even have a chance of communicating with this man. "You remind me so much of my daughter," the man told her. "She was so brave."

"Why are you doing this?" she whispered again. The man's eyes were glistening.

"Grayson deeply disturbs me. This monster he's created disturbs me more. I can't go against her. I can't."

"So you're scared," Cassidy observed. He gave a quick, embarrassed nod. "Listen, sir, if you just help us, we can change her back to herself. Please let me go."

The man shook his head.

"I can't do that, young lady. I won't be like that man in the cave." Cassidy nodded.

"I understand. But listen, please be brave. Please don't be a coward. Is that how you would want your daughter to remember you?"

His eyes looked at her with pain.

"I'm sorry child. I can't." Cassidy began to feel some frustration.

"Yes, I realize that you are scared. But my friends are too. Don't make your life like this," she pleaded. He just shook his head once more. Without warning, Cassidy tried to tear herself away from his grasp. She lunged away from his body, but his strong hands clamped down on her arms.

"Stop," he said, almost desperately. "I don't want to hurt you, child. Please don't make me."

"So that's it then," Cassidy said, a hollow feeling in her stomach. "You're just going to follow Blisse's orders. You're going to spend the rest of your life as a coward."

The man began to walk, but Cassidy swore she heard a weak sob escape his lips. Cassidy's helpless expression turned to Aiden. Ever since their trap, she almost felt as if that had made them stronger together. He returned the same terrified look as his guard pushed him as well. Cassidy's eyes shot to Blisse. She was standing at the cave's entrance, her arms folded triumphantly. With a hopeless sigh, Cassidy walked forward.

31

Ethan awoke in a room.

"Hello!?" he called. *Where am I?*

All of his prior memories flooded back into his brain. He could still feel the lingering sting of the white-hot pain caused by Blisse's gun. He could still feel the dread he felt when he saw the man propped up against the wall. "Where is everyone?" He felt a flutter of panic in his gut. *Hope.* He finally noticed Blisse, snickering in the distance. He forced his memories away. Finally, his mind could finally focus. Ethan noticed his whole group of friends, gagged and tied up. Hope's eyes were wide, looking to see if he was ok.

"He's fine," Blisse said, sounding bored. "Relax."

Aiden struggled against his bonds to no avail. "You won't get out," said Blisse.

"Why are we here?" Ethan asked. Blisse's mouth perked up.

"That's the fun part." Ethan nervously took his eyes off of hers and peered around the room. He noticed a gigantic sheet in the middle with a chain coming down from high above.

"Where are we?" he asked cautiously. He noticed what looked like two crudely carved doors in the brown walls.

"A volcano," Blisse answered. Ethan looked at her, feeling dread throughout his entire body.

"What's the sheet for?" Blisse was walking around, viciously yanking the gags and ties of everyone. "And why were they tied up?"

"I didn't want them to escape," she explained. "That's a bit obvious." She walked over to Hope. "Come here, girly," she demanded. Hope shook her head, whimpering. Blisse sighed exasperated. "Ugh, fine, I'll do it myself." She roughly snatched Hope's arm and dragged her closer to the sheet. Blisse pulled her close.

"What are you doing?" Hope asked nervously. Blisse ignored her as she dug for something in her pocket. Ethan gulped.

Blisse released Hope, roughly pushing her aside. The evil girl pulled out a shape. Cassidy gasped; she was holding a gun. Blisse pointed her gun straight at Hope. A real gun with real bullets that could kill her in the blink of an eye. She was cowering, her eyes looking for help. Haylee's mouth dropped open, her wide eyes terrified.

"I'm going to kill you Hope," Blisse sneered." She turned toward the terrified crowd. "If anyone wants to save her, here's what you need to do." She turned toward the huge sheet, which was covering a massive amount of space. Fire's breath caught in her throat. She knew that the sheet covered something very, very bad. Blisse bared her evil grin, enjoying the suspense she was creating. Suddenly, she yanked it off with unnecessary force.

Hope threw her hand over her mouth. Ethan gasped before he could help it. Even Fire was terrified and shocked. Beneath the sheet was an impossibly deep hole. Although it was painfully obvious, Hope realized now why they were trapped in a volcano. She could clearly see the bubbling orange lava below. Above the hole was a chain that hung from the top of the deep brown volcano. Attached to the chain was a large metal cage, blocked by metal bars. Blisse laughed at their shocked expressions.

"To save her, one of you must get in the cage," she explained sinisterly. "Choose, or Hope here will be fatally shot. Tick-Tock." Ethan looked on, his eyes widened in sadness. The way Blisse explained her horrible thoughts were so matter-a-fact that it made him sick. It was at times like these that he couldn't even remember that his kind friend was trapped inside this monster. Hope had never seen Ethan look this vulnerable and helpless before. He looked absolutely and utterly sad.

Haylee watched, her auburn eyes filling with tears, despite not knowing the girl in front of her. Cassidy's muscles in her face were scrunched up. It was obvious that she was holding back a storm of tears.

"I'll do it," stated Ethan. His voice was devoid of emotion as he took a step forward.

"How noble," Blisse sneered.

"No!" Hope exclaimed. "You are not going into that cage!" Ethan paid no attention to her. He walked over to Blisse. Fire clenched her fists in anger.

"No, Ethan!" she shouted. He weakly smiled.

"I'm sorry. I care too much about all of you guys." He turned his attention to Blisse. "If I die, you have to promise not to harm my friends." His sad eyes darted to Hope. "Do you understand?" Blisse narrowed her coal black eyes.

"I promise not to kill them," she said reluctantly. Ethan raised his eyebrows, not satisfied with her answer.

"I said I want no harm to come to them. If you don't give me your word, I won't go into the cage." His threat had no effect on Blisse. Her face grew into a twisted smile.

"That's fine," she said. "I'll just shoot Hope instead."

"I'll do it," piped a small, quiet voice from the back.

Hope knew that voice. Oh god, she knew that voice too well.

Haylee.

"Oh my god, Haylee. No," she demanded, her voice becoming higher. "No, you aren't. I'd rather be shot." Haylee just looked sadly ahead.

"Listen, I don't even know who I am. I have no memory of who you are or why I'm here. I don't want you to lose your friend, Hope. I see the way you two look at each other, and it'd be evil to tear you apart. It only makes sense that I do it." Hope quickly shook her head in protest.

"No Haylee," she said, her voice breaking. "I love you. I love you more than anyone else. I'm not losing you. I don't care if you don't remember anything, because I do. I'll tell you all the details of every single memory we have together. But please, you can't die." Hope felt a single tear make its way down her cheek. She quickly wiped it away, not wanting to look weak in front of the smirking Blisse. Haylee's eyes filled with tears.

"I'm really sorry!" she cried out. "But who am I if my mind is gone?" Hope had no answer to her pitiful question. Her glistening tears were falling down freely. Blisse laughed, infuriating the sad girl. Hope gulped, and let out a huge, shaky breath.

"Haylee," she whispered in a trembling voice. It took everything in her to not run over and grab her step-sister in a huge, tight hug. Haylee weakly smiled through her pain.

"It's ok, Hope," she whispered back sadly. "I'm not afraid of death. I'll be fine."

"But what if I won't be?!" Hope yelled. In the horrible silence, you could hear a pin drop. Haylee looked at her, a million years of pain plastered across her face. "Haylee, you're all I have left," she pleaded. "Mom, dad, and I were never close. It was you who held us together. If you leave I'll…I won't know what to do." Hope had never shared her feelings like this before. She hated the sympathy in Ethan's eyes, the way he knew what the outcome would be. Fire was watching the scene, her eyes focused on the floor. Although Haylee was crying, she took her steps to the cage. Hope desperately lunged for her, but Ethan roughly pulled her back.

"LET ME GO!" she screamed at him, thrashing around in his arms. He kept his firm grip on her, his eyes filled with unshed tears.

"Hope…" he began, trying to stop her struggles. Haylee shot her a look that made her heart snap in two.

"I wish I knew you," whispered Haylee. Blisse used her newfound strength to pull the metal cage toward her.

"Step in, girly," she demanded, snickering. Hope screamed in Ethan's arms, thrashing for dear life. There was nothing that would stop her from getting her sister back.

"Haylee, NO!" she yelled. Haylee ignored her begging as she stepped into the cage. Blisse violently slammed the cage door shut. Ethan finally let Hope go, but it was too late. Haylee was locked in the cage for good.

"Kill me, kill me!" Hope pitifully cried out to Blisse. She didn't listen as she cranked the lever down. The cage began slowly lowering into the lava with Haylee trapped inside. Hope ran as close as she dared to the edge. She was now sobbing freely, her blotchy face a mess. Haylee's eyes stayed locked on Hope's as she traveled down.

Suddenly, she shook her head. Haylee rubbed her eyes with her fists. Her eyes open, pure horror slowly making its way across her face.

"Hope?" she whispered. This time, her tone was different. It was full of familiarity and kindness and *love*. Hope felt her heart drop to her stomach.

"Oh my god. Haylee?" she asked. Haylee nodded, tears streaking her face.

"Hope!" she said again, joy filling her voice. Then, she got a glimpse of her surroundings. She realized that she was trapped. A glance downward showed that she was suspended over lava. She screamed, banging on the cage door. "Let me out, let me out, let me out!" she shouted desperately. Hope sobbed, looking helplessly down at her friend.

"HAYLEE!!" she screamed. Blisse smiled.

"Well, it looks like she remembers you just in time, huh?" Hope put all of her pain and hatred into a piercing glare. Blisse wickedly smirked. Hope peered back over the edge and gasped. Haylee was suspended right over the lava.

"I love you Hope," Haylee yelled from down below. Haylee's eyes flooded with recognition and sorrow. All her memories flashed before her.

The time Hope had locked her out of the house once, when they first met. She vividly remembered pounding on the door, shouting to be let in.

She remembered when Hope had stood up for her when she was being made fun of about her braces in high school.

She remembered Hope's determined look back on the plane when she was about to skydive.

She remembered her first birthday party, her first day of middle school, her first dance, her first boyfriend, her first kiss, everything. Haylee didn't even scream as she came face to face with the lava. She made eye contact with her sister for the last time. Her hands weakly rattled the bars.

I love you, Hope. You'll make it. I love you.

Impossibly, she didn't struggle or even attempt to escape. It made Ethan even sadder to watch as she just accepted her death. She didn't look so young anymore as her eyelids slid shut forever. The sound of creaking chains filled the air, marking the end of a young life. Hope watched as the lava swallowed up the only person she had ever loved.

Hope faintly heard the heartbreaking sob that came from her throat. And there she stayed for what seemed like forever, with the screams that cut her vocal cords like a knife. Blisse was watching Hope with a look of triumph, a look of accomplishment. It made bile rise up in Ethan's throat. Cassidy was shaking, her energy drained.

"Well, that was interesting," Blisse mused. Ethan held his middle finger up, staring daggers at his turned friend.

"Blisse," he said. "Go jump off a volcano." Blisse smirked.

"Whatever you say, pal." She walked over to Hope, roughly putting a hand on her shoulder. "Wow, Hope, you don't look too happy."

Without warning, Hope twisted her body. She grabbed onto Blisse's wrist, her right foot slamming into her knee. Blisse screeched as she dangled in the air above the lava, only Hope's grip keeping her alive.

"Go to hell." Her voice came out surprisingly steady and firm. Blisse clawed at her hand, but Hope didn't pull her up. "If you scratch me again, I swear I will let you go, and you can die just like Hay-" she broke off, not able to say her name. "Just like my sister did. It might just be me, but I don't think dying in lava is my cup of tea. So, *Blisse,* I wouldn't claw me again if I were you." Blisse stopped immediately, despising taking orders from Hope. The blonde adult bared her teeth. "Good choice."

Hope didn't know what to do next. As badly as she wanted to drop Blisse to her death, she couldn't. She knew that her real friend had to be inside the evil girl somewhere, however impossible it was to believe.

"Just drop her already!" Fire snapped. Hope turned her head and shook it side to side.

"I can't, Fire," she said urgently. "If I drop her, the real Blisse will be lost forever. Do you really want her die knowing that all she did was cause us pain? If that were me, I would be miserable. There has to be a way to bring her back." Blisse's black eyes were looking up in annoyance.

"I really hate all of you guys," she muttered. Hope responded by dropping her hand an inch. Blisse shrieked, instinctively tightening her grip on Hope's hand.

"I wouldn't insult us anymore," she said, snickering at her surprise. Fire sighed impatiently.

"Well then, what are we going to do? We know you're bluffing. Hope, we all know you won't drop Blisse, ok? So quit with the tough act or actually do it. I honestly don't care what you do as long as we leave in under five minutes." Suddenly, Hope felt her wrist snap. She screamed in pain as Blisse flipped up onto the surface.

"You should've dropped me," she said smugly. Hope cradled her wrist, feeling tears fall for the umteenth time that day. Ethan pulled at his knife, jutting the point out. Blisse dramatically sighed. "You know you won't kill me." She sashayed over to the side. Ethan's eyes were focused on her, not missing any of her movements.

"Geez, don't look so tense! I won't kill you. Right now," she added. "It would be foolish of me to fight you right now, I'll admit that. But you can't run forever. I'll kill you all. I promise." She backed up more to the far side of the volcano. Ethan raised his eyebrows, ready to strike if needed. Blisse bumped her hip on a part of the wall, opening the poorly cut door. She gave them a sly smirk. "I'll be back to kill you soon!" She slowly walked backward out of the door carved into the volcano. She slammed it shut, leaving them. As soon as she was gone for good, Ethan dropped his weapon, running over to Hope.

"Hope, are you ok?" he asked, concerned. She looked at him, her eyes full of nothing but pain.

"Do you really think I'd be ok?" She gasped suddenly. "I think she broke my wrist."

"Can you move it?" he questioned. Hope weakly shrugged. "I can try." She slowly moved her wrist up. A second later, she winced. "Ouch, no I can't. I definitely can't."

"Uhh, I hate to add to our problems," Fire began, "but I think we're locked in here." Ethan let out an annoyed breath.

"Are you serious?" Fire walked over to the door, pulling on it with all her might.

"Yep, I'm serious. It's not opening." Aiden came over to her. With an exasperated sigh, he roughly pushed the door with his palm. To her surprise, it creaked open. Fire's face turned beet red as she lowered her head. Ethan raised his eyebrows.

"Wow Sapphire, you win the award for smartest person," he told her sarcastically.

"Well, I- shut up, Ethan," she retorted in defense. "And my name's Fire." Her face was getting redder by the minute.

"Well," said Hope, "let's go, then." Ethan nodded, helping her support her wrist. All of the events before were beginning to flood her brain. "Ethan, distract me," she suddenly ordered. He cocked his head.

"What do you mean, Hopie?"

"I don't want to think about you know who. Just distract me." She desperately waited for any source of forgetting her dead sister. Her chest felt tight and her breathing sped up. Ethan rubbed his neck, visibly uncomfortable.

"Uh, ok." He thought about what to say. "Well, nice weather we're having, huh?" Hope gave him an annoyed look, slapping his arm with her uninjured hand. He grinned, lightly hitting her back.

"Quit flirting!" Fire called over from the door. Hope blushed, but Ethan didn't skip a beat.

"I don't know Fire, there's no need for flirting when Hope's already obsessed with me. I mean, she won't get off of me!"

Hope rolled her eyes.

"Stop," she muttered. Ethan nudged her with his elbow.

"Oh come on, you know I'm funny," he half heartedly joked. Fire's eyes darted over to them.

"Are you gonna come, or are you just going to stand there and enjoy the view?" Ethan grabbed Hope's good wrist and pulled her to the door.

"After you, element," he said, affectionately, ruffling Fire's hair with his free hand. She skipped out the door, gripping Aiden's hand. Ethan walked out as well. Although he tried not to show it, he was peering around the corner of the volcano, looking for a sign of Blisse.

"Ethan, you're thinking about Blisse, aren't you?" Hope asked. He smiled wryly.

"How can you tell?"

"Dude, you're fidgeting like crazy and you keep looking around. It's not that hard to figure out," she said. He squeezed her hand. She cocked her eyebrows. "What was that?" He chuckled.

"Oh, sorry, I was just thinking about something." She raised her eyebrows, expecting him to continue. He grinned. "That's my girl, persistent as always. I was thinking about something Blisse told me, a long time ago."

"What did she say?" asked a curious Hope. His gaze moved down to the ground.

"I asked her what her life goals were, what she wanted to accomplish." Hope put her good hand up.

"Oh, I can tell this is going to be really sad," she said, only half kidding. Ethan nodded grimly.

"Yeah, pretty much. She told me that she wanted to help people. She said that she didn't care what she did as long as it benefited people in need. I asked her why." Hope rolled her eyes.

"What do you mean why?" she questioned. He put a finger to her lips.

"Now now, save your questions for the end," he said condescendingly. "So I asked her more about it. She said that she didn't want to only survive. I was confused what it meant then, but I know now. And nothing makes me sadder than knowing that she's doing exactly what she always feared doing. Hope, I got to know her a lot before you arrived. She's the nicest person I could ever hope of meeting." Hope smiled softly.

"I know."

"What do you mean?"

"Well, remember when I first met you, and you were introducing me to everyone?" She paused, waiting for his nod. "I remember the way you looked at her, like she was someone you loved. I can tell that you love her. As a friend, of course," she added. He nodded.

"Well aren't you just observant?" he asked. She only nodded.

"So where are we gonna go now?" Suddenly, a shadow passed over her face. Her eyes looked to the ground.

"What's wrong, Hopie?" She looked up at him.

"It won't go away," she whispered.

"You'll be ok," he said, stroking her arm. It was difficult for Hope to hold back the flood of tears that threatened to spill over her lashes. She didn't think she would ever feel truly happy again. She could feel the void in her heart now. It would never be filled and Hope would spend the rest of her life with a numbness that would never go away. She avoided Ethan's gaze as she walked through the jungle. It didn't escape her that the once beautiful trees looked like rotted dirt to her eyes.

Haylee is dead.
Haylee is dead.
Haylee is dead.

32

"I have to get out of here," Hope gasped, running her fingers through her hair. Ethan looked at her, full of confusion and concern.

"What do you mean?"

"I just can't talk right now, I need to run, I need to-" Hope stopped speaking, feeling her breathing accelerate. She couldn't talk, she could feel a hole in her chest getting larger and larger, her throat gulped for air but she couldn't breathe…

"Hope," Ethan said, gently but firm. "Just breathe. Don't think about anything right now, just clear your mind." Hope's panic was to the brim. All she wanted to do was rip out her heart.

"I need to sprint," she almost begged. "If I just walk, I'll go insane. I need to run."

"Alright," Ethan told her, looking at her with sadness in his eyes. "Go ahead." Without a glance behind him, Hope took off at top speed.

The trees blurred past her as she ran and ran and ran. Her tears blinded her vision, turning everything into a mess. The only thing she could think about was Haylee, the way her eyes had looked so pure and innocent before she died. She absolutely hated Blisse. She wanted Blisse to feel the worst pain possible. She wanted to hear her screams. In a way, that thought disturbed her more than Grayson ever had.

Before she could comprehend what had happened, Hope was sprawled on the ground. Her foot was twisted up in a root, and it was then that she *broke*.

Hope screamed into the ground, letting her greasy hair wave around in all directions. She shrieked and shrieked until her voice was hoarse, and Hope could sense everybody around her. Ethan's face looked so innocent and sad, it made her weep even harder.

She spent five minutes this way, beating the ground with her cut-up fingers and screaming. She ignored the awful pain in her burning wrist as she punched and punched the ground.

Finally, Hope stood up and rolled her shoulders back. She sniffed, looking firmly into everyone's eyes. Nobody dared to say anything at all. Hope looked as though she could kill anybody with her bare hands at that moment.

"What," she said, her voice sounding robotic. "I can't cry too?"

"Where do we go?" Fire asked. Her voice broke, but she didn't care. Seeing Hope just fall apart threatened to rip her heart.

"I guess we can go this way," Ethan whispered. He grabbed Hope's good wrist, pulling her roughly to the right. Cassidy quickly changed her direction as well. Hope stopped at once, her feet planted firmly on the ground.

"Shh," she demanded, her finger flying over her mouth. Ethan looked at her oddly.

"But why…"

"Shut up!" she snapped, her eyes growing wide in urgency. Ethan shot her the same weird look, but he fell silent. *Nobody move,* she mouthed slowly. It was clear that Fire despised taking orders from Hope. It pained her to keep her mouth shut, but she decided that Hope had had to deal with more than enough for the day. For her whole lifetime, probably.

"Why'd you make us stop?" Belle whispered, slightly annoyed. Hope darted her eyes around nervously. "You look like you're insane."

"I hear something," Hope whispered back. Belle shut her mouth, looking around as well. A few minutes passed. Hope was still cautiously looking around, positive that she had heard a noise.

"This is stupid!" Fire exclaimed. Her eyes were wide in annoyance. Hope shot her a glare, something that she never would've done when they first met. Fire squinted her eyes, but she didn't comment back. Ethan sighed.

Snap.

Hope froze. She shot him a look that said *I told you so!* He took a small breath, and Cassidy's eyes grew terrified. Hope knew what they were all thinking: Blisse. If it was her, Hope didn't know if she could be emotionally stable. There would never be even the slightest chance of escape if the noise belonged to Blisse.

Ethan held his hand up, silencing everybody. He heard whispering from around the corner. Fire shot him a glance, a small amount of fear in her eyes. Very, very slowly, Ethan peered around the corner.

"AHH!" someone yelled. Ethan threw up his hands in pure annoyance.

"Don't worry guys," he said in a frustrated tone, coming back around the corner. He was holding the hair of a very terrified girl in his strong hand. Her copper eyes were wide in fear, and her mouth opened wide. "It's just some girl. Her friend is behind her." Another girl followed his steps, her gray eyes frightened.

"Please don't hurt me!" the girl pleaded. Ethan sighed, rolling his eyes.

"We won't hurt you. Quit whimpering and tell me who you are, and why you scared me and my friends that way." Ethan almost aggressively tore her hair from his grip. She wiped her moist eyes with her dirty hands.

"I didn't mean to scare you," she said, taking long breaths. "A few days ago, our friend got angry and left us. She's blown up before, but she always comes back. We went out to look for her." By now, she had calmed down a little bit. She could talk and explain with her voice steady. Fire walked in front of Ethan, her eyes set on the girl on the ground.

"And what might your name be?" she asked, her tone tinged with suspicion. The girl's golden eyes focused on her hard blue ones.

"I'm Genevieve, but you can call me Gen, if you want." She pointed over to the other scared girl. "That's my friend Aspyn." Ethan nodded.

"Got it. Why exactly did your other friend stalk off?"

"It was her birthday," Genevieve began. "She had plans with her boyfriend, before she came here. She was angry about it and for some reason, she got all mean and snarky. I warned her not to walk alone at night, but she didn't listen. And now, I don't know where she is." She suddenly put her head in her hands. Her body shook with sobs, and Aspyn gently put her hand on her shoulder.

"She's just worried," explained Aspyn. "She and Selena were closer than I was with her."

"I take it Selena is the name of your friend?" Fire asked. Aspyn nodded.

"Yep. I-" she stopped speaking, her eyes darting to Genevieve. "Hey, can I talk with you for a minute?" Aspyn gestured toward Fire. She raised her eyebrows.

"You know, I really don't like that sentence," she said, her lips pursed. Aspyn cocked her head to the side.

"Why not?"

"It reminds me of this guy we knew," Fire explained, remembering Gabe. "Those were pretty much his exact words to Hope." Aspyn slowly nodded, confused.

"Ok, sorry. But I need to tell you something." She pointed around the corner. Fire looked at her with suspicion in her eyes, but she walked around the corner. Aspyn followed, pointing up ahead. They took a few more steps.

"Well, what's so important?" Fire asked impatiently. Aspyn's light gray eyes darted around, making sure that they couldn't be heard.

"It's about Selena," she said. Fire looked at her, her face in an expression of annoyance.

"Ok, get on with it."

"I think something happened to her," Aspyn began. "I don't think that she wouldn't have come back. Selena can be a bit dense sometimes, but even she would never stay out at night. I think we should look for her, or at least investigate." Fire snorted.

"Yeah right. Listen, I think you might be onto something, I'll give you that. But if you think my friends and I are just going to drop everything to help you, you're crazy. We're already doing something important, and we don't have time to help you." Aspyn frowned. She twirled her pink hair angrily.

"What are you doing that could be so important, huh? If you won't help us, I want an answer."

Fire grinned slightly. In a way, Aspyn's anger and stubbornness reminded her of herself.

"We're kinda running from some psycho maniac who wants to kill us."

Aspyn looked at her with fright, her eyebrows scrunched together.

"Come again?"

"My friend, well, not anymore, got transformed into some monster. She's hunting us now, and believe me when I say she's terrifying. I'm not going to help you find your little friend, sorry. We have higher priorities. Don't take it personally."

Aspyn put her hands on her hips in annoyance.

"So what, you aren't curious about what happened to her? Not even a little bit?"

"Not really," Fire answered casually. "People go missing and die all the time. Unless it's Ethan, Aiden, or Cassidy, I really can't be bothered with anyone else." Fire shrugged. "That's life on this island, pink hair."

"But that's just stupid!" Aspyn retorted. "If I were you, I'd be terrified and curious about what happened to my friend."

Fire rolled her eyes dramatically.

"I don't care. I'm going back with Aiden now." Fire turned to go away, but she was stopped by Aspyn's firm grip on her arm. "I *don't* like to be touched," Fire growled. "Let go."

"No. I need to know what happened to Selena, whether you like it or not. Help me find her." Fire ripped her arm from Aspyn's hold, but she didn't stalk off. What if she was in place of Aspyn? What if instead of Selena, it was Ethan? She would be beyond mad if someone completely refused to help her. Fire sighed, turning around.

"I'll see what I can do, pink hair." Aspyn looked at her suspiciously.

"Really?"

"Yeah," Fire said warily, nodding. "I'll try to think of something, ok? I'll try." Aspyn's emotions changed like a light switch. Her frustrated face turned into a look of hope.

"You will? Do you promise?" Fire exhaled, suddenly aware of how exhausted she really was. Whatever Aspyn wanted, she would deal with it later.

"I promise."

"How was your little conversation?" Ethan asked, bounding over to Fire. She gave a weak smirk.

"Wouldn't you like to know?" Genevieve looked over suspiciously at her friend.

"Aspyn, what *did* you talk about?" Aspyn shot her friend a knowing smile.

"I just asked this girl about the island. No big deal, Gen."

Ethan gave Fire a look. She gave a quick nod of her head, and Ethan knew she would tell him later.

"Do you mind if we stick with you?" Genevieve suddenly asked. Cassidy and Belle locked eyes awkwardly. Hope looked at Ethan for help while Fire turned to Aiden.

"Yeah, can we?" Aspyn piped up. "I don't feel safe going back to our old place. Besides, there's safety in numbers, right?"

Ethan nodded uncomfortably.

"Well, yeah, but I don't think we can really afford to add more people to our group."

"We won't slow you down!" Genevieve told him eagerly. "Please, I really don't want to go back. I know we have food there, but it just doesn't seem safe."

"Wait," Belle ordered, putting out her hand. "You have food there? How much?"

"A lot," she said. "Like, in piles. We are all about stocking up."

Aspyn nodded, but she looked at Genevieve with discomfort.

"Oh, yeah, that's right, we do. But still, what if the thing that… took Selena is still by our place?"

"Then they'll have to go up against me," Belle stated, puffing out her chest. "I have been so damn hungry the past couple days. Take us there and you can stay with us."

"Is that a deal?" Aspyn asked Ethan. He shot Belle a hesitant look, but he nodded.

"Yeah, sure. It's a deal." Genevieve's face broke out into a grateful smile. "Thank you! I can show you the food."

"Wait," said Ethan. "What way did you come from?" Genevieve pointed to the right, confused.

"That way, why?"

"Let's go left then," he replied. Belle stared at him, appalled.

"That's the longer way, you idiotic walnut." Ethan's eyes twinkled as he chuckled.

"Idiotic walnut?" Belle crossed her arms, her hazel eyes staring at the laughing Ethan in anger.

"Why do you want to go the longer way?"

"There might be more clues about their dead friend, Belle. We need to look for evidence about what could have happened to her."

"We never said we would help them," Belle retorted. "I want my food, and I won't take a long way for some of your crap."

Aspyn fiercely raised her hand in the air.

"Actually, you did say you would help us," she stated. Belle narrowed her eyes at the angry girl.

"No, actually, we didn't."

"*She* did!" Aspyn responded, pointing almost accusingly at the now regretful Fire. "She promised that she would!" Belle snickered.

"No, she didn't, did you Sapphire?" Belle held her head high, her smirk wavering when Fire stayed silent. "Fire, you did not promise, did you?"

"Yeah, yeah," she muttered as her face grew a deep shade of red. Aspyn turned back to look at Belle, and there was a concealed smug expression on her face. Ethan put his arm around Belle's shoulder playfully, pulling her in.

"See, looks like we do have to go the long way after all," he teased. Belle glared at him, throwing off his arm aggressively.

"Fine, I'll go with you. Oh, and Ethan? If it takes too long, I'm eating you."

Ethan shrugged comically.

"Whatever the maiden says."

"Don't call me a maiden," she snapped back. "Now let's go. The faster you are, the less danger all you guys are in. Don't think I'll just stop at Ethan."

33

"Ethan, I'm getting hungry," Belle warned. The group had been walking for 30 minutes, each step sending a knife of pain through Belle's stomach.

"We're almost there," Aspyn reassured. "I've been over here before."

"I think I have too," Genevieve added excitedly. Her golden eyes suddenly lit up when she looked up into the deep sky. "Guys, look! It's raining!"

Fire let out an audible groan.

"It's the jungle. It rains all the time."

"It's so beautiful!" Genevieve twirled around in the now falling water. Her blonde, silvery hair seemed to spread out, making her look like an ecstatic ballerina.

"This sucks," Belle muttered, rolling her eyes at the girl's attitude. "Now I'm gonna get all wet, *and* I'm gonna have to murder and eat Ethan."

"Gen hasn't been out much," Aspyn apologized. "Selena wanted us inside our shelter."

"I think it's sweet," Cassidy said kindly.

"Well, I think it's putting Ethan in more danger," Belle replied, looking at Ethan almost greedily. "I'm getting very, very hungry."

Ethan bowed, looking at Belle with a challenging glance.

"Go ahead, Belle, eat me." She sighed, looking back at Genevieve. Deep down, Belle was jealous of the way the grinning girl could just leave everything behind and dance in the rain. Her expression looked so innocent when the water splashed off of her eyelashes, it gave Belle flashbacks of when she was a tiny child. Back before her life had turned darker and darker.

Sniffing away the sudden sad thoughts, Belle turned to look at Ethan again. Ethan was the only person in the group who didn't remotely annoy her. For some reason, Ethan was the one who Belle didn't have to strain to like.

His eyes were focused on Hope, who was standing next to him. At first glance, it looked like rain water was falling down her face. However, upon further investigation, it was clear that the liquid was pouring from her eyes.

"Hopie?"

Her head looked up at him. Her eyes looked clear and utterly sad in the rain. "What's wrong?"

Hope sniffed, more water coming from her light eyes.

"Haylee loved the rain."

"Well, Haylee isn't here." The snappy voice belonged to Fire, who had wandered over to Ethan. Hope gulped, looking at Fire in anger and hollowness.

"I know. Thanks for reminding me."

"Sapphire!" Ethan snapped, aghast. "Why would you say something like that?"

"Sorry, sorry," she mumbled, her hands running across her arms. "I just can't think straight with that idiot girl twirling like she's a rockette."

"Rockettes don't twirl like that," Belle said lowly, rolling her eyes. "You're thinking of a ballerina."

"Speaking of facts, who wants to hear one?" Aspyn asked brightly.

"No one," Fire muttered. Aspyn paid no attention to her as she cleared her throat.

"Genevieve is what one would consider a pluviophile," she started. "A pluviophile is someone who likes or enjoys being in the rain."

Belle looked at her darkly.

"I really wanna shove a pluviophile right up your big-"

"That's an interesting fact," Aiden said loudly, shooting Belle a look. Belle sighed, the loudest one of all.

"What can a girl do to get some food around here?" Her angry eyes darted to Ethan. "You know what? Screw all of you. I'm eating Ethan."

"It's right over here!" Genevieve shouted to them. "We just have to get past this tree." Belle let out one last exasperated sigh as she went to follow the now soaking wet Genevieve.

Gen stopped moving at once. A piercing, terrifying scream came from her open mouth. Fire jumped, looking over almost angrily.

"What?"

Genevieve couldn't move. Her body seemed to be paralyzed in shock. Ethan tore his gaze away from Hope and dashed up to her.

In front of them was a girl.

A dead girl.

Someone who had once been a lively, pretty African American girl was now sprawled on the ground with a deep red slash on her neck. Genevieve fell to her knees, shaking. Aspyn soon did the same.

"Selena," she choked out. Cassidy looked on, her eyes opening wide.

"Wait, that was Selena?"

Belle looked at Ethan almost helplessly.

"I told you we shouldn't have taken the long way, Ethan."

"Who- who did this to her?!" Genevieve screeched. Her hands were tearing through her hair now, small strands coming out in her quivering hands. "We could've been killed!"

"Well," said Fire, "you learn to deal with it once you've been on this island for awhile."

"Sapphire," Ethan snapped, holding her gaze. "Stop it."

"I'm not going back there," Aspyn whispered, her eyes filling up. "I'm never going to that shelter again."

Hunger tore savagely at Belle's stomach. It almost physically hurt to keep her comments back.

"Then where will we go?" Fire almost snarkily asked. "It's pouring rain, I'm freezing cold, and I'm about to eat Ethan too."

"Selena just *died,*" Aiden said, anger seeping into his tone. "Sapphire, not everything is about you."

Fire's head slowly turned toward her friend. Her eyes got smaller and smaller as her head lowered.

"Sorry, sorry," he said hastily, putting out his hands. "You're just being a bit insensitive."

"I'm just tired of watching people break down," she said lowly. "You know what my dad would've done, Aiden? He would've slapped me across the face twice, giving me something to cry about. Death is just a part of life, people get way too worked up about it. I want to leave now."

"Fine," Aiden said, suddenly cold. "I'll remember that when I do this."

Fire's narrowed eyes grew more confused and furious.

"Do what?"

Before Aiden could answer, he suddenly spun his body around toward a tree. To everyone's surprise and horror, he slammed his head against the tree once, twice, three times, loud enough to create a booming sound.

"Aiden!" Fire shrieked. "What the *hell* are you doing?"

Aiden's swaying body slowly moved back toward his friend. His pupils were large enough to scare Fire, and his head couldn't quite focus. He uttered two terrible, terrible words that made her sanity waver.

"Who's Aiden?"

34

"No, no," Fire muttered to herself crazily. Her heart dropped down to her knees once those awful words had escaped his mouth. "You did not just do that, Aiden."

Hope's mind immediately snapped to Haylee. If he lost his memory too, if she was forced to watch him suffer as Haylee did, she knew for sure that she would go absolutely insane.

Cassidy was standing there, motionless. Her body seemed to be flooded with ice, each breath sending waves of fear through her mind. The way Aiden looked around filled her with terror. She couldn't lose him too.

"Aiden," Fire shouted, hysteria creeping into her tone. "Aiden, you remember me, right?"

He just stared at her, confused. His head full of blonde highlights cocked to the side.

"I… I don't know…"

Fire could almost tangibly feel as her heart sped up. Her vision seemed to blur together in the drenching rain as she stared at her friend who could be gone forever. She had seen the tragic events that had happened to Haylee. She had watched as Hope had broken at the edge of the volcano. And now, that could be her place instead.

"Please tell me you remember me, Aiden," she begged, her voice shaking. Belle stared in disbelief at Fire's vulnerability. The small, hot-tempered girl was now freely sobbing in the rain, a sight that Belle would've never imagined happening. With Genevieve and Aspyn weeping over Selena and Fire crying over Aiden, the scene was the saddest thing she had ever laid her eyes on.

"Aiden, no." Her tiny body fell on the ground, her knees roughly hitting the soaking wet ground. There she stayed for what seemed like much too long.

"Sapphire," he said softly. Fire looked up, hiccuping and trembling. Her watering eyes grew wide.

"Aiden?" she whispered. She started to clench her fists, hot breaths coming from her mouth. "You lost your memory." He looked at her, almost as though he was regretful.

"You said people get too worked up over death? Well, I wanted to show you that that's not true."

Fire slowly felt her blood boil. She aggressively wiped her eyes, her face burning in pure humiliation. Aiden's face looked down.

"Fire, I'm sorry, but you needed to see that."

"Aiden." His head looked up eagerly at her voice. "Don't you ever talk to me again," she whispered. "Don't you ever think about me, don't even look at me. Whatever we had, you can consider it dead." She gave him one last look before she turned her back on him.

All the times she had dreamed about him, the times she had thought about him wonderingly, those had all been wiped away from this one act. He had embarrassed her in front of her entire group. Belle had seen her as she had broken down. Ethan had seen his partner's body quiver in sadness, seen her look vulnerable.

She was done with him.

"Hey!" Blisse snarled. Her dark eyes narrowed in on one of her men. His pant leg had gotten caught on a thorn, causing his large body to crash on the ground. "You're too loud."

"Sorry, Blisse," he murmured in embarrassment, forcing himself to get back up. Blisse bared her teeth, turning her entire body toward him.

"You will call me your master," she demanded. "You will not call me that pathetic name."

"Of course," he muttered. Blisse walked toward him, placing her fingers under his chin. The pure fear in his eyes absolutely filled her with delight, there were no words to describe the feeling she felt in her chest. She was in power.

She was in control.

"Of course, *master*," she cooed in his ear.

"Master," he said quickly, trying to sneakily move his body away from her. Of course, Blisse noticed this. The serum coursing through her very veins allowed her reflexes to respond faster, and every little movement didn't escape her vision.

But she let him move. She would not let him see everything she was capable of yet. The element of surprise was always welcome.

"So, let me get this straight," another man began. "You want us to kill a group of 20 year olds?"

"Yes," said Blisse, walking back to the front of the line. "Now that I have you as well, I will be able to kill them without any harm coming to me."

"What about us?"

"You are expendable," she said cooly. "You were not Grayson's chosen person, I was. You'd better hope that you succeed, because if you don't, something very bad will happen to you if you are still alive."

"That's not very fair," he muttered under his breath. To any normal person, his words would've been too quiet to decipher.

Blisse was not a normal person.

"What's your name?" she asked, her eyes staring into his. Although he was clearly trying to hide it, Blisse could tell that he was scared of her.

Of what she could do to him.

He looked up as he lightly scratched his beard.

"Tyrand," he hesitantly replied. Blisse slowly grinned.

"Well, *Tyrand,* have you ever heard that life isn't fair? Shut your trap, or you'll really see how unfair I can be."

He didn't reply. Tyrand hated the way this little girl seemed to threaten him with her large black eyes. They were impure. They were unholy.

He wished that he could take her pretty little neck and just break it. He wanted to break *her.*

But of course, he had seen what Blisse had done to that poor man. He had watched as his arms were ripped off, as the blood had spurted from the wound. It had been redder than anything he had ever seen.

That... that was what he had enjoyed. He had liked that. What he didn't like, though, was the way Blisse had looked at him afterwards. Her smile had been huge and sadistic and *crazed.* He didn't like how Blisse looked at all of them as though they were just a pile of meat. Tyrand knew that Blisse only wanted to see people suffer. He also was aware of how disturbing he was himself, but Grayson had shown him how much fun pain could bring when you are watching someone else. The sense of power he could feel was... indescribable.

But with this new, purely evil Blisse, he wouldn't be able to be in control. The little black eyed devil would never let a man take over, and it was clear in her expression. Whenever she had locked eyes with Tyrand, he could clearly see her challenging glare that dared anyone to take her on. Of course, no one dared to.

And until he could kill this infamous group of young adults Blisse wouldn't shut up about, he would never be in control.

Ara was not a normal child.

She was a six year old girl who had been the kid of some of the most terrible people on the planet.

Her mother, who went by the name of Ida, loved to kill people. Her father was dead. Ida never spoke of him, but Ara knew that he had been murdered by his own wife.

Whenever Ida would become angry, it was like a firework. That one vein in her neck would pulse as Ara would feel her cheek burn from the multiple hits she would receive. She couldn't yawn without feeling as though the skin on her face would snap.

However many times she was hit, Ida never brought out the knife. She reserved that knife for the men she would kill. Ara never was threatened by the blade. In some sick, twisted way, Ida loved her child. Sure, tiny little Ara with her chocolate hair and sunken in eyes was a handful, especially when she was a baby. Now, she had learned to fend for herself. Ida was away most of the time, and in that span, she would be alone.

Alone in the jungle, where bloodthirsty murderers hid away.

The first time someone had come at her, she had run. There was no way on earth she would've fought the guy with his crusted axe. When Ida had finally found her, she had received the worst beating of her life. Ironically, it was because Ida was worried for her safety.

Now was one of those times.

In her path was a bunch of old men, all with weapons and sharky grins. Ida was out hunting for food. Or people, sometimes it was hard to tell with her.

In the front of the group was a small girl. She was short, but Ara had to admit that she had muscle on her arms. The combination looked humorous.

But still, she was a small girl. And small girls on the island meant kindness, usually. The only alarming thing about her were her eyes. They looked like lightless pits dug into her tan face. Her hair was the same deep shade, which made her look frightening. Her lips were odd, too. They were very red, and Ara didn't recall anyone on the island owning any lipstick.

"Hi," Ara said simply. She was very observant and mature for her age, but she didn't see the point in running. They hadn't threatened her yet, and she was curious about the strange girl's dark lip makeup.

"Well hi there," the black eyed girl cooed. Her red lips went up in a grin. Ara could feel some sort of tingling in her gut when she locked eyes. Where was Ida? Why wasn't she back? Although their mother and daughter relationship wasn't perfect, she wanted her mother by her side.

"Where's my mommy?"

"Your mommy won't be joining us, sweetie," the girl said. She seemed happy, but Ara didn't know why. What was so funny about her question?

"Why do you have red lips?" she asked.

"I like to eat different things," the stranger mused, "and let's just say that I'm not a vegetarian. Your mother was the same way, child. She… joined me for lunch today."

"Why won't she be coming back?" Ara whined. The girl's dark eyes set.

"Just kill her," she murmured to the front man. "I want Hope."

"But she's a child," he began hesitantly. "She can't do any harm." The stranger's eyes grew angry. Finally, Ara knew something was up. That was a replica of Ida's expression.

Right before she hit her.

"What did I just say, Tyrand?" she asked through bared teeth. The man with the odd name looked at Ara with annoyance on his face.

"Alright, alright." He slid a knife from his belt. He took steps closer and closer to the wise six year old. Before she could run, before she could even move, he had thrown out a sharp blade into her chest.

That's when she started shrieking for Ida. The blood ran down her yellow shirt as she locked eyes with the black eyed girl. The stranger was smirking, mumbling something to herself.

Ara's consciousness slowly left her tiny body as her knees smashed into the ground.

"Well," Belle muttered, chewing on her bottom lip. "This rain is really... wet, huh?"

The group had made a crude shelter under a small, jutted out rock. The rain water still trickled down onto their skin. Aiden and Fire hadn't talked since their incident, and Hope didn't think that they planned to. Fire's icy eyes were locked onto the hard ground. Aiden's usually kind eyes were like daggers as he refused to look at his friend.

Aspyn's hands were wrapped around her knees. The image of her dead friend with her slit throat would not leave her mind. However many problems they had shared, Aspyn would give up anything to bring her back.

"I'm sorry, Aspyn," Gen whispered, hugging her tightly. All Hope could do was stare at the rain, thinking of Haylee. She willed her eyes to stay dry over and over as memories played back in her brain.

Ethan could only think of Blisse. She was ready to strike at any time, and she wouldn't let anything get in her way. She was willing to kill anyone in a heartbeat, and that's what made her so frightening. She had no conscious. None. There wasn't a slip of a human in her possessed body. She would do anything in the world to get her victims.

"Sapphire," Aiden mumbled, turning to her tiny frame. A snarl sound escaped her throat.

"No."

"Sapphire, please, just let me-"

"I said no, you psychopath!" She turned her back toward him once more. "You know what?" she asked loudly. "I want to get out of here. I want real shelter, not this crap."

"We can't do that," Ethan said in a patient voice. "You know that Blisse could be there."

"So? I want to go now. I'm cold."

"Fire," Ethan said through gritted teeth. "Shut up please." She squinted her eyes, glaring at him.

"Well, I'll go then. Alone."

"No!" Gen suddenly shrieked. Fire's head snapped toward her, alarmed.

"Why not?"

"That's how Selena died," Aspyn whimpered. "She was stubborn and she died. You can't go alone."

"Yes I can," Fire responded cooly. "I can do whatever the hell I want."

She pushed herself up, wincing at her stiff muscles.

"Fire," Aiden snapped. "You need to stay here. You could get hurt." Her cold gaze turned to him.

"What do you care? Obviously you don't really care about me at all."

"I do," he said, in an overly calm voice. Hope could feel the tension brewing in the air. "You have too much pride, Sapphire. I was just helping you see pain from someone else's point of view. I'm sorry."

"You're not forgiven." Her tiny body stomped away into the pouring rain. Aiden turned to Ethan, and Hope was surprised to see his eyes filled with tears.

"I made a mistake," he whispered. Ethan gently patted him on the back, looking out into the rain.

"You'll be ok," Ethan said sadly. "It'll all be ok."

Fire blinked the tears from her eyes as she sprinted on the wet ground. Rain blurred her vision, but that didn't stop her from dashing at top speed.

Stupid Aiden, she thought, her face burning. *I will never forgive him.*

She continued to run nowhere in particular until her lungs would burst if she took another step.

"Screw this stupid island!"

Fire slowly coasted to a stop as she leaned over, gasping for air. The only sound in her ears was her heavy breathing. She didn't recall the moment when her breathing turned into a sob.

Then, she saw something that made her throw her hands over her mouth. Her cries cut off immediately into silent shock. She saw a dead child, dressed in bright but dirt-crusted clothes. Her entire front was covered in red blood. Fire could feel her palms begin to quiver, but she took a step forward. She reached out her trembling hand onto the small girl's shirt, and it came away covered in blood.

Wet blood.

Fire's heart dropped to her knees.

This was the fresh blood that Fire had seen too many times. Whoever killed her, whatever killed her, still had to be nearby.

She had to warn Ethan. She had to warn Aiden.

Without thinking, she sprinted away with a sudden burst of energy. All of her exhaustion seemed to disappear in the blink of an eye.

Finally, after what seemed like much too long, she reached the pathetic shelter.

"Guys!" she bellowed fearfully. "We have to go!"

"I thought you wanted to be alone," Aiden replied coolly. Fire chomped her lip, glaring into his eyes.

"There is a murderer right by us!" she suddenly shrieked. She stomped right up to him, fighting the urge to punch him in the throat. "Do you want to die, Aiden? Do you want me to die?"

Her words seemed to make his fierce glare falter. His lip twitched as his eyes clouded with tears.

"Why are you crying?" she practically yelled. "Crying won't help us, Aiden! Now come on!"

Fire felt a firm hand fly on her shoulder. Spinning around, she saw Ethan staring at her with an authority-like look.

"Slow down there," he said calmly. "What exactly happened?"

"Dead kid," Fire choked out. "There was a dead child, and her shirt was covered in fresh blood."

"Are you sure it was new?" Aspyn questioned, getting shakily to her feet. Fire glared at her.

"Yes, pink hair. If you don't want to end up like your little friend, I suggest you come with me."

Aspyn let out a sob, covering her mouth with her trembling hand.

"I can't do this," Gen whispered, her eyes locked on the ground. "I just-"

"Oh, shut up," Fire snarled.

"Where do we go?" Cassidy piped up, looking around with terror in her eyes. "We can't just run off."

"A building!" Fire shouted, almost causing Aiden to slam his hands over his ears. "We need to go to a building, like I've been saying all along!"

"Shut up!" Aiden snapped. "If there is a murderer by us, they certainly know where we are now!" Fire braced herself to hurl an insult at him, but she hesitated. Her eyes stayed locked on his, but she didn't scream back.

"Alright," Ethan stated, nervously looking between the two of them. "We'll go to a building."

"We'll get killed," Hope muttered, wishing more than anything that her sister was with them. Fire's furious gaze turned to her. For a moment, the only sound was the soft rain pattering on top of the rock. Then, Fire threw all her weight into a lunge at the blonde girl.

Ethan clawed at Fire, putting scratches all up and down her small arms. Fire was swearing at the top of her lungs with spit flying from her lips. She looked like some sick psychopath as she shouted and shouted.

"Sapphire," Ethan said firmly into her ear. "Stop it. This isn't you. This isn't you."

She thrashed around in his grasp, but she seemed to calm down a little. She finally fell limp into his arms. Hope narrowed her eyes, scared and disturbed. Ethan calmly released her sore arms.

"Ok then," she breathed out. She stole a look at Aiden, and she immediately wished she hadn't. His face was just gazing at her, mixed with fury and longing.

"I'm going insane," Fire murmured to herself. "Jesus, I'm going insane."

35

"Ethan," Belle muttered. She was sitting, shivering, inside a dimly lit building that provided no heat at all. Fire was asleep, but Belle could see her small body trembling from the cold.

Ethan's hard eyes turned to Belle. "What are we going to do?" she asked quietly. Ethan squinted his eyes, his stare flickering down at Hope.

"What do you mean?"

"Everything," she said almost helplessly. "We are going to die soon."

"No we aren't," Ethan harshly snapped. Belle just sighed.

"If we don't get off this island, we will. We can't just spend our lives running from that freak. Sooner or later, we'll get caught."

"I don't know," he finally said in a deflated tone. "I just don't want to give up that easily." Belle rubbed her bare arms, attempting to warm up her goosebump-covered skin.

"Well, Ethan, I would rather die than get captured by her."

"Ok," he said. "Let's all just go jump off a cliff, if that's what you want." Belle looked at him intently as he looked at the floor. "I didn't mean that."

"I know." Belle looked down at the sleeping Hope. Her dirty hair was sprawled out on the dusty floor. "Poor kid," she murmured. "She doesn't deserve this."

"None of us do," Ethan stiffly replied. Belle bit her lip, tasting blood.

"Yeah, but she's different. She isn't screwed up like the rest of us."

"You never did tell me about yourself, Belle," he said. His tone turned surprisingly gentle. Belle let out a dry chuckle.

"I don't plan to, buddy." She pushed herself up from the ground, firmly patting Ethan on the shoulder. Her hazel eyes looked cold and dull as she locked eyes with him. Ethan noticed her cracked lips and sunken in skin. The corner of her mouth went up in the smallest, saddest smile he had ever seen. "Have some good dreams, Ethan. We all need them tonight."

Hope woke up simply. She rubbed her sore eyes as her mouth stretched open in a large, long yawn.

"I need a shower," she muttered, her words cut off by the loud rumble in her stomach. Hope forced herself off the hard ground, and she found herself wishing that she had at least a had a pillow. Her back ached like nothing else.

She gazed around the grungy room at her still sleeping friends. Fire was gone, which wasn't a surprise. She had most likely gone off temporarily to clear her mind. Hope wanted to do the same.

She quietly pushed open the doors, careful not to disrupt Belle, who was lying near the exit. As Hope walked out, a breeze of warm air blew through her hair. In front of her was the old, cracked road, with the now beautifully deep green jungle behind it. She turned her head to the side, looking at the ancient, abandoned buildings. They were about as small as her old apartment.

Her old apartment. With Haylee.

Hope could feel her eyes burn at the thought of her old home. To think that was barely a week ago sent chills down her spine. Just two weeks ago, she had been with her mother.

My mother, Hope thought in sudden horror. *My mother has nobody now. Haylee is… she's not here, dad's gone, I'm gone.* She would no doubt fall into a depression without any of her daughters by her side.

Haylee's death was like a physical knife in Hope's chest. Before she really knew what she was doing, her body was shaking with sobs. She forced her fist into her mouth. The last thing she wanted to do was wake up her friends. They all desperately needed sleep.

Hope covered her mouth as her body shuddered and her heart broke. And for the first time in her life, she genuinely wondered if death would be better than this pain.

The original idea for the island was clear now as Hope gazed at the early morning sky, wiping water from her eyes. If she had to guess the time, she would've said around 6:00. The small amount of light made the island look beautiful. Magical, even. Clearly, the island had been meant for an earlier town with better people. How sad it was to think that this gorgeous island had been polluted with terrible, terrible humans. Hope could have even come here on vacation in another life, another time.

The blonde adult jumped and hastily wiped her eyes when she felt a tender hand press on her shoulder. Turning around, Hope saw Cassidy.

"Hi, Hope," she said. "I didn't think you'd be up right now."

Hope lightly grinned, catching her breath.

"Yeah, well, sometimes I just need to think." She paused, looking at the direction Cassidy had come from. "Hey, Cassidy, where were you?"

"Just the jungle," she muttered, turning away. As she released her arm, Hope saw a trail of blood trickle down her friend's wrist.

"Cassidy, wait," Hope said firmly. The brunette spun around curiously. "What happened to your wrist?"

"Oh, that?" Cassidy asked, her other hand flying over the smudged blood. "I just got cut on some thorns, no big deal." Hope nodded uneasily, coming closer to the visibly uncomfortable Cassidy.

"Cassidy," she said, looking closely at her arm, which she now saw was covered with thin white lines. "What are all of these scars from?"

"Just different plants and stuff," mumbled Cassidy, silently opening up the doors to the building. "I'm fine." Before Hope could speak again, her friend had entered the structure. With a tiny sigh, Hope rested her back against the building's wall and slid down into a sit. It was amazing that this purple sky and the starry one she had seen before were so different, yet so breathtaking. Hope watched the sun slowly rise with a sad, watery smile on her face.

Blisse awoke. She had been forced to conserve her energy and sleep in a tree. Of course, she wasn't even remotely nervous that she would be killed. She was the killer. Not the other way around.

"Tyrand!" she called down. Her beetle-black eyes found his. "Let's go, we will not waste precious time."

He didn't answer her as he and the other men reluctantly moved.

"I'm still tired," Tyrand muttered to himself. "She can deal with waiting a few hours."

"Wow," a voice in his ear breathed. Tyrand felt his body turn to lead right on the spot. "You don't learn, do you?" Blisse cooed into his ear. "You really need to keep your opinions to yourself, darling." Blisse gracefully hopped from the branch she was on, landing with a grin.

"Hey," another man began to Blisse, "why haven't you killed him yet?" Tyrand's blazing eyes turned on him. Blisse smirked at the man.

"Your name?"

"Jay," he immediately responded. His dark, graying hair was chopped up at his ears, and he was shorter and more plump than the other guards, giving him the appearance of an elf.

"Well, Jay," she said, "I need guards with me."

"To do your dirty work?" he asked. Blisse narrowed her deep eyes, and Jay quickly regretted what had come out of his mouth. Blisse slithered toward him, her teeth on full display.

"Jay, if you don't watch that pretty little mouth of yours, you may find that you can't speak at all." She made a motion with her dirt-crusted finger, sliding it menacing across her tongue. Jay got the disturbing message.

"Now," she proclaimed, "for each day that goes by without finding Hope's group, I will kill one of you. I don't need six men's mouths to feed. Understand?"

Tyrand slowly nodded, looking around at the other men. If it came down to it, she would probably kill the skinny, short man with his hair falling out in patches. Tyrand didn't even bother to find out what his name was, as his malnourished body would most likely be dead in less than a week, considering the condition he was in.

"Hey, Blisse?" Tyrand asked. "What will we do when this is all over?" She set her haunting eyes on him.

"What do you mean?"

"I mean when we have killed this group you're on about," he smugly replied. "What is your plan once we've stopped hunting them?"

"'I'll figure it out once they're dead," she said coldly.

Of course, she'd thought about it every night since she had taken her new form. She had meticulously planned every single detail of what she would do, but she couldn't dare tell these worthless men that whatever they chose to do, they would all be dead or taken captive by their very own master.

Tyrand stopped walking.

"Well then, I want to know what will happen. If I'm going to follow you and worship at your feet, I want to know my fate."

"Do I detect a hint of sarcasm, Tyrand?"

"You know what?" he loudly asked. "Yes, you do. I'm tired of doing your bidding when you won't give me or anyone clear answers. We are not your guinea pigs, Blisse."

"Well, you are stubborn," she muttered. "That's relatively good." She paused, her eyes slithering around at her men. "Fine Tyrand, I get it; you're brave. But you don't talk to me that way." She walked up to the one skinny man, who was literally shaking in her presence. "I won't kill you, because you're useful," Blisse began to Tyrand, "but this man here won't be so lucky."

She slowly brought out a dagger, stealthily hidden on a band on her thigh.

"Please don't," the short man begged silently. "Stop her, Tyrand." Blisse smiled like a maniac.

"Look at yourself, you'll die in less than a week. I'm doing you a favor." With her eyes locked on his, her hand shot out and slit his throat. He fell to the ground without a sound. "Aw," Blisse mocked humorously to herself. "Nobody ever even knew his name." She cackled, staring at Tyrand. He noted to himself sickly that Blisse's continuous killings didn't even bother him anymore.

"Morning, Hopie," Ethan said, stretching his scraped up arms over his head. Hope lightly grinned as she walked through the old door, noticing that Belle had gotten up and moved. Ethan sat up slowly, his face open in a long yawn. His sleepy emerald eyes found hers, and he smiled.

"Is Sapphire back?" Cassidy asked from the back of the room. Hope shrugged.

"Yep," a voice said from outside the door. Ethan laughed, getting to his feet. Fire waltzed in gracefully, striking a pose inside.

"Did you wait out there until you could make an entrance?" Ethan asked, laughing slightly. Fire smirked, answering, "You know me so well."

"Where were you?" Cassidy questioned, now coming closer. Fire bit back a smile.

"Nowhere important. Anyway, what are we going to do today?"

"Wow," Aiden chimed in, "you really seemed to have calmed down from yesterday."

"Shut it, Aiden," Fire and Ethan both said in unison.

"Oh, would you look at that," Cassidy said wryly, pointing to a corner of the room. "There's a mirror here. I haven't looked at myself in forever."

"None of us have," Ethan replied, walking closer to the corner. Fire dryly snickered.

"I'm not gonna look at myself, I know I look like I've been run over by a truck eight times." She especially glanced at Aiden, who was looking at the floor.

"Can I look?" Gen timidly asked. Ethan smiled kindly.

"Sure, Genevieve. You can too, Aspyn." The pink haired girl smiled gratefully as she gazed at her own face for the first time.

The first thing she noticed was her piercing gray eyes. They were too gray, it seemed. Her faded hair matched them in a strange way, but they seemed to work together. Aspyn saw her tan face covered in dirt and blemishes, but for the most part, she thought she looked alright. Relatively attractive, even. Her eyes darted over to Gen, who was biting her lip, smiling at her own reflection.

"Wow," Gen murmured, tears in her eyes. "I haven't looked at myself since I was home." Aspyn nodded in agreement, tears welling in her own eyes as well.

"Can I look?" asked Cassidy. She pushed her slightly curled hair out of her face.

Cassidy's mouth spread into a weak smile, but it went away when she moved closer to the nearly shattered glass. She prodded a red spot peeking out from the dirt covering her face, and she tried to straighten out her hair that naturally curled at the bottom. She poked her split lip, wincing when pain shot through her mouth.

"I look disgusting," she simply said, looking at the ground. Aiden put his hand on her shoulder gently.

"You don't look horrible," he reassured her. Her eyes darted to his.

"Wow, thanks."

He frowned, looking at her with regret.

"Ok, judging from your voice, I said something wrong." She shook her head quickly.

"No, you're fine. It's nothing," she said. She sighed softly, walking over to a corner. He helplessly looked at Hope.

"What did I say?" he asked. She shook her head, smiling slightly. He moved closer, his mouth perking in a confused smile. "What?"

"It's just, that's not what you should tell a girl," she explained, chuckling. When he greeted her with a blank stare, she laughed aloud. "Listen, if a girl asks how she looks, you *never* just say what you said. That's pretty much like an insult." He tilted his head to the side. She finally let out a huge laugh, bringing Fire over to the both of them.

"What's so funny?" she asked. Hope laughed again, looking at Aiden's expression.

"Aiden here doesn't know jack about girls," she told her. Fire looked at him, dramatically rolling her eyes.

"Really?" Fire asked. He shrugged in defense.

"What did I do?"

"You say something else besides the word fine," Ethan piped up, amused as well. Aiden's hazel eyes grew wide in confusion and anger.

"*What?*"

"Here, I'll show you what to say," Ethan stated. He strolled over to Hope as she looked at him in confusion.

"Wait, what are you doing?" she asked nervously. He laughed, looking at her confused expression.

"I'm using you as an example of what to say to a girl," he told her, his grin growing wider. "Is that alright with you?" Hope nodded, her face beginning to burn in embarrassment.

"I guess so," she said, blushing. Aiden looked at them, crossing his arms in pretend annoyance. Ethan's face suddenly put on a warm, flirty expression, causing Hope to turn even redder.

"Oh Hope," he began. His voice was so silvery and light that Fire burst out laughing. "You are the most beautiful woman I have ever had the pleasure of setting my eyes on." Fire wiped glistening tears of laughter from her eyes.

"Ethan, you're so stupid," Fire said, her voice barely heard over her laughter that pierced the air. Ethan's focus turned to Hope again.

"Your hair makes the sunrise turn its head in jealousy, the golden wheat fields look away in shame. Your skin makes even the smoothest rock envious to the point of insanity, the softest pillow doubt itself." Hope's face was turning a brilliant shade of maroon, her eyes intently focused on the concrete floor.

Ethan, oh my god, stop, stop, she thought silently, desperately avoiding his stare. She could only hope that the burning feeling inside her didn't show on her face. Cassidy had wandered back over, watching Ethan flatter Hope. His gaze was completely focused on the girl standing before him. His light voice was now flowing naturally, his words pouring out of his mouth.

"Your golden eyelashes frame the radiant pools underneath. And your eyes, oh, they could break someone's heart just by looking at them. They are glittering green seas, deeper than the vastness of space. Golden honey specks are intertwined with beautiful dark emeralds, and the dark frame around them holds in the beauty. Your lips are pinker than the brightest tulip, redder than the wisest rose. And when you smile, my world is brightened beyond words." His gaze lingered on Hope, and her face seemed to be hotter than the sun. Fire had ceased laughing. Her look was an expression of wonder, of shock.

"Wow Ethan," Cassidy said, breaking the silence. "That sure was something." Aiden chuckled at Hope's face. *Quit staring at me,* she pleaded silently, hating the feeling of everyone's eyes on her.

"See, Aiden?" Ethan asked, his eyes still on Hope. "It's not that difficult." His light eyes darted over to Fire. "Aiden, try it on Sapphire."

Fire's gaze turned beet red.

"Ethan, I swear. No," she stated firmly. "I don't want him to. Not after what he did." Aiden's face grew into a smile. "I'll literally cut off your arms," she warned.

"I can't say no to Ethan." Theatrically, he got down on one knee. Before she could dash away, he snagged Fire's hand in his. Her eyes were piercing in anger, but she didn't try to pull away. "Sapphire Aurora Smith," he began, in a parody of Ethan's heartwarming voice. "You are the prettiest girl I have ever seen. Your eyes..." he shot a glance at Ethan, who was giving him a thumbs up with a gigantic grin. Aiden winked. "Your eyes are deeper than the darkest cave, and more blue than the most radiant sea. They reach into your soul, which no words can describe how deep and amazing it is. The gold in your eyes are like a million jewels, which is what you are. You were named Sapphire for a reason; the stunning jewel matches you."

"Shut up," Fire said, her face an extremely deep shade of red as well. Cassidy looked at the two guys, her mouth hung open.

"Geez guys," she simply said in awe. "You sure know how to compliment someone." Ethan nodded, his mouth perked up at the corner.

"Yep. I had plenty of practice when I was locked in my room as a kid. I just acted like I was proposing. I guess it helped." Hope finally mustered the courage to look into his eyes. Embarrassingly, her eyes were watering. His eyes flooded with concern right away. "Hopie, what's wrong?" She shook her head quickly.

"No, don't worry, I'm not upset," she reassured him, tears brimming over. "No one's ever said anything to me like that, fake or not." He slowly put his arm on her hand.

"It wasn't fake," he whispered softly, only to her. Hope's mouth dropped open before she could help it. Quickly, she turned her back to them, making sure that nobody could see the gigantic smile that was plastered across her face. *He meant it,* she thought, his words giving her a jolt of butterflies. *He meant it.*

36

Hope was still smiling when Aspyn screamed.

"Guys, guys," Aspyn whimpered, shakily pointing toward the door. Ethan squinted his eyes at the clouded glass, but there was nothing there.

"What did you see, Aspyn?"

"A person," she replied back. Her tone sounded high pitched and forced. "They just ran across the door."

"Are you sure?" asked Fire. "I don't think so."

"I promise."

A noise boomed through the air.

Hope and Cassidy both flinched, looking fearfully toward the door.

Fire accidentally chomped her lip hard, causing the taste of blood to fill her mouth.

Aiden and Ethan's bodies both tensed up, staring at the outside world, while Genevieve and Aspyn clung onto each other. Belle roughly sighed, clenching her fists.

"If it's Blisse, I swear I will kill her," Fire growled, her gaze never leaving the entrance. Ethan shook his head half heartedly. *Don't let it be Blisse,* Hope pleaded silently. Her previously burning face was now drastically losing all color. A single person had never terrified her this much before. Blisse was straight out of a horror movie.

Hope did know one thing for sure, however; if it was Blisse who walked through, she would try her hardest to kill her. She was done trying to protect the girl inside. This Blisse deserved to die, although it would mean the destruction of her former friend.

Suddenly, a delighted shriek pierced the air. Hope gulped, grabbing onto Ethan for support. Aiden held his knife out in front of him, his hand firm and steady. His hard eyes were intently focused on the door. Hope felt something prod her back gently.

"Take this," whispered Cassidy. Hope closed her hand over something rough. She brought it close to her, seeing that it was a small but sharp silver dagger.

The doorknob rattled. Hope felt her face go ashen, and her palms began to sweat. No matter how many times she had seen a criminal, she was absolutely terrified.

Something hit the door. The noise echoed throughout the room. Genevieve and Aspyn were holding on to each other, both their faces as white as a sheet. Hope remembered that they had never actually had an encounter with a criminal before.

The knob rattled once more. Everyone tensed up. Fire made a snarl noise through her bared teeth while Aiden narrowed his eyes dangerously.

The door flew open. A person came running in, his eyes red and wide. Hope scrunched her eyebrows together when she realized that he had no clothes on, and his bald head was bloody and scratched.

"Stop," Ethan commanded, his voice loud and firm. The person paid no attention as he picked up speed, running towards them. "Stop!" This time, he shouted it. If the man didn't listen, there would be no third time.

The person continued dashing to them, the words not reaching his brain. Ethan looked over at Aiden. His mouth tightened. Aiden stiffly nodded once, and Hope saw his grip on his dagger become stronger. He reared back his hand, and the knife sailed through the air like a shooting star. It landed with a *thunk* in the middle of the man's chest. He fell to the floor, his head making an audible crack when it hit against the hard floor. Hope gasped, watching the floor beneath him turn red. Although she had had more than enough experience watching people die, the sight of death still made her queasy and horrified. Ethan looked down at Hope, who was digging her nails into his wrist.

"That was freaky," Fire stated, breaking the silence that followed death. Genevieve nodded, her face in a look of uneasiness.

"You ok?" Cassidy asked. Genevieve shook her head, looking at the floor.

"I think I'm gonna throw up," she choked out. Cassidy gently put her hand on Genevieve's shoulder.

"I'm sorry," she softly whispered. Genevieve just shook her head, her golden eyes staring uneasily at the corpse in the middle of the room.

Hope screamed. Another man ran through the doorway, more horrible looking than the previous man. His eyes were crazed and bloodshot, with the same bloody bumps on his head. But something about this man was much more terrifying; he was holding a knife.

"What the hell do we do?" Fire practically shouted, staring at the man in front of them.

"Watch out!" Genevieve shrieked as the stranger lunged toward them. Hope could see that tears were trickling down her face. Aiden swiftly stabbed him in the chest with a spear given to him by Ethan. The man fell to his knees, his mouth making the same horrible gurgling noises as the previous man. Finally, after what seemed like far too long, he fell to the ground.

"What if there are more?" Hope whispered, eyeing the doorway cautiously. Aiden shrugged heartlessly.

"Then I guess there are more people to kill," he replied stiffly. Fire opened her mouth, but closed it once more.

A large *crash* sounded from the distance. Hope felt fear flood her system. There was no way that anybody should ever have to go through encounter after encounter with some of the freakiest people on the planet.

A face popped through the empty doorway. This time, it belonged to a woman. She stepped into the room, revealing the face of a bloody and insane lady. Hope's breath caught in her throat. Another man's body followed hers. Then another. They all slowly walked into the room, the light brightening up their mangled faces.

"What would you say is scarier?" Ethan whispered to Hope. "These freaks or Blisse?" Hope weakly chuckled.

"If you ask me, both are pretty terrifying. But I guess I'll still have to go with Blisse." Ethan nodded, his eyes locked on the crazy people in front of him.

"Yeah, me too. I think that-"

He was cut off by a loud thud. Hope's eyes grew big, looking for the source of the sound. She felt her skin erupt in chills when she saw a knife buried in Genevieve's chest. The girl clawed at the knife, finally pulling it out. But it was too late; the damage was done. Aspyn's face slowly grew into a mask of horror.

"Oh god oh god, oh my god. Gen, no no no no." She kept repeating her statement, a tear making its way down her face. "This is not happening, this is not happening." Hope felt like crying too. It pained her to watch Aspyn watch her friend die. With a stab in her chest, she thought of Haylee. Hope saw that the lady in the front was the one who had thrown the knife. The stranger's perfect aim greatly scared her. Maybe they weren't as detached as they thought.

"That's it!" Hope screamed suddenly. Everybody turned to look at her. Ethan held his breath as he stared at her. She kept her eyes on his, her hard look not wavering. She then turned her head to the people in the middle of the room.

"I'm sick of it!" she shouted angrily. "I'm sick of all of this, I just want it to end!" Hope was glaring at the group of insane people in front of her. The lady was watching, almost seeming confused. Hope was ready to pour out her rage on the group ahead of them. "Ethan," she said, her grip on her dagger tightening. "Let's kill them."

He looked at Hope with a surprised expression.

"I thought you weren't at all for death, and now you want to *murder* them?" he asked, still shocked. She firmly nodded as she gave a snarl that scared even her.

"They aren't real people anyways. Look at their eyes, they are maniacs, Ethan. And I don't know about you, but if I were one of them, I'd want to be put out of my misery. You're right, death makes me feel all sorts of emotions, mostly sadness, but these people aren't exactly people anymore, so it's ok, sort of." Ethan raised his eyebrows, but Hope saw the hint of a smile.

"Oh yeah," Cassidy said, her eyes growing wide in shock. "That makes it ok."

"Cassidy, look at Genevieve! That woman just *killed* her, ok? I never think violence is ok, let alone taking someone's life, but we need to defend ourselves!" Cassidy rubbed her neck uncomfortably.

"Yeah, but I don't think that I can kill anyone," she said, biting her lip. Fire looked at her, her face in a gentle yet firm expression.

"You killed Grayson."

Cassidy put her hand over her mouth. A pitiful sob came out of her mouth.

"I had to!" she exclaimed. "He was horrible and twisted and Blisse was gone and it was our only chance and-" she broke off, tears streaming down her face. She couldn't stop the waterfall of sadness as she remembered killing Grayson. Fire looked at her softly.

"I know, Cassidy," she said. "I'm sorry." She gently put her arm on her shaking friend.

Hope shrieked. Her terrified eyes grew wider and wider.

"Oh gosh, oh gosh," she said, starting to hyperventilate. She threw her hand over her ear. "That knife went right here." With a trembling hand, she pointed to the side of her head. The woman had thrown another knife, and she felt the breeze as it swiftly sailed past her head. The lady was pouting, her arms crossed. Hope was horrified yet greatly relieved at the same time. *I almost died. I could be dead.*

Her thoughts were cut off by another loud sob. Hope's head snapped around, looking for the source of the sound. The scream belonged to Aspyn. She squeezed Genevieve's limp hand desperately, her eyes full of water.

"Gen, Gen, no!"

Hope couldn't stop a single tear falling down her cheek. She couldn't help thinking of Haylee. She thought with a pang if Aspyn was how she had looked. She wondered if the way she was crying was exactly how she had done. Aspyn suddenly slammed her hand on the floor roughly. Her face contorted into a look of pure fury. With a jolt of fear, Hope realized that she wouldn't let Genevieve's death go unavenged. Ethan clearly sensed this as well.

"Aspyn," he said warningly. Her glare snapped to him.

"We need to kill them," she said angrily. Belle chuckled dryly.

"That's what we've been saying all along."

Cassidy's mouth opened in shock.

"Am I the only person that doesn't want to kill someone?" she practically shouted. Hope looked at her sympathetically. "Can't we just injure them or something?"

"We can't," Hope replied. "They would still be out there. I'm sorry, but this is our chance." Hope slowly was becoming annoyed with Cassidy's stubbornness.

Well, I don't want to kill anyone either, she thought, *but I'm willing to do what it takes to survive.* Cassidy sniffed once. She put her head down for a moment, and her hands were folded together. Finally, her head went up. She turned her body to look at Hope. Her red eyes were still shocked, but her face was in a firm expression.

"Fine," she said, devoid of emotion. "Whatever you say."

Aiden ripped the spear from the man who he had killed. He held it out in front of him in a position of defense. Fire's hand tightened around her dagger.

"Well, would you look at that," she stated dryly. "There's a lunatic for each of us." With her confidence sinking, Hope realized that Fire was correct. Deep down, she was hoping that she could help someone defeat a person, not take one down on her own. Cassidy looked like she would throw up at any moment.

"I can't do this," she whispered, terrified. "I can't fight these people." Hope gave her arm a comforting squeeze.

"You'll be fine, Cassidy. I know you will." The brunette girl's hands began to quiver. Hope looked at her gently and said, "Remember how we felt when Blisse was turned? Do you remember how you felt when Haylee-" she stopped speaking for a moment. *Hope, stop.* "Well, I can recall those things with great detail," she continued. "Remember Gabe? Remember how annoying and arrogant he was? Well, I don't know about you, but I absolutely despised him. Did you?"

Cassidy nodded. Tears were falling from her puffy eyes, and Hope was beyond thankful that the crazy people hadn't made a move yet.

"Ok Cassidy. Use that rage right now. I know that you don't want to kill anyone. Believe me, that's the last thing I want to do. But think of all those moments when you're trying to survive, ok? I know that you won't die. You can't." Cassidy's body racked with sobs. Ethan softly put his hand on her back. She took another sniff, and she tensed up her body. She swiftly slid another dagger from her boot. Biting her lip, she held it out in front of her, mimicking Aiden. She gave Hope a warning look.

"Are you ready?"

Hope nodded, looking hesitantly at the people ahead of her.

Oh god, she thought. *I'm going to die.* She smacked herself on the cheek, hard. *No Hope, don't think that way. Do it for Haylee.* The name felt like a nail being driven into her skull. She choked up, her sister's face getting in the way of her confidence.

Do it for Haylee.

Hope looked at Cassidy. She could suddenly imagine her as a young child at home, before she was thrown into this mess, before she was banished to the island. She could almost imagine them as childhood friends, growing up as neighbors until they graduated. Hope knew now that Cassidy's life was even more messed up than her own. She gave her arm another nudge.

"I'm ready."

"Move!" Fire shrieked. Hope's head snapped up, revealing a knife flying straight at her face. It was like everything was in slow motion. Impossibly, she dropped to the ground, just barely avoiding its tip. Hope stood up with her dagger.

"Hopie," Ethan whispered. She turned her attention on him, but the corner of her eye was still watching the woman who had thrown the knife. "Her knives are gone. You take her." Hope nodded firmly. Her previous confidence was now greatly diminishing.

Who am I kidding? she thought, dread filling her body. *I can't kill someone! I can't even stand the sight of killing a bug! How the hell am I supposed to kill a person?* Ethan must've noticed her wavering attitude, because he said, "Just relax, Hopie. Don't watch their faces, ok? Just...do it and move on." Hope cringed.

"I can't do that," she retorted. Ethan threw his hands in the air in surprising anger. "Well, you're the one who suggested it in the first place!"

"I know! But that's only because I don't have another option!" Ethan looked at her, and she could see some annoyance in his tired eyes.

"Listen, Hope. Let me say something. Don't talk, ok? Don't interrupt me." He paused, waiting for her nod. By now, everyone was watching them. The insane people were staring off into space, as though Ethan's group wasn't even there. "I'm just...tired," he began. "You want to do this. It's bad, I know, but we can't afford to debate about it all the time. Just don't think about it, and know that you are doing whatever it takes to survive."

Hope felt her face burn in anger and humiliation. She narrowed her eyes, and she forced herself to keep tears from them.

"Well I'm sorry that I'm not a heartless robot," she snapped. "Maybe it's just me, but after Haylee, I can't even think of death." He looked at her, his expression gentle yet weary.

"Hope, I know that Haylee's death was awful and tragic, ok? Believe me, I know what it's like to watch that, but just think about that later."

Calm down, Hope. You don't want to say something you regret. It almost hurt to keep her waterfall of tears from splashing over her lashes. She felt her fists clenching.

"Think about it later?! Really? Sorry, I forgot that I could just put it out of my mind as easy as goddamn running. And it's horrible of you to accuse me of talking about Haylee too much. I've been there for you." Ethan snorted, but it was far from a laugh.

"You mean like when Martha died? Yeah, you were a real therapist."

"No," she said coldly, surprised of why she was so angry all of a sudden. "I was there for you when you told me about Carter, and how he died in the street! I was there for you when you told me how much you hated your parents, and how much they hated you. I took care of Martha's goddamn body while you just sat there!"

Hope slapped her hand over her mouth. Ethan stared at her in shock, hurt and anger evident in his falling face. *I can't believe I just said that,* she thought in horror. *I can't believe I just said that.* Ethan looked sadly at her. "Ethan..." He shook his head.

"Kill them," he told her, his voice robotic. She looked down, greatly ashamed. And then, the barrier holding back her tears *broke.* Water poured down her face. She buried her face in her hands. Hope felt a sharp pain in her broken wrist, which made her yelp. Faintly, she felt her body shake in sobs. Ethan turned away, which made her weep even harder. Fire watched the scene, desperately wanting to take Ethan's side. But she realized how upset Hope was, and even she didn't find pleasure in that.

"I think we should go," Aiden suggested. Belle punched him in the arm, too hard to be playful. "Ow!" he exclaimed. "What was that for?" Belle looked at him as though he was the biggest idiot on the planet.

"Can you not see how sad she is? That was terribly insensitive of you, Aiden." He threw his hands up in the air.

"Well, what do you want me to say when there's a group of crazies advancing toward us?"

This statement made Hope's head snap up. Aiden was right; they were slowly but surely walking for them.

"This is a zombie apocalypse if I ever saw one," Fire joked halfheartedly. *I can't do this,* Hope thought, panic flooding her mind. *I'd rather die.* Ironically, that's what she would probably do anyway. Hope laughed grimly at her humor. Fire looked at her, an almost pleased expression on her face. "Were you laughing at my joke?" she asked. *No,* Hope thought.

"Yes, Fire. I thought your joke was great," she said. There was no point in making her sort-of friend angry. Fire's mouth turned up in a pleased smirk.

"Now," she said, bringing up her knife, "let's get this fiesta started."

37

Hope squeezed her dagger tighter. All the fear, humiliation, pain, and sadness she had felt were now bubbling to the surface. One last look at the cold and pale Genevieve was all she needed.

Without warning, the crazy lady threw herself at Hope. She shrieked, but she brought out her dagger in front of her. Ethan chose a large, muscular man to fight while Belle decided to take on a woman with stains of blood covering her lips. With a crazed look, Fire rushed at a woman with a threatening mace, who was swinging it around and around. Because of her tiny size, Fire was able to duck and dodge the sharp spikes. Aiden used his spear to defend himself, jutting out the point whenever anyone got too close to him. Cassidy was breathing deeply, trying to calm herself. Suddenly, a lady locked her bloodshot eyes with her chocolate ones.

Cassidy froze.

"Stop," she said, her voice coming out high and desperate. The woman paid no attention as she prowled closer and closer. "Stop, please." Cassidy put out her hands. The lady pulled back her lips in a delighted snarl. She came closer, closer, closer. Cassidy let a whimper escape her mouth as she brought up her dagger. "Please," she begged one last time.

Her pleading had no effect on the woman in front of her. Cassidy freely cried as she stared at the person she would have to kill. She took a few steps toward the crazy stranger as well. "I'm so sorry," she whispered. Cassidy was full of terrible remorse, but she wasn't idiotic. As the lady lunged toward her, Cassidy twisted her body away. She spun around and stabbed the woman in the back, hearing the *thunk* as it entered her body.

Cassidy buried her face in her hands as the lady fell to the floor. "I'm so sorry."

Aiden's eyes narrowed as he got in a defensive stance. A tall, slim, deformed man was holding out a bat with nails on it, menacingly pointing it toward him.

"Back away," Aiden growled out.

"No," the man simply replied. A large vein on his forehead seemed to pulse as he brought up his bat. He swung it, and Aiden jumped out of the way. He was a second too late.

Part of the bat slammed into his shoulder, the nails piercing his skin.

He screamed, tumbling to the floor. He swore under his breath, angry at having such slow reflexes. He put his hand on his right shoulder. Aiden pulled it away, rewarded with the sight of dark blood. The insane man grinned, baring back his bloody lips. He held up his threatening bat. Aiden braced for the pain that would surely come from the pointed nails.

Aspyn came out of nowhere. She threw herself on Aiden, not being able to pull him away with her weak muscles. She screamed in agony as the nails came into contact with her skin.

Aiden gasped, but now was not the time for shock and sadness. He twisted out from under her body, the bat still stuck in her chest. The man was thrown to the side, as his grip was still tight on the dangerous weapon. Aiden jumped up and ran to get his spear with all his might. Without a second thought, he began to heartlessly stab the man, desperately trying to keep him away from the screaming Aspyn. The man choked up, falling to the ground. Aspyn was heaving, her hand pressed over the holes embedded in her skin.

"Aspyn," Aiden whispered, sounding concerned. Cassidy came over, tears spilling from her eyes.

"Aiden, what happened?" Cassidy asked, sounding alarmed. Aiden slowly kneeled down, gently setting his hand down on her wound.

"She saved me," Aiden said softly. He pushed Aspyn's pink hair from her eyes. Her body was writhing on the ground. "Will she live, Cassidy?"

Cassidy set her shaking hand on Aspyn's forehead.

"I think so," she whispered back. "I don't think it hit her heart. I think she'll be alright, Aiden. I think she'll be alright."

Fire grabbed a medium-sized rock in her hand. She got in a stance, a rock in one hand and a dagger in the other. Fire made sure to keep a good distance from the threatening mace in the air. The woman she was fighting seemed to be off in her own little world. Fire knew she could take her once she got the weapon out of her hand.

Ok Fire, how can you get the mace? Her eyes were darting everywhere a hundred miles an hour. She saw some girl lying in a pool of blood, surrounded by Aiden and Cassidy. Judging from her unmissable hair, the injured girl was Aspyn. *Wonder what happened there.* She saw Ethan grappling some man for a knife. Hope's eyebrows were scrunched together nervously as she held the shaking knife out. A man was stalking toward her, and it was obvious that Hope was trying to avoid a bloody situation. Her grip on the knife was all wrong, and her hand was shaking too much to actually cause any damage to someone else.

Fire's woman was still looking dazedly off into space. Her icy eyes were analyzing every move of her opponent, a million fighting strategies running through her frantic mind. Clearly, her mental woman was not planning on fighting any time soon. With a huff, Fire turned to go help Hope.

"Die, die, die," he was muttering to himself.

Hope was shrinking back. Her heart was pounding too much for her brain to think clearly. There was a mentally not right man with an axe coming right for her. She couldn't imagine anything else more frightening.

"Listen," Hope pleaded, bringing her knife back in a bit. "Look at me in the eyes. I don't want to hurt you. I really don't."

The man took a sudden swing of the axe. He looked as though he was drunk as he swayed it back and forth, back and forth. *I can't kill him. I can't kill him.*

The man cornered her against the wall. Hope had been moving backward farther than she had thought. She felt the *thud* as her back slammed onto the cement. Hope could see every single jagged edge in the axe as it was so near to her. The man's bloodshot eyes locked with hers. A shiver of pure fear went down her spine. The man looked so crazy and *pained.* She could almost see begging in his milky eyes.

She was cut off from her thoughts as the axe swung toward her face. Hope shrieked as she instinctively ducked to the ground. She heard the weapon enter the wall.

The man went flying to the side. Hope covered her face, thinking he was lunging for her. However, he flew as though *he* was the one being knocked over. With confusion and dread, Hope lifted up her face to look at him.

Fire was on top of him. The scene looked like a feisty and scrappy squirrel fighting a pitbull. She screamed disturbing sounds as she clawed at his face and stabbed him in the throat.

"Die!" Her body twisted and contorted as she struggled to get off him. The man was laying there in a pool of his own blood. Hope gagged slightly as she reached to help Fire up. With a sharp look, Fire ignored her hand as she pushed herself up from the ground.

"Thanks for helping me," Hope told her, feeling stupid at the patheticness in her voice. Fire was panting as she ran her trembling hands through her hair.

"Well, it was obvious that you couldn't muster the strength to kill him on your own. If you died, Ethan would be pissed, and then where would I be?"

Hope looked at her strangely.

"Just the same, thanks."

Hope limped over to Ethan, who had been victorious in defeating his foe. His once chestnut hair was now drenched in blood, and she had to tear her eyes away from it.

"You ok, Hope?" he asked gently. She bit her lip, nodding.

"Yeah, I'm fine. Actually, I didn't really have to kill anyone," she admitted sheepishly. "Fire came over and did it for me. I'm so sorry for what I said about Martha, I didn't mean it. I'm sorry I couldn't do it, Ethan. You were right; I could never kill someone. I'm too weak."

Ethan snickered.

"Hopie, I didn't mean it. I was mad, ok? Not wanting to kill someone is never a bad thing. Hell, that practically makes you a saint on this island. Don't ever be sorry because you don't want to take someone's life."

Hope smiled reluctantly.

"Thanks. That made me feel better, I guess." What Hope saw next almost gave her a heart attack. A woman with a mace was barreling right toward her.

"Ethan!" she shrieked. Ethan's head spun around as he locked eyes with the insane lady.

"Aiden!" Ethan shouted. Aiden looked up at once and threw Ethan his spear. Ethan angrily thrust it forward, and it stuck in her chest. Her hand went limp as she dropped to the floor. Ethan hesitantly reached down and plucked the weapon from the now dead woman's grip. "Maybe we can use it later." With a wink, he threw it at Hope. She jumped back, but one of the spikes caught on her hair.

"Ethan!" she yelled, but she was laughing. "That wasn't funny!" With a wince, she tore it out of her hair. With a fake disgusted look, Ethan shook out the strands of hair onto the floor. Hope made sure the lady was dead before she turned around. Her eyes looked over to Aspyn, who was being cradled by Cassidy and Aiden. As she hesitantly walked over to the trio, she asked, "What happened to her? Is that blood on her chest?"

"Yep," Aiden responded, dabbing at Aspyn's wounds with his shirt. He looked at the gasping girl with admiration in his eyes. "She jumped in front of a bat to save me. I could've died."

"You could've?" Fire asked. Her voice sounded rough like it always did, but Hope could hear some hysteria. Aiden nodded, looking at Fire curiously.

"Yeah, the bat might have hit my heart. My reflexes were just too slow."

"Well I'm beyond happy that you lived," said Ethan, "but we can talk about it later. We have to get out of here. There might be more of those freaks."

"And who are these freaks exactly?" Belle asked. "Obviously something was wrong with them, we all know that. But what? What on this island could've possibly contaminated so many people?"

"I think I might know," Fire said darkly. Everyone's heads turned to her. "Think about it: what or who on this island likes to test things on people? What or who on this island likes to watch people succumb to madness?" Ethan locked disturbed eyes with her.

"Grayson," everyone said in unison. Hope slowly put her hand over her mouth.

"Wait, so you think that Grayson developed some serum and then tested it on those people?" Fire looked at Hope blankly.

"Well," she said, "it is what I'm implying here."

"It makes sense," Ethan chimed in. "He tried out his freaky stuff on Blisse. Maybe he tried it on his victims until he perfected it. I think it did what he wanted it to to Blisse; I think that is probably what happened to them. It's the most logical explanation."

"At least he's dead," Aiden said encouragingly. Belle sadly shook her head.

"And now there's Blisse. And in some way, she's worse than Grayson. We know Grayson would do the most psychotic thing, but I have no clue with Blisse. She seems so unstable, I think she's the true baddie." Cassidy shook her head in agreement.

"Yeah, that's true. I just think it's so sad. This is exactly what Blisse wouldn't have wanted for her, and for us. Just think of when she comes back. She'll probably hate herself." Belle nodded.

"You're right. It's so beyond awful."

"How would you know?" Fire retorted. "You treated her like crap, Belle. Don't act like you care about her."

"I do care," she mumbled quietly, but nobody heard. Aiden had already started toward the door.

"Well, let's go then. Where do you fellows have in mind?" Hope started to speak, but Fire cut her off.

"I swear, if you say a damn tree, I will-"

"Chill out," Ethan said, putting a firm hand on her shoulder. "Let Hopie tell us her idea."

"I'm not a five year old!" Fire snapped at him. "Don't talk to me like I am one!" Ethan heaved a sigh.

"Sapphire, if you're going to act like one, I'm going to treat you like one." Fire threw off his hand and stared hard into his eyes.

"Screw you, Ethan." Fire stalked off out of the door. Ethan locked eyes with Cassidy, and they both shrugged.

"Wow," Aspyn said, breaking the silence. "That was uncalled for, huh?"

"Uh, I'm sorry?" Hope said hesitantly. Ethan shook his head.

"No Hopie, don't apologize, there's no need. She's just in one of her moods, she'll get over it."

"Yeah," Hope said, but she wasn't entirely convinced. "I was going to say that we go back to the hole in the ground. I know Blisse knows about it, but it was one time, really quick. I honestly doubt she'd remember it. It's safer than another building; do you guys agree?" Ethan put his hand on his chin thoughtfully.

"Sure, I guess there's no harm in it. The only thing is that we could be cornered if she finds us there," he warned. Hope shrugged, nudging his shoulder.

"What's life without a little risk?" A reluctant smile pulled at Ethan's mouth.

"Ok then, let's get a move on." Belle dashed up to the front, followed by Cassidy and Aspyn. Aiden ran ahead all of them to catch up to Fire. Ethan prodded Hope along, grinning, as he walked out of the door. Hope made sure to not look at all the mangled bodies that lay behind her.

"Hey!" Blisse shouted behind her. She viciously whipped her head around. "What is taking you guys so long?"

Her guards looked up in fear.

"I'm sorry, we were just-"

"I don't give two damns what you were gonna do," she snarled at them. "I need to find Hope's group, and you will *not* slow me down. Would you like to die?"

"No," the first man quickly piped up. The two hastily caught up to their horrible leader. With a roll of her dark eyes, Blisse turned back around. She crossed the clearing of the jungle into the old town. Her eyes squinted, carefully analyzing where her prey could've run off to.

An open door caught her eye. With a quick grin, Blisse took off sprinting toward a building. The middle aged men tried their absolute hardest to keep up with her. Blisse threw the door open more as she dashed in. What she saw wiped the confident smirk off her face.

There were various bodies thrown around, all of them clearly murdered. Blisse got down on her knees, carefully searching each body. As she was walking to an impaled woman, something caught her eye. Curiously, she bent down, picking up a strand of hair. With a spark of interest, Blisse held it up to the light.

Just as the guards walked in, Blisse swore in a scream.

"Those little *bastards* were here! This is Hope's hair, I know it!" Blisse dashed over to her guards who were gawking at the doorway. She threw her strong hand over the first man's long hair, pulling him close to her.

"I could've gotten them," Blisse growled in a low whisper, "but you idiots slowed me down." Blisse threw him to the ground as she began to shake in rage. "They were here not that long ago!" Her angry voice rose to a scream. "I COULD HAVE TAKEN THEM, BUT YOU MADE WE WAIT!"

This time, Blisse grabbed the other man's shaggy beard. "You have no idea how furious I am." The man gulped nervously. Blisse aggressively tugged on his long facial hair. "I work better alone, but I brought you imbeciles with me!" She seemed to think for a moment. "Well," she started, a gleaming smile coming to her lips, "luckily I have more men working for me. That way, I can do this." Before the man could speak, Blisse's hands were already wrapped around his neck. He wheezed for air, his lungs aching for oxygen. Blisse squeezed tighter and tighter, satisfied by the light purple color he was turning. The second guard froze. He watched as his friend got weaker and weaker, until there wasn't an ounce of strength left.

Blisse menacingly turned toward her other guard. He had his hands out in a pleading gesture.

"Please don't kill me," he begged, burning tears coming to his eyes. "I don't want to die." Blisse stared angrily into his wide eyes.

"You should've thought of that before you denied me Hope," she replied coldly. The man shouted in terror. Blisse grinned as her hands shot out around his throat.

It felt as though his brain would explode. Pain erupted throughout his whole body as the tendons and arteries tore. Blisse's grip savagely tightened on his neck, causing his body to shake. Her inhuman strength slowly sucked the life out of her guard. "And *that* is for slowing me down." She threw his barely alive body on the floor. Her hands were off of him now, but it was too late for him. His body shook with spasms as he died.

Blisse's body turned to the door with a deep breath. Her hands still slightly shook with rage as she slowly walked out of the building, leaving her guards behind with the murdered bodies. Blisse only had one thought on her mind: Hope. She could still recall with joy what the blonde's face looked like when her step-sister was drowned in the lava. That was the one thing that had kept Blisse from losing faith. *Come on girl, you can find them,* she angrily told herself. *Where would they go?*

The first idea that came to her mind was a tree. Would they risk going up in a tree? Ethan certainly wasn't the brightest, but he was smart enough to not climb in one. *Where else could they be?* Blisse resisted the urge to smack her head. *Think!*

A light bulb went off in her mind. They wouldn't go to another building, they wouldn't climb a tree, they wouldn't risk a cave… but where else could they go? Blisse smirked smugly to herself. She began to jog.

38

"Go, go!" Ethan yelled, ushering everybody through the dark jungle. "We need to hurry!"

"I got that!" Belle replied, huffing for breath as she sprinted.

"How much farther?" Aspyn gasped out. Hope ran up beside her, putting her hand on her arm.

"About five more minutes," she replied. "Hang in there, Aspyn." They all continued dashing with the dead bodies and Blisse on their mind.

Finally, Ethan tore from the jungle into the clearing that contained the hole.

"Hopie!" he called. Hope was grasping her side, heaving deep breaths.

"I'll never know how you can run so fast," she huffed out. Ethan's eyes glinted as he answered, "I told you, I was on a cross country team. Now Fire, get in the hole."

With a grunt, Fire pulled back the large cement circle. She leaped in gently, followed by Aiden.

"Hope," Cassidy whispered. "I need your help." Hope paused, looking into her fear-filled eyes.

"With what?"

"I think something's happening to me. I feel like I'm about to faint." Hope bit her lip in thought.

"Uh, do you know why?"

"All those bodies," she whispered. "Like the massacre." Everything clicked into place for Hope. Her friend was at her breaking point.

"So, do you want to talk about happy things? Do you think that will get rid of it?" Cassidy simply shrugged as her breathing became more rapid.

"Maybe. Ask me a question."

"Um, ok. What do you like?"

"What do I like?" Cassidy gave a small laugh. "I like to write."

"I know," Hope said quietly. "What else?"

"I- I guess I don't even know. I haven't had time to do anything fun for the past week." Cassidy's eyes lit up a fraction. "I could help you write something. That's fun for me."

"I can't write to save my life, Cassidy," Hope replied. Cassidy snickered kindly.

"Sure you can! I can help you. Just think of something important to you, and go from there." The first image that popped into Hope's mind was Haylee. Nobody had ever mattered more than her blonde best friend. The name still painfully shattered Hope's heart.

"Well, there is Haylee," she muttered. Cassidy's face took on a look of sympathy.

"You don't have to do that. You can choose something else if you want."

"No," Hope said, in a tone that sounded too rough and firm. She cleared her throat, lowering her voice. "No," she repeated. "I can write if the topic is something close to me. I'll do Haylee." Hope took a deep, deep breath, willing herself not to cry.

"Ok then. What did you admire about Haylee?" Cassidy asked. Hope shrugged, thinking about the qualities that made up the person she loved. "Well, she made me happy when I was sad. Is that any help?"

"Yes, it is," Cassidy replied. "Can you compare Haylee to anything? Something like a metaphor? Something, say, that can be beautiful?" Hope thought for a moment with her hand on her chin. What could be pure enough to describe innocent Haylee? The small, weak Summer popped into her mind. Haylee and her were so alike, yet so different. They both had that look in their eyes, the way that their emotions showed clearly on their face.

Haylee had been stronger, though. She had lived her whole life dealing with pain, dealing with built up anger from her dad's divorce. She had dealt with much more than she let on. In a way, she was like a hurricane. Hope had seen Haylee when she had snapped, when she had blown up in anger. Her personality was like the eye of the storm. When pushed, she could be much more furious than she let on.

"Weather," Hope stated. "Weather is beautiful like her." Cassidy's face went up in a smile.

"Now think of weather that is pretty to you."

"Sunrises," Hope immediately responded. "And rain. Thunderstorms, sunsets, and even things that aren't weather, like honey, oceans, meadows, stars..."

"Great," Cassidy said encouragingly. "Now, think of a poem using those words."

"I can't do that. Words can't just flow from me like they do from you. Can you help?"

"Of course," Cassidy told her, grinning now. Her eyes were lit up in a way that only writing could do to her. Her brown eyes no longer looked sunken in and dull, but rather bright and *alive*.

"Ok, let's see. *'You were like a golden sunrise, a gentle autumn rain.'* Cassidy paused, her eyes looking up in thought. *'You brought me joy everyday as you erased the pain.'* Cassidy locked eyes with Hope. "How does that sound?"

"Perfect," Hope complimented. Cassidy squinted her eyes, back in thought. *'You were like a dark thunderstorm, beautiful and deep. You were a shimmering diamond that I had always intended to keep. Your eyes held the glow of a million suns. The world had no obstacles you couldn't overcome.'*

"Good, let me try," Hope said. She wracked her brain for the perfect poetic line. "Um, maybe, *your voice was like the stars, your mind as bright as the moon-*"

"Your soul was like a rare, mysterious monsoon," Cassidy finished. Her freckled face was stretched in an eager smile. It was almost possible to think that Cassidy wasn't even upset anymore.

"Your hair was gold like honey," Hope continued, *"and you belonged to me. My heart was full of happiness, and only you owned the key."*

"Really good job, Hope." Cassidy paused, considering something. "Do you think I could add something about... you know..."

"Her death?" Hope asked. Her tone had gone uncomfortably flat. Cassidy hastily shook her head.

"No, no, really.."

"It's fine," Hope answered. "I want to help you, so why not?"

"Alright," Cassidy said, in sort of a warning tone. "How about, *'My world started to crumble as my masterpiece fell apart. The lock was torn open as glass shattered in my heart. Your eyes lost their light, and soon so did mine. My sunrise withered away as I slowly saw you die."* Cassidy stopped immediately, looking at Hope in shock. "Oh gosh, I didn't mean to say that, it just came out as a rhyme, I'm sorry." Hope looked at Cassidy kindly.

"I understand. You can use that line, it sounds sad enough. Now let me try." Hope cleared her throat, sniffing away her burning eyes. *"My purple sunsets turned to shadows as my rain turned dark. My perfect built up world began to fall apart. My stunning meadows and gorgeous oceans soon turned into a yawn. What happened was my worst nightmare; you had truly gone."*

Cassidy looked at Hope with an expression of sadness and love.

"Nice poem, huh?" Hope shrugged, forcing her face into a grateful smile. Cassidy returned the look.

"Hope, thank you."

"We should probably get inside the hole now, you know," Hope said. "There could really be another crazy person right by us." Cassidy quietly snorted.

"I doubt that, but let's go. Oh, and Hope?" she asked as they moved to the hole. Hope looked up. "You do have a way with words. I don't think you realize that, but you could be a poet." Hope snickered.

"Now there's something that I *absolutely* doubt."

"Glad you could join us," Ethan joked as his blonde friend fell into the earth. She brushed the dirt off of her now permanently stained blue shirt. Cassidy followed not far behind, her body just nearly missing Hope's.

"It's about time," said Belle. She sat down, pressing her back against the cool, dark wall.

"We wrote a poem," Cassidy said excitedly.

"About what?" The voice belonged to a curious Aiden. Belle flipped her light long hair, running her fingers through it. Cassidy was just about to answer Aiden when Ethan said, "Hey, Belle, what's that on your neck?" Belle scrunched her eyebrows together.

"Huh?"

"There's something on your neck," he repeated. Belle laughed awkwardly.

"Oh. That."

"Hickey?" Fire asked impatiently. Belle shot her a look. She turned her attention back on Ethan.

"It's a scar," she stated. Ethan nodded.

"Yeah, I can tell. What's it from?"

"One time, I was at a party in my first year of college," she began. Ethan pretended to wince.

"Oh, this can't be good," he observed. Belle uncomfortably nodded.

"How right you are. Anyway, I went to a party," she continued. "This one popular girl was drinking beer and wine the entire time. Other people started to drink too." Ethan raised his eyebrows.

"Belle…"

"I wanted to drink too," she retorted in defense. "So, I did. A lot more than I should have. I was walking down some stairs, and I totally wiped out. I couldn't see straight and my vision was all blurry. There was a nail hammered into a wall, and I hit my neck on it."

"Really?" Ethan asked with mock disappointment.

"What?!" she exclaimed. "Everyone else was drinking!" Ethan rolled his eyes.

"If everyone jumped off a bridge, would you?"

"Duh," said Belle. "There would be a big pile of bodies to land on." Fire snorted before she could help herself. Belle glared at her, but the look melted off her face. It turned into an almost… pleased expression. Ethan nodded, chuckling.

"Well, I guess that's one way of thinking," he said. "Well, while we're running from that maniac Blisse, we might as well make it fun. Anyone else have any crazy stories?"

"Oh, oh!" Fire yelled, receiving a shush from Ethan. "Sorry," she sarcastically whispered. Hope moved over to them, falling down into a sitting position. Ethan did the same, and he affectionately put his arm around her.

"Ok Fire, we're ready," said Ethan. Aiden looked at her almost sadly, and Hope knew why; her perky blue eyes were no longer focused on him. Her embarrassment had destroyed their friendship, or whatever it had been. All of her attention was on Ethan, and even a blind man could've seen Aiden's pain in his dull hazel eyes.

"Ok. So see my hand?" She crawled over to Ethan, shoving her small hand in his face. "See this?" She pointed to her thumb. On it, there was a jagged scar running across the length of her thumb.

"Yes Fire, I see your thumb," Ethan told her, using both hands to gently push her away. "One time, my cousins were driving me to McDonald's when I was about seven. I got out and bought some fries." Her mouth watered as her stomach growled. "Oh, what I wouldn't do to eat just a single fry again."

"So interesting," Ethan said, gently nudging her with his leg. She smacked it jokingly and continued her story.

"So I opened the door and a bee flew in. I tried to shoo it out and my cousin was freaking out. I got the bee out and she slammed the door shut, but she didn't see my finger there." Ethan winced. Belle bit her lip in fake pain.

"I have a story," Hope piped up quietly. All heads turned to look at her, causing her face to get redder and redder.

"What kind of story is it?" Belle asked.

"Well, it's a time when I was mad," Hope replied sheepishly. Ethan grinned.

"Oh, this is gonna be interesting," he said. Hope weakly smiled.

"Well, it's definitely surprising. One time, I was with my best friend, Sabrina. Her dog was sick, and she was really upset about it. He died, and she was heartbroken. She was crying about it in the hallway, and this one little idiot came up and told her to get over it." Her smile was growing wider and wider as the memories poured out of her mouth, making her forget about Haylee. "So I went up to him and called him out. He said some pretty sexist things to me."

"I already hate this guy," Belle said, clenching her fists. Hope nodded, genuinely chuckling.

"Yeah, I know. Anyway, he wasn't even listening to me." Her embarrassed smile got bigger and bigger. "I walked into a classroom right across from me. I picked up a stapler and walked back into the hall."

"Hopie," Ethan laughed.

"I threw that stapler at his ugly face."

Fire started hysterically laughing. A huge smile spread across Hope's face. "I got suspended for a week, and my mom was furious. On the bright side, Sabrina absolutely loved me."

Ethan started to laugh as well.

"Wow Hope, I didn't know you had that in you," Cassidy said, smiling. Hope grinned.

"I didn't either." Ethan pretended to wipe tears of humor from his eyes.

"Well, I don't know if anyone can top that, but does anyone else have a story about when they got mad?"

Cassidy raised her hand, embarrassed. "I do." Ethan's mouth spread into a massive smile.

"Wait, little miss perfect snapped?" She rolled her eyes, making him happier.

"Oh, shut it."

Fire was leaning forward, her small elbows supporting her weight. She was ready to listen perfectly. Hope thought of when her family had all sat together by a campfire, making s'mores and singing songs. That's what it felt like now, with everyone crowded together in a circle, telling stories and making people laugh. It took her mind off Haylee and her horrific end.

"I dated this guy, and for a while he was really nice," Cassidy began. "I knew a girl who was gay. She was hilarious and sweet, such a good friend of mine. My boyfriend, Mike, came over once when she was over too. He liked her at first, until she told him she was gay." Her eyes were looking up, remembering the days before the island. "It was like a bomb went off. He screamed at her about how God hated her and she would never go to Heaven and that she was impure, all this stupid stuff. She started to cry, and this jerk wouldn't stop shouting at her. I got really angry with him, but I didn't say anything."

"Why didn't you cuss him out?" Fire asked. Cassidy smirked.

"I had a better plan. I went over to his house once, and told him how sorry I was. He accepted my apology. He went into his room to get something, and that was my chance."

"Oh christ, Cassidy," Ethan said excitedly. Cassidy's mouth spread into a smile.

"I hid his project for school. A huge one that was a very important assignment. He never found it, and he failed it." She paused to take a breath. "He had to retake the class over the summer. On the very last day of summer vacation, I told him what I did. His mom rang my doorbell to talk to me. I said some very rated-R things," she said, laughing. "I'm not ashamed."

Belle put out her hand for a high five.

"Wow Cassidy," Aspyn said in awe. "Are you sure that wasn't a bit much?"

"Not at all," she answered. "No one deserves to be treated as less than a human. That… imbecile deserved every single piece of crap he got."

For the first time in what felt like forever, Hope didn't feel on edge. She could forget about Blisse, forget about Haylee. She looked around at all of her friends. Fire looked happier than she had looked in a very long time, Ethan's smirk that she adored was plastered across his face, and even Belle was just barely concealing a grin.

Aspyn no longer looked like the depressed, hollow-faced girl she had looked like when she had found her friend dead on the ground. In some part of her mind, Hope knew that this peaceful moment wouldn't last for long. She knew that they would be back in their routine, running from Blisse, terrified. But she didn't want to dwell on that. With Cassidy telling her story and everyone laughing, Hope felt at home. For the first time since she was on the island, Hope really, genuinely felt *happy*.

"So what's the plan?" Fire asked. Although she was attempting to hide it, it was plain as day that she didn't want to stay sitting for long. Ethan looked at her, an amused smile on his face.

"I'm not sure," he answered. "I guess it depends on if we are found or not." Hope tensed up.

"Wait, what if we *are* found? What then?"

Ethan's gaze turned to her. His eyes stared at her with a look of protection and admiration. Hope's eyes looked down in embarrassment.

"If someone comes down here, we'll strike them where it hurts," he finally said. Hope felt a look of longing show on her face.

"Ethan, I wish I were like you. You're so fearless and I can't even hurt someone." Ethan's expression turned a bit sad.

"Oh, I'm not fearless," he replied. "There are people who I am terrified to lose."

"Like me?" Fire asked, striking a pose theatrically. Ethan chuckled, throwing a pile of dirt at her.

"Yes my little Sapphire, just like you."

Blisse could feel her already torn up clothes snag against thorn after thorn as she stalked through the jungle. Just thinking about the damage she was about to create sent a shiver of pleasure up her spine. She could imagine Ethan's face as she slowly dragged a knife up his skin, the way his crimson blood would so ever slowly, excruciatingly pour out, the way his screams would echo joyfully in her ears....

Not now, she chided herself. Blisse couldn't yet let her fantasies take her over. Once she got her hands on them, she could do whatever she pleased.

She could feel in her heart as Normal Blisse tugged on her brain, trying to stop her from doing the unspeakable things she longed to do.

Normal Blisse, who would loudly cry each time someone's body went slack.

Normal Blisse, who would try to stop her very own body from moving to harm someone.

Yet, she would never succeed.

Psycho Blisse would never leave now. The black in her eyes had now become a part of her soul, and that part was something that would never leave.

It had taken control of her heart.

It controlled her brain.

And Normal Blisse was no match for the new, reigning Psycho Blisse.

Before she knew it, her foot hit the first sign of clear ground. The dense plants and trees disappeared as Blisse took her first steps into the clearing.

"Hopie, Hopie, Hopie," she mumbled cheerfully to herself, the annoying blonde girl's face popping into her mind. She would target her first.

Oh yes, she would.

She would start with Hope's legs. The knife would slide and slide over her flesh until nothing was left. Ethan would be watching with his face in a mask of pain and fury.

Blisse would then go for the eyes. Hope's oh so beautiful eyes would be blind as she continued to mutilate her body with her precious knife.

She would then get Belle. That stupid little brat would regret ever messing with her in the first place.

The girl with the pink hair and Aiden, they could starve for all she cared.

Voices were heard under the dark soil. How stupid they were to choose this place! Not that Blisse was complaining. This time, her victims would not leave. They would never escape her clutches now.

A scraping sound pierced the air. Blisse slid her flexible body behind a close tree trunk, curious at the sound. Was somebody coming out?

Blondie's face popped up. Little Hope's green eyes circled around, looking for a clear coast. How surprised she would be when she found that her worst enemy was right around this very tree. Blisse could feel her palms shake with the excitement of it.

She then had a thought that almost made her snap the tree in two.

Blisse couldn't fight the entire group alone. She needed some more expendable old men to help her get her victims.

Hope's stupid face taunted her. How badly she wanted to just run over there and slice it clean off her pretty little shoulders.

But if she did that, Ethan and Aiden would be on her in a second. She needed to kill one of them off. She knew that Ethan and Aiden both had admirers, that was obvious. One of them would break if their love died.

This thought filled Blisse with immeasurable delight.

She could break two birds with one stone.

Hope's head froze. Blisse's head was sticking further out of the tree than she had imagined. Hope's spring green eyes grew larger and larger, becoming filled to the brim with fear. Blisse mentally cursed herself. Hope's head suddenly dropped down, back into the ground.

Well it's too late now! she angrily thought. Stupid Blondie was probably blabbing her big mouth to Ethan about how their biggest fear was right by them.

Blisse couldn't fight them now. They all had weapons, and even she could die if they hit her in just the right spot. She would *not* go through the embarrassment of being defeated by her very own prisoners.

"Ugh, screw it," she muttered, backing away from the tree. She had to go find more guards. Killing the other two was a mistake. A very bad mistake.

Her rage had overpowered her at that moment, and she couldn't let it happen again. She also knew that this could've been her only chance to kill the very people that had escaped her. Now, the element of surprise was gone. They would all be on their best guard now.

Well, no reason to dwell on what could have been. With one last longing glance toward them, she reluctantly went on her search for more guards.

39

No, no, Hope thought in pure fear, any happy thought completely wiped away from her mind. She had seen Blisse's eyes stare right at her. There was no way she would have imagined that look of utter sadistic joy.

Hope's quivering body slammed back onto the ground. Ethan grabbed her good wrist, pulling her up oddly.

"You good, Hopie?"

"No." Her voice came out as embarrassingly shaky. "We have to get out of here. Blisse is up there, I just saw her eyes looking at me."

"Woah there, slow down," Fire stated. Hope paused, not realizing how fast her tone was. Well, hyperventilating in terror tended to do that to a person.

"It's Blisse," Hope repeated, deliberately slower this time. "I just saw her behind a tree, but she just ran away. I don't know why, but we need to leave."

Aiden looked at her with a concerned expression.

"Hope, are you sure? You have been quite traumatized the past couple of days, are you sure that you didn't-"

"I did *not* imagine it," Hope snapped at him. "If you won't follow me, I'll go alone. I'm not going to die by the hands of Blisse."

"Alright Hope," Ethan reassured, giving her arm a squeeze. "We'll go with you."

Hope thought about when she had been confined to the small helicopter. She had thought she could never experience more fear than she had been feeling at that moment. Clearly, she was wrong. It was almost funny to think that she had still been innocent then. She hadn't been put through watching real, genuine death. Hope never would have thought that her life on the island would be spent running for her life, away from someone who she couldn't even bring herself to kill. And if the chance clearly presented itself, she didn't think she'd be able to actually take a life away anyway.

Before she knew it, she was out of the large hole. Her hurt wrist painfully fell onto the hard ground, but Hope bit her lip hard and wished the agony away. She pushed off her knees, lunging up from the ground, getting as far away from the hole as possible.

"I can't believe she was so close," Cassidy whispered, coming up next to Hope.

"Neither can I."

"She will kill us," Cassidy confessed, giving Hope a look. "She won't capture us again."

"She might," Hope replied.

"You guys are right," an intelligent voice stated behind them. Turning around, it revealed Aspyn. "I studied psychology when I was still in school," she continued. "Blisse hasn't succeeded yet, so I'm 99.9 percent sure that she'll capture you guys again."

"But that hasn't gotten her anywhere yet," Cassidy pointed out. "She wouldn't be dumb enough to attempt to kidnap us yet again. It makes no sense."

"Just think about it," Aspyn persisted. "She's tried multiple times and she's failed at each one. The human mind always wants to feel accomplished. She has not succeeded yet, and she won't stop until she gets what she wants: control."

"You don't even know who she is," Fire said coldly, coming up to join their conversation. With a quick glance back, Hope saw that it was Aiden who was pulling himself out of the hole. His eyes were glued to Fire, in a sad, puppy-dog way. It made Hope's heart want to break. "You haven't been taken by Blisse, Aspyn. You don't know what it's like." Fire's eyes were hard. "You don't know what it's like to fear for your life every second of the day when a black-eyed sociopath is haunting you day and night. Don't act like you can understand. You'll never understand us."

By now, Ethan had made sure that everyone was out of the hole.

"So," Belle began, "where do you lads suppose we go?"

"A building," Fire stated. Ethan shook his head.

"No, I don't think that's-"

"Yes we are!" she interrupted. "I'm tired of sleeping with mosquitos biting my face, I'm tired of feeling all wet and disgusting under the trees, and I'm tired of tossing and turning from the heat! We are going to sleep with real shelter tonight."

Ethan paused, looking at her. It tugged at his heart when he remembered how emotionally weak Fire had been when she had arrived on the island. He knew about her dad, the way she had flinched whenever someone had made a sudden movement. Her time on the island had changed her, and Ethan wasn't sure if it were for the better.

"We can go to a building," Aiden piped up. Fire just stared at him coolly, her dark blue eyes glaring up at him. He stopped speaking, and the same heartbroken expression took over his face.

Just make up! Hope wanted to scream. It hurt her soul that Fire and Aiden could've had something together, she knew it. Now, Fire couldn't have hated someone more.

"Alrighty," said Ethan, staring at Aiden with some concern. "We'll go to a building. I don't know how safe we will be, but it's something."

"Oh, screw safety," Belle snapped. "I want Blisse to come at us. I want to get rid of her stupid little black eyes."

Cassidy stared at her, appalled.

"Wait, you wouldn't actually kill her, right?" Belle chuckled sardonically.

"Hell yeah I will. I'm tired of not being able to sleep too. Screw my safety. At the end of the day, I want to see her filthy little blood on my hands."

"We won't be stopping you," said Aspyn hesitantly. Fire dramatically rolled her eyes.

"Well, let's go," Ethan said. Hope noticed him lightly pat Aiden on the back as they turned to find shelter.

"So, where *are* we going?" Tyrand gasped out. All of his energy had been exerted in their long trek through the jungle. Blisse turned, but she didn't snap back. Her eyes looked around thoughtfully and angrily. She would not admit that she hadn't thought of their destination. Originally, she had planned to stomp back into the hole in the ground, and take them all by surprise. Of course, now she couldn't do that. Stupid Hope had spotted her.

Just the thought of losing her victims sent spots of red into Blisse's vision. Anytime Hope's stupid blonde hair popped into her mind, she would later find that her hand was covered in red, stinging nail marks. Where else could they possibly go?

A tree popped into her mind. They had always chosen trees for a safe spot. But would they risk it again? After all, Blisse had been correct about their idea of finding the hole. However, she didn't think that they would choose a tree. They would be cornered if they did that, and Hope probably knew she had made a mistake about the hole.

They might choose a building again, but that would be a huge risk. They probably wouldn't go to the other side of the island now, it would be too far and not as familiar as the place they had lived in for years.

Come on, Blisse, she commanded herself. She angrily knocked her fist against her forehead repeatedly.

Then, she turned and looked at Tyrand. He was bent over, gasping for oxygen to fill his lungs. His big, fat lungs that were… expendable.

Blisse's mouth slowly went up in a smile. She could use him against the kind people in Hope's group. They wouldn't be too suspicious of him if he ran around crying, claiming that Blisse hurt him. They would let him join their group out of pity, and then Blisse could strike.

She knew Ethan. Although he could be very untrustworthy when he felt like it, he wouldn't completely reject a victim of Blisse.

At least, he would think he was a victim.

Her giddy smile grew bigger and bigger. She bared her teeth at the line of guards behind her.

"I have a plan," she declared. Tyrand hesitantly looked up, his faded brown eyes looking into her pure black ones.

"Oh no," he murmured. "She has a plan."

"Shut up, Tyrand," Blisse snapped coldly. "And you will act on my plan."

"But why?"

"Because I am your master!" she screeched suddenly. "I am your master, you piece of scum! Not you, *me!*" She stomped up to him, and suddenly she appeared to be much bigger. "And if you *ever* question my plans again, I will rip out your tongue!"

"Sorry," Tyrand muttered, slowly trying to back away. Without warning, Blisse gripped the edge of Tyrand's ripped collar on his shirt. For a moment, it looked as though she would lose all control. Her vision was red as she breathed deeply, trying to regain her sense of self control.

"You will be my plan," Blisse said, deliberately calmer this time. "You, Tyrand, will help me get my victims back."

"I hate all of you," Belle muttered to herself. Instead of piles of food like she had originally hoped for, she had gotten a piece of rotten fruit from an old tree. Ethan was starting to genuinely look like a source of food.

"Hey, at least we aren't running," Aiden brought up. "You'd be much more hungry if we were."

"Thanks for the tip, smart one."

They continued trudging through the jungle, heading toward a building where they could stay.

"This sucks," Fire muttered. "I don't even know why we have to be on this stupid island in the first place."

"You know why," Ethan told her. "It's because you are so smart."

"That doesn't mean that I should be shipped off to some island, though. I thought being smart was a good thing."

"Not to the government," Aiden said darkly. "I don't know why, though."

"I didn't ask you," Fire replied coldly. Aiden's face flushed a deep red as he turned away.

Soon, Hope could see the first sign of a building. The sky was slowly growing darker, and she knew that they had to reach it quickly. Who knew if Blisse could be hiding out in the darkness?

"Finally," Belle breathed out. She took off in a dead sprint, exerting the rest of her energy into the run toward the building. When she finally reached it, she was panting on her knees. "Wow," she gasped. "Am I really that out of shape?"

"No," said Cassidy, who had been able to keep up with her. "You're just starving, and it's harder to run on an empty stomach."

"Why so fast?" Hope asked, as she finally reached the doors of the building. Before she could walk in, Ethan pulled her softly aside.

"Look," he whispered. Hope turned her head to see what he had been pointing at. In front of his scratched up finger was the burnt remains of the place that was once their home. It looked so sad there, with some stray ashes being swept away from a breeze.

"I am so sorry, Ethan," Hope whispered back. Ethan shrugged as his light eyes stayed glued to the charred structure.

"You know," he began sadly, "that building was where I spent my very first night on this hell they call an island. I sobbed in that place so much, Hope, you don't understand. I don't even know why I miss it."

"You know, it's all my fault that the building was burned," Hope suddenly said. Ethan just stared at her.

"Hopie, don't be stupid, you weren't responsible for it."

"Yes I was," she argued. "I was the one who had to follow that stupid smoke when I first got here, I'm the one who started all the trouble with Grayson, and I'm the one who started this fight with all the guards. If I hadn't escaped from him in the first place, they would've left you guys alone."

"It's *not* your fault," he stated firmly. "You needed to survive."

"I never should have come here." Hope's lip started to tremble, and she mentally stopped herself. She could not cry here, not right now.

"Hope, do you really want to play the blame game? Fine, I was the one who was responsible for Carter's death. I threw the ball badly, and he suffered for it. If it weren't for me, he would still be here."

"But it's not your fault that he ran into the road."

"Now you know how stupid you sound." Although the words were harsh, his voice came out in a kind tone. "Don't think about what could've happened, it'll drive you crazy."

"But still," she persisted. "I'll have to live with the knowledge that I hurt you all."

"Fine," Ethan said flatly. "If I had never snapped at Cassidy, then she would have never run away, and I would have never run away. Then we never would have gotten separated, and we wouldn't be caught in the first place."

"And if I hadn't suggested we stay at the tree you had shown me, Martha wouldn't have died!" Hope shot back.

"Oh yeah Hope," Ethan snapped, "your existence caused all this. See how ridiculous that is? We are all responsible for things, but that doesn't make us who we are."

"Haylee would still be alive," Hope forced herself to say. "She would still be here if it weren't for me." Ethan took a deep breath.

"Hopie, everything happens for a reason." His voice came out as oddly strained. "I believe in fate, and I think there's a purpose for each thing we go through. Don't torment yourself thinking about 'what ifs'. It'll only kill you."

She looked at him for what seemed like hours. *Please let him be right*, Hope pleaded in her brain.

"Thank you, Ethan."

"Guys!" Aspyn screamed from inside. "Come in! This thing's deluxe!" With a small laugh to himself, Ethan walked in, holding open the door for Hope.

"Look!" Fire said excitedly, grabbing his arm. "There's more than one room in this place!"

Ethan snickered.

"Wow, that's what we consider luxurious now."

"Hey," said Aiden, "it beats staying up in a tree like sitting ducks. No offense, Hope," he added hastily. Hope grinned.

"None taken."

"I call getting the other room!" Ethan screamed, comically pushing past Fire, knocking her to the floor. With a joking snarl, she dashed after him through the door. Aiden watched her with a sad smile. Hope noticed and said, "Aiden, I'm really sorry."

"It's my fault," he answered. "I wanted to teach her a lesson, but I guess she took it in cold blood."

"No, I think it's just because you embarrassed her in front of everyone. I don't really know her all that well, and even I can tell that she is not someone who likes humiliation. Don't get me wrong, nobody does, but especially Fire doesn't like it at all. I know why you did it, and I think she'll forgive you."

Aiden darkly chuckled. "Not if one of us dies first." Hope snickered, but she didn't like the way he dragged down the mood.

"We'll all live, I swear."

"Then I guess I change my mind," Aiden said. "She'll forgive me as long as we aren't all psychologically damaged."

"We'll be ok," Hope persisted. "Hey, I'm just trying to make you happier, Aiden. You know that Fire isn't your whole life."

"She might as well be." He said the last part in a hushed tone. "I love her, Hope. Just like you love Ethan."

"No I don't!" she automatically exclaimed. Aiden sighed.

"Yeah, you do. He loves you too though, don't worry. You should see the way he looks at you."

"You're just saying that."

"No, Hope, I'm not."

"He doesn't love me," she responded firmly with a flushed face. "There's nothing about me to like. Now, if you'll excuse me, I'm going to go to sleep after I eat something."

Aiden watched her go away, but not before he heard his favorite laugh echo in the other room.

"Tyrand," Blisse whispered, not even trying to hide the excitement in her tone. As she had been walking along the jungle line, she had seen a light flicker on in a building. It was very faint, but she knew that Hope's group had to be there. "I want you to put my plan into action."

"So you want me to betray them?" Tyrand asked. Blisse slowly nodded, the very thought of it sending pleasure into her mind.

"Yes. Now hurry. I'll sneak around the back later tonight, and you can signal me in."

"Ok." Blisse squinted one eye at him. "Master," he added, full of embarrassment. Blisse nodded in approval.

"Now go." As she watched him sprint away to the building, she felt something in her heart. It was Normal Blisse, trying to get her to stop. A very, *very* small part of her original mind was peeking through, begging for this monster's body to stop. It was one tiny ray of light in a cavern of darkness.

Blisse angrily wished the thought away.

Tyrand dashed through the rapidly fading sunlight. He had to get to the building before nightfall, or this group would never let him in. The thought of an angry Blisse made him pick up even more speed.

He reached the door as the first star had become visible. Tyrand stopped, staring at the silver orb in the sky. It was so strange that those were the same stars from when he was young.

Before he had been sent off to the island because he was wicked.

Whatever strange theories and rumors he had heard about geniuses being sent to the island, he didn't believe. Of course, he did have a sadistic part of him. The test memories were a bit blurry, but he remembered hurting people in it. He enjoyed every minute of it.

No, he wasn't smart. He was dangerous. And that was fine with him. As long as he was with Grayson and the other men, he was content. Sure, he didn't go as in depth with his killings as Grayson had done, but he enjoyed it very much. There was something about holding someone else's life in your hands that made life worth it. And now, he was controlled by a stupid little child. He had spent over half his life on the island, and now he was dominated by a *girl*. Who cared if she was some new and improved person? At her core, she was still just a weak girl who deserved to be killed.

By him.

He knew Blisse would come back at some point, and he made sure he would be the one to kill her.

He would take that fragile little neck of hers and twist it.

Then, he would have control once again.

He grinned to himself as he turned away from the single star. Walking through the door, Tyrand slightly clenched his fists, thinking of the demise of the oh-so-powerful Blisse.

40

"Holy hell!" Aiden screeched, jumping at a man in the doorway. He quickly grabbed his spear. "Get outta here or I will put this through your head!"

Hope just gasped. The man scared her, but he was nowhere as terrifying as Blisse. Still, whenever some seemingly crazy man barged in, it would disturb anyone.

"Wait!" he cried out. The man immediately put up his hands. Aiden squinted his eyes, walking closer with his spear pointed out. Hope tried to force her eyes away from the crusted blood on the metal tip.

"I'll go get Ethan!" she yelled. With brewing confusion, Hope ran into the second room of the building. Everyone else had found their way into the room. They were all around in a circle, talking.

"Hope!" Cassidy said in surprise. Her face grew red in guilt. "I'm sorry we didn't grab you, we just thought that you would want to speak with Aiden."

"It isn't about that!" Hope almost screamed. "There's some strange guy in here, and I have no clue who he is."

"We are in the middle of a game," Fire snapped, her eyes growing in annoyance. "Now, Aspyn, would you rather jump off a ten story building or get run over by a bike?"

"I don't care about your stupid game!" Hope yelled. Fire jumped up, putting her tiny hands on her hips. "There is a strange man that could be a threat. Get over yourself and come with me." Fire smiled a cruel smile.

"Oh, you are the biggest bit-"

"Ok Hopie," Ethan said loudly over Fire. "What's he doing now?"

"Aiden's holding him off," she answered. Fire was still acting smug and annoyed, and it rubbed Hope the wrong way. Just for her satisfaction, Hope said, "I know, he's so amazing and brave. Aiden would be the perfect boyfriend, don't you think?" It was almost funny the way Fire's face seemed to flood with anger.

Ethan roughly pulled himself up and rushed through the door. Belle sighed, but she didn't seem too angry.

"What a shame," she said, deliberately making her voice monotone. "I was having so much fun."

Hope chuckled and followed Ethan out of the door.

The man was there, and he didn't dare move with Aiden's spear under his neck.

"Thanks bud," Ethan said kindly, gently touching Aiden's shoulder to get rid of the tension. "I can take it from here."

"I've got it," Aiden said, almost fiercely. Ethan nodded with surprise evident in his eyes.

"Okie dokie then."

"Why are you here?" the angry hazel eyed adult interrogated. "You had better talk fast."

"I'm not here to hurt you guys," he pleaded. "I'm here because of Blisse."

That wiped Aiden's hard glare off his face.

"What is your name? And how do you know her?"

"Tyrand," he answered. "Blisse forced me to work for her. The stuff she did was despicable." He pretended to shudder. "I just escaped from her."

"She's here?" The voice belonged to Hope, who's hysteria was rising. It was unhealthy the way she would shake even at the mention of that name.

"No," Tyrand lied. "By just, I mean I just got here. I escaped a day ago." Hope audibly breathed a sigh of relief.

"Ok, that's awesome. So what, you want to stay with us?"

"Yes," he answered. "Please, I can't go back to her."

"I understand how you feel," Aiden said. His tone had completely changed from suspicious to sympathetic. "You can stay."

"Hell no he can't!" The person who had spoken was Belle. She was looking at him almost accusingly. "You can't trust someone who was involved with Blisse, you just can't. Look at him. Does he look like he's been emotionally distressed?"

Tyrand was growing nervous until Aiden answered, "Not all people scream and cry when they have been hurt, Belle. You should trust him."

"No," she said coldly. "You shouldn't."

"For once, I agree with her," Fire chimed in. "I don't want him here." It was clear that she expected him to agree with her. Instead, Aiden looked at her smugly.

"Well, the world doesn't revolve around you, love."

Fire just stared at him, his words shocking her into silence. Finally she spoke.

"Fine then. Go be an idiot and get yourself killed. I don't trust him, and neither should you."

"He hasn't given me a reason to not trust him," Aiden retorted. Belle looked at him almost helplessly.

"Aiden, when you've gone through as much crap as Fire and I have, you learn that you shouldn't and can't automatically trust everyone you meet. He hasn't given you a reason, but he shouldn't have to. And if you just let him in, you could get hurt."

"You guys are just too judgemental," Aiden replied coolly. "It's not my problem that everyone in your life was a bunch of jerks. We need to give him a chance."

"I'm not stopping you," Belle said, "but when he murders you painfully, don't come whining to me, crying about how he betrayed you."

"He won't betray me," Aiden said proudly, looking at Tyrand. "You won't, right?"

"Of course not," he said, feigning innocence. Fire sarcastically snorted.

"Yeah Aiden, ask him if he will. He looks just like a little angel."

"You shut it Sapphire," he snapped. "Now go get your beauty sleep or whatever it is you do." Fire bared her teeth at him. She suddenly didn't look so pretty as her middle finger went up in the air.

"Go screw yourself." She stomped back into the other room, slamming the door as hard as her tiny frame allowed. Aiden's eyes burned, but he forced himself to remain sane.

"Well Tyrand," he said in a strained voice, "I guess we can go to sleep."

"Just curious, is there a back of the building?" he asked. Aiden nodded.

"Yeah, just behind that door. Why?"

"Just wanting to know the layout of the place," he lied. "Well, I am so grateful for this. Thank you." Aiden gave him a warm smile, but it looked forced to Hope's eyes.

"No problem. You know how girls can be sometimes."

"Aiden," Belle warned. He just sighed.

"Sorry, I just… sorry." He rubbed the back of his neck as he went to lay down against the wall. Tyrand went to the wall by the door while Cassidy went to a corner. Aspyn watched everyone with sad eyes, and Hope got a sudden urge to go and give her a huge hug. She hadn't given much thought to the fact that Aspyn's two closest friends had died in just the past few days. Finally, the pink-haired girl just sat down right where she was and laid down. Ethan's eyes lingered on Hope as she put her back up against the wall.

Very much to Hope's surprise, Belle slid down next to her.

"You can tell she's killing him."

"What?" Hope asked. Belle shot a glance toward Aiden, who's back was toward them.

"Sapphire- she's killing him. He can't be with her, and it's driving him insane."

"Yeah, I know," said Hope, "I tried telling him that. He doesn't believe me." Belle shook her head.

"No, he knows it. He just can't stop himself from feeling the way he does. I think that's what's killing him the most. He can't stop what he knows is hurting him."

Hope moved her eyes to look at Belle. Looking closely, she could see the way her eyes didn't seem to have the same spark that she saw in Ethan. Her hair was knotted and full of dirt and grease, and her nails seemed to be stained with blood. It was horrible what this island had done to her.

"You know, Belle, for the kind of person you are, you really say some deep stuff." Belle nodded.

"Yeah, I know I do. I guess I just have a way with words." Hope could tell that she was just joking, but she nodded anyway. "Hope, you are an interesting person."

The blonde adult squinted her eyes in confusion.

"Really? I haven't heard that before."

"I can't decide who you are," she continued. "Aiden's generally sweet, Blisse-well, the normal Blisse- seems nice, Cassidy tries to be nice and happy, Ethan's just Ethan, Fire's aggressive and, well, fiery, and then there's you. I can't tell what you're like, and that's good. Use that to your advantage."

"How?"

"It's good because you are unpredictable," she answered. "Nobody knows what decision you'll make, and that's smart. I don't know if you do it on purpose or not, but whatever it is, it works." Hope lightly chuckled, but she didn't really understand what Belle meant. Who cared if she didn't fit one label? She didn't want to annoy Belle, so she kept quiet. Belle stood up with a sigh, patting Hope's knee.

"Well, kid, you should probably get to sleep. I'll go now." She walked away, and Hope found that she had developed a new liking for the girl. She gently set her head on the ground. Before Hope had the time to think of anything else, she had fallen asleep.

Tyrand stood up. The light from the moon showed through the glass windows of the building, allowing his vision to work almost perfectly. Careful not to wake anyone, he crept through the door of the structure. He had the skills to open it silently.

Sitting there was the small brunette girl who had yelled at him earlier. Why was she still up? Luckily, her back was facing him, and she was the only one in the room. He could hear stifled sobs coming from her mouth, and the noise provided him with an advantage. Maybe she wouldn't hear him walk to the door.

He took a step. Then another. The girl was still crying into her hands. He continued tiptoeing silently, his excitement growing larger and larger with each step.

And then, that's when he stepped on a hidden twig.

He winced as the twig snapped. The girl in front of him spun around so quickly, her vision blurred for a moment.

"What are *you* doing?" Fire snapped at him. She hastily wiped her eyes with her palm. She couldn't look weak in front of this man.

"That's none of your business," he stiffly replied. Fire stood up, facing him with groggy fury.

"I was right about you," she realized aloud. "You're up to something." Tyrand smirked, putting out his hands.

"And nobody believed you." Fire squinted her eyes, bringing up clenched fists.

"Whatever you're doing, you won't get away with it." Tyrand smiled a hard smile.

"I believe I will."

He moved past her toward the door. Fire shoved her small body against his large frame.

"No," she growled out through gritted teeth. "Stop."

"Get off," he simply commanded. He roughly threw off her body, but she attempted to pounce on him once more. This time, instead of hitting her, he grabbed her arm. She bit back a scream as she thrashed against his grasp. His gritty, calloused hand covered her mouth. She shrieked, but the sound was muffled in his grip.

Fire couldn't breathe.

Her hot breath stayed forced in her mouth, and her throat burned and screamed for air. This brought back memories of being submerged underwater, which sent panic through her body. Suddenly, she was back in the cold, freezing water, begging for oxygen but nothing could get through…

And before she knew it, she was unconscious and limp in his arms. Tyrand smugly threw her down on the ground, and he heard the thud of her bones hitting the floor. He opened the door, and standing there was his master.

"Tyrand," Blisse cooed affectionately. She rubbed his arm, and he greatly fought the urge to punch her in the face. "Thank you. Now, get me some rope from one of the closets in this place. We are really going to have some fun."

Blisse looked around in victory at her victims. The sunlight streamed through the windows, allowing her to get a good look at the people she hated for so long. After she had knocked them all unconscious with a rock, she and Tyrand had spent a tiring half hour tying each of them up. Even with her improved strength, the task had greatly diminished her energy. Blisse had then been forced to go hunting for some food.

She had killed five birds with her bare hands and eaten them raw. She wouldn't waste her precious time starting a fire. When Blisse had returned, her prisoners were still asleep. She had used too much force knocking them out, and that had been a mistake. Blisse wouldn't be able to watch them suffer and beg for mercy to let them go.

Oh well, she would do that later that night.

"Tyrand, I left the other guards back at the tree we were last at," Blisse told him. "Why don't you go join them." Tyrand shook his head in protest.

"What? No way! I got them all ready for you, I should get to watch them too!"

"Who makes the rules here?"

Tyrand scoffed.

"You do, but I want to watch them suffer just as much as you do. Maybe even more."

Tyrand shouldn't have said that.

Blisse stared daggers at him, her hand snaking across his arm. This time, he did flinch away. The sight of those unnatural eyes just gave him the chills.

"You think you want this more than I do?" she dangerously whispered. "I have spent the last moments of my life tracking them down, just for this moment. I have exerted myself to get them, and they have escaped. You think you want this more than I do?"

"No," Tyrand said quickly. "I'm just mad, sorry."

"You can be mad, but I don't care. Now go join the other guards." She lifted her hand at his protesting face. "And *don't* make me ask you again."

Muttering to himself, Tyrand stomped out of the building. Then, he broke into a full sprint to join the other workers.

Aiden groaned. He forced his eyes to open. He reached for his pounding head, but he found that he couldn't. Confused, he pulled harder and harder. He stopped when a smiling Blisse came into view. *But that's impossible, she isn't here.*

And suddenly, the memories came crashing back to him. He remembered seeing her gleaming, sadistic eyes looming over him as pain had slammed into his head.

"You," he growled. At least, it would've been a growl if his voice had been working. Instead, it came out as a raspy whisper. Blisse heard his attempt at speaking, and her eyes found his.

"Aiden," she whispered in delight. He forced himself to look away. After Aiden, Ethan was the first to stir. He groaned as his eyelids slowly opened. As soon as he got a glimpse of Blisse, everything had fallen into place as it had for Aiden. Afterwards, Belle and Cassidy awoke. It was great to see their faces just fall as they realized they had been tricked. Hope and Aspyn woke up, and finally, Fire was the only one left. As she stirred, Aiden suddenly got an icy pit in his stomach. She had been right about Tyrand, but he hadn't listened. She would be beyond furious with him now, and there was no way she'd ever forgive him.

His theory was proved when she did awake. Her groggy eyes locked with his, and they soon turned to ice. Her body shook in rage, and all she wanted to do was scream. Blisse seemed to read her mind, because she said, "Go ahead, little gem. Let him have it."

And she did. She hurled every vile swear word her mind could muster up. The saddest part was, Aiden just stood there, ashamed. His head hung low as she verbally attacked him, letting out all the rage in her system.

It took five minutes for her to calm down. Fire deeply breathed, glaring at Aiden and then Blisse.

"So what do you want?" she hissed. Blisse gave her a knowing smile.

"Is it that hard to guess?"

"You want to hurt us," Aspyn whispered, shaking. "You want us to feel pain." Blisse grinned.

"Right on, pinkie. Don't worry, I'll save you for last. I don't know you as well as I know these fellows here, so I don't have anything to do with you. I'll still kill you, darling."

"So, how are you going to kill us?" Belle asked casually. A smile tugged at Blisse's mouth.

"Quite painfully, if that hints at it." She not-so-stealthily pointed to her knife. "Now, I'm going to go get ready for my night."

"Wait!" Cassidy yelled. "How is it night again?"

"You were knocked out for awhile, my dear friends," she answered. "Bye bye!"

"Wait!" Belle called desperately. She noticed how needy her voice sounded. "Wait," she said again, her voice much more firm. Blisse spun around.

"What do you want, girl?"

"Let me help you," Belle pleaded. "I can be your assistant. I'll do anything you want me to do, I promise."

Ethan's mouth dropped open in surprise. He shot her a look.

"Belle, you're kidding, right? Please tell me you're kidding," he said, his eyes narrowing. She shook her head.

"Nah, I'm not kidding. I never actually liked you guys anyway."

"Belle!" Hope exclaimed. "Remember what we talked about? Does that mean nothing to you?" Belle shrugged, devoid of emotion.

"Eh, not really. Sorry guys, I'd rather side with Blisse. If I can't stop her, I might as well join her." Blisse's face spread into a large smile.

"Yeah, an assistant could work. You're a feisty little one." She paused, seeming to think better of something. A smile came to her face. "Ok, Belle, if you're telling the truth as you say, I want you to do something for me."

Belle gulped, but she nodded. Blisse's black eyes grew wide in happiness. "Tell blondie that you're glad her sister died."

Hope's mouth dropped open in a gasp. She had done everything possible to forget about Haylee. Now, the picture of Haylee's pleading eyes flooded back into her brain.

"Belle..." Hope whispered. *You can't do that!* Belle thought silently. *You'll break the poor kid's heart!* Blisse looked at her, her eyebrows raised.

"Do it or I'll keep you tied up and leave you to die!"

Belle averted her gaze to the plain gray ground. Putting on the most blank expression she owned, she said, "I'm happy that Haylee died." Blisse clapped in delight. Her eyes lit up in pleasure.

"Oo, now say that Haylee deserved it! Tell Hope that Haylee was a slut who deserved to die!" Belle's eyes darted to Hope in spite of herself. It pained her to see Hope's sad puppy-dog face. Her green eyes were full of water. Belle couldn't bring herself to do it. However, one look at Blisse made her want to freeze. Her previous delighted face was now dangerously impatient.

"Haylee deserved to die," Belle said, devoid of emotion. "She was a stupid slut and I'm glad she's dead." Hope looked at her, her lower lip trembling. Blisse grinned, her face bright.

"Very good!" she exclaimed. "Now I know that you can follow directions!" Blisse came over and put her knife against the rope, swiftly cutting it. Belle stretched, rubbing her sore wrists.

"You coward!" Fire screamed angrily after a moment. "You filthy coward! I can't believe you! We'll never trust you again, and don't *ever* speak to me again. I never liked you anyway, you disgusting *coward!*" Belle didn't even glance at the group as she walked out of the door. Blisse did.

"Yikes, looks like something didn't work out," she said through a grin. "Must suck. See you in a moment!" She sashayed out of the door.

"It's like Grayson's shack all over again," Cassidy mumbled miserably. Hope was much more nervous this time around. She was absolutely terrified of Blisse. Grayson was terrifying, but he at least was still human. Blisse's serum had completely wiped out any trace of humanity. Her heart raced just thinking about her. Everyone gave each other helpless looks.

We're screwed, Fire thought. *We're so very screwed.*

41

"So girl, when did you decide you wanted to help me?" Blisse asked, her black eyes sizing her up. "You didn't seem very cordial toward me on that trail."

Quick Belle, think of something, she thought. Blisse put her cold hand on her wrist, making her gulp.

"Is it because you're scared?" she whispered in her ear. "Are you scared of me, little Isabelle?"

"No, I'm not scared," she said quickly, hoping her lie sounded convincing. "I just got tired of the whole group. They are so obnoxious and I can't stand them. And what's the point of going up against you? We all know you'll win." Blisse pretended to wipe a tear from her eye.

"Thanks for the compliment! Yes, I like your thinking." Blisse grabbed a knife off of a concrete slab next to her. "Well, let's go hurt them!"

"No!" Belle yelled. Blisse cocked her head.

"No? I thought you didn't care about them," Blisse said, bringing the knife dangerously close to Belle. "Who's side are you on, girly?"

"Trust me, I'm on your side," Belle said hastily. "But here's what I'm thinking."

"This better be good," Blisse warned. Belle nodded.

"Trust me, it is." Blisse crossed her arms, her black eyes impatient.

"Well?"

"Ok, so I say we wait," Belle began.

"Wait?"

"Only until tomorrow," Belle added quickly. "I think that by waiting, we create more suspense and fear. I can honestly say that I was really scared back at Grayson's when he made us wait until the next day. You can go down to them, tell them anything you want. I think by waiting, we'll create more terror, and that will bring you, I mean us, joy. What do you think?" Belle tried her hardest not to look too hopeful. Blisse eyed her thoughtfully.

"Yeah, I like it," she finally said. Belle greatly resisted the smile that threatened to break out across her face.

"Ok, great. So what do you want to do?" Belle asked. Blisse grinned.

"Let's just say that mutilation isn't too tough."

Belle tried extremely hard to not let her disgust show on her face.

"Ok, great. Don't tell me anymore, I want to be surprised." Blisse nodded.

"Ok girl. I'll respect your wishes." She walked out of the doorway. She opened the door, and the group of friends were glaring at her. "I have an announcement!" Blisse proclaimed. "I've decided to prolong your deaths until tomorrow!"

"Whoopee, lucky us," Cassidy muttered. Fortunately, Blisse didn't hear her statement.

"I just want you to know that your deaths will be excruciating," she said with a smug grin. "You'll wish that you had never escaped from Grayson in the first place." All of the color drained from Hope's face. Blisse snickered at her fear. "On that happy note, sleep tight!" She walked out of the room, but not before shooting one last glare at all of them.

Belle was standing in the room, going over her plan. *This has to work,* she thought. *It has to.*

"Well, don't you just look in thought?" Blisse said, startling her out of her thoughts.

"What? Oh, no, I'm not thinking of anything. Nothing at all."

Blisse gave her a strange look as she crossed the room. She then climbed into a messy pile of dirty blankets, located in the corner of the room. Clearly, she must have set up camp while they were unresponsive. Belle bit her lip uncomfortably.

"What are you doing?" she asked. Blisse looked at her and sighed.

"It's late," she said, as if that explained everything. Belle nodded, still confused. Blisse rolled her eyes. "I'm going to sleep, stupid."

Belle greatly resisted the urge to shoot back with a snarky comment. Instead, she asked, "Wait, you sleep? Aiden thought that you couldn't."

"Of course I sleep, you idiot," she snapped. "I'm not a robot, girl. I need energy, just like you do. I thought you'd at least have some common sense." Belle's face turned light red.

"Sorry." She mentally cringed at how pathetic her voice sounded.

"Shut off the light," Blisse commanded. Belle did as she was told.

"Goodnight," Belle said stiffly. Blisse didn't answer. *Wow, thanks.* Belle awkwardly laid herself on the hard concrete floor. All she had to do was wait until Blisse's breathing became heavy enough.

Ok Belle, she thought nervously. *If this goes wrong, you'll be dead. There's no way she'll let you live.* Belle chuckled grimly. *Wow, way to make yourself feel better.* She debated whether she should actually go through with her plan.

Of course you're doing it, she told herself angrily. A half hour went by. She felt her eyelids become heavier and heavier. Finally, against her will, she fell asleep.

"Mom, mom!" chirped an ecstatic Belle. She was bouncing up and down in excitement, her loose pigtails flying all over her face. She waved a paper up and down. She tugged on her mom's leg, as her head could barely see over the tall marble counter. "Mommy, look!"

Belle felt a sharp kick in her small calf. She fell over, her tiny hands automatically covering up the area. She hopped back up, her excitement ruling over her pain. "MOM!"

Her mother lazily picked up her head, revealing a face full of smudged makeup and messy hair.

"What do you want?" she asked, her words slurring together. Belle grinned proudly.

"Look mommy, I got all A's!" Her mother carelessly snatched the wrinkled piece of paper out of her daughter's hand.

"Lemme see this," she mumbled. Her unfocused eyes skimmed across the page, much too quick to be a genuine look. "What's so special about this?"

"Well," squealed Belle in pure happiness, "I worked really hard!"

"Isabelle, you are in kindergarten. This isn't something to be proud of," her mother said, ripping the paper in two. Belle shrieked and dove for the pieces of her accomplishments. Her mom's foot came slamming down on them, preventing Belle from reaching them.

"Ow, mommy, you stepped on my hand!" Belle cried out. Suddenly, her mother's hand swooped down and grabbed the collar of her stained pink shirt. She pulled her face right against Belle's.

"You listen here," she growled quietly. The stench of alcohol flooded into Belle's face. "Did you make any money?" Belle shook her head, her gaze on the ground. "Does this help me at all?" Tears came to Belle's eyes as she shook her head again. "Does this get me a job?" The small girl's head shook once more, ashamed. Her mom's mouth contorted into what was a shark-like smile. Her beer-stained teeth were bared in anger. "Exactly. Next time, show me something that matters."

She practically flung Belle away. Her head hit the jagged edge of a nearby table, causing her to cry in pain. Her mother picked up the two torn up pieces of paper and swiftly threw them in the trash.

"But my grades," Belle whimpered. Her mother smirked.

The scene flashed forward two years later. Belle was at the same counter again, this time her face able to see over the tall edge. In her hand was a treasured piece of paper that had her poem written on it in special red ink.

"Mommy!" she exclaimed, holding the piece of paper up. Her mother's same judgemental eyes flashed her way. She was holding a bottle of cheap wine in her tattooed hand.

"What is so important, Isabelle?"

"I wrote a poem!" the young girl boasted. Her missing front teeth altered her pronunciation a tiny bit. She was proud of her lost teeth, as if that somehow made her older and more mature. Her mother squinted her eyes.

"I see. Why did you write a poem?"

"It's for Mother's Day. Wanna read it?" Her mother snatched the paper from her hand to read it.

"Really?" she finally asked, her attention focused back on her wine. "You act like that's some Shakespearean shit right there."

"What's a Shakespearean, Mommy?" Belle asked, looking proudly at her piece of writing.

"Isabelle, come here," her mom demanded. Without warning, she grabbed Belle's french braid. She pulled hard, making Belle cry out.

"Mommy, what are you doing?!" she asked, her eyes producing tears. Her mom roughly let go, and she fell to the ground.

"That's for your idiotic 'poem'," she answered, picking it up from the ground.

"No!" Belle yelled, as her mom shoved it down the garbage bag. The woman shrugged.

"The garbage is where all the trash goes, isn't it?"

The picture moved two years later. This time, Belle came walking through the door with a ponytail tied tight on top of her head. She was wearing mascara and the tips of her hair were dyed black. Behind her back, she held a permission slip for a field trip to the zoo. She knew that her mother would never in a million years sign it for her. The teachers had sadly said that they couldn't sign it and her mom's signature was required.

"Mom?" she asked timidly as she walked into the kitchen. Her mother's head was resting on the faded marble. Belle took a few more steps and lightly touched her arm.

"WHAT?" she viciously yelled, her head snapping up from the table. Belle jumped back, but kept her feet firmly on the ground.

"Will you sign this slip for me?"

"What's it for?"

"The zoo," Belle said bravely. "I'm at the top of my class in school and I've been doing really well and I just think that-"

"No," her mother interrupted. "I'm not signing a damn thing for you. I already do enough as it is." Belle nodded.

"Yes, that's true, but this is just something that-"

"I'm the reason you have clothes on your back and a roof over your head," her mom screamed in her face. "You should be grateful that you even have that! Now shut your trap, there is no way in hell that I'm signing that thing for you, you ungrateful child."

Belle nodded, fighting to keep back her tears.

"It's ok," she said, her voice wavering. "I understand." She ran to the back of the house where her father's study was located. She tentatively walked in. Her dad raised his eyebrows in anger, his square glasses falling to his nose.

"I thought I told you to never interrupt me during my work," he said in his raspy voice. Belle bit her lip nervously.

"You did. I was just wondering if you could maybe sign this permission slip for me. I just feel like it would be a good reward for how well I'm doing in school." Her dad looked curiously at her.

"I guess it couldn't hurt," he finally said. Belle mentally did a high-five with herself. "Have you asked your mother yet?"

Belle felt all her hopes crumble. Should I lie?

"Well, I, um, showed her the slip," she squeaked out. Her dad looked at her suspiciously.

"And what did she say?"

Suddenly, heavy footsteps echoed throughout the room. With a nervous gulp, Belle turned toward the doorway. Her mom was standing there, an empty vodka bottle in her hand.

"I just knew this little rat would come to you," she snarled. "I already said no."

"But why!" Belle shouted. "It doesn't even cost you any money."

"Don't you dare yell at me, young lady," her mother snapped quietly. "How dare you come to your father when I specifically told you no?!" Her gaze snapped to her husband. "Jared," she said, looking dangerously at Belle, "get the belt."

Belle was now in seventh grade, her blonde hair pulled into a messy bun at the nape of her neck. Her mascara was running down her cheeks, and there were nail marks in her hands from when she had squeezed them. She ran through the door, aggressively kicking off her cheap broken shoes.

"Isabelle!" she heard her mom yell. Belle flopped herself on her bed, burying her head into her pillow. She loudly sobbed into it.

"Isabelle Rachel Pratt, get your ass down here now!" Belle dared to ignore her. She heard stomps coming up the creaky stairs. Somebody pounded roughly on her door. "I will take your door off its hinges if you don't open it this instant," her mom angrily threatened. Wiping her eyes, Belle forced herself off of her bed. The door showed her angry mom, her bleached blonde hair thrown all over her head.

"What the hell are you crying about?" she demanded. Belle sniffed, turning away.

"I'd rather not talk about it." Her mom's hand grabbed her shoulder and roughly spun her around.

"Don't turn your back on me," she snarled. "Now tell me why you're crying, or I'll give you something to cry about!"

"It's...it's Jay," she said between sobs. "He...asked me out as a joke!" Her whole body shook, remembering his friends taunting her, teasing her for feeling so excited. She had been humiliated in front of the whole school. Her mother heaved a sigh.

"Isabelle, why on earth would someone actually like you? You were an idiot for believing that he was real!"

"This is why I don't ask you for things!" Belle screamed back. "You are so mean to me! I hate you!" Her mom's eyes narrowed.

"Is that so?" she asked, her voice dangerously calm. Belle sniffed, nodding.

"I'm sorry, I didn't mean to say that."

"Don't bother," she snapped. "I don't need apologies from an ungrateful child." Her back turned to walk out the door. Through her tears, Belle spotted a new tattoo of a quote on her upper neck. Suddenly, her mother turned back around. "And Isabelle?"

"What?"

"You are an utter fool for believing that anyone would think of loving you."

Belle lazily threw open the door. She kicked off her worn out boots and flung her backpack across the floor. She heaved a sigh as she threw up her dirty hair into a messy bun.

"Isabelle!"

Belle flinched as she heard the voice that she had grown up with for so many years.

"What?"

Her mother walked in, holding an almost empty bottle of beer. Her torn up slippers clicked against the hardwood floor.

"Do you have any homework?" she asked, almost in a snap.

"No," Belle lied. "I finished everything at school." Her mother stared at her suspiciously, but she couldn't find anything to yell at her for. "I'm going in my room." Her mother quickly grabbed her wrist roughly.

"Not so fast. Your teachers have been emailing me about your grades, and you have been greatly falling behind, Isabelle. I'm not happy."

"Why aren't you happy?" Belle muttered. "It's not like you even care about my life at all."

"For the first time, you're right. I don't want to look bad to the school." Belle nodded, sighing.

"There's the mom I know." Luckily, her mother didn't seem to hear her. "Ok, I'm going upstairs."

"I'm not an idiot, Isabelle," her mom snapped. "Take your backpack with you. I know you have work in there." Belle sighed.

"Whatever." She carelessly picked up her old bag. She stomped upstairs to her room. Instead of doing her work, she chucked it at the other side of her chipped wall. Belle moved over to her bed, which she hadn't bothered making. She jumped onto it. Her face roughly landed in her pillow, but she didn't care. She didn't recall the exact moment she felt her mind shut down.

Finally, Belle walked into her kitchen again. She lazily snatched a bagel from her cupboard that she could never reach for so many years. Her mom walked in, watching her daughter suspiciously. Belle shrugged as they made eye contact. She didn't even bother saying hi.

"I got a letter from one of your teachers today," her mom said casually.

Uh oh, she thought, taking a bite out of her plain bagel. Here we go again.

"Oh yeah? What's it for?"

"It says here that your grades are D's," her mother replied, looking at her angrily. "How embarrassing is it that my child's grades are D's! You won't get accepted to any college, and you'll have to spend your whole life living here!"

"I won't do that," Belle mumbled. Her mother raised her eyebrows.

"Excuse me?"

"I won't do that," Belle repeated softly. "If I don't get into college, I have other things I can do." Her mother snorted.

"Like what?"

"I can get a job." Her mother rolled her eyes.

"Not with that face you won't. You need an education or you'll be stuck here forever."

"You don't think I can get a job?" asked Belle, not really caring about the conversation. Her mother shook her head.

"No. What other options do you have now?"

"I can become dangerous."

Before she knew it, her mother's hand flew across her face. Her hand slapped up to cover it, her cheek bright red.

"If you do that," said her mom angrily, "you would be the biggest disgrace our family has ever known." Belle shrugged halfheartedly.

"It's better than living here."

Her mother's eyes narrowed. Belle flinched back, thinking she was going to hit her again.

"Isabelle." Her mom took a deep breath. "I wish you were never born."

Belle sat upright. The awful visions of her mother lingered in her brain. She peeled her lids open, feeling tears slide down her cheek. Belle then felt a bullet of panic enter her mind.

Oh god, what time is it? Her mind raced with panic until she looked over and saw that Blisse was still asleep. Ok, she reassured herself. It's still nighttime. She calmed herself down from her dream.

It's fine, that's over now. It's over.

Belle forced herself up from the floor, wincing at the stiffness in her muscles. She slapped her face hard, hoping that it would wake her up. Instead, it just made her face burn in pain. There was no way she could go back to bed.

Minutes passed, full of heavy breathing. Belle coughed, looking to see if Blisse showed any reaction to the noise. *Ok Belle*, she thought. *You got this.* She silently creeped over to the sleeping Blisse. Holding her breath, she quietly bent down. She lightly grabbed a corner of the filthy blanket and pulled it toward her. She about had a heart attack when Blisse took a loud, deep breath. Belle froze, breathing as quietly as possible. Minutes went by, and Blisse didn't wake up. Shaking slightly, Belle pulled the covers more until Blisse's hand was visible. She could faintly see the bronze knife nestled tightly in her hand. Belle reached over and picked up a loose piece of cement.

Come on, this has to work. She slowly moved her hand toward the knife. Finally, her finger came into contact with the cold metal. Praying, she softly placed the piece of cement in Blisse's small hand. Quick as a ninja, she picked up the knife. She held her breath, biting her lip, looking for any signs of Blisse waking.

When it was clear that she was still sound asleep, she quietly stood up. Belle quietly pushed open the metal door. She cringed at the creaking sound that it made, and her head whipped around to check on Blisse. The crazed girl was still asleep, thankfully. As softly as possible, she tiptoed through the doorway. Belle could taste blood as a result of chomping her lip too hard. Fire groggily opened her eyes at the sound.

"What the…" her crystal eyes widened when she saw Belle standing there. "It's you!" she yelled. "You piece of-"

"Shut it!" Belle snapped. Fire cut off instantly, seeing something in her hand.

"Is that a knife?" she whispered back, a tinge of fear in her voice. Belle shook her head.

"Yes, but I'm here to help you," she said. Fire sighed. Her eyes widened when Belle stayed silent.

"Wait, are you serious?" she asked, trying desperately to keep the hope out of her voice. She saw Belle nod in the darkness.

"Yes Sapphire, I'm serious. I can't believe you didn't trust me." She walked over to the other end of the line, which started with Aiden. He opened his eyes when he felt his rope shake.

"What's going on?" he asked loudly. Belle slapped her free hand over his mouth. His fearful face relaxed when he realized what she was doing. She did the same to Hope, who didn't wake up. Her sleeping body fell onto the cement below her. By now, Ethan had awoken as well. As soon as he was freed, he ran to wake up Hope.

"Thank you Belle," whispered Ethan. She weakly shot him a grin. Hope's eyes were slowly opening. She groaned as she forced herself to sit up.

"What are we doing?" she asked Ethan sleepily. He gestured toward Belle. Hope gasped, remembering the events just a few hours prior. Before she could speak, Belle put out her hand.

"Hope, listen," she said softly. It was obvious that Hope wanted to speak, but she shut her mouth tightly. "I didn't mean anything that I said, ok? I knew it would kill you to hear those things, and I didn't want to do it at all." Belle paused, looking at Hope's reaction. She sniffed quietly, but she didn't say a word. "I had to get Blisse to trust me," she whispered. "If I didn't do it, she would've gouged your eyes out." Ethan's eyes grew wider in disgust. "Anyway, we need to get out of here *now*."

"Hold on," Fire said, her voice a loud whisper. Everyone's heads turned to look at her. "Shouldn't we, you know…"

"No, we don't know," said Aiden through a yawn. "What should we do, Sapphire?" She scrunched up her face in embarrassment.

"Well, Blisse is asleep, and she is dangerous," Fire said, trying to communicate her point. Ethan sighed.

"Are you suggesting that we kill her?"

She nodded. "Well, yeah, I am."

"It's not a weird idea," Belle said in agreement. "Blisse is our biggest threat. Now is really the only time she's available to kill. Honestly, it's now or never." Hope looked up with a pained expression.

"Yeah, it's just that I don't want to kill the real Blisse," she said. Fire heaved a huge sigh.

"Are you still on this crap again?"

"It's not crap," Hope retorted. Belle shrugged.

"I mean, yeah, you have a good point. But should we really save her with the possibility that the serum is irreversible? If it's not, she could kill everyone on this island, including us. And if we escape her *again*, our deaths won't be pretty, I can guarantee that much. I know she's your friend and all, but killing her is what we need to do."

"So there's no way that we could find a cure?" Hope asked, feeling helpless for yet another time. Ethan pushed his dark hair from his face.

"No, not necessarily," he stated quietly. "Usually, no one ever creates something if they don't have a solution to it. Yes, Grayson's evil, but he's a genius. I don't think even he would make this kind of monster without something to stop it." Fire squinted her tired eyes.

"So what is it you're suggesting?" she asked. A hint of a smile touched his face.

"I say we go back to the shack and look around. We never had anything close to a chance to look around there. With Grayson and Blisse gone, we'd have the perfect chance." Cassidy wrinkled her eyebrows.

"It sounds risky," she warned. Ethan ruffled her messy hair.

"What's life without a little risk?"

Belle nodded thoughtfully.

"Yeah, it makes enough sense. But this is our last opportunity to get rid of her once and for all," she said. "Are you sure you just want to pass that up?"

Ethan thought of the moment when he had first met Blisse. When she arrived, her large eyes had been full of fear. Ethan had taught her how to take risks, how to play games, but most importantly, how to not let life on the island break you.

He remembered the time when Cassidy, Blisse, and him had made their own rope swing out of vines and other plants. They had failed miserably, but they had all fallen down laughing. He remembered when Blisse had had her first encounter with a criminal. He had protected her, and she hid cowering behind his shoulder. The next time she had seen one, she was still terrified, but she hadn't shook as hard. The third time, she didn't need to hide behind him. There was no way that he could let that sweet, innocent, loving girl die because of a monster inside her. He would not lose her because some lunatic stuck a needle into her neck. Ethan nodded firmly.

"Yes," he said, getting to his feet. "I'm sure. Now, we're gonna save Blisse, even if it kills us. Does everyone understand?" He put his hand out. Getting the memo, Belle put her hand on top of his. Then Fire, Cassidy, and Aiden put their hands out. Ethan looked over at Hope, who was watching the floor. "Hopie," he called softly. "Put your hand in the middle."

With a reluctant smile spreading across her face, she put her hand on top of Aiden's. "Deal?" Ethan whispered. Everyone locked eyes with each other.

"Deal," they all said in unison. Ethan's face broke out in a grin.

"Perfect. Now let's go save our Blisse."

42

"Ok guys, look quickly!" Ethan told them. Belle nodded grimly.

"You think?" She bit her nail nervously as she tapped her foot. Ethan looked oddly at her.

"Belle, are you ok?"

"No," she said simply, looking at the ground. "Blisse will get me first, I'm the one who betrayed her. I don't want her to kill me." Ethan nodded, looking at the floor.

"Belle, do you remember when you told me you killed your sister?" he asked. Cassidy looked up in shock, her eyebrows scrunching together.

"Ok, *what?"*

"I lied," Belle finally said. "I never even had a damn sister in the first place." Belle looked hesitantly up at him.

"Why'd you tell me, then?" Ethan asked. "That was my first impression of you." Belle weakly chuckled.

"I don't know. I guess I just wanted to seem tough or something." She took a deep breath. "Ethan, I never say this, but I'm sorry." Ethan grinned.

"Sorry, could you repeat that?" Belle rolled her eyes, lightly punching his arm.

"I'm never saying that again."

"Guys," Hope called, interrupting their conversation, "I think I found something!"

"Is it another syringe?" Ethan asked excitedly. She shook her head, causing his hopes to fall a little bit.

"No, but it might be of interest to us!" With a sigh, Belle walked over to Hope.

"Hope, it's a book," she said in a bored tone. Hope earnestly shook her head, pointing to it.

"It's not just any book, it's a diary. I think it might have belonged to Grayson." Fire burst out laughing.

"Wait, a grown man wrote in a diary?!" She imagined Grayson going to his room after a long day, writing *dear diary.*

"Why are you laughing?" Ethan asked with a grin. "Writing in a diary is a very masculine profession."

"You guys, it might help us," Hope told them, a bit frustrated that they weren't taking it as seriously as her. "It could tell us something about Grayson." Cassidy shrugged.

"Well, Hope, read us the first entry." Hope nodded, carefully opening the wrinkled page. For a moment, she was terrified that the pages would be empty. But the faded yellow paper was full of ink, all neatly lined up in rows.

"Ok. *Dear-"* Hope stopped right away, knowing that if she said the words 'dear diary', Fire would start loudly laughing again.

"When was it written?" Aiden piped up in interest. Hope squinted her eyes, trying to decipher the small print.

"It says July 8th, 2026. So it's 2060 now, that would be…" Hope paused quickly. "34 years," she stated. She glanced down at the diary that could hold so many answers.

"Ok, I'll start now. Here I go…

The government just announced something new. They are going to empty out all the prisons and put everyone in some remote location. I thought I would write everything down that's happening in case something happens to me. Apparently, anyone over 18 must take a test very soon. My mother is terrified for Alice and I."

"Who's Alice?" Aiden asked. Belle shot him a look.

"Aiden, use your head. She's most likely Grayson's sister. Now shut up, because I want to hear his little story." Aiden shut his mouth, gesturing for Hope to continue. She cleared her throat.

"*This concept scares me. I'm scared of being sent to this place. My test is scheduled for tomorrow. So help me God.*"

"He actually sounds sane here," Fire observed, no longer grinning widely. Cassidy nodded sadly.

"I wonder what went wrong."

Hope turned the next page. She noticed a few wrinkled dots on the paper.

"I think these are tears," she realized aloud. "This is the next day." Hope began to read the next words.

"*I'm on a bus right now. I'm dangerous. I'm going to some island. I have no clue where it is, but it used to be called Hawa.*" Hope looked at Ethan in confusion. "What's Hawa?"

Aiden snapped his fingers suddenly.

"Hawaii! That's what he had to have meant! So that's where we are!"

Hope looked at him oddly.

"I'm sorry, but what in the world is Ha… He… Hawi..?"

"Hawaii," Aiden corrected with a smile. "I learned about it. I came from Florida, and we talked about it a ton in history." Hope slowly shook her head.

"I've never heard of Hawaii before." Aiden shrugged.

"Well, not many people know about it anymore. After all, it was obliterated a long time ago."

"What happened?" Hope asked curiously. Aiden flashed a smirk.

"That's for another day, friend. Now, I want to hear more about our little buddy, Grayson." Hope smiled.

"As you wish." Hope's eyes turned to the next rows of ink. "*I snuck this book onto the helicopter. I am absolutely terrified now. I don't know when-*"

"Wait, helicopter?" Aspyn asked. Hope nodded.

"Yeah, this is later," she responded. "Then the writing just stopped here for a second. It's probably because of the mist."

"Mist?" asked Fire. Hope nodded.

"Yeah, didn't that happen to you? About four hours after I was on the helicopter, some weird mist filled the air. It knocked me out. I think it was so I couldn't find the island's location."

"This is July 11th," Hope stated. *"I'm hiding in a small building in some town. I was almost jumped by a group of guys who wanted to kill me. I'm going to die soon."*

"Poor guy," Cassidy said, biting her lip. Fire looked at her, astounded.

"How can you feel sorry for that psycho?"

"Because he was like us once," Cassidy said quietly. Ethan patted her shoulder lightly. "And it's sad to me that he was once a nice guy. He used to fear people, not be feared. Isn't that just horrible to think about? Life on this island changed his mind. That's just terrifying to me."

"Well," said Aiden, "when you put it like that, I do feel a little bad."

Hope gasped, throwing her hand over her mouth. Ethan looked at her immediately in alarm.

"What is it?"

"It's the next entry," Hope answered, her eyebrows scrunching together. "Look what it says." Ethan looked over her shoulder curiously. When he saw what the writing said, his eyes grew dark.

"What is it?" Fire asked impatiently. Ethan took a breath.

"I met a girl today," he read aloud. *"I almost injured her out of defense, but she promised she wouldn't hurt me. She is now hiding with me as an ally."* He paused, looking especially at Fire. *"Her name is Martha."*

"No," Fire said slowly, her eyes wide in shock and disgust. "My Martha was *not* acquainted with Grayson. No way."

"That's repulsive," Aiden agreed, his eyes narrowing.

"I can't believe it either," Hope said in shock. "Ok, this next entry is from July 13th. *"Martha and I are in the jungle now. Somebody set fire to our building, and we nearly died. I'm keeping watch right now while Martha sleeps in a tree."* Hope paused. *"I think I hear something. I'll write later."*

"This gives me the shivers," Cassidy said, hugging her legs.

"At least we know what the outcome is," Aiden told her. She shrugged.

"That's even worse."

"Well, no wonder they tried to set fire to our little building a week ago," Ethan observed. "Grayson had it done to him."

"This next page is dated July 17th," Hope chimed in. She continued reading.

"We're captured. I'm stuck in some wooden building with Martha. There's a saw in the room that we are locked in. There's some other boy, too, who looks my age. I don't think anything good will happen with the saw, and I'm going to try and escape."

"The saw," Ethan whispered in horror. "He was in the saw room. He was in the room where you almost died, Hopie."

"I know," she said dryly. "This is from July 18th." The writing was written messily and lightly, sending chills down Hope's spine. *"The boy was killed! He was sliced in half! Martha and I were forced to watch. This is going to happen to me tomorrow. I am going to die tomorrow. This is my last entry. If anyone finds this, goodbye."*

"Well, we know he doesn't die," stated Belle.

"That's good and bad," replied Aspyn.

"This is July 19th," Hope said, turning the page. *"I have an hour until my death. Martha is watching me write right now. She thinks it's cute that I write in a journal. I just asked her out before I die, and she said yes. At least I can date her for one hour."*

Fire made a puking motion.

"They *dated?!* He asked out my Martha? *My* Martha?" Hope nodded, showing her the page for evidence.

"This next part is written later," Hope told everyone. She took a deep breath and began to read. *"Martha and I escaped. As some guy was coming in to tie me up, I choked him and put him under the saw instead. When I watched him die, I felt a sort of pleasure. His screams somehow brought me triumph. Martha wanted to get out right away, but I wanted to stay and watch. She looks at me a little different now, like I'm not the same person. We are hiding in another room, getting ready to jump someone else. I'll write more later."*

"And thus, a villain was born," Ethan said darkly. Cassidy looked at the ground.

"So, that was his light bulb. I guess that was when it happened. That moment changed him." Hope shook her head in agreement.

"Yeah, I know. Do you guys want me to continue?" Cassidy reluctantly nodded. "Ok then. This is written on July 20th. '*Two men found us. We were almost captured again, but I locked them in a room. I don't know when or if we will be found, but right now we are hiding in some closet full of tranquilizers. Martha is sleeping right now so I can write. I think that I have an idea of what I'm going to do to the people who captured us. They wanted to see us burn, but now they will.*

"Oh my god," Ethan whispered, stopping Hope. "I think that he means the fire room. You know, where Summer died."

"Who's Summer?" asked Belle. Hope's eyes grew large as she realized Ethan was right.

"She was this sweet, innocent girl who was thrown into Grayson's prison." Hope told her. "She ended up being… well, burned to death." Cassidy shivered.

"She was burned?" Hope sadly nodded. Aiden looked at Ethan in disgust.

"Well, screw me over sideways. Grayson burned some innocent girl?"

"Why does that surprise you?" Fire asked. "Out of all the sick ideas in his head, that's the one that disturbs you most?"

"He called it his death sauna," Ethan chimed in. "It was actually pretty disturbing, Fire. Of course, you weren't there."

"Don't act like I can't comprehend anything just because I wasn't there," she snapped. Hope turned the next page.

"Shall I continue?" Everybody's heads nodded. "This is from July 22nd. *I did it! I rewired the thermostat on the wall to only change the temperature inside the room. It can now go up to deadly heats, just like fire. The men who captured us paid with their lives. Martha begged me not to do it, but I don't care. I used the tranquilizer guns to knock them out. They are now dead. Time to find the other people. I will write later.*"

"This is sick," Cassidy said, her eyes looking disturbed. "This is so sick."

"Yeah," Aiden agreed. "What started as survival became something so much more gruesome."

"This gets even worse," Hope said in a horrified tone as she silently read the next words. "I don't even think I want to read it out loud."

"I'll do it," Belle offered, plucking the book from her hand. "Ok, this is from July 24th. *I found the rest of the men. I've shot them with my tranquilizer guns. I've found an amazing discovery, a room that has a moving floor. There is a huge amount of acid below. I don't know how it got there. I shot Martha too, so I can do what I please. I had one guy positioned over the acid. I slowly lowered the rope, until he was completely submerged. I felt powerful as I listened to him scream. I wish I had it on video so I could watch it over and over. The other guy, I forced him into a pile of razor wire. I watched as he bled. Martha is still asleep right now. I think I will make my new home here. The men are all dead now, thanks to me. I believe I have found my place on this island. I found pleasure in the men's pain. This island was a blessing. This is my last entry I will write. I am now free to do as I please. Goodbye, journal.*"

"What the hell?" Cassidy choked out, holding her throat. "I've never heard anything worse. Oh my god."

"Grayson is terrible," Aiden whispered. "I can't believe he was so young when he started." Hope had chills all up and down her body.

"I guess Martha eventually broke up with him," Fire stated. "She probably was really disturbed with him. I can't believe she never told me."

"She probably didn't want us to be scared," Ethan told her. "Or maybe she wanted to forget him. If I were her, I would want to forget that I had dated a psychopath."

Silence filled the air. Ethan thought of Blisse at that moment.

"Shouldn't we be looking for that syringe?" Ethan reminded them, forgetting his goosebumps. "That's why we're here."

"Yeah, but what do I do with this diary?" Belle asked. Ethan held out his hand.

"Give it to me. We might be able to find a use for it later. Maybe we could use it to jog Blisse's memory, if she doesn't try to kill us first." Belle plopped the book in his hands and began to look around some more.

"Eureka!" Fire screeched excitedly, holding up a container.

"Syringe?" asked Ethan in the same tone. Fire was grinning ear to ear.

"Yessiree!" She held up the clear liquid proudly. "I found it in this mouse hole over in this corner."

"Aren't you just observant?" Ethan said, smiling largely. "Well, now we can go get our Blisse back!"

"Where do we go?" Aspyn shakily questioned. "How will we find her?"

"Easy," he replied. "We go to a clearing."

"Are we really doing this?" Cassidy asked, trying to hide her anticipation and fear. Ethan nodded, his smile not leaving his giddy expression.

"Yes, we are. Now let's go."

"Isabelle," Blisse murmured through a yawn. "Isabelle, turn on the light." The room stayed full of pure darkness. "Isabelle, I said now," she warned. Still, the room stayed without color. "Dammit, Isabelle." Blisse forced herself up and limped to the light switch on the other side of the room. Turning it on, she found that Belle was not in the room. Blisse pushed open the door that separated her and her hostages.

Molten lead poured into her stomach. She could feel the moment when her body started to quiver in pure rage.

Blisse screamed every vile word she knew as loud as she possibly could.

"ISABELLE!" she shrieked manically. The exit door had been left open, and it was clear that nobody had stayed behind. Blisse screamed until her vocal cords ached.

Tyrand popped into her mind. She needed to find him. *No, screw him,* she ordered herself. *I need to find them.*

With pure fire erupting in her system, Blisse threw the door open with a dark glance.

"And now," said Ethan, "we wait."

They had found a clearing nestled in the deep jungle. They were in a wide open space, open to anyone. Blisse had to go there at some point. At least, that's what Hope kept telling herself firmly.

A half hour passed. Then an hour. Fire was beginning to chomp on her lip in anger and nerves.

"She should be here by now," she repeatedly muttered. Aiden watched his friend from the hard ground. He missed the way she would talk to him, the way she laughed. And suddenly, as he longed for her warmth again, he couldn't take it.

"Hey, Ethan, I'm gonna go take a walk," Aiden quickly said. Ethan shrugged with a limp nod. "Just so you guys know, I'm going for a walk," he announced loudly. Fire's icy eyes shot up.

"Does it look like we care?" Aiden frowned, sighing with sad eyes.

"Don't get killed," Ethan said. He meant this as a joke, but it came out bitter and sad. Before Aiden left into the trees, he took a good look at his friend's faces. Cassidy looked bored, Hope was staring at the ground in thought, Fire was angry, her face fuming, and Ethan was fiddling with his nail. *I can't believe we're the only ones left*, he thought sadly. He greatly missed Blisse, but he knew that in her current state, she would kill him without a second thought. It made him depressed to think that the kind girl was now roaming out there, somewhere in the deep jungle, looking for victims.

He also knew that his group was as good as dead. After all, he was positive that she was beyond angry about their escape. Aiden knew that it wasn't the best idea to go out into the jungle alone when a killer was stalking him, but he didn't care at this point. He was tired of being around Fire. She was sucking all of the happiness out of his life. Well, all the happiness he had left. He gave a small, weak salute behind him as he took steps into the jungle.

Right away, three-quarters of the sunlight disappeared. The young adult walked on a crude trail, his mind clear. He didn't want to think; he just wanted to stop thinking of anything at all. Stop thinking of Fire, who now hated him, thinking of Haylee's eyes as she faced the realization that she was going to die, just thinking of everything. Aiden walked on for about 15 minutes until he turned a corner.

Suddenly, he stopped dead in his tracks. He couldn't move, he was so petrified. Standing right before him was Blisse on the ground, peering closely at footsteps. When she heard his breathing, her head snapped up. The biggest grin he had ever seen was spread across her face. She slowly stood up, her teeth bared.

"Well well, I'll be damned," she barely whispered. Aiden's heart was racing, and he couldn't move his legs. "If it isn't little Aiden, the person I've been looking for! And to think, you've been close to me this entire time." She took a small step closer, her crazed eyes taking him in. "Come here, boy, come to me." Aiden had stopped breathing.

Oh god, kill me, kill me before she puts her hands on me. He had never felt this level of pure fear before.

It was almost funny to think that they had all thought that their real enemy was Grayson, maybe even Gabe. He would've never in a million years thought that his beautiful generous friend would make him turn crazy.

"Hi Blisse," he choked out. Her black eyes were amused as she watched his eyes light up in pure terror.

"Well now, don't just stand there, old friend. Don't you know that not greeting someone is very rude?" She sarcastically put her lip into a pout. "Come on boy, don't be shy," she taunted. Aiden somehow forced his paralyzed legs to take a step closer to her. She curled back her lips.

"That's a good boy," she cooed. "Come closer." He didn't think he could move again. He could see her eyes becoming impatient.

"DO IT NOW!" she shouted without warning. He jumped at her sudden shouting, but he followed her demand.

Her grin came back as he came closer and closer to her. Blisse heaved a sigh as she forcefully grabbed his wrist. Aiden was stunned at her incredible strength. This person was so unlike Blisse that it made him want to cry. His arms were cut by thorns as she dragged him off of the trail. Finally, they came to a different clearing with one large tree in the middle. There was a bed of leaves right under it and a bowl of dried leaves holding water; it was clear that this was where she had been staying. It gave Aiden chills to know that she had been so close to them this entire time. She took a quick look back at him and snickered when she saw how pale his face had become.

She laughed loudly as they neared the single tree. Blisse stopped moving abruptly, causing Aiden to almost crash into her. She quickly turned around. Blisse wrapped her small hands around his forearm and slammed him against the tree. He grunted in pain as his back came into contact with the thick trunk.

Blisse pressed her body against Aiden's, preventing him from getting away. Before she had been possessed, she was weak and small, giving her the appearance of a 13-year-old. Now, with her coal black irises and her impossible strength, she was an exact replica of the devil.

"Time's up, boy," she purred into his ear. Before he could shout for anyone, she clamped her strong hand over his mouth. "No, no, I'll do the talking. Your friends won't get you, boy. Even if they heard you, you know they are scared of me." His emerald eyes blazed. Blisse laughed, a sound that made his hair stand up. "You're scared of me too, Aiden, I can see it in your eyes. Your pretty, pretty eyes. I can't wait to watch the spark go out of them," she said, her split lip curling into a sinister smile.

"Blisse," he pleaded, his eyes filling with terror. "I know you're in there somewhere, I just know it. Look into my eyes, Blisse. Please." Her dark eyes bore into his. Although he was down-right terrified, he didn't break eye contact. His hazel eyes stared into hers with urgency. He greatly resisted the urge for his eyes to move, to show vulnerability. Finally, after what seemed like an eternity, Blisse blinked. Instead of opening her dark eyes back up, she kept them shut. Her eyelids were still, which was impossible for a human. *Oh my god,* he thought with horror. *She's not really human.* Suddenly, her eyes snapped open. When her gaze focused on Aiden's, her mouth dropped out in horror, but her eyes were still black. Aiden's eyes widened in astonishment.

"Blisse?" he asked, his hopes rising. A soft smile spread across her face. "Yes?"

"Oh gosh, Blisse!" Aiden exclaimed. "You're back!" Blisse grinned, but her eyes still weren't turning back to her golden color.

"Ok Blisse, you can let me go now," he stated. The smile stayed on her face, but she made no move to follow his command. He laughed uncomfortably. "Geez Blisse, you're still really strong," he observed. Her smile grew wider, and she moved her hand down to her waist. Any other time, Aiden might've noticed this weird gesture, but right now he couldn't believe that she was almost back to herself.

"Aiden, I missed you!" she exclaimed. Her voice sounded like her old self, but there was something off about it. It almost sounded...strained.

"I know, I missed you too! But can you let me go?" Her hand lingered at her waist.

"Hey Aiden, can you answer something?" she asked sweetly, completely ignoring his question. He shrugged, then nodded. "Where are the others?"

"Oh, they're over there, about 15 minutes away," he said. Blisse nodded.

"Which direction?" she asked, gently stroking his arm. She was still giving him that kind smile. He pointed behind Blisse.

"That way." He went to scratch his forehead, but she put her hand on his arm forcefully. "Ok Blisse, I really need you to let me go," he said, feeling more and more weird about her. She locked her awful eyes with him, smiling. However, she didn't move a muscle. Aiden chuckled awkwardly, getting an odd feeling in his stomach. "Uh, Blisse, are you alright?" he questioned nervously. She gazed at him, her fake smile transforming into a twisted one.

"No, Aiden," she said, putting her hand behind her back. "I'm not alright." She swiftly brought up her right hand. In it, she was holding a glinting blade. Aiden felt his hopes completely drop.

"I'm an idiot," he whispered simply. She nodded, a smirk making its way across her face.

"And I told you where they were," he realized in horror. A corner of her mouth perked up.

"Yup, that's right. You're so dreadfully oblivious. You've always trusted people too easily, kid." His eyes were widened, knowing what was coming.

"And now, you're gonna kill me," he said dully.

"You're really great at stating the obvious." She brought the blade up to his face, showing him every angle of the tool that would end his life. "Any last words?"

"Yes, I actually have two last words," he said. She glared at him, waiting for the last words that he would ever say. "Ready to hear them?"

"Get on with it!" she snapped impatiently. He made a big scene of clearing his throat.

"Screw you."

"Oh, I really can't wait to kill you."

"I apologize, friend."

Her black eyes blazed. She pushed her elbow into his gut, holding him against the tree with her miraculous strength.

"Lights out, Aiden."

With a smile on her face, she plunged the knife into his chest. He gasped with surprise.

Then came the pain.

He screamed as she watched with sick pleasure. He swore at her with each breath that he gasped out.

"It's not fun getting stabbed, is it?" she asked, her terrible smile growing larger. He faintly noticed blood trickling out of his mouth as his vision became blurry. Aiden choked and gagged on it as he fought for oxygen. He tried to desperately look at his wound, but Blisse held his chin up.

"No no, keep your face up," she commanded. "If you look down, I can't watch as you die!" The pain in his chest was like a million nails, but he wouldn't give her the satisfaction to watch him scream again.

"Tell Sapphire that I... that I love her," he choked out. "That I'm sorry."

She laughed, twisting the knife deeper into his body.

"Ah, I always thought you would make such a cute pair," she mused. "How sweet! Yes Aiden, I'll make sure to tell her that you spent your last moments on Earth nobly proclaiming your love for her." He groaned in pain.

This is it, he thought. *I'm actually dying. Sapphire, I'm so, so sorry.*

The last thing he saw was Blisse's sadistic smile as she watched him get weaker and weaker.

Then, he saw nothing at all.

43

"Oh my god!" somebody shouted. From the shrill sound, Hope knew that the voice belonged to Cassidy. Ethan's head spun around. Blisse was standing on the line that separated the trees from the clearing. Fire's hard eyes looked up. Blisse walked closer and closer, her trademark smirk plastered across her face.

"Well, friends, I finally have you," she whispered. Blisse saw Fire standing behind Ethan, looking incredibly weak compared to everyone else. Her black eyes looked ecstatic. "And Sapphire, your little boyfriend and I crossed paths."

Fire let out a small gasp of fear and anger.

"You're lying," she said, saying it more to herself than to Blisse. "You never saw him." Blisse let out a horrible laugh.

"Oh, but it's the truth. Your Aiden's gone," she said sinisterly. "And Sapphire, he asked me to deliver you a message."

"What?" Fire asked harshly. Judging by the grin on Blisse's face, Hope knew that the message would be far from good.

"He wants you to know that he's sorry," she said mockingly. "He loved you, gemstone. Your name was all he could think about."

Suddenly, Fire opened her eyes wide, forgetting to look angry. Hope could see some fear and sadness nestled in her blue iris.

"Where is he?" Fire's tone was mixed with hesitation and dread.

"He's dead, little jewel," Blisse said, still walking closer. "I put a knife in his chest. He screamed, Sapphire. He screamed for you. I saw as life fled from his terrified, beautiful eyes. He is gone."

Fire clenched her fists. *He's not dead,* she thought, her emotions bubbling. *He can't be.*

Blisse seemed to read her thoughts, because she said, "Oh, you had better believe it darling."

"So he's dead." Fire's voice came out in a hollow whisper. "He died thinking that I hated him. Thinking that I never loved him." Blisse smirked, taking a couple more steps.

"You never deserved a boy like him, gemstone. He was too good for you. Too pure for a girl who had a drunk daddy."

"I loathe you," Fire snapped. "I want you dead." Blisse shrugged.

"Well that makes two of us. I wonder, Sapphire, how does it feel knowing that you never got to say goodbye to the man you loved? How does it feel to know that your mother and your precious Aiden are dead?"

The question made Fire snap. Without warning, she snatched the syringe away from Ethan's hand.

"Give that back," he whispered angrily. Fire took a step, her eyes dead set on Blisse.

"No."

Ethan saw her tense up. Before his best friend could put herself in danger, he lunged at her. His force roughly threw her onto the ground. Blisse opened her mouth in delight as she started a sprint toward them. Hope was utterly *terrified*. The sight of Blisse's gleaming black eyes set for Ethan was something that made her stomach turn.

"Ethan!" Belle screamed. "Behind you!"

Faster than lightning, Ethan turned his head around. He screamed in shock when he saw her lunging toward him. He almost aggressively pushed Fire off of him as he grabbed Blisse's small wrist. He forcefully pulled her to him. He flipped his body over, using Blisse's smaller frame to his advantage.

Ethan pinned Blisse roughly on the ground.

"Get off me," Blisse snarled. Ethan dryly chuckled.

"Oh, if only it were that simple." Even surprising himself, Ethan slapped her face. He never would've dreamed of wanting to ever physically hurt someone before, but Blisse had just turned that switch on.

"I will kill you," she growled in a voice so low that Ethan had to lean in. "I will kill you and your friends."

"Hey, why do you hate us this much anyway?" Ethan asked, still holding onto her. "It's just a serum in your body. Give me one good reason why your hate for us is justified."

Her evil glare seemed to pierce his entire body.

"I don't owe you an explanation, boy. I feel my hatred for you in my bones. I need to murder you." Ethan looked at her, his mouth in a smug smirk.

"Have you ever considered taking therapy?" She tried to buck him off, but his adrenaline was too strong to just be thrown off of her. Fire suddenly came dashing over, the bright liquid sloshing around in the plastic syringe. The needle looked menacing in the glinting sunlight. Fire gave Blisse the coldest stare she could muster.

"Ethan," she said angrily, "give this garbage a good, hard stab." Ethan laughed.

"Will do, element." She forced the container into his hand. He held it tightly in his hand, not daring to let the struggling Blisse get it away from him. Blisse's dark eyes focused on the syringe in his hand. They grew wide, and her thrashing suddenly became much more desperate.

"NO!" she screamed. Ethan swung the needle into her neck. He watched as the sharp needle penetrated her skin. Hope watched in excruciating anxiousness.

Blisse let out an inhuman shriek. Her nails clawed at Ethan's arm. Hope could see him wincing, but he was obviously trying to hide it.

She was still thrashing like a rabid animal, but her voice was beginning to sound strangely autotuned. Hope could only wish that meant Blisse was transforming back into the friend she loved. Ethan desperately emptied out almost all of the clear liquid in the syringe.

"Why the hell isn't it working?!" Fire screamed. Ethan shrugged angrily as he pressed all his weight on Blisse's wrist.

"I don't know, but it needs to work!"

"I'll murder you," Blisse snarled. Her voice was clearly becoming weaker and weaker. Ethan blinked.

"I'll murder you too, if this doesn't work." Blisse's devilish black eyes bore into Ethan's.

"Go jump off a cliff," Blisse snapped. Ethan chuckled, putting even more pressure on her arms.

"You wish."

A minute went by. Blisse was still angrily glaring at everyone, especially Ethan.

"This is ridiculous," Cassidy muttered. "She should be turned back by now. Why the *hell* isn't she?!"

"It could be the wrong serum," Fire suggested. Hope threw up her hands.

"Well, you could've said something when we, you know, *were at Grayson's freaking shack!*"

"I'm just being logical," Fire retorted. "You should try it sometime, Hope. Maybe I'd like you better." Hope rolled her eyes.

"I have better things to do than wonder or care if you like me or not."

"You guys really aren't helping!" Ethan's voice rose to a scream. "This was the only syringe in there! I may not have a degree in common sense, but I'm pretty sure this is the only thing that could work!"

"Did your plan not go as you thought it would?" Blisse asked innocently. Her eyes were twinkling. "What a shame."

"Shut up, Blisse," Ethan snapped back. "I know this will reverse you back. I just don't know how the hell to do it."

"Look at the syringe itself!" Hope told him. "Maybe there's something that might help us!" Fire looked at her, annoyed.

"Oh yeah, because I bet Grayson would put the instructions right on the front of the freaking bottle. Wow Hope, what would we do without you?"

"Belle, come here," Ethan ordered her. Belle smirked.

"Sorry, I don't take commands." He rewarded her with a glare. "Yeah yeah, sorry, not the time." She walked over to him, still holding the struggling Blisse. "So hot stuff, what do you want from me?"

"*Belle.*"

"Ok, ok. What?"

"Hold Blisse for me," Ethan stated. Belle looked at him as though he were crazier than Grayson.

"Not a chance. I'm not touching that… thing."

"Belle, if you don't, we'll set her loose. She'll go for you first, you know. After all, you did say it yourself; you were the one who betrayed her." Belle was taken aback.

"I did it to help you bums!"

Ethan nodded, exasperated. "I know, I know. Just come hold her. I want to look at the syringe like Hope said. There might be a clue. But I can't do that when Blisse WON'T STAY STILL!"

Belle sighed.

"Ok, fine. I'll help you one last time. So how do I do this? Do I just… get on top of her?" Ethan grinned slightly.

"Exactly. Put your hand on her wrist, like I'm doing. Whatever you do, *don't* let her hands free." Belle nodded, only feeling the slightest of nerves in her body.

"Ok then, here I go." Awkwardly, Belle sat on Blisse's stomach while Ethan carefully got off.

"Ok Belle, grab her wrist in 3…2…1.."

Belle's hands slammed down onto Blisse's wrists. Their transition was perfect, as Blisse struggled roughly but didn't escape their clutches. Hope, Fire, and Cassidy rushed over to Ethan, holding the syringe in his hand. His eyes looked confused and wary.

"Well Hope," he said, "you were right. There is something scribbled on it. Look." There were numbers sloppily written in very small print. Hope had to squint her eyes to see.

"Ok, there's a 2, 4, 6, no, that was an 8. 2,4,8,7, and 1," Hope read. "What does that mean?"

"Having fun there?" Blisse called to them. Her coal eyes settled on Belle. A shiver went down her spine.

"You," she growled. "You betrayed me."

"Yep," Belle muttered. "Sorry pal. I had to do it."

"You ruined my plans."

"And you wanted to kill me."

"Not anymore," Blisse taunted. "If you let me go, I won't kill you. I won't even hurt you. Let me go, and you can help me. I'll get you food and you will be protected by my guards. Let me go, and I can guarantee that you will live."

Belle savagely bit her lip. *Think about it,* a voice whispered in the back of her head. *You could live! Blisse won't hurt you! You can live the rest of your life knowing that you'll be safe!* Another thought popped into her mind. *But your friends… they'd die in some of the worst ways possible. Is it really worth it to live with the guilt for the rest of your life? Would it make sense for me to throw everything away to save myself?*

If this had happened even a month ago, she would've let Blisse go without hesitation. But now, as she looked at Ethan's determined look, Hope's scared expression, and Fire's pained face, she knew that she could never live with herself if she chose to let them die. The old Belle would've said yes in a heartbeat. But she was not that Belle; her friends had awakened something inside her that she thought had died long, long ago. And as she glanced at Blisse's amused stare, she knew what she had to do.

"Blisse," Belle began. Blisse's face looked genuinely hopeful. Her black eyes were haunting and evil, but Belle didn't back down. "I'm never going to let you go. I'm never going to be a coward again."

Blisse's face slowly darkened sinisterly.

"Is that so, Isabelle?"

Belle firmly nodded, her eyes squinting in hatred.

"Yes. Now do me a favor and go jump into the ocean, because I'm done with you, Blisse."

"I got it!" somebody suddenly exclaimed. Everyone's heads turned to Aspyn, whose eyes had gotten brighter. "I studied something like this in high school! It's a super rare and expensive drug called *salvatore auxilium,* and it has specific things it can do. I have no clue how Grayson got it, but it's so helpful. We experimented with it, and we used something where you had to click it. It was used as a code or something when people were in the military. Try clicking the syringe in between the numbers!"

Ethan gave her an odd look.

"You do it," he finally said. Aspyn's face immediately turned white.

"No, I really don't think that I should do anything, honestly." Fire looked at her with an angry expression.

"Just do it, Aspyn. We don't have time for your crap right now! Clearly, you're the only person here who knows anything. Don't you dare be a coward. Put the damn syringe in her neck and like it!"

Aspyn looked taken aback. With a nervous breath, she walked over to Blisse, who was still pinned down by Belle.

"There's not much left," Ethan warned. "Make sure that this little plan of yours works, ok?" Aspyn firmly nodded.

"I know it will."

As quick as a wink, Aspyn stabbed Blisse with the syringe. She quickly pulled it out, roughly shaking it twice. She stabbed it in once more, then pulled it out and shook it four times. She did the same thing, shaking it eight then seven times. Finally, it was the last number. With her hands slightly shaking, Aspyn stabbed it in once more.

It was as though a switch shut off. Blisse's body instantly went slack, and her eyelids closed. Belle hesitantly pulled herself off of Blisse's frame. Cassidy watched, frightened but intrigued.

Blisse's eyes opened. Everyone held their breath.

Blisse suddenly grabbed the knife that had fallen onto the ground. Ethan tensed up, putting his hands in front of him. He dreadfully expected her to lunge at him once more. Her eyes locked on his, wider than ever. She was frozen, resembling a statue. He saw her grip on the knife tighten. He stepped further away.

Then, something strange happened. She didn't point the knife at Ethan. With shattered caramel eyes, she gently set the blade over her own wrist.

44

Ethan saw the girl he had first met, so long ago. His eyes opened wide. Suddenly, Blisse's whole body started to shake. Sobs screamed from her mouth, and tears poured down her face like heavy rain.

"I killed them!" she shouted, her vision blurred. "Kill me! Kill me!" She held the knife firmly over her vein.

"Blisse, no!" Cassidy screamed, moving toward her. "You're back now, it's not worth it! Don't you dare move that knife!" Blisse pressed down the knife with heavy pressure. Ethan could see the small beads of blood coming from her wrist. She was crying hysterically, hiccups coming from her open mouth. Fire forced her face to look sympathetic, but Hope could see the hardness in her eyes. Clearly, she was feeling beyond guilty about Aiden. *Haylee...*

Hope snapped herself out of her thoughts. After all, Blisse still had the sharp blade dangerously poised on her vein. One swift movement could end her life.

"Don't kill yourself," Fire snapped. Blisse's teary eyes turned on her friend.

"B-but, you should hate me!"

"Oh, I do," Fire answered angrily. "But you would be the biggest coward on the planet if you end your life right now. Think of everybody who you murdered!" This statement earned a pitiful cry from Blisse. "Don't you dare kill yourself after all the pain you caused," Fire growled. "You won't escape the misery, Blisse."

Blisse's quivering arms set the knife down. Almost smugly, Fire put her hands rigidly at her side. Blisse buried her face in her dirty hands, her weeps loud and clear. Hope felt a tear slide down her cheek, although she didn't know exactly why.

Maybe it's because you're watching your friend have a mental breakdown, she thought. *Is she even your friend anymore? Can you still be friends with a person who has done such despicable things?* She stopped thinking about that, because she knew her answer.

Cassidy slowly took steps Blisse's way. Her honey eyes were wide in caution.

"Blisse...," she said, almost sympathetically. Blisse brought up her head, ashamed.

"Is there any way you guys will ever possibly forgive me?" Ethan looked at her sadly, but he and nobody else nodded.

"Just give us time," Hope suggested. It shocked her how empty her words sounded. No matter what anyone tried to think, their relationship with Blisse could never be mended.

"I can't ever express how terrible I feel and how sorry I am," Blisse kept repeating through tears. Fire crossed her arms.

"Your apology won't bring him back." Blisse's face scrunched up in sadness.

"I swear I tried to stop," she said in an urgent tone. "I tried to stop my arm from moving, I promise."

"Was it fun?" Fire asked in an empty tone. Blisse wiped her eyes, confused.

"Was what fun?"

"Watching as you forced Haylee into a metal cage, listening to her cries as she was burned."

"Sapphire!" Hope screamed angrily, slapping her arm. Fire swiftly turned around, her eyes tinted with a dangerous glint.

"Did you just *hit* me?"

"Yes," Hope snapped. "How dare you bring Haylee into this!"

"I want to die!" Blisse shrieked back. "Does that answer your question, Sapphire? I. Want. To. Die. Simple as that."

"Well," said Belle, "that was sweet and all, but I want to know what happened to those guards. Where are they?"

Blisse's trembling hand slowly moved over her mouth.

"They're hunting you."

"They're *hunting* us?" Cassidy repeated, alarmed. Blisse sadly nodded.

"They think I'm still bad. I told them to meet me back at the hole in the ground."

"So that's it then," Ethan said emptily. "We're going to spend our whole lives running from these guards." Blisse shrugged encouragingly.

"Maybe not, when they see that I'm back to normal…"

"Oh shut up, Blisse," Fire interrupted. "When they see that you're back to normal, they'll hurt you. Why in the world would they let you go after what you did?"

Blisse's shoulders fell.

"Oh, right." She sniffed. "Well, we can go back to the shack."

"I can't believe you," Fire hissed as hot tears fell down her face. "Aiden and I can't be together. Because of you. He never knew."

"Don't blame Blisse," Aspyn offered. Fire turned around almost crazily.

"I don't!" she shrieked. "I hate myself! I'm the one who cut him off, I'm the one who hated him!"

Blisse looked at her with sadness and sympathy.

"Don't blame your-"

"And I do blame you too," she hissed. "You killed him, and I will never forgive you."

Blisse's newly light eyes fluttered to the ground in pain.

Tyrand was fuming.

Blisse hadn't returned yet, and neither had her captives. "Guys," he proclaimed, standing up with effort. "We can't stay here any longer. We need to go find Blisse."

"No," said a man hastily, getting to his feet as well. "Staying here keeps us safe. If we move without her orders, she'll be angry." He looked around fearfully. "I'm not ready to die."

"We've been here for hours," Tyrand declared. "I wanted to help her. I want to see her captives suffer just as much. Is it fair to us?"

"I don't care about fair," the first man responded. "If we're with her, we're safe. That's all that matters."

"She'll kill us in the end," Tyrand said, coming close to the man. "You know she will. She won't keep us. She kill us and eat us, like she did with that girl's mother. We can't stay with her, you know that. She's just a little girl."

"Grayson created her," the man said with a shiver. "She's not just a tiny girl anymore. We've all seen what she's capable of. Those black eyes..." he trailed off.

Tyrand suddenly looked up, a malicious smile coming to his lips.

"We could kill her, you know. If we left this place and hid, we could gang up on her and kill her. She wouldn't control us anymore."

"Yes," said a stocky man called Mace, the nickname inspired by his neck tattoo of his favorite weapon. "I'm tired of her getting all the food. Grayson is dead. Gabriel is gone. This girl is the only person standing in our way of domination. We can kill her."

"She's strong," the man fearfully piped up. "Her strength is improved by the serum."

"If we make a plan," Mace said, "we can catch her off guard."

"Make it slow," Tyrand said viciously. "I want to watch the blood drain from her body. We can all do it together." His blackened teeth spread into a massive grin. "She'll be the new Caesar. But it will be so, so much worse for her."

Blisse's mind seemed to collapse any second. The knife in her hand wouldn't stray from her skin. Sometimes, she could almost feel the serum creeping in her veins, getting ready to hurt her friends. There was no way she would ever be able to feel truly happy again. Absolutely none. For a short time, she had been the most dangerous person on the island. She had been the most dangerous person in the entire world. Blisse couldn't bear to look into Fire's eyes anymore. She could almost physically see what had broken in those blue eyes.

"You guys keep walking," Blisse gasped, stopping in the middle of the trail. "I need a minute alone."

"No," Cassidy immediately replied. "You'll kill yourself."

"I promise, as much as a person can promise, that I won't do that," Blisse said quietly. "I need to breathe for a moment."

"Better keep an eye out," Fire muttered from ahead. "She might stab us when our backs are turned." Ethan gave her a nudge that was much too rough to be playful. Blisse didn't reply. She gulped back a sob as she pleadingly stared at Cassidy.

"I know how you feel," Cassidy whispered. "Hurry back." With that, Cassidy jogged up to the front with her friends, leaving Blisse to fully break down on her own. It could've been five minutes or five hours, she didn't keep track of the passing time as she ripped plants in pure sadness and pain. Aiden was her best friend. He was practically her brother. His eyes had been so full of the worst fear possible. Blisse would never, ever forget that look.

A gasp was what brought her back to reality.

Blisse stopped crying for a moment. Her golden eyes moved up in fear as she locked her gaze on the one person she never wanted to see again: Tyrand.

45

"Blisse," Tyrand said, his voice clearly surprised. "I didn't expect to find you here." His scared look then turned to pure enjoyment as he stared hard into her eyes. "Wait, your eyes aren't black anymore." He laughed aloud. "Looks like your little friends figured out a way."

Tyrand paused, seemingly lost in thought. He licked his lips, smiling in pleasure. "You know, Blisse, I was going to make a plan with the men. A plan that would catch you when you weren't ready. But it looks like that won't be necessary." He gave her a grin. "Now, you're back to yourself. You won't be able to fight me off. And since you're here, I might as well finish you off now."

"Oh," she gasped out. *Ethan, please turn around. Please.*

"Now," he began, "I'm going to hurt you. I'm going to kill you. You've been the little boss of me for far too long. It's time for things to go the other way around."

"I'm so sorry," Blisse whispered. "It wasn't me doing those things, you know that."

"But it was your body," he coldly replied.

"I've apologized. I never wanted to do what I did." Blisse's eyes were now filled with burning tears. Tyrand stepped closer, his hands coming reaching for a knife in his belt.

"I don't care about your apologies," he snapped. "Don't worry, *master,*" he said sarcastically. "It really is too bad that your servants couldn't be here to watch this. I'll make sure to tell them how you screamed. I am going to enjoy this, Blisse." His hand shot out, but Blisse was already dashing through the jungle at top speed.

"Ethan, help!" she shrieked. She could sense Tyrand at her ankles, and she could hear the wind gliding off his weapon. His growls echoed in her ears, and she knew he would outsprint her in a matter of seconds. "Stop, please!"

His body weight slammed into her, knocking her to the ground. Blisse shrieked as she felt the blade slash across her leg. Her body twisted around, bringing them face to face. Blisse's chest heaved as she reached for her concealed weapon. "Don't make me do this," she begged. Tyrand's mouth curled. His hand moved to strike.

Before the blade could pierce her, Blisse tilted her head to the side. Her arm sprung up, plunging her blade into his gray eye.

Tyrand gave a scream of pain as he brought up his hand to cover his eye. With a sick noise, Blisse pulled out the blade and jammed it into his other eye.

Blisse shrieked and shrieked at his face, where two bloody holes now stayed. Memories of Psycho Blisse surfaced. Her mind wouldn't stop telling her that she could never be normal now. The screaming Tyrand showed her that.

Then the thought that almost made her sanity crumble came to her- *should I just kill him and get it over with?*

She had never considered killing someone before. Never.

"I'm sorry," she whispered over and over, too quiet for him to hear over his screams of agony.

She left him there as she ran through the trees, not being able to stand the sight of him any longer. She had left him vulnerable without eyesight, which was almost worse, but Blisse had no strength left to murder another.

The island was poisoning her.

Kill me, Blisse begged inside her mind. *I deserve to die in the most painful way possible.* If another minute continued of this torment, she would go crazy.

Mercifully, her broken brain welcomed unconsciousness as she fell across the ground and didn't find the drive to get up.

Ethan had heard Blisse's terrified screams from up ahead on a trail. They all dashed back to her, afraid to find her dead or mutilated body. Instead, they had found her slumped on the ground with tears still rolling down her cheek.

"She has actually gone crazy," Fire unnecessarily stated. "Maybe we should kill her anyway." Ethan glared at her in a way that he never had before.

Before she could reply, Blisse lifted up her head in shame.

"My guard," she whispered, almost too quiet for them to hear. "I hurt him."

"You hurt a lot of people, Blisse," responded Fire, "like the person I loved."

"Sapphire," Ethan muttered dangerously. His eyes turned warm again as he looked back at Blisse crumpled on the ground. "Blisse, you know it wasn't your fault when you hurt them. You couldn't control yourself, we all understand that."

Blisse shook her head as more tears fell.

"I did it just now," she whimpered. "He was attacking me, and I blinded him. Please, please kill me."

Ethan looked taken aback for a moment, unsure of what to say. Then, he composed his face back into a mask of kindness.

"It's ok, I promise. Those guards are evil at heart, Blisse. You aren't. You never have been, and you never will be. Let's go to the shack."

With a shaking body and broken eyes, Blisse forced herself up.

"I'm so sorry for the pain I caused you, Ethan," she said. "You might not have to kill me if the guilt does it first."

She began walking toward the trail with everyone behind her. It occured to Hope that Blisse was truly back now, that she would have to look into the same face that murdered her sister. Hope didn't know if she could do it without hurting her, but she had to try. Blisse was back. Real Blisse was back.

But despite that, Hope knew what she would do, what she had been keeping in the back of her mind since Haylee died. She choked back her tears until it was time.

The group continued to trek through the jungle. The only sound belonged to the small breeze blowing through the air. Fire didn't think that she could speak to Blisse again, nor did she ever want to. If only she hadn't yelled at Aiden the way she did. Fire thought that she would apologize to him later, once she had the chance to talk with her love again. She forgot that on this island of murderers, tomorrow may never come for some people.

Hope lagged behind. She veered off of the trail onto the coast where the tall edge of a cliff stood, overlooking the ocean.

Hope gazed out from the cliff as her eyes filled with tears. For a moment, the solitude was almost too much to take. Sadness threatened to engulf her entire being. It felt as though the edge was calling her, taunting her; she knew what she must do. The girl looked ahead at her friends one last time. Slowly, she took a step. Then another. For a minute, all she did was take small steps towards the edge, her body racking with silent sobs.

Hope thought about what the falling sensation would be like. She would hit the water, feel horrible pain for a split second, but then it would be all over. She would be done with sorrow, done with pain, done with life. The girl kneeled down, feeling the cliff's rough surface. The thought that she might never feel this again was terrifying and welcoming.

"I'm sorry," she whispered, her voice breaking. She glanced behind her one last time as she took a shuddering breath. She turned around, ready to take her last steps that she would ever take.

"Hope!" she heard a voice call from far up ahead. She realized that she had to move quicker. The footsteps were sounding much louder. "Hope!" shouted the same voice again, much nearer. In her damaged mind, Hope noticed the voice belonged to Cassidy. Only a few more steps, and it would all be over.

"Hope, there you are!" panted an exhausted girl. "I didn't notice that you fell behind!" Cassidy looked at her with a small smile. "Come on, I know the view is nice, but we have to go!" She turned to start running again, but faltered when Hope didn't move a muscle. Cassidy's eyes grew larger when she really looked at Hope. She saw that her friend's normally bright eyes were now full of pain, her face was blotchy from the tears sliding down her face, and her hair was thrown all over her face without care.

"What's wrong?" Cassidy asked, full of concern right away. Hope just shook her head, her dull eyes forming more tear drops. "Hope, come on, everyone else is way up ahead! What are you doing?" she questioned. The blonde girl just stared at her sadly, and her eyes darted to the edge, hoping her friend would get the message.

Suddenly, everything clicked into place for Cassidy. Her dark eyes filled with realization as it dawned on her. Her mouth dropped open in horror. "No, you are not doing what I think you are," she said, her voice filled with sudden urgency. Hope took short, shaky breaths as she nodded. She couldn't trust herself to speak. If she did, she would burst out crying, and then Cassidy would think she was insane. She should have jumped sooner.

"Hope, get back over here right now," she demanded in a tone that reminded her of her mother. "I said now." She pronounced each word slowly, as if Hope was mentally not right. She took one more step toward the edge. If she took another, she would fall off, ending her life that seemed worthless without Haylee in it. Her pupils dilated as she looked out into the crystal sea. It looked so beautiful and amazing and *free*. She could be reunited with Haylee and feel that way once again. She chewed her already cut up lip as she looked at Cassidy. Now, her friend's eyes were shining. "Hope," she began, her voice starting to tremble.

"Did I ever tell you where I got these from?" She pointed to large white scars on her wrist. Hope nodded, remembering the conversation that they had about her marks only a short time ago. To her, it seemed like years. Hope took one breath, willing her shaky voice not to break.

"Yes, I remember. From the plants." Her voice came out raspy. Cassidy bit her lip as well.

"Well, the story I told you, it was- it was a lie. Do you really want to know what happened?" Before Hope could reply, Ethan came bounding over.

"Cassidy, what's taking so long? I thought you were-" he faltered when he noticed her expression. His green eyes grew wide when he noticed Hope's devastated face. "Guys, what's wrong?" he asked. Hope closed her eyes for a moment, taking a calming breath. *Just one more step, Hope. Just one more.* "Hope, why are you on the edge of the cliff?" he asked, exasperated. She opened her eyes, clenched her fists, and delivered him an intense look.

"Ethan, I lost my best friend, my other friend now has issues because she was taken over, I was almost sawed in half, I watched Summer die, and I'm standing at the edge of a cliff. The real question is, what do you think I'm doing?" Her voice came out sounding strong, but it broke at the end. It took everything in her to not start crying again. Ethan's eyes narrowed in anger and fear when he realized what she was implying.

"No, you *are not* going to jump off this cliff. Do you hear me, Hope?" he demanded. She shrugged helplessly.

"Ethan, you can't stop me from doing this." He took a long step closer, which caused Hope to tense up and almost fall out of surprise. "If you take one more step toward me, I swear I will fall right off this cliff. Do you understand?" she asked, glaring at him. He stopped moving at once.

"Hope, I asked you if you wanted to know what my scars are from," Cassidy said, her sad eyes overflowing. The girl nodded, keeping a careful eye on Ethan.

"Well, like I said, I lied. It wasn't really from a plant. When I first got here, I-" She broke off for a moment, clearing her throat. Ethan was now looking curiously at her. "When I got here, I met everyone in this group. I met a boyfriend named-"

"I know," Hope cut her off. Cassidy narrowed her moist eyes.

"How do you know? I never told you this before." Ethan's face was turning a bright red.

"I might've told her," he admitted. Cassidy shot him an angry glare through her tears.

"Well then, I guess I don't need to go on. I assume you know what happened to him then?" Hope nodded. "Well, after he died, I, well, I wasn't the happiest person around. I was depressed. And, um, ok I'm sorry, I've never talked about this before," she explained, wiping her eyes with her palm. "One day, I just couldn't take it anymore. I, well, I hurt myself." Cassidy said the last part softly and quickly. She said all of this while purposely avoiding Ethan's shocked gaze.

"You did *what*?!" he exclaimed. Her tears were coming back.

"You heard me. I did it for a while in secret."

"I can't believe you never told me, Cassidy Jane Tamer," said Ethan angrily.

Before Cassidy could speak again, Hope put up her hand. It wasn't a dominant or angry gesture, but the other two stopped talking just the same.

"It's not just Haylee," she whimpered. Cassidy cocked her messy hair to the side.

"What do you mean?" she questioned, her nails digging into her palms. Hope mentally calmed herself. She needed to stay sane, at least for what she was about to say.

"Haylee isn't the only reason I want to jump. It's just… my whole life. I'm just so tired, but it's not the kind that sleep can fix."

That's when all of her mental preparation crumbled. She wept as she looked back on her life. All of her secrets she had never told. All of her anxiety and fear of looking into Grayson's terrible eyes. Hope somehow grasped onto the fact that she was an absolute and utter *mess*. Cassidy looked at her, her face contorted in a look of sympathy.

"Hope, I'm so sorry. I never realized how much you were hurting," she said softly.

"And now the person I love is…. they aren't here anymore," Hope murmured. "And I just can't deal with it." Hope sniffed, putting her hand limply over her heart.

"See this, Cassidy?" she asked. "That's where it hurts. There's a hole in my chest now, Cassidy. It's almost like physical pain, except it's worse. It's so, so much worse because I can't fix it. Sure, if my arm was stabbed, it would be painful. Heck, it would be excruciating, but I would bandage it up and be happy little Hope. But this? How can I fix this?" she hopelessly yelled. "They don't make a bandage for the injury I have. The only bandage is to jump and forget this. To actually heal the thing Blisse did to me."

Awful, awful silence followed that.

Cassidy finally cleared her throat. "Hope," she said kindly. Hope lifted her head in shame. Her expression was so pained, it made Ethan want to hurt Blisse and never stop. "Hope," she said again.

Hope wobbled dangerously, which could make her fall even before she chose to.

"No Cassidy. I don't want to live," she stated quietly. "And if I jump off of this cliff, I won't feel that way anymore." Ethan pointed his finger at her.

"No, Hope. Absolutely not."

"Ethan, let me speak," Cassidy said, sounding dangerously calm. "I know now that I should never have harmed myself after Brandon died. And I hate admitting this, I really do, but I want to tell you. Suicide is *never* the answer, Hope. I know that you feel really upset and depressed right now, and I understand it, probably better than anyone else. But please, Hope, come back away from the edge. Please."

Hope looked at her, imagining her friend screaming and crying as she dragged a sharp blade across her arm. She imagined her running through the woods alone, blinded by tears from seeing her boyfriend hung from a lifeless tree branch. This made her feel so sad, she was almost angry. Hope subconsciously took one step in Cassidy's direction.

"I know that you feel like you want to die, but really, you don't," she continued. "If you really wanted to, you would have jumped already. Listen, Hope. We're all just imbeciles in this crazy thing called life, but I can promise you one thing; I will always be here for you, and I mean *always*. I can't do that, though, if you choose to end your life now. You'll be ok, Hope, I mean it. Everyone always is, it's just life. Please, come back to us, Hope. We're here for you." Cassidy held out her arms. Hope stared, shocked at her long speech. But before she knew it, she was in her friend's arms. She was crying up a storm, and Ethan stood uncomfortably watching.

"I'm sorry Cassidy!" she cried out, squeezing her tighter. The two stayed like this longer than was normal. Finally, Hope was the first to pull back.

"Hope, in the most platonic way possible, I love you," the brunette girl said in between laughing and crying.

"I love you too, you know, platonically," Hope told her, sniffling through her laughs. Ethan smiled awkwardly.

"Uh, guys, not to interrupt this lovely, um, talk, but I think we should go now." Hope looked up.

"Yeah, I guess you're right," she admitted. "We need to get to safety." The two friends stood up, leaning against each other for support. The trio all walked together, Hope beginning to smile in spite of herself with tears in her eyes. She was glad now that she hadn't jumped after all.

46

The sun had gone down soon after they arrived at the shack.

Fire's eyes had turned to ice now. It was impossible to see any slip of happiness in her. Just the sight of it filled Blisse with immense guilt and pain. She had killed her love. It didn't seem as though Fire would smile ever again.

Aspyn didn't seem to have any light in her eyes anymore. The thrill of saving Blisse was gone. All Blisse did was sulk and sob, which made Aspyn wish that she had done nothing. Her friends were both dead. These people she was with, they all had a history together. She knew she didn't belong there. Her will to live seemed to be dimming. She knew, from every part of her heart, that her life was no longer valuable. That was the saddest realization she had ever come to.

It now seemed that for the rest of the group, nighttime was the only time there was ever peace. Sleeping provided a chance of escape.

Except when the nightmares came.

Hope couldn't close her eyes without seeing the eyes of her sister. She couldn't get rid of orange lava enveloping her vision. The girl had lost hours and hours of sleep. That's why she was up talking to Cassidy at one o'clock in the morning inside the shack.

Hope had told her friend every single thing that she could think of about herself. She told her about her first kiss. It had been a hot, sweaty kiss in the car on a summer's day with her younger neighbor. She winced as she told the embarrassing tale, but it was sort of refreshing in a way to pour her thoughts out to the girl in front of her.

Cassidy returned the favor by telling her stories of the greatest natural wonders she had ever seen. She used her words to describe fields of magenta tulips and the pure white snow of mountains. *Once a writer, always a writer*, Hope thought to herself as she dreamily imagined Cassidy's words in her mind.

Cassidy was describing a golden desert when her words drifted off with uncertainty. Hope opened her eyes, looking at her friend. Suddenly, Cassidy's eyes squinted in confusion. She was peering at something behind Hope's back. Hope stared at her, dread and worry beginning to fill her mind.

"Is everything ok?" Cassidy bit her lip even harder, but Hope didn't want to turn around. Her friend's anxious confusion made her scared. Hope heard a noise behind her. It sounded almost like a step. *Chill, Hope. If something's wrong, Cass will tell you.*

Cassidy's mouth slowly lowered open, her brown eyes growing bigger. All of a sudden, she screamed. Her face was in a look of more terror than Hope had ever seen before. Her shaking hand was pointing to something behind Hope. With chills all over her body, Hope quickly spun around. In her path was Blisse, her eyes jet black again. In the dimmed light, she looked like a bloodthirsty demon.

"I thought she was turned back!" Cassidy exclaimed, fear overpowering her voice. Hope felt panic throughout her body. *No no, this can't be happening. The horrible Blisse is gone. She's gone.*

"Ethan!" Hope shrieked. "Fire! GET UP!" Ethan groggily picked his head up. "What?"

"It's Blisse!" Cassidy shouted. "Help!" His head snapped up at the word Blisse. Fire did the same. She aggressively brushed her tangled brown hair out of her eyes.

"What the hell is going on here?" she asked angrily. "I'm tired! If you didn't know, I was the one who was deprived of sleep!" Cassidy gave her a stern look.

"Sapphire, what's more important, your sleep or *your survival?*" Fire finally got a good look at Blisse. Despite her sleepy state, she felt goosebumps erupt all over her skin.

"I thought she was cured!"

"That's what we all thought!" Belle shot back. "But apparently little Blisse needs to make our lives as miserable as possible." Blisse bared her teeth. Ethan held his knife out in front of him, but it wavered the tiniest bit.

"This isn't possible," he muttered to himself.

"WATCH OUT!" Hope threw herself at Cassidy, knocking the poor girl down. It was just in time, as Blisse's knife would have penetrated her throat if Hope hadn't done anything. Blisse's momentum from her lunge launched her painfully into the wall. Before she could turn back around, Ethan suddenly leaped onto Blisse's back. She gave a wild shriek, almost like an animal. She used her strong arms to slap him, but he grabbed her in a choke hold. Forcefully, he slammed her back onto the ground. Before she could spring back up, he sat on her stomach and pinned her wrists down.

"Get off me!" Blisse yelled, in her manic voice. Ethan's mouth perked up.

"Yeah, because I'll listen to you." She struggled, but even her crazy strength couldn't throw Ethan off of her. "Hope, get her knife!" he yelled. She got up from the floor and dashed over to him. Hope narrowly avoided being slashed from the flailing knife in Blisse's hand. Quickly, she reached for the handle. She closed her grip around it, and strongly pulled it out of her hand, feeling the pressure on it lessen. Aspyn covered her shocked mouth with her hands.

"What the hell is this thing?" she exclaimed, frightened. Ethan looked at her sympathetically.

"She's an infected girl who is my best friend." Aspyn looked at him, an expression of fear mixed with confusion.

"But I saved her." Fire sighed.

"She was saved, but now I have the tempting urge to stab her and throw her off a cliff," she said through her teeth. Belle looked at her with an amused expression.

"What? She killed the man I loved," she said simply. Belle's eyes almost looked sympathetic.

"Listen kid, I don't really know much about love. My mom was too drunk and my dad was too stressed to pay any attention to me. But I do know affection when I see it, and I knew that it was only a matter of time before you two lovebirds declared your love for each other. I want you to know, from the bottom of my heart, that I'm sorry that he was killed. I know it doesn't mean much, coming from me, but I hope that it makes you feel better."

Fire gazed at her. She was shocked to hear such an apology come out of her mouth. She wouldn't have believed it if she didn't see Belle's mouth move.

"It does mean something coming from you. Thank you."

"Stop talking and help me get Blisse back to normal!" Cassidy shrieked.

Ethan nodded.

"Yup, right as always."

"Well, what do we do?" Hope asked. She looked at Blisse's twitching body, which was desperately trying to get out of Ethan's firm hold.

"I honestly don't know," Ethan confessed. "I used all of the serum to cure her. I thought that it would do the trick. Clearly, it didn't."

"But I thought she was fine before," Aspyn said, still watching Blisse's twisting body with wide eyes.

"Well aren't you Miss Observant," Fire said sarcastically. "She was fine before, but now she's not. And frankly, I don't give two craps about what happened earlier. I only care about not being killed."

"I will kill you," Blisse said angrily, her insane voice piercing the air. "I'll kill you alright, every last one of you. There will be no chance of escape this time."

"What happened to you?" Ethan demanded. "Why are you like this again?"

"Like what?" she asked innocently. He roughly slammed his elbow into her throat. She choked before she started laughing hysterically. "I won't ever be the girl I was before," she snarled, her voice coming out in gasps. "Now, you have something to lose. You know your friend's back, you've seen her and talked to her. You won't kill me," she said to them, looking especially at Hope. "I know you won't."

"I think you're underestimating me," Hope shot back. "You don't know what I'll do." Blisse chuckled darkly.

"If you wanted to truly kill me, you would've let me go when you held me over the lava." Her mouth grew into a sinister smile. "Remember that day, Hope? The day your sister died as the lava slowly swallowed her up? The day you watched the light in her eyes flicker, and then go out completely? What was her name?" She found pleasure in the way Hope grew red in fury "Ah, yes. Haylee."

Hope clenched her fists. *Don't think about it,* she firmly told herself. *You can't cry now. You can't.* Miraculously, the memories didn't bring any water to her eyes. Blisse's smirk slowly faded away, and her body began to cease struggling.

"What is she doing?" Fire asked, watching her with disgust. Ethan shrugged, looking back at her.

"I haven't got a clue, element."

Minutes went by, and he started to loosen his grip the tiniest bit. Her eyes suddenly snapped open, and he just barely stopped himself from slapping her face in surprise. He immediately relaxed when he saw the golden color in her eyes staring back at him. Ethan prepared himself for another hysterical crying fit when she realized what she had done. However, she only blinked at him, confused.

"Why are you sitting on me?" Blisse asked, her voice drowsy. "Was it because of my nightmare?" Now it was Ethan's turn to be confused. Hope leaned over eagerly.

"What do you mean nightmare?" Ethan asked. Dread was slowly seeping into his veins. She bit her lip in confusion.

"I had a dream that I had a knife in my hand. I probably was twitching around, but that doesn't explain why you are on top of me." Her eyes darted over to Hope and Fire. "And why is everyone crowded around me?" Her eyes found Aspyn. The poor girl was staring at Blisse, obviously still afraid. "And why does she look scared of me?"

"Wait," Ethan said, clearly sensing that something was off. "You don't remember anything?" She tilted her head.

"Ethan, I'm sorry, but I truly have no idea what you're talking about. Can you please get off me now?" He hesitantly pulled his body off of hers, his eyes still locked on her nervously. "Why are you looking at me like that?" Blisse exclaimed. "What's going on?" Ethan turned out, almost sadly, to the small crowd of gathering people.

"She doesn't remember anything," he announced.

"Remember what?" This time, annoyance was evident in her tone. Ethan looked at her, calmly putting out his hands.

"What I'm about to tell you might freak you out a little. Please, just relax. No one's mad at you," he reassured her. She looked at him, her eyes squinting the tiniest bit.

"Ok," she said hesitantly. "Tell me."

His gaze looked at Hope for second. She gestured with her hand to tell him to go.

"Well, you kinda went all Psycho Blisse on us again. You almost killed Cassidy, and you tried to kill me." Her mouth dropped open with every horrible word that came out of his mouth.

"You're lying. You have to be lying." She put her hands through her hair, taking quick shallow breaths. Ethan softly put his hand on her shoulder.

"I wish I was lying, but I'm telling the truth. Are you sure that you don't remember anything?" Blisse began to hyperventilate.

"You have to kill me," she said, looking at the knife nestled in Hope's hand. "I'm a danger to you guys. I told you, it was just like a dream to me. The details are already fading. You need to get rid of me while I'm still... me, and not that other freak who is in my body." She took a step toward Hope. Automatically, Hope swiftly put the knife behind her back.

"No," she said firmly. "We aren't killing you."

"You're like Dr. Jekyll and Mr. Hyde," Fire murmured. Blisse looked at her, her eyes huge.

"This isn't funny, Sapphire. I need to die. Please. I can't live with this thing inside of me. I don't know what Grayson did, but it's working. He's turned me against you, and you've watched me become a monster." She looked at Ethan sadly. "His plan has worked perfectly. The next step is to kill me."

"Grayson's plan didn't do anything," Belle snapped. "Who gives a damn what he wanted anyway? Do you want to let him win?" She suddenly stomped her foot down, hard, on the concrete floor. She held her middle finger up to the sky. "Screw you Grayson!" she screamed. "Screw your plans, screw your life, and screw you!" She stopped, realizing something.

"Oops," she said. "Wrong direction." She pointed her finger down to the earth. She swore louder, causing Blisse to wince slightly. "Why is the world like this?" Belle asked to no one. She suddenly felt burning tears behind her eyes. Gulping them back, she looked back toward the devastated Blisse.

"Hope, please give me the knife," Blisse said, her voice only a little gentle. Hope looked at her, her eyebrows raised.

"Blisse, no offense, but I'm not stupid. I know that you want to die, but we will find a way to help you."

"Don't any of you realize what I'll do?" Blisse practically shouted. Ethan looked at her, his arms folded.

"Realize what, Blisse?" he questioned. She turned her full attention on him.

"When I first came out of my little trance, I remembered every single detail." She shivered, thinking of the memories. "Like I told you, it was like I was there, but I couldn't do anything to stop it. This time, it wasn't like I was trapped in this body anymore. I wasn't even aware of what I was doing. Think about it. If I can't remember anything, maybe this… serum is taking me over. What if it takes me over for good?"

Ethan opened his mouth, but no words came out. She snorted dryly.

"You know I'm right. What if I can't control what happens to me?" Her words came out faster and more panicked as she spoke. "What if I use my strength and hurt you? What if I *kill* you? What if Psycho Blisse captures you again? I know what that girl was going to do to you guys, and trust me, it's some awful, awful stuff. I can't transform back into Psycho Blisse again." Her breathing became short and fast again. "What if I stay longer than this time? What if it's *permanent?* It would basically be impossible to kill me with my strength, and then you would be stuck. It's not like you can swim off this island."

Hope looked at her, upset.

"What if we could find a way to get off the island?" Fire suddenly asked. Blisse blinked tears from her copper eyes.

"What are you talking about?"

"I said, what if we could actually get off this damn island?"

Ethan lightly sighed, looking at his friend.

"You know that there's no way to do that. If there was, we would have done it as soon as we got here."

"It makes me so sad," Aspyn said suddenly. Ethan stopped speaking as everyone turned to look at the girl who hadn't spoken in so long. "I'll never be able to get married. I can't ever have children or even go to college. I always dreamed of falling in love." She sniffed. "I'm not even dangerous. It's terrible for us to be here. There had to be a mistake in our tests. I've always wondered why my friends and I were forced to come here."

Blisse looked anxious. Her copper eyes now were dull and scared.

"This still doesn't answer what you're going to do to me," she said.

"We aren't killing you," Fire snapped. "You need to get that through your head." Blisse sighed. She threw her hands up in the air.

"I'm worried for you guys! I am going to *murder you!* Fire, get that through your head!" Fire crossed her arms and jutted out her hip.

"Clearly, she wants you to kill her because she doesn't want to kill you. Imagine how awful she would feel if she killed all of us and then came back to herself," Cassidy interjected. "We'll make sure it doesn't happen next time."

"There might not be a next time," Blisse whispered in a warning tone. Ethan cocked his eyebrows.

"Don't think that way, Blisse." She looked at him, her lips in a straight line.

"I won't be happy for the sake of it, Ethan."

"Blisse, if you say any more crap about you getting killed, I will punch you," Fire threatened. Blisse huffed a breath.

"Kill me instead."

"Let's compromise," Hope suggested. Fire threw her hands up with a hint of exasperation.

"How do we compromise on something like this?" she asked. Hope looked her her, nodding.

"Well, if you let me finish, you could hear what I have to say." This made Fire's face turn dark red. "As I was saying, let's compromise. Blisse, can you feel when a Psycho Blisse moment is coming on?"

"No," Blisse answered sadly. Ethan shrugged.

"Maybe it was just because you were asleep," he said encouragingly. "If you're awake, you might be able to tell us."

"Yeah, maybe." Her tone wasn't very convincing.

"If you hurt more than two people, we… we will kill you." Hope forced the cold words out of her mouth. Blisse shook her head in protest.

"More than two!? If I even slightly harm somebody, I need to die. Why can't you understand that?"

"Ugh, shut up!" Fire screamed. "Get it through that stupid head of yours that we *aren't killing you!* If you try to do anything to yourself, I swear that I will tie you down and keep you there until you have an ounce of common sense in your mind. Do you hear me?"

Blisse chuckled dryly.

"Are you threatening me?"

"I don't know, did you murder Aiden?"

"I hate this," Blisse said quietly. "I hate this so much. Remember in elementary school how we were taught that everything that was black was evil and that everything white was good? When my eyes turn black, my world is full of misery. When my eyes turn black, your world is full of terror and panic. Soon, my world could be black permanently. I just… hate this, so, so much."'

"You have a good point," Cassidy observed. "But I think you might be wrong there." Blisse looked at her oddly.

"How so, Cassidy?" Belle asked. "I think that Mr. Hyde has a point."

"How am I wrong?" Blisse asked curiously. She looked thoughtful.

"Well, think of it this way. Grayson was so violent, so beyond help. You could say that his heart was made of ice. His personality was like lightning. Not the fascinating, bright lightning, but the type that burns and chars every old tree. White light reminds me of the artificial light that people see when they wake up in labs. It reminds me of bleached, lifeless places. It just doesn't scream 'peaceful' to me." Blisse put her hand on her chin.

"I guess so."

"But the darkness is the opposite of that," Cassidy continued. "Darkness brings us the stars and the stunning moon. It reminds me of chocolate, something amazing I haven't had in forever. Yes Blisse, your eyes do turn black. But that's a different, man-made substance that Grayson created. I think that our life now is white. Our life is full of running away from a poison that is injected into everyday. White brings the inevitable while darkness brings the infinite."

They all sat there in silence for awhile. No one knew what to say to Cassidy's poem that was heartbreakingly true. Belle was the first to speak.

"You know, there might actually be a way to get off this island," she finally said. Ethan opened his mouth before Belle put up her hand. "No, listen. I thought of a good plan, for once." To her slight surprise, Ethan nodded and shut his mouth. Belle took a breath.

"Ok, so you know how people are supposed to check up on this island once a year? Does anyone remember the last time they did their little check?"

"The last time they were here would have been when Hay- when my sister got here," Hope replied. Fire huffed a sigh.

"We already know that. Did they search around the entire island, Hope? That's what we care about." Hope's face burned bright red as she looked down.

"Sapphire, *stop,*" Ethan commanded loudly. "What's your problem?" She scoffed.

"You know, if murder was legal, half of you would be dead," she muttered.

"The funny thing is that it is legal here," Aspyn piped up.

"Thanks for reminding me, pink hair."

"Let me finish my brilliant plan," Belle said loudly. She cleared her throat. "Ok, so when did they actually check on the island? Does anyone have even a slight date to go on?"

"July 17th," Ethan proclaimed. Blisse looked at him with wide eyes.

"How do you remember that?" she asked. He grinned, showing them something from inside his pocket. He pulled out a very wrinkled piece of paper and a small, almost nonexistent piece of lead. "I've been making a tally mark for each day, like a calendar. According to this handy thing, today is July 13th."

"Ok," said Belle, slightly smiling. "Assuming they come on the same day each year, like they mentioned to me when I first got here, we can jump them and their helicopter."

Fire snorted before she could help it.

"Sure. Let's attack the government, who has guns and technology. Great idea, Belle."

"You raise a good point," Ethan said to Belle, "but Fire's right. We wouldn't stand a chance against them. We would just be killed."

"Not necessarily," Blisse murmured from the floor. "If we hid, we might have a chance. I have something we could use." Cassidy looked at her curiously.

"What do you mean?"

"Ethan knows," Blisse answered. He cocked his head.

"I don't think so, Blisse."

"The electric gun," she whispered. "There's a whole stash of them in here somewhere."

Ethan froze, forgetting to breathe for a second. He could all too easily recall the feeling of being shocked to the bone with electricity. Doing that to someone else seemed completely inhumane.

But they were the people who sent them to this hell. He never would have been beyond hurt if he hadn't been forced to come to this island. Some sick part of his mind *wanted* to see those government officials in pain. Ethan would do anything to get off this island, and if that's what they had to do, so be it.

"Ok, Blisse," he said firmly, "we can get the guns."

"Are you sure you'll be ok with it?" she asked, concerned. "It will be hard to watch them get shocked if you know what it feels like."

"I can do it."

"Ok," Blisse said. She paused, looking him in the eyes. "I'll only show you where they are on one condition, though. If I have another Psycho Blisse episode, I want you to shoot me with it."

Ethan gasped. He shook his head profusely.

"I won't do that to you, Blisse. It's too painful."

"Then I won't show you where I put them." He looked at her with a mixed expression of anger and pain.

"Blisse…"

"Promise me," she said, getting herself up from the ground. "I need your word that you will. I will not harm one of you guys during one of my episodes again. If my eyes turn black, you will shoot me with the gun. Promise?" She looked into his eyes intently. "Promise?"

"I promise," he said reluctantly. Cassidy stared around at everyone with a small smile.

"Well, I guess that's it then," she said. "Let's get the hell out of this place."

47

The group had everything perfectly planned out.

They had spent days doing nothing but creating strategy after strategy. Finally, they all decided on the simplest idea of all: old fashioned combat. The electric guns and the element of surprise were sure to provide them with an advantage.

Blisse had three more terrifying episodes of Psycho Blisse. The serum was running its course, leaving her with moments of craziness that were getting better and better. She had finally gone through a day where all she felt was a pang of rage that went away as quickly as it came.

"We'll go tomorrow," Ethan had finally said, on the night of July 16th. "We can do this."

Hope couldn't believe that she could soon be back to civilization. She hadn't told anyone that she would do anything to find her mom somewhere out there. Unless she hadn't died from a broken heart yet.

They were to camp at the edge of the sand, where green meets gold. Then, they would attack.

"I can fly a helicopter," Blisse reassured everyone again and again. "I learned how to when I was young."

Finally, they all left Grayson's shack behind for good. They would never have to step foot in that terrible place ever again. Grabbing their guns full of electricity, they set off to sleep in the trees.

Their plan might not work. They might be forced to spend the rest of their lives on this beautifully disguised island. They might get captured by the guards and live in unimaginable pain. But Hope wouldn't allow herself to think that way. She would get off the island. She would be reunited with her mother once again. She would do it.

She would do it for Haylee.

They later reached their spot for the night.

"Ok," Ethan said, his eyes glowing orbs in the darkness. "Tomorrow is what we've been waiting for, ever since we got here. We can do it, guys." He lightly grinned. "Goodnight."

The group closed their eyes on the last night of their stay on the island of danger.

Hours of the night passed, yet Hope found that her nerves wouldn't give her sleep. She tried shutting her eyes, but there were too many thoughts running through her mind.

She sat up, staring up at the stars. With surprise, Hope noticed that Fire was also up. Her small back was turned toward her. Hesitantly, Hope stood up.

Fire's large eyes were fixated on the ground. Her hands were intertwined through her knees, and her hair was up in a messy ponytail. Her head was sitting on her kneecaps. Hope silently came over, but she knew that Fire was aware of her presence. Hope sat next to her in the darkness, the sound of crickets filling the air.

"April fifth," she whispered. Hope's head turned to look at her.

"What?"

"April fifth," she repeated softly, "was when I came to this island. I was a small afraid girl, terrified of meeting someone like my dad. He was the first one I found." Hope didn't need any hints to know that she meant Aiden.

"He thought I was a little kid at first. He brought me to Ethan, and I was beyond scared. I thought they were going to kill me or something. I later realized that they had taken me in. I became close with Cassidy, as close as sisters. I told her all about myself, but not my dad. I got more comfortable with everyone, and they became the family I never had. I never got along with Blisse that well, because we have such different personalities. Maya at first didn't really like me all that much. Then, we became an unstoppable duo. I remember when I killed my first criminal. I thought I would go insane from the guilt, but Aiden comforted me, told me it was ok. I talked with Ethan, and I found him so fascinating. After all he had been through, he was still the bright, funny, and smart person he was.

"The first time I really talked with Aiden was when I had a dream about my dad. I was screaming and crying, I guess, and he woke me up. I told him everything that night. He was the only person who I had ever really shared anything that personal with. He told me all his secrets too. He told me about how he lost his grandma to cancer, about how his dog got hit by a car when he was 13. He told me incredible things too. He told me about his home in Miami, he described his favorite sunrise. He dried my tears and told me everything was alright.

"It was that night that I fell in love with him, Hope. I had never felt like that about anyone before. I dreamed of telling him. And now I never can. I'll never have the chance to tell him how much I loved him. He's gone, Hope. He's gone."

In the darkness, Hope could see that her eyes were full of water. Her irises looked like blue glass in the clear liquid.

"I'm so sorry," Hope said, trying to make her voice as understanding as possible. "He never deserved to die. He truly was a good person."

Fire sniffed as she nodded.

"You didn't deserve to lose Haylee either."

Hope looked up in surprise.

"Wait, really?" she asked. "I thought you didn't really care all that much. You seemed not to. I thought you were annoyed with me." Fire looked up as well, locking eyes with Hope's green ones.

"No, I did care. I just didn't know it." She paused, seeming to think of something. "Hope, I'm going to tell you something that I really don't want to, ok? Just don't say anything." Hope nodded curiously. Fire took a hesitant breath.

"It's just that I was... jealous. I was jealous that you still had someone to care about, that you had someone that you loved. Yes, I had Aiden, but that was different. You had a family that you cared about. You had someone that you were willing to die for, someone that made saying goodbye hard. And that made me so sad, Hope." She took a long breath. "I'm sorry that it came out as me not caring. I was sad, I just didn't know how to show it. I'm sorry, Hope. I'm really sorry."

Hope was staring at Fire, her mouth open slightly. Fire was twiddling her fingers, looking at the ground.

"Fire, I don't know what to say. Thank you." Fire nodded, tears trickling from her crystal eyes. Hope hesitantly moved closer to the curled up girl. Fire looked up. Her face was glowing in the star light, and Hope could see all the sadness in her tired eyes. Fire bit her lip, her arms outstretched. Hope didn't know what to do. It finally clicked in her mind that her tough, fiery, aggressive small ally was leaning in for a *hug*. Without hesitation, Hope wrapped her arms around Fire. Her small head only reached just below Hope's shoulders.

"Thanks," Fire said through her breath. Hope smiled, feeling tears form in her own eyes as well.

"No problem, Fire."

Fire sat down hard. Her eyes slid back to the ground.

"I don't enjoy killing, you know," she mumbled. Hope could barely hear the girl in front of her, so she got down as well. "I don't like killing people at all. It makes me feel like my dad. The look in people's eyes, I just... it kills me. And Hope, I didn't mean to get mad at you back in that room. I know you didn't want to kill anyone. I was just mad."

"It's ok," Hope replied gently. Fire aggressively shook her head.

"But it's not though! I can't believe what I said to you, and I'm sorry. I was just like my dad in that moment, and I hate myself now, Hope. You can't imagine how much I hate myself. Hope, don't ever kill someone, ok? A part of me dies every time somebody takes their last breath. I don't want that to happen to you. Anyone, actually. I don't care what I say, murdering someone makes me sad. I hate having to stab someone, ok? I mean, it's just... ok, I don't really know how to say this, but-"

"I understand what you mean," Hope said with a soft smile. "And thank you for apologizing."

She sniffed.

"Yeah, yeah. But if there's one thing that I've learned on this island, it's that even the sweetest person will do anything to survive. The first time Blisse had to kill someone, she was hysterical. But she did it. And you might have to someday, Hope. Ethan's killed more people than any of us have, but he's never let it affect him." She paused for a moment, the sound of soft rain beginning to fill the silence. "You know, Hope, I'm kind of... jealous of him too. After everything that has happened to him, he's the brightest person I know. I wish I could be like him."

"He is a great person," Hope said with admiration.

"I can see you two together," Fire said suddenly. Hope's face blushed immediately.

"Huh?"

"You do like him, don't you?"

"Well," Hope said, embarrassed, "I, um, I guess I do. I don't really know." Fire smiled despite her feelings.

"Are you sure? You don't find him hot? Not even a little bit?" Hope chuckled uncomfortably.

"Do you?"

"Well, yeah," Fire said, sounding as though it was completely obvious. "But don't worry, I don't like him like that. He's my best friend." Hope nodded, and she knew her face must be as red as a tomato.

"Hey Fire, where did you live?"

"You sure changed the topic quickly," Fire said, but she didn't sound angry. "I lived in Michigan. Detroit, to be exact. It wasn't the best place for a child to grow up, let me tell you that. That's how I learned to fight so well, I guess. Fights broke out at school all the time." Fire picked at some dirt on the ground. "Where did you live?"

"New York," Hope answered. "I went to one of the best schools in the state. I grew up in the city too. At first, I hated my small little apartment, but now I really miss it. Not that I don't like you guys, of course," she added hastily. Fire slightly snorted. Somehow, the sound made Hope like her more.

"No, I get what you mean. I wish I could say the same, but I'm glad to get away from my old house. Too many bad memories." Hope nodded understandingly.

"I really am sorry about your life, Fire." Fire's silhouette shrugged in the dark.

"Don't bother, it's not your fault." Hope gave a small smile her way. "You know, I've always wondered who I would be now if I would've had a normal childhood."

"Well, you wouldn't be yourself," Hope reminded her, "and aren't you glad that you've survived this long? You, Fire, are honestly the bravest person I know."

"Really?" Fire couldn't hide the amount of pride that had made its way into her voice. "You think I'm brave?" Hope nodded encouragingly.

"Hell yeah! You do have your bad times, but you haven't resorted to almost jumping off a cliff. I mean, after Haylee died, I wanted to kill myself. I feel bad now." Fire lightly smacked her arm.

"Don't feel bad, Hope. It's ok. I actually stopped living after my mom's death. I didn't sleep, didn't think, didn't eat. I… I wanted to die too. But I didn't, obviously. And now, I guess I've already accepted my life."

"Well, that's great." Fire snickered.

"Yeah, I know, I'm real deep that way."

The rain was falling harder now. The rain wasn't like cold bullets, but rather the temperature of a gentle summer pour. Hope felt at peace as she laid under the tree, listening to the sound of the calming rain around her.

"Hey, Fire, what was-" Hope cut off when she saw that the tiny girl had impossibly fallen asleep. When her face wasn't in a yell or snarl, Hope had to admit that Fire was actually not bad-looking at all. In fact, she was quite pretty.

Hope thought of Blisse up above her. Blisse was finally back to herself for good. Even though her friend's kind nature had returned, Hope knew that nobody's relationship with her could ever be the same.

She thought of Aiden. His corpse was probably still lying out there, propped up against a tree for eternity. It truly was a shame that he had to die, especially by the person Hope called her friend.

Her mind turned to Cassidy. Strong, beautiful Cassidy who had been through much more than she let on. Who had survived against all odds. Everyone in the island group was extremely strong mentally and physically in every way. *I'm so lucky to have found these people.*

Hope lightly patted Fire's shin.

"Goodnight, Sapphire," she whispered.

48

Hope's head was full of nightmares.

The first time around, she was shocked to the bone with the terrible electricity from the gun. Her skin was peeling and all she could smell was the awful burning of her flesh.

In the second dream, blood was streaming out of the many bullet wounds that the government had shot into her. It was like a movie. A terrible, awful movie where she could only sit there and watch herself die. Over and over and over.

The third dream had been the worst.

She had seen Ethan screaming and writhing on the ground with a bloody stump for an arm. An official from a government helicopter had laughed at him with a snake-like smile and black, black eyes. Then, he electrocuted Ethan. He wouldn't stop. Ethan's eyes rolled up into his head but his shrieking, oh his shrieking, it wouldn't stop. The only thing Hope could do was watch and watch and it was just like Haylee and she had lost two people she loved....

Finally, she woke up with wet eyes. How long it had been, she had no clue. The smallest sliver of the sun was visible on the horizon.

So, Hope thought to herself, *today's the day. The day I die or find my freedom.*

For one terrible moment, she had a strong urge to get up and run back into the jungle. Everyone was asleep. If she took off now, she wouldn't face the same fate in her dreams. Even now, the idea was seeming less and less realistic. The crazy adrenaline of fighting the government was fading rapidly, and it was only a matter of time before she was shot and Ethan would scream.

Hope pinched herself as hard as she could, drawing a little blood.

You won't run. You'll get off this island for your mom. You'll get off for Haylee.

It was almost sad, in a way, that her life would change before night fell again. She would be dead, hurt, or somewhere far away from Grayson's shack.

Hope sat there alone, staring at the calm waters, wishing more than anything that she was never called dangerous.

The sun eventually rose. By now, the island group was awake, on high alert for a helicopter.

"I'm so hungry," Fire complained. The rumbling of her stomach had gotten louder and louder after each excruciating hour. Hunger was like a roaring animal that threatened to eat her from the inside out.

"We can always resort to cannibalism," Belle joked darkly. Blisse gave her look so full of sadness and pain that Belle's heart gave a jump. "Wait, Blisse, did you.... nevermind."

Hope's anxiety set in once the sun was at its highest point in the sky. Maybe the stupid helicopter wouldn't come. Maybe it would never come. Maybe they would just get kidnapped by the poor guards who had been terrorized by Blisse.

"So, Aspyn," Belle started shakily. "What's your favorite color?"

Aspyn let out a small anxious laugh.

"We're about to get murdered, and you want to know my favorite color?"

"Yeah," she said. "I guess I do."

"Gold," Aspyn finally said with a sigh. "I love gold. It's so beautiful." Belle smiled a rare, kind smile.

"Great. Cassidy?"

The brunette looked up in fear.

"What?"

"Your favorite color," Belle said through a chuckle. "Don't worry, it's not a scary question." Cassidy seemed to relax a little.

"Sorry, I was just thinking about ...nothing, sorry. My favorite color is brown."

"Brown?" Fire asked with disgust. "Brown is the color of dirt."

"It's the color of the earth," Cassidy answered quietly. "I like that."

Ethan's sharp intake of breath made Cassidy pause. "Ethan, what is it?" Ethan's finger was shaking slightly as he pointed straight ahead. Fire froze. Belle gasped. Hope felt a wave of relief and dread. Ethan was pointing at the helicopter that they thought would never arrive.

"They're coming," he said. "They're finally coming."

"I can't believe we're actually doing this," Hope whispered.

"Well, we are," chimed Fire, who had listened to her worried statement. "Blisse, got your gun?"

"Yes," Blisse answered quietly. "Right here." She swiftly brought it out of her pocket. Ethan slightly winced, remembering the feel of the electric weapon.

"And Blisse, you're *sure* you can fly a helicopter?" Aspyn asked, looking up at the official vehicle with wide eyes. Blisse eagerly nodded.

"Oh yes, I am absolutely positive. I promise that if our plan works, I can get us off this place." Fire narrowed her eyes.

"You had better be sure, or I swear I will-"

"I can," Blisse said almost angrily, cutting Fire off. "Please don't be like this right now." Fire's narrowed eyes grew even angrier.

"Don't scold me, murderer." Fire was rewarded with a look of anger, pain, and sadness from Blisse, making her smirk. "Lets see. There was Aiden, that man without an arm, countless guards..."

"Sapphire, shut up," Ethan demanded, his voice low. Fire's expression turned shocked.

"Excuse me?"

"You know what you're doing," Ethan replied, clearly not amused. "She has apologized, and she's gotten over it. You should too." Fire didn't reply back, her face turning red in fury.

"Guys," Belle muttered. Fire shot her an angry look.

"Zip it Belle."

"But guys," Belle said again, her voice louder.

"I said stop talking!" Fire snapped back, throwing her hands on her hips.

"Guys!" Belle yelled once more, her voice rising to an angry scream. "Shut your damn mouths and look!" Ethan looked to where Belle was pointing. A bullet of adrenaline raced through his body.

The men were on the island.

"Take a quick scan of this spot and we can leave!" one of the men announced to the group of 5 men. "This place gives me a bad feeling, we might as well get out as soon as we can." Thankfully, his eyes skimmed over the large plants that the group was hiding in.

"But they aren't even checking the island!" Aspyn angrily hissed. "They're just looking at this one spot and taking off!"

"I know," Ethan responded in the same tone. "It's ridiculous, they are supposed to check the whole damn place, not one stupid piece of sand."

"We need to hurry, then," Cassidy told them. "If we don't go now, they'll take off." Ethan shook his head in agreement.

"Well, I guess we gotta go now." Despite his announcement, everybody stayed still. Hope was nervously biting her nails.

"Well, that's it then, huh? We just... go attack?" she inquired. Ethan grinned.

"You aren't feeling regret now, are you? What, do you want to stay on this crappy excuse of an island or something?"

"No," Hope retorted in defense. "I just... like you guys, and I don't want you to die." Fire gave a rude sarcastic snort.

"Wow, thanks for that lovely piece of encouragement, I really needed that." Hope looked at her oddly, not seeing how the fragile, sniffling Fire from just the night before could look at Hope as though she hated her. Ethan gave Fire a stern look, but it melted slightly.

"My dear Sapphire," he said, "use that anger against these government imbeciles. Make them feel your wrath." Fire's mouth reluctantly went up at the corner as she gave a mocking salute.

"Will do, sir."

Ethan gazed around at everyone, pure love in his eyes.

"Guys, I just want to say-"

"We don't need a death talk, Ethan," Belle interrupted. "We'll all live, so there's no point to make everything all sappy." Ethan smiled.

"Alrighty then, I'll skip the part where I was going to kiss everyone of you." He suddenly put his hand in the middle. Belle rolled her eyes.

"No, you've got to be kidding. I'm not putting my hand in the middle of a circle." Cassidy's hand slammed down first.

"Well, I will," she proclaimed. With a small grin, Hope set down her hand on her friend's. Next followed Blisse, then Aspyn. Fire and Belle looked at each other with exaggerated pain in their eyes.

"Come on," Ethan said mischievously. "Put your little hand in the friendship circle." With a sigh, Fire set down her tiny hand. Everyone's eyes were locked on Belle.

"Oh, for the love of…" she muttered, setting down her hand on the pile. Ethan looked firmly into everyone's eyes.

"Gentlemen," Ethan started, in an exaggerated tone, "it's been an honor serving with you." Hope rolled her eyes, chuckling, as Belle quickly lifted off her hand. Blisse reached into her pockets and grabbed out a small electric gun for each of them.

"Now normally I wouldn't condone this, but let's go get them," Blisse stated, grinning. Ethan patted her on the back.

"Now that's some spirit, baby." He grabbed his weapon. He looked at Hope, who was gnawing on her lip. "You alright there, Hopie?"

"Just nervous," she replied. "I sort of have this thing where I don't really want to die." Ethan chuckled.

"Oh, we all have that, it's called common sense." He brushed a stray piece of golden hair from her face. "You won't die, Hopie. You've survived too long to die now." Hope weakly smiled.

"Okie dokie then," she said, looking back at the jungle for the last time. "Let's go hijack that copter."

49

The first person out of the jungle was Fire, who looked as though she had been shot out of a cannon. With her own crazy battle cry and her fist pumped up in the air, she looked like some maniac warrior. The government officials froze. Fire was followed by Belle, Aspyn, Blisse, Ethan, Cassidy, then Hope. The men sprung into action. They took out small pistols from their pockets.

There were six men in total. Five were on the sand while the last one was in the pilot's seat of the helicopter.

"Blisse," Ethan hissed, causing her head to spin around. "I'll distract them, you go to the helicopter and try to take it over."

"No," she whispered back. "You go. I'll charm them or something." Ethan looked at her firmly.

"Blisse..."

"No!" she snapped. Ethan stopped. "I can act, and no offense, but they are more likely to believe a sweet, innocent girl instead of you." Ethan paused, pondering her offer.

"Ok, fine," he finally responded. "Go work your little charm." Quietly, Ethan tried to sneak out of the commotion and get to the back of the helicopter.

Fire was on a rampage. She darted all of the knives and bullets that came her way. Instinctively, she could tell where the men would shoot before they shot. She could see their plan in their hectic eyes. Hope was in the background, holding out her gun in case of an emergency.

"Stop," the front man commanded. "In the name of the law!" Belle snarled.

"Well," she said, "you see, there aren't any laws on this island." Fire firmly nodded in agreement.

"You wanna know what else isn't fair?" Fire said. "Sending off all the smarties to a deserted island, hoping to get them killed off!"

The first man's gun rose. It was pointed straight at Fire.

"Get down on your knees or I will shoot you."

"Wait!" Everyone's head turned to the source of the plea: Blisse. Tears were streaming down her face, and her hands were desperately up. Fire let an extremely annoyed sigh, throwing up her hands.

"Please, hear me out," Blisse begged. The man's grip on the weapon tightened.

"And why should I do that?"

"So you can better understand our situation," she replied, still more tears trickling. "We were kidnapped by some psycho old man who hurt us and broke us. When we saw you, we got scared that you were trying to hurt us." Fire loudly snorted.

"That's a bunch of BS!" she yelled. Blisse ignored her, turning her attention back on the man.

"We saw your helicopter, and we thought that you wanted to harm us. This is just an automatic reaction, considering what we have been through. Please don't shoot us, just leave us alone."

Fire gave Blisse the meanest look she could possibly form.

"You are such a coward!"

Fire was cut short by a loud thud. The first man spun around, revealing the slumped body of another official. Behind him was Ethan with a crowbar in his hand. He had fallen out of the pilot's seat.

"Blisse!" Ethan yelled. Blisse looked his way, wiping away her tears. "I have them, go start it up!" Fire's angry expression also turned confused.

"What the… ?"

"I'm a pretty good actor, aren't I?" Blisse asked, smirking at a gawking Sapphire.

"ETHAN!" Cassidy shrieked. Ethan spun around wildly, coming face to face with a man's knife. He could see it heading for his eye, heading to kill him…

The man dropped to the ground, spasming. Cassidy was shaking, her trembling finger still on the trigger of her gun.

"Cassidy?" Hope asked in a tone that was part awe and part fear. "You shot him?" Cassidy quickly wiped away her tears.

"He was about to kill Ethan."

The front man angrily looked at Cassidy as he held his gun. He then grinned.

"This one's for you, princess."

And he pulled the trigger.

Hope shrieked.

Fire's hand went over her mouth.

Cassidy screamed in agony as her legs went out from under her. The bullet had hit her leg. Her blood was flowing much too fast, and it didn't seem to be stopping.

Hope crouched down in terror, hectic tears beginning to fall.

"No, no, I can't believe he shot you, oh my god Cassidy." The man's face had a smug grin plastered across it. Fire took her chance.

She lunged at the official, her momentum knocking him down. She clawed crazily at his eyes, grappling for the gun. Before the other men could help their co-worker, Ethan shot his gun full of white-hot electricity. One of the nameless men fell into a pile, twitching and shaking on the ground.

Blisse ran around the other side of the helicopter. Quick as a wink, she hopped up onto the side of the vehicle, climbing into the pilot's seat.

"You guys!" she screamed.

That was the wrong thing to do.

One of the remaining men heard her shout. His eyes perked up to look at her as she felt her body freeze. She hastily reached into her pocket to get her gun.

A hollow pit dropped in her stomach. *Blisse, where is your gun?* She looked out, and she could see it on the ground. Through all the commotion, she must've dropped it there. She mentally cursed herself for being so idiotic.

The man was sprinting toward her now. Blisse could feel her hopes fall. His gun was pointed to her, getting ready to shoot her with a metal bullet in her heart.

"No!" Ethan screamed. He chucked his gun at the running man. The metal handle slammed into his knee cap. He yelled, falling down on the sand. Blisse could feel tears of joy in her eyes. She wasn't dead yet.

Before the man could pop back up, Ethan dashed toward his gun. As his hand reached out to grab it, the man snatched Ethan's wrist, pulling him to the sand. Ethan screamed for help, but nobody else could hear him with their attention all on someone else. Blisse saw the man's hand clamp around Ethan's throat. Ethan desperately thrashed around, his hand clawing at his neck. Blisse could see his face turn a deadly shade of purple, and if no one helped him, he was going to pass out.

Ethan's bulging eyes locked with Blisse. Blisse felt a bubble of panic. If she didn't go and fight the man, Ethan would die. *Ok Blisse,* she prepared herself. *Don't look at his face. Just don't look into his eyes.* Ever since Blisse had come back to herself, she never wanted to fight anyone again. But as she looked at her friend hanging onto life by a thread, she couldn't hesitate any longer. Blisse rushed out of the helicopter, throwing her body onto the government man. He released Ethan as his hands found a new target; her. Ethan went on his knees, desperately gasping for air.

The man's hands went for her face. He scratched and clawed at her, causing Blisse to scream. She went at him too, punching and punching his throat.

The man slapped her nose. Blisse could faintly feel the blood flow, but her anger kept her from feeling too much pain. She let out a grunt as her head snapped back. Ethan's face was losing its purple color, turning back to his normal light skin tone. He took the butt of his gun and smashed it on the man's head. He let out an inhuman snarl as more blood gushed from his nose. Ethan hysterically smashed and smashed the gun until the official fell unconscious.

Blisse held her throat, her lungs aching for air.

"I can't believe I did that," she whispered. Ethan lightly patted her on the back.

"It's what we had to do."

Four men remained. Fire was still aggressively trying to slip the gun out of the government official's hand. Belle angrily sprinted over to the two.

"Move, Sapphire!" she shouted. "I can't get a clear shot!"

"I'm... trying!" Fire yelled back, in between gasps. "And... it's... Fire!" With that sentence, she reared back her fist and sent it at the man's eye. He grunted in pain. As his head whipped back, Belle seized her chance. She shot him, the electric spark hitting his ear. Fire hastily hopped off as gurgling sounds came out from his mouth.

"Thank you," Fire mumbled, looking away. Belle smirked, her eyes glinting.

Three men remained.

Hope was still kneeled down beside Cassidy, her hands using cloth from her shirt to plug up her wound. Hope about fainted when she saw a man stalking toward them. He lifted up his gun at Hope, the hole looking right into her face.

"Wait!" she cried out. "You can't shoot me. I haven't harmed you at all since you were here. I haven't even touched you. Killing me right now, when I haven't done anything to you, is straight up illegal." The man paused to consider this.

"But she shot a gun," he whined, pointing at Cassidy. Hope nodded.

"Yes, but now she has a bullet in her leg." Hope braced herself to say the next words. "She'll die anyway, right? There's honestly no point in wasting a bullet on her when she's as good as dead." Cassidy gasped in shock and hurt quietly. The man's eyes squinted at Hope, trying to decide if there's anything he could find that was wrong with her proposition. Finally he said, "Alrighty blondie, you've got a point there. I won't shoot you or your friend." Hope mentally gave a sigh of relief. Cassidy's body was beginning to shake as the blood soaked through the cloth.

"Hope," she gasped out. Hope refused to let her speak in that tone. Her voice sounded defeated and hopeless.

"No," Hope snapped, staring hard into her friend's eyes. "You will not die. I'm sick and tired of my closest friends just dying in front of me. You are going to live. Do you hear me? And if you die, I swear I will kill you." Cassidy weakly chuckled.

"But Hope, it's pointless to save me. The cloth is already soaked through. I'm going to bleed out."

"Cassidy!" Hope practically yelled. Cassidy's expression turned shocked. "What?"

"Why are you this way?" Hope exclaimed. "You're talking like you *want* to die!" Cassidy's sad eyes avoided her gaze. Hope stopped breathing. "No, you do want to die," she realized aloud. "You don't want help. You really want to die."

"I'm sorry," she whispered. Hope couldn't believe what she was hearing.

"You want to leave me? Are you really going to do that?"

Cassidy sniffed.

"I don't enjoy this, Hope." Hope snorted.

"Shut up, Cassidy. Do you know how many people close to me have died? My parents split and now Haylee is *dead!*" She stopped speaking. That was the first time she had said the dreadful truth aloud. She hated how blunt and cold the words sounded coming from her mouth. Cassidy's eyes clouded. "If you die Cassidy, I won't be able to live. Simple as that."

"But you have Ethan," Cassidy whispered. Hope threw up her hands.

"So what? Yeah, I have Fire and Blisse too, but who cares? You were the first person I met on this island, Cassidy, and ever since then I've come to like you a lot. You were the one who begged me not to jump off that cliff, and now I'm the one begging you to not let yourself die. You die, and it's all over. You die, and I have nothing left to fight for. You die, and I die."

Cassidy stared at her, shocked into silence. Finally, her trembling hands moved to cover her wound.

"Ok Hope," she said softly, almost too quiet to hear. "I'll live. For you."

"Ethan, go in the pilot's seat," Blisse commanded. "You need to be closest to the men in case they shoot." Ethan nodded as he climbed into the seat. Aspyn and Fire saw this, and they both went strategically in front of the men, blocking their view of the helicopter.

"Hey boys!" Aspyn called, drawing the attention to herself. One of the men looked angrily toward her.

"You, missy, are in a lot of trouble." Aspyn shrugged.

"Well, that makes two of us." The man looked at her suspiciously.

"And what do you mean by that?" She smirked. As soon as she gave her que, Fire shot the man in the back. He fell down into a spasming mess.

Two men remained.

They both held out their guns menacingly. Nobody could shoot them while they still had their guns. Real guns, not just filled with electricity, but metal bullets that could kill in the blink of an eye. Luckily, they hadn't yet seen Ethan and Blisse in the helicopter.

"Darn it," Blisse muttered under her breath. "I need the key." Ethan felt a sinking pit in his stomach.

"And how on earth are we going to get this key?"

Blisse suddenly grinned.

"I think I have an idea, old friend. Ethan, give me your gun," she ordered. Ethan gave a perk of his mouth as he handed it over.

"Go get that key." Blisse nodded at him, looking at the buttons of the complicated vehicle.

"Ethan, when I get the key, I'll need to give it to you right away, ok? Be ready when I do." Ethan gave a firm nod of his head.

Stealthily, Blisse slid out of the front seat. She put her own gun in her hand while she tucked Ethan's gun in the band of her pants.

"I surrender!" Blisse pleaded, showing the palms of her hands. Fortunately, one of the still standing men had the key inside his pocket. She could see the shape bouncing around whenever he moved.

"And how do I know that you aren't faking?" the man asked accusingly. Blisse held up her electric gun for proof.

"Because I'll give you my gun."

Fire looked over suspiciously, but she kept quiet.

"You will?" The official's tone was shocked and excited. Blisse nodded her head in a pretend look of defeat.

"Yes, I will. It's clear you have us overpowered. I'll give it to you now." She held the gun away from her, trying hard to pretend that she meant no harm. The man grinned in victory.

"I'll take that," the man said, not trying to conceal his smug tone. Blisse gently set the gun in his hand. As he was reaching for it, she sprung into action.

She ripped the set of keys from his pocket as she grabbed her hidden gun from her waist. She held it right against his side as she held them tightly in her hand.

"Move, and I'll shoot," Blisse warned, not looking directly into his eyes. His body froze, not knowing what to do. As quick as a wink, Blisse sprinted away from him, toward the helicopter. She could hear the bullets exploding out of the gun as she dashed for her life. She could hear the sound of someone's footsteps behind her.

"Ethan!" she shrieked. His head popped up immediately at her shout.

"You called?" Blisse showed him the keys.

"Take these!" With perfect aim, she threw the keys into his hands. It was just in time, as she felt the large shape of a man slam into her back. She fell into a heap on the ground, the wind knocked out of her.

Ethan caught the keys, just barely wrapping his fingers around the ring.

"Get... off... me!" Blisse shrieked, batting at the man's back. She hit her gun against his face, which allowed her time to slip through his grasp.

"Ethan!" she yelled. "Start the helicopter!" Ethan looked at her in hectic confusion.

"I don't know how!"

Blisse sighed quietly. She heard more pounding behind her. Terrified, her head whipped around, revealing a charging official.

"I'm sorry," she yelled to him, pulling the trigger of her gun. The electricity slammed right into his chest. Blisse dry heaved at the gurgling, wet sounds in his throat.

One man remained.

The other men were on the ground, still spasming.

One man left.

One man left until they could leave the island.

One man left until they could worry about guards no longer.

Cassidy was still sprawled on the ground, Hope not leaving her side. The final man didn't dare to believe anyone's offers of surrendering, as his other workers had been deceived.

"I will kill all of you," he growled. Fire smirked.

"Yeah, here's the thing. If you shoot us, we still will live long enough to shoot you. If we shoot you first, you'll fall immediately."

"Let's make a deal," Hope compromised. "How about you come back with us to the next dangerous station, back on the mainland. Let us come with you, and we won't shoot."

The man looked at her as though she had just suggested that they all jump off a cliff.

"Are you crazy, blondie? Why in the world would I take criminals with me?" Belle snorted.

"There are more of us than there are of you, buddy. Shoot one of us and you die." The man sneered.

"I won't die."

And he did in fact pull the trigger.

But the bullets had all been released.

The man's eyes widened as Belle's grew smug.

"Looks like we are in fact going on that damn copter," she said, her tone victorious. Without a second thought, she pulled the trigger. She watched in pleasure as the electric spark hit his chest.

"Hope," Ethan shouted from the helicopter. Her head spun around. "Bring everyone here." Hope's eyes shot down to Cassidy, whose face was turning dangerously pale.

"Um, I think I need your help!" she shouted back. Ethan jumped from the seat and jogged over to his friends on the sand. His eyes widened as he got a look at Cassidy.

"She… she was shot?" Hope nodded.

"Yeah. Can you carry her?" she asked. Ethan nodded quickly.

"Heck yeah I can." He bent down to his best friend. Cassidy slightly smiled.

"Don't I just look ravishing?" Ethan chuckled.

"Yep. Red really suits you." He swooped her up in his arms, walking her back gently to the helicopter.

"You know, you had great ideas," Fire admitted to Blisse, her eyes looking down. "I didn't mean to scream at you like that, I was just mad." Blisse smiled.

"It's ok. Really. I've been mad before too." Fire laughed.

"When have you ever been mad, Blisse?" Blisse grinned uncomfortably.

"Right now, actually. I was furious with the government guys right now. I even made them bleed." She winced. Now the feeling of regret was coursing through her veins. Fire patted her arm.

"I'll forgive you," she said quietly. "For Psycho Blisse. I'll get there eventually. It wasn't you, I know that. I'll forgive you." Blisse smiled gratefully.

"Thank you. I guess I just have to learn to forgive myself." Fire stopped, looking into her eyes.

"You will, Blisse."

Ethan set Cassidy down gently in the back of the helicopter. He slid away the separating metal wall so he could speak with his friends. Blisse sat herself in the pilot's seat, using the key to start it up.

"Wait a second," Ethan began. "I'm not the smartest man in the world, but I thought that helicopters don't need keys."

"They don't," Blisse replied, "but the government specially designed them so that they are almost impossible to steal." Ethan nodded his head in thought.

Blisse stuck the key into a small hole on her right. She turned it, and a green light came on. Ethan watched, mesmerized, as she pushed and toggled the millions of small buttons in the vehicle.

"How in the world do you do that?" he asked in awe. Blisse shrugged.

"I taught myself when I was ten. I was bored, and machinery always came easy to me." Ethan grinned at her.

"I guess that explains why you're on the island, then. You've got crazy smarts for machinery." Blisse smiled to herself.

"Yeah, maybe."

A moment later, the helicopter began to rise. Hope looked at the window as the golden sand became smaller and smaller.

"You guys," she said in horror. "Look."

She pointed to the still unconscious men on the sand. There were numerous guards circled around them now, and Hope could see them being gagged and bound. Blisse suddenly screamed, causing the helicopter to sway to the side. Hope's head smashed painfully against the window.

"They don't know I've turned back to normal," Blisse realized aloud. "They still think they're working for Psycho Blisse." Ethan steadily guided her hand to keep the helicopter straight.

"It's alright, they'll probably learn that soon enough," he told her calmly. "We need to worry about us now, not them."

And they did.

As they flew across the vast ocean, the sky began to turn dark. The silver stars were soon visible in the sky. Ethan turned around and tapped Hope's knee.

"Hey Hopie, remember the first time I showed you the stars?" Hope smiled, nodding.

"Hey Blisse?" she asked

"Hmm?"

"Where exactly are we going now?" A nervous pit seemed to settle in Hope's gut. "We're still considered dangerous by the government. Where can we go?"

"Michigan," Fire answered immediately. Belle looked at her oddly.

"And why exactly Michigan?"

"We can go to the Upper Peninsula," she replied. "I know that to take your test, you had to travel down into the Lower Peninsula, which means that there aren't any dangerous-testing places there. We have a high chance of not being found if we go there."

"Alrighty then," said Blisse. "The old Mackinac state it is."

"I'll help you navigate," Ethan offered, his tone excited. "I can guide us by the stars. Of course, follow that star right there." He pointed to the brightest star in the sky.

"That's the North Star, right?" asked Blisse. Ethan gave her a nod.

Hope stared out the window, looking at the beautiful sea in the starlight. She felt a weak prod on her knee. The touch belonged to Cassidy.

"Hope," she whispered, tears in her eyes. "Are we really free?"

Hope didn't reply right away. In a physical sense, they were free. They were no longer tethered to the island in the middle of the ocean. Emotionally, though, no one was really free. Aiden, Haylee, Genevieve, Martha, and the countless guards' deaths would stay with them as long as they were alive. As she looked at Cassidy, though, she knew that their rough times were over, at least temporarily. She gave her an encouraging smile.

"Yes, Cassidy," she said. "We're free."

Hope looked at Ethan, who was staring at the stars. She loved the look of giddy happiness on his face as he stared into the sky. She looked over at Fire. Her tiny friend was curled up against the wall, sleeping. Hope looked at Belle and Aspyn, who were slumped against the sides, looking at the ground. Blisse was still flying the helicopter, her eyes set on the starry sky.

"I love you guys," Hope whispered, thinking nobody could hear. That's why she was surprised when Ethan responded gently, "I love you too."

Hope didn't know where their next threat would come from. She had no clue whether their danger was truly over or not. But she had her friends with her, and they were all happy and relieved and *safe*.

And for now, that was enough.

Acknowledgements

Wow. Writing this book has been a heck of a journey, and I couldn't have done it without multiple people.

I want to first start off with my parents, Bonnie and Dan Gretzner. They've always been my number one fans and have been there for everything. I've forced them to listen to my piano songs, poems, and story ideas, and they are always there to fuel my creativity. Without their undying support, I would have lost passion in creating things a long time ago.

Next, I want to thank one of my favorite teachers to ever exist, Mrs. Manders. I needed someone outside of my family to provide feedback on what I could change and improve in this book, and she was right there when I asked. Being a teacher is so hard, and she managed to give me wonderful feedback while also teaching English and drama. It meant so much to me that she would take her time to read what I wrote, and I'm forever thankful.

Another person who was monumental in this writing process is my forever friend, Adriana Christner. She was the very first person to read this story in its entirety. She helped me make my characters more dynamic and gushed over them with me. Her continued love and support has helped me more than she will ever know.

I also want to give a shout out to my long time best friend, Alyssa Eubanks. She gave me great feedback in the very early stages of this book. It would have turned out different and of a lesser quality if she hadn't been there to help me and talk about the details. I love her with all my heart.

Finally, I want to give my thanks to any people in my life who have helped me on this journey or have been there along the way. This includes Matthew Day, Grace Teachout, Alexa Brzyski, Faythe Miller, and countless others. Thank you for inspiring my creativity beyond words. Even Grayson would love you all.

About the Author

Jordan Gretzner is a 15 year old who has always loved to read. She was born in Michigan and she's a highschool sophomore. Along with reading, Jordan loves theater, writing, and composing her own songs on the piano. One of her major passions is traveling. She has visited Australia and Iceland, and she plans to explore many more countries when she's older. Along her journey, Jordan has also become much closer with God and has been working on her spiritual relationship and finding her purpose in the world.

A beautiful music artist called Sleeping at Last has inspired Jordan's love for space. One thing that can always distinguish her is her Saturn necklace. After this book, she plans to write more and create a series. Jordan owes much of her creativity and a love for life to her friends and family, who she loves very much.

Made in the
USA
Lexington, KY